This book is dedicated with love, respect, and gratitude to my husband, John Marshall Morton Jr., a true Virginia gentleman, whose deep roots in the Old Dominion first stirred to life my ever-growing interest in the state's glorious history; to my beloved aunt, Jean Ring Cude, who so graciously shared her "writer's genes" with me and has always been a loving, lively inspiration and a top-of-the-line "booster cable;" and last but not least, to the wonderful physical therapists throughout this country who daily practice their caring "hands-on" profession and help, coach, prod, and cajole us to be as strong and able as we can be.

# Time-Spun Treasure

## THOMASINA RING

LOVE SPELL  NEW YORK CITY

LOVE SPELL®

August 1995

Published by

Dorchester Publishing Co., Inc.
276 Fifth Avenue
New York, NY 10001

Printed in the United States of America.

# Chapter One

The afternoon got off to a rotten start.

Patrick Henry arrived with a bad case of laryngitis, George Washington's fly was missing two buttons, and Thomas Jefferson's wig had sprung a curl.

Clucking like a mother hen, Meredith Davis searched through her oversized leather shoulder bag and within seconds had everything under control.

For Mr. Henry, Meredith found a package of herbal cough drops. "Suck two of these slowly and another two shortly before the big speech—they should do the trick," she assured him.

Mr. Washington received a couple of safety pins and an admonition. "Please, for God's sake, pin them on the *inside* so they don't show."

A strategic placement of a small clip and a whiff of hair spray took care of Mr. Jefferson.

They were beholden, they told Meredith.

With a warm grin, she dipped a mock curtsy and left the men standing amid the gravestones behind the small church. She couldn't help but chuckle as she hurried around to the front. Lord, even the Founding Fathers were depending on her now. The irony struck her. Back there stood the so-called "Voice, Sword, and Pen" of this country's noble struggle for independence, and without her assistance they surely would've made a sorry spectacle of themselves today.

Rounding the corner, she saw Kelly McGee already stationed in St. John's open doorway. Meredith glanced at her watch and frowned. She was five minutes late, thanks to the delay out back. Even as she quickened her steps she remembered to unfasten the black-strapped watch and stuff it into her bag—it would have added a jarring note to her colonial garb.

Scurrying through the door, she offered Kelly a shrug of apology, tossed her purse into the corner of the vestibule, grabbed a handful of programs, and joined her fellow docent out by the entrance.

The bright, sunny day was unusually warm for late March, and early arrivals for the afternoon's performance chose to linger outside, many of them wandering around the old graves in the historical churchyard.

"Like your new costume," Kelly complimented her in a properly subdued voice while they waited. "Fits you better than that brown thing you wore last year, and the lower neckline is becoming as all get-out."

"Even managed some tantalizing poofiness, I hope you noticed," Meredith whispered with a wicked smile. "Found an underwire push-up bra at Victoria's Secret that works miracles."

Kelly lifted an eyebrow. "Am I hearing right? *You?* Ms. No-Nonsense, Professional-Image Davis into tantalizing and shopping at bimbo heaven, of all places! Did you get a personality transplant during the winter?"

Meredith's cheeks warmed though she'd expected Kelly's teasing. Good grief, she'd long ago proved her levelheadedness and professional competence. Now, at 29, she figured an attempt at a bit of feminine allure would hardly create the impression she was an airhead.

"The personality remains the same, Ms. McGee," she retorted. "It's just that I've decided to stop hiding my drop-dead beauty from the impoverished world."

Kelly tilted her head and gave her an appraising look. "Hmmm. A dynamite new blunt cut, obviously a first-class salon job. Green contacts—startling green, like a cat in heat, I'd say. A touch of matching shadow, a hint of mascara, a light brush of blush, lip color." She giggled. "Not drop-dead, Meredith, but you show some promise. Estee Lauder or Clinique?"

"Lancôme. And, if you can believe it, I splurged on a set of violet contacts, too, for a change of pace."

"You needed one, girl, and it's about time." Kelly's hazel eyes sparked a saucy twinkle. "And way past time you started looking for a man."

Meredith bristled. "I'm doing this for me, Kelly, not for a man. I've found I like being a touch more attractive, and it's something I feel secure enough now to come to grips with—a big something I've had to work out for myself. Besides, the last thing

11

I'm interested in at the moment is a man. *Any* man. When Sam and I broke up last year, I swore off involvements." She wrinkled her nose. "Shoot, they're all wimps these days—half-baked wimps, the lot of them."

"But your eyes, love," Kelly said with a wry grin before turning to face a group of people heading their way. "Definitely like a she-cat in heat," she tossed over her shoulder in a low voice.

*Blast her*, Meredith grumbled, though she had to admit that perceptive Kelly had punched a sensitive button. It had been a year since Dr. Sam Whitson had crawled out of their stormy relationship to marry that simpering, docile nurse. But Meredith hadn't missed him a minute, if truth be told. Like the pitifully few other men she had ever let get close to her, Sam had protested her strong will and independent ways, but whimpered like a lost puppy if, God forbid, he had to exert some gumption on his own.

She was a hard woman to please, she guessed. What she wanted in a man simply wasn't out there to be had—someone who would love her for her strength because it dovetailed with his strength. Someone she could respect, for Pete's sake.

She shrugged. Since such a paragon didn't exist, she'd decided she could get along just fine without a man.

True, her hormones had been rebelling a tad lately; but, like the rest of her well-ordered life, she had those primitive urges under complete control.

She lifted her chin a resolute notch higher. Despite her new vivid-green contact lenses, she was *not* a she-cat in heat. So there, Kelly McGee!

12

Meredith greeted a trio of elderly ladies with a pleasant smile and led them inside to a pew near the front. "Please leave this seat at the end here vacant," she said in a conspiratorial whisper, knowing that the gray-haired women would be thrilled beyond measure when the actor playing George Washington, resplendent in his bright red coat, would enter soon and take his seat there beside them.

She hoped like the dickens his fly was suitably closed.

After the audience had been seated, filling the tiny white wooden church, the annual anniversary reenactment of the proceedings of the March 23, 1775, Second Virginia Convention got under way. Kelly had stayed inside for the performance, saying she'd never tire of hearing those wonderful words.

Meredith felt the same way. Today, however, the church was sweltering, and she hated crowds. She'd opted to stand in the vestibule near the open door where she could benefit from the fresh breeze that had kicked up. Besides, she could hear well enough, and she practically had the thing memorized.

Like Kelly, she got tingles in her spine every time Patrick Henry stood to deliver his immortal "Liberty or Death" speech, though she'd heard it in dozens of similar reenactments by dozens of Patrick Henrys—none of them bearing the slightest resemblance to portraits of the gaunt redheaded Virginian, but all of them gifted with proper verve and silver tongues.

Being a Richmond native, Meredith loved history, especially Virginia history, so she'd happily taken on this part-time job as a docent for the Patrick Henry Association. Lord knew, it wasn't the little bit of money she was paid that attracted her. Her small physical therapy private practice was doing exceedingly well. Referrals from orthopedists and other physicians had grown to the point that she'd have to expand soon and increase her staff.

She truly enjoyed ushering at these St. John's reenactments, and the activity took little time away from her busy schedule. Other than this anniversary performance every March, the events were held only on Sunday afternoons during the three summer months.

A grumble of thunder disturbed her thoughts, and she stuck her head out the door to study the sky. Uh-oh. Angry clouds had gathered in the northwest and were fast approaching.

*"The question before the house is one of awful moment to this country. For my own part, I consider it as nothing less than a question of freedom or slavery."* Mr. Henry had started his speech. Her cough drops had worked, thank heaven. His voice was as clear and resounding as the Liberty Bell. She prayed the storm would hold off till he finished.

But it didn't look promising. A strong wind buffeted the trees lining the church's narrow brick walkway. Maple seeds and dried magnolia leaves skittered across the weathered gravestones.

*"I have but one lamp by which my feet are guided; and that is the lamp of experience. I know of no way of judging the future but by the past."*

Grimacing as a speck of dirt blew into her left eye, lodging beneath the contact lens, Meredith quickly grabbed for her shoulder bag and dug for the bottle of saline solution. She squirted a few drops into her eye and blinked away the irritation. A sharp spear of lightning flashed through the vestibule, triggering an added blink.

*"Sir, we have done everything that could be done to avert the storm which is now coming on."*

As if on cue, a loud clap of thunder provided a dramatic response. She tightened her lips. "Hold back," she muttered her plea to the turbulent sky.

The actor's voice rose for the soul-stirring climax. *"Gentlemen may cry, 'peace, peace'—but there is no peace. The war is actually begun. The next gale that sweeps from the north will bring to our ears the clash of resounding arms!"*

She leaned against the paneled wainscoting and closed her eyes. He was nearly through. For a moment, the wind quieted, the thunder stilled. The voice back in the crowded church lowered; the audience was hushed, waiting. The small building itself, like the storm above, seemed to be holding its breath. *"Why stand we here idle? What is it that gentlemen wish? What would they have? Is life so dear, or peace so sweet, as to be purchased at the price of chains and slavery?"*

And then, that glorious primal shout: *"Forbid it, Almighty God!"* Meredith loved the poignant pause, knew the actor's arms were stretched high. *"I know not what course others may take; but as for me, give me liberty or give me . . ."*

A blinding stab of lightning pierced her closed eyelids, a blast of thunder tore through her ears. Jolted, Meredith stiffened against the wall. But the wall wasn't there! She fell backward, through dark nothingness, landing on her rump with a teeth-shattering jar.

15

Stunned, still clutching her bag, she sat in the darkness, unwilling to open her eyes. Dear God, had a tornado struck? Was everyone all right? Was she all right? Nothing hurt; she could move her arms and legs, wiggle her fingers and toes.

She opened her eyes and gasped. Wherever she was, Meredith Davis was no longer in the vestibule of St. John's Church.

She took a quick, deep breath, trying to ward off the icy panic that gripped her. *Where am I? Good God, what's happened?*

Ordering herself to stay calm, though her thumping heartbeat refused to obey, she did what she could to assess her situation. She was seated on weed-covered ground beside a small white clapboard building. On a dreary hillside. Alone. The day was heavily clouded, the wind brisk and cold, like winter. But the scattering of trees on the steep hill bore the tenuous green sprouts of spring.

Her astounded brain raced, searching for a logical explanation. Had the storm swept away Richmond and left her the lone survivor? Had she been swept up and transplanted, like Dorothy, only to a far less colorful Oz?

She shook her head. *Be logical, for heaven's sake!* But nothing around her made logic easy—or gave her a glimmer of useful information. Pure and simple, she was sitting like a dolt on the hard, damp ground of a strange place.

The dolt part might be permanent, she feared, but at least she could do something about the sitting. Awkwardly she pushed herself to her feet. Though her knees were weak, she was relieved to find they held her upright.

Good. She was physically intact, but hopelessly confused. And, no denying it, her pulse was racing.

Forcing herself to be practical, she checked the back of her new green calico dress. After brushing away the few sprigs of clinging weeds, she tugged at the skirt to straighten it over her starched petticoats and took another deep, steadying breath.

*Okay. Now let's get this situation under control.* There *had* to be an explanation.

She reached down for her purse and slung it over her shoulder. With tentative steps at first, then with purposeful strides after determining that her legs worked fine, she walked around the corner of the clapboard building, studying it.

Nondescript was her first thought. *Totally unknown to me,* screamed the overriding second thought. She blocked out the scream, reminding herself firmly that she'd never find answers if she allowed hysteria to take over.

The el-shaped structure had tall, black-shuttered windows. The roof was pitched high, and atop it perched a squat open belfry, complete with bell.

A church? Meredith's brow crinkled.

Moving forward, again commanding her pounding heart to slow down, she went around to what she figured was the front of the building. Its narrow four-paneled oak door was closed, an old-fashioned iron latch where a knob should be.

With some reluctance she pulled at the latch, but the door was locked. She knocked, but no one answered. Probably just as well, she thought. Whatever had happened, wherever she was, she didn't want to confront anybody. She might start babbling like an idiot.

She backed away from the door. The front of the simple church did look familiar. She had seen it before. Where?

She gnawed at her lip, struggling to remember. And then it came to her. This building looked similar to a drawing she'd seen of an earlier St. John's.

It had fronted on the west back then, she remembered. Not that any of that knowledge helped, considering she was standing in front of something she'd only seen in a drawing.

But at least it was something she had seen. Part of her brain's memory store.

Like the blow of a hammer, the truth hit her. *That's it! None of this is real!*

Her sigh of relief collided with her gasp of concern, nearly choking her. She hadn't gone crazy. She was dreaming—or whatever people did when they were unconscious.

Her concern was for her physical condition. Obviously, she had been injured in that storm— stunned by the lightning bolt or struck on the head by something. Even now, she might be on her way to an emergency room.

Just her unconscious mind was wandering around this desolate churchyard; the rest of her— the real her—was being tended to by medics. She was probably in shock. That would explain the cold; and it might explain the lack of aches and pains, too.

Lord, she hoped she hadn't broken anything important. She hoped fervently she wasn't in some kind of coma.

Attempting to calm herself, she tried a few deep-breathing exercises. The crisp, fresh air in her lungs convinced her they were operational; for

18

sure, her heart was pumping. Heaven only knew what the emergency squad was discovering, but her vital signs still seemed vital.

Gradually she relaxed and felt an odd sense of resigned comfort. Since her body was in the control of others for the time being, there wasn't a thing she could do but wait for the return of consciousness.

In the meantime, she might as well check out this fantasy she was having. She would experiment with those lucid dreaming exercises she'd read about. All she had to keep in mind was that nothing could hurt her (nothing more, she amended), and she could control the events to suit her own needs.

Feeling stronger, she gave the church a challenging reappraisal. So she was imagining an earlier St. John's? While she was at it, why hadn't she conjured up its big event?

Now, *that* could be exciting! Why not? Since she was in control, all she had to do was imagine the shutters open, populate the churchyard with spectators, horses, and a few carriages, lift the windows, and she could hear the original proceedings of Virginia's Second Convention.

"So be it," she ordered.

But none of those things happened. St. John's remained shuttered and silent. Except for a few lopsided gravestones sticking up out of the weeds, the churchyard was empty. Her imagination was less colorful than she'd thought.

Well, surely she could make the day warmer. Seventy to seventy-five degrees would be perfect, she decided, willing the temperature to rise.

But even that small adjustment was beyond her. Fretfully she scrunched up her shoulders, longing for a wrap. The lucid dreaming concept had obvious limitations. She wished she'd read that book with more attention.

*I must be in an operating room. They keep them at refrigerated levels. Good grief, I hope they're not finding something serious. I hope to heaven they know what they're doing!*

She shoved away the thought. Better that she keep moving; better to explore this fantasy world further. Maybe she could discover some important things about herself, being in her subconscious this way.

"Beats analysis," she mumbled. Not that she'd ever considered analysis or had reason to consider such a thing. She was the most well-adjusted person she knew.

Oh well, she was far from perfect. Her subconscious might be more interesting than she realized. She should consider this ordeal an opportunity and, meanwhile, pray the ordeal would be a brief one.

Walking beyond the church, she found that the steep, windswept hillside provided a clear vantage of what she supposed was her own concept of early Richmond. Again, her imagination disappointed her. The dreary day she'd chosen made everything look like an old sepia photograph. She wished for technicolor, but couldn't manipulate the transformation.

Way down at the bottom of the hill lay the James River, dull as dishwater under the leaden sky. The scattering of buildings she saw were flimsy gray things—some down by the water, some over where she figured Shockhoe Slip lay, several on the hill itself.

Those below possibly were warehouses, shops,

or taverns. The structures on the hill looked like small houses, and smoke came from their chimneys. She considered approaching one of them, but decided against it.

She walked slowly, a pace she considered appropriate for someone in a trance. When the toes of her Capezios reached a wide path, she stopped. Was this a rudimentary street? She looked up and down its cleared but unpaved length, noting narrow wheel tracks and hooofprints in the rust-brown dirt.

Glancing back at the church and judging her distance, she guessed she'd arrived at Grace Street—in its earliest form, as produced by Meredith Davis.

Suddenly she wanted to cry. Blast it all, this whole thing was ridiculous! She didn't care what the street was; she wasn't interested in seeing old Richmond; she didn't want to know what her stupid subconscious mind might reveal.

All she wanted was to wake up and tell somebody, please, to give her a blanket or, for God's sake, to turn up the blamed thermostat!

Meredith hated being out of control of everything in her world. She felt pitiful and lost, and she didn't like that either.

Exasperated, she leaned against the trunk of a gnarled oak and heaved a sigh. What should she do? Go back to the church and wait till she woke up? No, she'd freeze up there. But she'd freeze here equally fast, she realized, and wandering about like a homeless waif in search of subconscious treasures was no longer the tiniest bit appealing.

Wearily she pushed herself away from the tree. She might as well head back up the hill.

But as she turned, she nearly collided with a wild-eyed young woman who had rushed to her side from God knew where.

"You take it," she said, thrusting a bundle into Meredith's arms. "And God help ye and forgive me, but I'll not go to that benighted house! Had ye not by the grace of God been here, I'd have left it alone on the ground."

After her strange outburst, the woman fled, leaving Meredith stupefied and sputtering fervent pleas for her to return. But the cloaked figure disappeared over the crest of the hill.

*What on earth?* Meredith's brain whirled in confusion. The fur-wrapped bundle she held, though a touch of welcome warmth against her beating chest, compounded the confusion.

Her first instinct was to drop the unwanted thing and run like mad back to the church. But an impulse of curiosity compelled her to inspect the contents.

Reminding herself that all of this craziness was but a figment of her imagination, she opened a small gap in the fur with trembling fingers.

A baby!

She was standing alone in the middle of nowhere with a sleeping baby in her arms!

*Okay, now, enough's enough!* It was high time she woke up. Her dratted subconscious wasn't even revealing anything she didn't already know. Of course she'd love to have a baby. But the normal way, thank you, after marriage, should she ever be lucky enough to find Mr. Right.

Anxiety mingled with her impatience to regain consciousness, and consternation quickly set in. What should she do? What *could* she do?

The fantasy baby, contentedly cocooned in its

fox fur wrapping, felt as solid and real as the bag on her shoulder. She was unwilling to rid herself of either burden, though both, she knew, were ephemeral as air.

Even in a dream she wouldn't abandon an infant. The reliable bag, filled with the essentials of her daily organized life, was such a part of her she'd be lost without it. That her subconscious believed the same thing and had kindly brought it along surprised her not at all.

She snuggled the baby closer, relishing the warmth of the fur and feeling a rush of something she might have called contentment under different circumstances.

The sound of hooves and the clatter of wheels shattered the heavy quiet, startling her. She jumped alert and stared to her left with apprehension. A horse pulling a half-covered cart galloped down the road toward her.

She backed against the tree and held her breath. *Go on by, don't see me!* she commanded the vision.

But the horse and two-wheeled buggy stopped directly in front of her.

A tall man stepped from the antique conveyance. As he approached her, she gaped, paralyzed with foreboding. A specter? He was dressed in black from his high leather boots to the top of his tricorn hat. An ascot-like white wrapping around his neck and a narrow strip of white braid on his hat provided the only interruptions to the somber black. Even the wide-lapeled cloak flung over his broad shoulders was black, adding to the spectral quality.

She had conjured up a colonial gentleman! An ominous-looking one at that. He held a whip in his black-gloved hand.

23

Meredith pressed harder against the tree and clutched the baby tighter, too terrified to blink and forgetting to breathe.

And then he stopped, towering over her. She saw brass buttons, smelled leather and wool, bit her lip, and slowly looked up—into a pair of incredible blue eyes. No, not blue. Turquoise. The valued gem variety, set in an angular, stern face that was, without doubt and despite the sternness, the most impossibly handsome face she'd ever seen.

She couldn't think straight. She couldn't think at all.

The specter spoke. "Joshua was to be with you and the babe at the appointed hour, Miss Wetzel. Do you know where he might be?"

# Chapter Two

"Hmmm?" was all Meredith could manage.

Not one word he'd spoken in that rich, deep voice made a grain of sense.

"Where's Joshua?" he asked, apparently repeating himself.

She shook her head.

His firm jaw tightened, sending a mesmerizing ripple up his smooth yet rugged cheek. Oh my, she'd conjured up quite a man.

"Well, then, we'll go on without him," he said, reaching for her elbow. "He's dallied somewhere, I wager. He'll follow soon enough."

His gloved hand on her arm was persuasive, electric. She wanted to protest, tried to hold back, but the intriguing prickly sensation he'd set off clouded her already-clouded brain.

This captivating specter had somehow converted her usual steel resolve into a puff of smoke.

What difference did it make? He as well as everything around her was nothing but smoke. Dream smoke.

She let him lead her to the buggy.

"Have you no cloak?" the Dream Man asked.

She'd forgotten the cold. "Uh, no." Her words had the power of a couple of dropped cotton balls.

But he must have heard them. "Here, take mine," he said, and soft warm wool fell across her shoulders, circling her with the light scent of camphor mixed with a headier masculine aroma she found both comforting and appealing.

Her subconscious was indeed more interesting than she'd realized.

"I'll hold it while I hand you up."

He was talking gibberish, but it hardly mattered. His voice held the dark resonance of a well-played cello. She sensed he expected a response, but all she could muster was a puzzled stare. Mercy, but his eyes were beautiful!

"The babe," he said to her. "Let me have him and I'll help you up into the chair." Impatience colored the cello's tones.

"Oh." She'd dropped another cotton ball. Her head felt stuffed with them, but a trickle of comprehension worked through. She handed him the baby.

With his help, she got up into the buggy. She'd expected to float, but the process was tricky. The toe of her shoe tangled with her skirt's hem and she would've fallen backward had his large hand not been there to boost her up. By her fanny!

She plopped down on the hard leather seat with

an undignified grunt and felt her face flaming. She was chagrined by her clumsiness and thoroughly unsettled by this man's presence. *He* wasn't real— why did his touches feel so real?

In fact, what could explain the vivid qualities of this strange dream? The sharp smells of leather, damp wool, and horseflesh; the firm pressure of the buggy's seat against the back of her knees; the chilling brush of wind across her heated cheeks. The sight, dear God, of that tall, handsome man holding a fur-wrapped baby and waiting with strained patience for her to get organized enough to take it back from him.

Where on earth was he taking her? Who did he think she was? Who was he? *What was she doing?*

She was stranded without answers, but a thin thread of rationality told her she might as well go along for the ride since she had no alternatives at the moment. She wiggled around to straighten her skirt, positioned her bag by her feet, and adjusted his cloak over her shoulders. After her resigned signal to him that she was ready, he placed the baby in her arms and walked around the buggy.

He took his seat beside her with a fluid grace she couldn't help but notice. He oozed confidence.

"Do you have the necessary documents in your valise?"

"Valise?"

The corner of his mouth twitched, making a lovely dimple form in his left cheek. Her continuing display of stupidity annoyed him, she guessed. Who could blame him? She watched the dimple vanish.

"That satchel you brought," he said, nodding toward the bag by her feet.

27

"Oh." Good heavens, she sounded like such a fool! Appalled by her uncharacteristic behavior, she pulled away from his probing gaze, ordering herself to regain a semblance of her natural poise. She stiffened her back, lifted her chin, and studied the rear end of the golden horse harnessed to the buggy.

She saw no reason to act other than assured. *Remember, it's only a crazy dream.*

The phantom wanted documents? She had documents galore in that bag—driver's license, Social Security card, credit cards . . .

"Of course I have documents," she blurted out. "Any and all that might be necessary, I'm sure." The crisp clarity of her voice strengthened her resolve to carry on as if she knew what she was doing.

"Very good," he said after a weighted pause. She suspected that her sudden coherence had surprised him. Out of the corner of her eye she saw him lift the reins. The wooden wheels creaked beneath them as the horse started forward.

Deftly the man maneuvered the animal to turn the wagon around and brought him to a gentle trot. As they clattered down the road in the direction from which he'd arrived, Meredith looked back. The oak where she'd stood had disappeared behind the cloud of dust kicked up by the wheels. What little there'd been of her early Richmond was fading in the dust behind her.

*Dust . . . smoke . . . they're one and the same. Air. Like this jostling buggy, the golden horse pulling us . . . that enchanting man. All of it is nothing but air.*

Though her mind swarmed with unanswered questions, she settled back on the bouncing seat, cuddled the sleeping baby in her arms, and kept her eyes straight ahead.

Now that she'd regained her composure, she hoped the handsome phantom would observe that she, too, oozed confidence.

Benjamin Foxworth was not impressed with the woman who was to become his brother's bride. How in Satan's name had Joshua gotten himself into such a coil? Oh, he knew well enough *how* he'd done it—his younger brother's scandalous behavior was as predictable as the phases of the moon. Joshua had an insatiable appetite for feminine pulchritude and took his pleasures with the fervor and conscience of a randy bull.

The rake probably had bastards of all colors running at the heels of their wench mothers throughout Virginia. And Benjamin suspected that more than a few youngsters of proper plantation ladies had Foxworth blood in their veins as well. Indeed, Joshua's wild oats had contributed mightily to the colony's rising population.

The question this time was *why* his brother had allowed himself to become entangled with the virginal daughter of a Richmond merchant and get her with child. Joshua should have known better. Herman Wetzel was a strict German Lutheran father, and despite the fact that he couldn't pry from his daughter the name of the man who had put her into a family way before the babe was born, once she'd confessed Wetzel did exactly what Joshua could have predicted from the beginning—demand a wedding.

Benjamin glanced over at the slender woman by his side. Sylvia Wetzel didn't even look like one of Joshua's preferred targets. "Aye, ripe dumplings bubbling with steam are to my taste," he'd heard his brother say numerous times. "Virginia's kettles are filled with the delicacies, and they pop right up out of the broth when I stir them up."

And so they did, apparently. Only this time he'd stirred up something other than a dumpling, and Joshua was soon to find himself in the confining iron kettle of matrimony.

It served him right. Though Benjamin couldn't help but feel a twinge of pity for his brother's bride-to-be. Joshua wouldn't change his philandering ways. This pale, befuddled woman was in for a life of hell, and she appeared to know it.

But Benjamin wondered how much she truly knew. She acted a mite like someone without normal intelligence. Dear God, he hoped she wasn't feeble-witted.

He cleared his throat. "It's cold for late March," he said, attempting to put her at ease. Perhaps mere apprehension made her so peculiar.

"It was extremely warm earlier. I had no idea a cold snap was coming."

*Cold snap?* He'd never heard the term. German, he supposed, though she spoke English with fair pronunciation.

"Maybe in Richmond the morning was warm, but in Hanover we had frost," he said.

"Is that where you're taking me? Hanover County?"

Her wide, questioning eyes searched his. They were a curious shade—a bright garish green. But the glint of concern flickering through that green touched him, and he felt a swell of compassion for her.

He tried for a warming smile. "Of course

Hanover. Have you not been told that Fox Haven is in Hanover?"

"No," she said, shaking her head. Her capless hair was the color of polished chestnuts and swung loose against her high-boned cheeks. He had never seen a woman's hair styled thus, flowing free yet in a controlled swaying manner. His fingers tingled beneath his gloves with a rebellious desire to touch the unfettered strands.

Benjamin chastised his improper thoughts, but realized at the same time that Sylvia Wetzel was far more comely than he'd allowed himself to note at first. Other than that odd tint of her thickly lashed eyes, she was indeed a lovely woman.

Something like a small wave billowed inside his chest. He tensed and quickly looked away. Had he been staring?

"No one's told me anything, as a matter of fact. I don't even know who *you* are," she said.

He tightened his hands on the reins. The arrangements had been planned at Fox Haven a week ago when Mr. Wetzel had made his unexpected call upon Benjamin's father. What kind of man would send his daughter and grandson to the assigned spot without telling her who was meeting her and where she was to go? And what kind of daughter would agree to such a thing? He worried once again about his future sister-in-law's mental capacities.

"I'm Joshua's brother," he said.

"And do you have a name?"

"Benjamin." Obviously Joshua hadn't wasted time discussing his family with the woman. Benjamin wished mightily that Joshua had done more talking and less dallying with her.

"And your last name?"

# Thomasina Ring

"The same as Joshua's, of course," he grumbled. Jesus, she was simple-minded!

"I don't know what that might be," she said with incredible nonchalance.

He glowered at her. "That's damnably unlikely, Miss Wetzel, since you knew his name well enough to give it to your father, or perhaps your wits are so feeble you can retain a complicated name like Foxworth for only a short period."

Spots of red colored her cheeks and her bright green eyes sparked with anger. "*My* wits are feeble? How about *yours*, Mr. Benjamin High and Mighty?" she exploded. "You're the one who picked up the wrong woman. I'm not your Miss Wetzel—I don't even *know* anyone with the stupid name of Wetzel!"

Astounded, he stared at her. She wasn't through. "Nor do I know any Joshua, so there! Now stop this museum piece at once and let me out."

Benjamin pulled on the reins to halt the horse. "What the devil are you telling me? You were there at the arranged time holding the babe—"

"The baby was dumped into my arms by a wild-eyed woman not more than a minute or two before you arrived, Mr. Foxworth." She was highly agitated. "Look, you can have it. I surely don't want it!" She placed the bundle on the seat and moved to step from the chair.

He grabbed her arm. "Damn it, woman. Explain yourself!" This was madness. She *had* to be Sylvia Wetzel.

"Let go of me."

Her words had the strength of a command, and the determined set of her face reinforced that command. But Benjamin felt no obligation to obey. He tightened his hold.

"You'll stay right here," he growled.

Her lips clamped together and her strange-tinted eyes narrowed. "I will *not*. Release me this minute!"

Her anger was palpable. His own was growing, fired by her startling revelations and unreasonable behavior. He relaxed his hold but maintained a firm restraint on her.

"You must tell me all you know, woman." He controlled his voice, keeping it low and steady, bolstering it with force enough to convince her that his will was not to be denied.

Her arm beneath his fingers tensed further. Then she shook her head and seemed to slump beneath the weight of his heavy cloak. "I've told you everything I know," she said with a weary sigh.

A glimmer of tears floated across her large eyes as she looked up at him. "Please just disappear into the smoke I know you are," she said incomprehensibly. "I'm tired of this whole silly whatever-it-is and want only to get back to reality."

Benjamin could make no sense of what she'd uttered. Her hot anger had melted away, damping his. But he continued his hold.

"You say you're not Sylvia Wetzel?"

"I swear to God I'm not Sylvia Wetzel."

"And you contend a woman unknown to you put the babe into your arms?"

She nodded. "I swear."

Could she be speaking the truth? If her avowals were correct, he could do naught but return her to Richmond and confront Herman Wetzel with the news that his daughter had foisted her babe on another and had run off.

The marriage, then, would have to be postponed

until Sylvia Wetzel could be found. And Joshua, too, now that he thought of it. The two of them could have worked up some nefarious scheme. Joshua had been far too placid these past few days. Benjamin should have known that his clever brother had planned a way to wiggle out of the wedding. This woman might well have been party to their scheme.

"Who are you?" he asked her.

"Meredith Davis."

He frowned. Davis was not an uncommon name; but a woman named Meredith? Truly unusual, though perhaps it was her mother's family name. "Where is your home?"

"Richmond."

"And why were you standing by that oak today?"

A shadow of hesitation darkened her eyes, and she shifted them just enough to put him on guard.

"I . . . I honestly don't know," she responded.

"That answer rings false to my ears, woman." He pressed his fingers into the firm flesh of her arm. "You agreed to be there, didn't you? Did they pay you?"

"Remove your hand this instant," she hissed. "You're hurting me."

"Answer me."

"I don't know what you're talking about," she said through clenched teeth. "Now let me go."

Benjamin glared at her. She glared back. The resistance in her eyes was as strong as the steely resistance he sensed beneath his fingers. Whoever this woman was, she was not easily intimidated.

He reduced the pressure of his grasp. "I have no choice but to return to Richmond, and you shall return with me, do you understand?" he said. "Perhaps Mr. Wetzel will be more successful than I at prodding the truth from you."

Her response surprised him. "That sounds like a dandy idea to me. Maybe Mr. Wetzel's a gentleman who won't manhandle me like you . . . you colonial bully! At least he'll know I'm not his daughter, and that matter can be settled once and for all."

"Do you promise to sit there if I release you?" He wasn't at all certain she could be trusted. *Did she call me a colonial bully?*

"Riding, even in this blasted contraption, beats walking," she said with a shrug.

She spoke the strangest English he'd ever heard, but he understood her meaning. Warily he removed his hand, poised to grab her if she attempted to flee. But she sat back with apparent cooperation and folded her hands on her lap. Her long nails were glossy, adding yet another peculiar characteristic to this puzzling woman.

As he straightened and reached for the reins to turn the horse, a muffled cry from the ball of fur beside him stopped him. He looked over at the woman, but she was blatantly ignoring the disturbance.

Benjamin lifted the bundle cautiously. He'd had little experience with babes. Catherine and Aunt Laura hadn't allowed him much time to hold Betsy when she was this tiny.

Stiff-armed, he jiggled the infant, hoping to quiet it, but the cries grew louder.

"Shhh." He jiggled harder. Bloody hell! The last thing he needed at this moment was a squalling child to tend to.

"You're doing that all wrong," the woman scoffed. "Here, let me have it."

He relinquished the babe to her with relief. She seemed to know what she was doing, and in but a moment she had the wee tyke quieted. Patting the fur and cooing softly, she held him up against her shoulder.

Women—even this unpredictable woman—had instinctive ways with children.

As he reached again for the reins, the sound of approaching hooves caught his attention. He looked back.

Joshua! Thank God. The ne'er-do-well had much to explain, but at least he hadn't gone into hiding. Feeling somewhat easier, Benjamin settled back in the seat and turned to the woman by his side.

"Our little mystery is about to be solved, I believe. Joshua should be able to shed some light on this murky situation."

Her head jerked around, and she eyed the nearing rider.

"Joshua?" Her expression was inscrutable, but Benjamin detected a hint of anxiety.

"Indeed." He felt like crowing.

"Has your chair thrown a wheel, Benjamin? I thought you'd be almost to Fox Haven by now." Joshua's cheerful voice was smooth as taffy as he drew alongside them and pulled his horse to a halt.

Benjamin scowled at his brother. "Where in God's name have you been? The wheels are fastened tight, but other matters seem to be unraveling. This woman here tells me—"

"I hope you two are enjoying your journey," Joshua interrupted with a broad smile, doffing his hat to the woman and sweeping an effusive bow. "Your beauty brightens this dreary day, Sylvia.

How are you, my dear? And I trust the babe is faring well?"

Stunned, Benjamin faced the woman. *What in hell . . .*

"So you *are* Sylvia," he said, layering his words with accusation to cover his astonishment.

# Chapter Three

Meredith was aghast. Why on earth would that Joshua person call her Sylvia? What kind of daffy plot was her subconscious cooking up? Lord, the seesaw of emotions she'd just gone through with Benjamin Foxworth had been dizzying enough for a dozen dreams—or nightmares, as she hastened to reclassify the wild fantasy. And now, another Foxworth had arisen from nowhere to vex her.

At a loss for words, she stared at this newest phantom. Astride a white horse, he, too, was dressed like a colonial but with far more flash and color than his stern specter of a brother. His splendid brass-buttoned coat was robin's egg blue, his knee breeches a powdery buff, and his high riding boots rich cordovan. The silver gray cloak over his shoulders sported a flamboyant crimson lining.

The two men were a study in contrasts. Joshua twinkled like a sparkler; Benjamin simmered with the deep, unfathomable shadows of a midnight sky. Beneath his floppy-brimmed hat, the younger brother's long, sun-streaked blond curls hung free; the elder's tied-back hair under his stiff tricorn was raven black. Joshua was as loose and jaunty as Benjamin was controlled and somber. The only clue that the two might be related was the shared turquoise color of their eyes.

Though in differing ways—Joshua's features were soft and devilishly youthful while Benjamin's had the chiseled strength of a mighty man— both were far too handsome to be human, and she wondered how she'd created such visions; and more importantly, *why?*

What in heaven's name was her subconcious trying to tell her?

A lusty wink from the phantom atop the white horse set off a warning buzzer in her head. Joshua Foxworth was up to no good and acting for all the world as though she were his accomplice. She glowered at him. Good grief, he'd had the gall to say she was Sylvia Wetzel!

And Benjamin, she could tell by his reproachful gaze, had swallowed the nonsense hook, line, and sinker.

Screwing up her face so that sourpuss Benjamin and the lying Joshua couldn't miss her displeasure with whatever was going on, she sat back and feigned a resigned calmness. What else could she do? This little drama she'd concocted would have to unfold in its own way until she woke up, she guessed. Though dejected, she was curious, too. This story had interesting possibilities, and it was no more real than a late-night movie. Why not stick around and see how it ended?

As the buggy lurched into movement, she dared a sidelong glance through her lowered lashes at the darkly tense Benjamin. Well, one thing was certain. Benjamin Foxworth, despite his irritating uppity manner, was definitely leading man material.

Joshua, now, she would cast in a secondary role. Comic relief, maybe—of the mischievous troublesome sort, she'd bet.

And what of the mysterious heroine Sylvia Wetzel? Why was she being taken to Fox Haven?

*I'm not Sylvia Wetzel*, she reminded herself. That wild-eyed woman in Richmond must have been Sylvia Wetzel.

So why did Joshua call her Sylvia? What kind of fool trick was he playing? How did the baby fit into the story? And what could she do about any of it?

Not a blasted thing, she realized. She wished like the dickens her subconscious would provide a script to guide her.

The trip to Fox Haven in Hanover County took nearly four butt-numbing hours. Joshua, claiming impatience with the "chair's slow pace," had sped ahead on his white horse long ago "to ensure the house is in readiness for the fair Sylvia and her bundle of joy."

Meredith had been relieved to see him go. His constant banter and flirtatious you-and-I-know-a-secret manner had set her teeth on edge. But riding alone with the taciturn Benjamin was no picnic either, she soon found. His stony silence made her increasingly uncomfortable—and, of all things, bored.

"I wonder what time it is," she said at last to break the monotony.

Without taking his eyes off the road, he reached into a pocket of his waistcoat and pulled out a large gold antique-looking watch attached to a chain. He flipped its lid open with his thumbnail, glanced down briefly, then closed it with a snap and returned it to his pocket.

"Half after five," he said and nothing more.

She'd lost all sense of time. Five thirty? The lightning bolt had struck around two forty-five, she figured. Had she been unconscious nearly three hours? Good heavens . . .

But dream time wasn't necessarily real time. To keep her mind as well as her fidgets under control, she reached down into her bag for her own watch, holding the baby cradled against her with one arm. Digging around among the hodge-podge of contents in the bag, she was heartened by the familiar feel of so many items she depended upon: her contact paraphernalia, wallet, makeup case, "emergency supplies" like scotch tape, sewing kit, and only the Lord and she knew what else.

Meredith liked to be prepared for any and all eventualities. Though the current one might well offer unique challenges she couldn't have predicted, she realized with a sinking heart.

Just then her fingers lit on her reliable no-frills Timex. Retrieving it, she worked awkwardly around the fur bundle and fastened the watch on her left wrist.

The Timex said five thirty.

She and Benjamin Foxworth were in sync, in the matter of time, at least—but unfortunately in nothing else she could think of.

41

"What's that peculiar device?" he asked, catching her off guard.

"A wristwatch, of course," she said without thinking. He was eying it with open interest.

Oh dear, a genuine colonial would never have seen one, she supposed. She shrugged inwardly. No reason she could see not to edify one who was only a phantom.

"It tells time, like yours," she explained, using teacherly tones and holding her arm outstretched for his perusal. "But far more convenient, being right there when you need it. They're commonplace as the dickens. I'm surprised you're not familiar with them," she added, unable to resist nettling him. She barely admitted to herself how pleased she was to see him enticed by *something* about her.

"Truly amazing," he said, quite taken with the miracle. He bent to examine it more closely. "Timex?" His cultured near-British accent made it sound like "Tom Mix." "Quartz?" he continued. "And the third hand that moves around so rapidly—could that be marking the seconds? Where is such a wonder made?"

"Uh . . . Japan, probably. Practically everything nowadays comes from there," she said, a bit dazed. His head bending over that way, so near that his warm breath brushed her arm, had become a delightful distraction. She found herself hoping he might want to touch the watch, and maybe her skin beneath while he was at it.

But he raised his head and looked at her, puzzled. "Japan? That's passing strange, if true. Are you certain?"

She wasn't certain of anything at the moment except that his eyes were turquoise. "Hnn-uh . . .

I mean no," she stammered. "I don't know where it was made, really. That was just a guess on my part."

When he turned his attention back to the road, she remembered to breathe again and folded her arm around the baby she'd juggled over to her right side. Boy, he'd sure discombobulated her. She'd better be careful. Benjamin Phantom oozed way more than confidence; he overflowed with sex appeal!

"The concept of a timepiece on the arm interests me, though it could be vulnerable to easy damage, I vow, uncovered that way," he said. "They're sensitive instruments and dearly priced."

"Not this one," she countered, back into the edifying mode now that he'd returned to his end of the buggy seat. "Cheap as dirt and sturdy as all get-out. Waterproof, shockproof, you name it." She wished she had something fancier to intrigue him—an Olympus or Rolex, for instance, with date, lunar phases, the works. Or, and the thought amused her, a Mickey Mouse watch would curl his colonial hair.

But the dark scrutiny her last remark had elicited from him gave her pause. Maybe she was overdoing the edifying and should exercise a bit more caution. His hair didn't need curling anyway. It had beautiful waves.

She changed the subject. "What's Fox Haven like?" she asked.

The hard lines of his face relaxed before he responded, just enough for her to detect she'd touched a soft spot. "It's our home—my labor and my love." His slipping from first-person plural to the singular she considered noteworthy, though somewhat strange.

43

"You should rest your fears," he continued, adding a low "about Fox Haven, that is" under his breath, disconcerting her. "There's no truth to its rumored curse. We've had our share of misfortunes, true, but surely no more than many of our neighbors. Even now the Henrys at Scotchtown lie under a shroud of sadness that—"

"Scotchtown? Is Patrick Henry your neighbor?" she interjected, trying for an enthusiasm that didn't quite make it. Naturally she would find a way to insert her favorite patriot into a fantasy set in the colonial period—that hardly surprised her. But the other thing he'd said. Fox Haven was rumored to have a *curse*? Her straightforward, see-it-as-it-is conscious mind abhorred gothic themes. Finding that kind of gloominess lurking deep inside Meredith Davis, PT, amazed her.

"Aye. You've heard of Patrick, then," he responded, pronouncing it *"Pah*-trick." "His reputation has spread widely since the Stamp Act resolutions back in '65, one might say—a firebrand he is, but an effective one."

*Back in '65?* Her next question was out before she could stop it. "What year is it now, do you think?"

"I beg your pardon?" He had that incredulous look on his face again.

"The year?" Her voice cracked, sounding woefully meek. "I was just wondering . . ."

"The date, Miss Wetzel, is March twenty-third, 1774. Wednesday," he said, pinching each word with a slow precision as if he were addressing an idiot.

And decidedly raising her hackles along the way. "Why, *thank* you, Mr. Foxworth," she said with a thick slathering of sarcasm. "The female brain does have to struggle so to retain all the information you men consider important. Our days are mostly the same, you know—one like the other, so it matters little to us whether it's Wednesday or Saturday or 1774 or . . ."

She clamped down on her tongue. *Blast it all, it does matter!* Why was she dreaming Wednesday when the day started out Saturday? And 1774 made no sense at all. 1775, now, she knew a little about; but 1774? A complete void as far as she was concerned. But her real body was lying on a treatment table in 1991. She had to keep that in mind and not panic.

Benjamin was studying her face, one of his handsome black eyebrows curved up like the top of a question mark. "Most females of my acquaintance manage dates quite well. You, it seems, are an exception."

"You bet your boots I'm an exception!" she retorted, spurred to anger by his supercilious way. She'd show him, by God. She'd knock him for a dizzying loop by telling him when and where her day began. And she had proof. She'd show him coins and calculator and dozens of other things that would blow his mind.

But before she could open her mouth, the baby's wailing cries cut through the air and sliced the hot wire of her anger into a sputtering fizzle. She turned away from Benjamin Foxworth and attempted to quiet the screaming infant, using every trick she knew. Nothing worked this time. She recognized the cries. The baby was hungry.

"He's hungry," Benjamin yelled over the racket.

"Tell me about it," she snarled. "Now, now . . . shhhh," she crooned into the fur. To no avail.

"Well?" he questioned loudly.

"Well what?" she shouted.

"Why don't you feed him?"

"*Feed* him?"

"Yes, feed him. You're his mother, aren't you?"

She glared at him and raised the decibels of her voice. "I told you I'm not his mother! And carrying around a bottle of baby formula is one emergency I never thought to prepare for!"

The relentless squalling was making her nervous.

"Do you mean you're dry, Miss Wetzel?"

"Dry as a bone, Mr. Foxworth!"

His disapproval was as sharp as the lash of a whip. She jerked back and slid away from him to the far end of the seat.

"Then why in God's name didn't you bring along a wet nurse?" he roared.

"I don't know any blasted wet nurse!" she screamed over her shoulder, exasperated to the point of tears.

And then she remembered. She did have something in her bag—something she'd bought yesterday for her silly, dumb-blond sister-in-law who believed crying was good for a baby's lungs. She bent and groped with one hand through the purse's miscellany until she found it. With dispatch, she tore away the plastic wrapper and placed the brand-new pacifier against the lips of the bawling infant. All was soon quiet except for contented little sucking sounds. The round white ring bobbed merrily above the busy rosebud mouth.

Meredith smiled and settled back.

"What is *that*?"

Oh, oh. Time for more education. "It's called a pacifier."

"A mock mother's teat, woman? That appears a highly unnatural method to quiet a babe."

"But effective, as you see."

His "hmmpf" reeked with criticism.

She didn't give a damn. "I trust there's a wet nurse in residence or a supply of milk and baby bottles at your Fox Haven," she said, her confidence restored. "How much longer till we get there? The pacifier won't satisfy him forever, you know."

"We should arrive in a quarter of an hour or so," he said tersely. "Your father said nothing about the need for a wet nurse," he added with a grumble, his intriguing lips drawn into a tight line, his beautiful dark eyebrows pulled together.

"An oversight on his part," she said with an it's-your-problem-not-mine shrug.

Clopping hooves, creaking wheels, and vigorous sucking noises were all quieter than the loud silence hovering between them. She sat complacently, waiting.

"Sukie will have milk," he said at last.

"Sukie?"

"One of the house slaves."

Meredith made a sour face. "You have *slaves*? That's disgusting. Absolutely immoral," she snipped.

Benjamin glowered at her. "You speak of immorality, Miss Wetzel? You, an unnatural mother of a bastard child, dare to accuse others of immoral acts?"

She contorted her face into a squiggle of angry objection. "Slavery is immoral, Mr. Prim and Proper. And I am *not* a mother, unnatural or otherwise. Please get that fact into your stubborn eighteenth-century head."

"The proof is in your arms, Miss Wetzel."

"I am *not* Sylvia Wetzel," she snapped back at him with the zing of a stretched jar rubber sprung loose.

His sigh was heavy with disgruntled impatience. "Your bridegroom says you're Sylvia Wetzel, and that's evidence enough for me." He looked at her then, disdain hardening the turquoise of his eyes to cobalt. "Your speech is pocked with insensible words, Miss Wetzel, your manner is troubling, and your fiery temper unseemly. I fear my brother's been trapped into taking a scold as his wife."

"What on earth are you talking about?" Her voice quavered over the lump of apprehension in her throat.

He didn't respond. He didn't have to. She'd heard his words—*bridegroom*—his *brother* . . . *wife*.

Meredith shivered. She was supposedly on her way to marry Joshua Foxworth? *Joshua?* The baby, then, was that rascal's. His and Sylvia Wetzel's. A shotgun wedding was planned.

*Over my dead body!* No, she shouldn't even think that phrase, not with her real body lying in a hospital back in Richmond. She wasn't superstitious, but she didn't want to tempt fate, either. She'd recover. She'd wake up soon. Until she did, she'd try to get better control of this crazy dream. Of course she wasn't going to marry Joshua Foxworth. She wasn't about to marry anybody!

*Think, for Pete's sake!* She wasn't Sylvia Wetzel; Joshua, certainly, knew she wasn't Sylvia. For some reason he was pretending she was. Why?

A dead end. She tried another path. Benjamin seemed to have the upper hand with Joshua. He was older, and probably ruled the roost at the "cursed" Fox Haven. But he was hardheaded and refused to believe her. Wasn't there some way she could reason with him? An idea struck her. She had I.D.'s in her bag that would prove she was Meredith Davis. Maybe their dates would upset Benjamin, but that was beside the point.

No way was she going to sit by quietly and let him marry her off to that brother of his, even in a dream state. Good grief, Joshua reminded her of an early-American Warren Beatty.

She made her decision.

Shifting the baby to her right arm, she reached down, hefted the bag up, and plopped it on the seat between them. *Was the purse lighter than before?* Nonsense—her imagination was working overtime. She took a deep breath and looked over at Benjamin.

"I have multiple items in this bag to convince you that I'm not your brother's Miss Wetzel." She sounded firm and steady, like a top-notch lawyer preparing to unveil her irrefutable evidence to judge and jury.

His eyes flicked down to the purse under her hand, then returned without a hint of interest to gaze at the road ahead. "The voice of God would be unlikely to convince me at this stage. I doubt that anything in that valise can do otherwise."

"Oh, but I do believe it will," she said with confidence. Wishing she had both hands free, she fumbled inside the bag with the less-agile left one to find her wallet. Strange. The bag's contents did seem somewhat diminished.

But her fingers surrounded the wallet's bulky contours; satisfied, she pulled it out, set it on her lap, and began working on the clasp.

Without even looking at what she'd retrieved, he spoke up, his words freezing her fingers into immobility. "Whatever you have there, Miss Wetzel, it will have to wait till another time. We're approaching Fox Haven."

"But you *must*—"

"Later, perhaps, though the only items I truly care to see are the babe's and your birth documents. We'll need them before the ceremony can be conducted."

When the meaning of what he'd said seeped through, she breathed a sigh of relief. Her problem was solved, then—just like that! She had no birth certificates of any kind, so the proposed marriage, for sure, was off.

Tossing her wallet back into the bag, she smiled, considerably less tense. She didn't have to ruffle this phantom colonial's staid feathers with twentieth-century evidence after all. And maybe tomorrow he'd take her back to Richmond where she belonged. Or, and she crossed her fingers as she got her first glimpse of Fox Haven, surely she'd wake up before then.

The house loomed ahead of her at the far end of a wide rust-colored dirt path bordered by dark green cedars. It was an impressive structure—a red brick two-and-a-half-story gable-roofed Georgian with stately chimneys and symmetrical one-and-a-half-story wings on either end. Candlelight twinkled from nearly all of its numerous windows, defying the gloomy dusk outside and issuing an invitation of warmth and genteel hospitality.

Despite its imposing dimensions and advertised "curse," the place was totally incompatible with anything gothic. For the second time in as many minutes, Meredith expelled a sigh of relief. Her subconcious finally had started behaving itself. Fox Haven was exactly the kind of elegant house she'd be likely to dream up.

As the buggy pulled up to the white-paneled front door, flanked with sidelights aglow with the golden light from within, Joshua and a young black man descended the three brick steps to meet them.

"Welcome to Fox Haven, Sylvia, my love." Joshua's baritone purr sounded like a tiger ready to pounce. He reached for her hand.

Meredith hesitated. She saw no easy way to maneuver bag, baby, and her stiff body down from the conveyance all at one time, even with his unwanted offer of assistance.

"I'll bring your valise," Benjamin said, leaping out the other side with the ease born of practice and reaching back for her shoulder bag. "Here, Jack, my good fellow," he said to the black man. "Take the chair back to the stable, unhitch it if you will, and give Croesus his well-deserved feed and water."

After securing the baby in her left arm, Meredith accepted Joshua's hand. Despite his smooth-as-silk help, she felt as if she negotiated her descent from the buggy with the grace of a three-legged elephant.

"Umpfh," she complained as her feet landed with separate thuds and her backside scraped against the buggy's protruding parts. To add insult to injury, Benjamin's cloak, as stubborn as its owner, had slipped off and stayed behind on the seat.

"Steady, now," Joshua said with a laugh, circling the sides of her waist with his hands. He was coming on far too possessively to suit her. Wiggling away from his grasp, she noted his impish gaze skim approvingly over her Victoria's Secret-enhanced bosom. It made her skin crawl.

*Keep your eyes to yourself, Don Juan,* she wanted to shout. Instead, she elevated her chin defiantly, shot a few eye-darts in Joshua's direction, and moved away from him, heading toward the door.

If Benjamin had seen the little tableau, he offered no comment. But suddenly there he was, walking beside her like a dark protective shadow. He'd retrieved his black cloak and had it slung, along with her bag, over his left shoulder. His right hand cupped her elbow lightly. Good thing. The man's nearness had a weird effect on her motor coordination, and Meredith found her normally surefooted self tripping over her own shoes up the wide steps. Without his support, she'd probably have fallen into the pungent boxwoods banking the entry and made a complete fool of herself.

The door swung open as if they'd triggered an electric eye. But an elderly black man stood there, holding it wide and bowing deeply. He was dressed to the hilt in crimson velvet coat, vest, and knee breeches, his crisp white shirt spilling ruffles around his neck and from his sleeves. White stockings met his shiny brass-buckled black shoes.

"Good evening, Robert," Benjamin said, guiding Meredith into the house with his hand ever so lightly at the small of her back. The warmth of his touch didn't match the frozen set of his jaw, but she did notice the gentle smile he offered the servant as he handed Robert his tricorn hat and cloak.

Nor did she miss the momentary flash of that charming dimple.

Joshua bounded into the entry hall behind them, his exuberance undiminished by her earlier put-down. "Ho, Robert, old chap," he exclaimed good-naturedly. "What do you think of my bride? I've landed a comely one, don't you agree?"

His hand rounded her upper arm and his thumb made goosey dents in the sensitive armpit area while its knuckle grazed annoyingly over the side of her breast. Her reprimanding frown was reflexive, and so, too, was her quick move away from him—closer to Benjamin.

The servant Robert dipped his white curly-cotton head politely. Judging from the slight jerk of his knee, she suspected he waited for permission to leave.

Benjamin dismissed him to "inform Aunt Laura we've arrived and tell my father we'll be up for introductions as soon as Miss Wetzel has rested from the journey."

Aunt Laura? *Father?* Hell's bells! Was she going to have to run a gauntlet of Foxworths before this charade ended?

She had to stop this runaway craziness dead in its tracks. She turned to Benjamin, determined to inform him once and for all that she wasn't Sylvia Wetzel, that she didn't possess one single birth certificate, and that he might as well face the fact right now that she was tired of batting her head against his mule-headed obstinancy. So there!

But she made a tactical mistake. She looked up into his face before she spoke. *Oh my.* Candlelight did magical things to his eyes. And the results took most of the starch out of her backbone.

"Look," she began after a deep steadying breath. "I think it's high time you listen to me." Good, she had his attention. Too much of it, maybe. Her knees felt funny. She swallowed around the drumming pulsebeats in her throat and continued rapidly. "Not only am I not your disgusting brother's Sylvia but, for your information, I don't have with me one blasted certi—"

She got no further. The baby renewed its high-pitched squeals and, without warning, a tall, wiry woman appeared before them as if she'd materialized on the spot.

"We'll need Sukie's services as a wet nurse," Benjamin shouted to Joshua. "Fetch her quickly!"

Meredith stood unmoving. She didn't attempt to reinsert the discarded pacifier to quiet the bellowing, for she was oblivious to the baby's cries. She hadn't heard Benjamin's command; she was unaware of Joshua's hasty exit.

Wide-eyed, she could only stare at the woman. Smoke. *This* apparition was surely made of smoke. Everything about the woman was in monochrome. She bore an uninterrupted cast of dull, smoky gray—from the gray cap atop her gray hair that coiled about her gray-hued face to the unadorned severity of her long gray dress and the pointed tips of her gray shoes. Meredith supposed the eyes beneath the short gray lashes were likewise smoky gray, but she couldn't tell for sure. They were narrowed, examining her.

The gray ghost wafted toward her, arms outstretched, and Meredith cowered.

"I'll take the poor child to Sukie, *Miss* Wetzel," she said in a prim, nasal tone that somehow was audible over the baby's robust cries. Not only audible but heavy with judgment. Each syllable embodied mistrust and stilted disapproval.

Meredith shuddered and pulled away, holding the bundled infant close to her breast.

"This is Miss Laura Preston, Miss Wetzel. She's the babe's great-aunt and will see that he's fed and cared for. Hand him to her." Benjamin's deep voice was calm and patient. Yet she heard the underlying order. *Do as I say, woman!*

She did, but not without difficulty. Even as she gingerly held out the squirming fur, the angry child's little legs and arms, whirling like miniature helicopter blades, pushed away the fox wrapping. Undeterred, Miss Gray Woman plucked the wailing baby from its plush cocoon and, with the poise of a lady-of-the-manor, held it protectively in her arms as she twirled around with a haughty sniff and left them.

She walked, Meredith noticed with amazement. She'd fully expected her to vanish in a puff of kindred smoke.

"I'll see you to your room," Benjamin said, breaking the leaden silence that had filled the richly appointed entry hall after the baby's departure.

Meredith's tongue wouldn't work. Nor any of the rest of her, she discovered. Too much had happened too fast.

So he steered her again, this time toward the sleek carved wooden staircase that ascended a formidable distance, then curved to continue up an equally impossible stretch to reach the second floor.

Standing there at the bottom, she shook her head and pressed back against his hand. "I'd rather stay here," she said, barely above a whimper, struggling to order her thoughts. What was it she wanted to tell him?

55

"Nonsense, you need to rest," he prodded. "Here, I'll carry the fur for you."

*Oh! That business about the birth certificates.*

But just as she turned and started to speak, he slipped the fur from her still-outstretched hands and flung it over his shoulder that already held her bag. The pacifier fell to the crimson flowered rug and bounced over to the polished oak floor. As he bent to retrieve it, two pieces of paper fluttered down from the fur, and he swept them up in one graceful motion.

"Ah, the birth documents," he said, giving them a quick once-over as he stood tall beside her. He tucked them beneath his elbow.

"The *what*?" she gasped.

"The only proof we need, Miss Sylvia Wetzel," he said, taking her arm and leading her toward the stairs.

# Chapter Four

The trip to the second floor was vintage dream-work. Meredith, dazed beyond reason, didn't know if she'd floated, crawled, or been carried.

*This isn't real, it isn't real, it isn't real* spinned through her head, more taunt than comfort.

She was standing before a closed door. No, an open door. *He'd* opened it, was speaking.

" . . . in . . . Lucy bath . . . trunks . . . hour . . . father."

"Huh?" Her own voice. Gauzy as her head.

Benjamin spoke again. This time his diction—precise, sharp—clipped through the gauze. Her mind cleared with a vengeance.

"This is to be your room until after the wedding, Miss Wetzel, and you must go in now. Lucy will bring up your bath and assist you if you so desire. Your trunks arrived yesterday with clothes enough for a dozen women, so you may wish to change before meeting my father and the rest of the family. I will be back in one hour to escort you to Father's room."

She grimaced. The commander had spoken. She clicked her heels and saluted. "Jawohl, Herr General!"

His turquoise eyes hardened. He didn't approve. Tough cookies. Neither did she.

"Your valise, milady," he said, dangling the bag in front of her.

She took it without a word and twirled away from him, entering the room. He didn't follow, but stood in the hallway.

"One hour," he repeated and walked away. Testy? Icy? Equal measures of both, she determined, fiercely slamming the door. The reverberating bang gave her a modicum of satisfaction. Kicking the fool thing felt even better. She wished it had been his blasted shin.

Sputtering a stream of select, twentieth-century oaths, she plopped down on a cushioned chair, took off her shoe, and rubbed her toe. What a god-awful mess! Through the looking glass, down the rabbit hole. Name it, she was there. And who would she meet next? The Mad Hatter? Tweedle-Dee and Tweedle-Dum? The Queen of Hearts?

Damn, damn, *damn*! She'd been handed those birth certificates along with the baby. Circumstantial evidence that she was Sylvia Wetzel kept piling up, and the whole world not only seemed content to believe it but stubbornly set against allowing her to prove otherwise.

Her anger slid toward frustration. No, she protested, trying to stop the slide. Anger was far healthier. Frustration led to rank confusion and helplessness, and she wouldn't accept either! She threw her shoe against the closed door.

The muffled thud was followed by two timid knocks.

"Who is it?" she bellowed.

"Lucy, ma'am. With yo' bath?" came the shy response.

Right on schedule, she grumbled. Like a dictator's trains, Benjamin Foxworth's Fox Haven apparently ran in perfect order and on time.

She limped over to the door, picked up her shoe, and opened for Lucy. The large black woman stood with her head bowed, awaiting permission to enter. Two huge wooden buckets, each filled to the brim and steaming like witches' cauldrons, hung from her hands.

"Good grief, come on in. That's some load you've got there—here, let me help," Meredith exclaimed, moving aside but automatically reaching out for one of the buckets to assist the woman.

"No, ma'am," Lucy demurred, her round ebony eyes registering astonishment and a glint of reproach. "Lucy fills the tub for the lady."

Meredith backed off, feeling as if she'd broken protocol and in no uncertain terms had been put into her place. Silently she watched the big woman lug the buckets behind a wood-framed screen that stood in the far corner. A torrent of splashes ensued, and steam puffed above the screen.

Her bath, she assumed, had been drawn.

She sat on the edge of a chair, suddenly drained, tired. Her glazed eyes skimmed the room, actually seeing it for the first time since Benjamin Foxworth had dumped her there. Though spacious and furnished with gleaming antique-style furniture, including a canopied four-poster bed, it had the seldom-used quality of a guest room.

Brass sconces on the walls and an array of candles here and there valiantly struggled to provide sufficient light. Cumulatively they achieved about as much brightness as one twenty-five-watt bulb. The cheery blaze in the fireplace promised a hint of warmth, but contributed more flickering shadows than light.

She had no idea what color the walls had been painted. Wainscoting, manteled fireplace, and trim reminded her of mustard that had gone bad. The walls could only be described as blah. The total effect was thoroughly depressing, despite the red coverlet on the bed, red cushions on stools and chairs, the deep red field of the large Tabriz rug on the floor, and the red damask draperies at the two windows. In the dim light, all of the reds took on the shade of drawn blood.

*Her* room, "until after the wedding," Benjamin had said. And then what? As Joshua's blushing bride, would she be expected to move in willingly with colonial Virginia's prize stud?

She wrinkled her nose. No way! She'd dot lipstick all over herself and claim an attack of virulent measles first; then she'd feign whooping cough, chicken pox, maybe even a long, drawn-out case of tuberculosis if need be. She'd design contagions enough that nobody would dare get within twenty feet of her. Until she figured how to convince these people she wasn't Sylvia Wetzel—or, bless heaven, until she woke up—she wasn't about to get into the same bed with Joshua Foxworth!

"Yo' bath's ready, ma'am. Will you be needin' he'p with yo' clothes?"

Meredith's clasped-together fingers twitched. She'd forgotten Lucy was still in the room.

"No, I'll manage," she responded, remembering

to tack on a "thank you." Her weariness weighted her words.

"We's hung yo' wedding frock in the back room so's it don't get mused; all t'other of yo' garments are in the trunks yonder, jes like they come to us." Lucy's ample black skirt rustled as she walked over to the trunks and opened them, bracing their domed tops carefully against the wall.

"Anythin' else I can do for you, ma'am?"

*Get me out of here!* Meredith wanted to scream, but she only shook her head. Her "nothing else, Lucy, thank you" was a mere whisper. She'd never felt more desolate.

After the woman left, Meredith rose from the chair, heaved a forlorn sigh, and bolted the door. A hot bath appealed to her. Every muscle she owned was tied into knots. She shed her clothes quickly and padded barefoot to the screen, peeking around it with some trepidation. Well-founded, as it turned out. The oval tin tub was short and narrow, and though deep and filled near to its top with water, it was hardly an accommodation for a luxury soak.

She climbed in, feeling like a contortionist as she sat, knees to chin, and finagled with the slippery bar of lavender soap and lopsided sponge to wash what she could reach. The rest of her had to make do with subdued swishing within the restricting confines of the tub's metal sides.

Anything as refined as a shampoo would have to wait till another day, a bigger tub, or additional practice. Nevertheless, the ends of her hair got thoroughly wet as she scrunched down to rinse off her shoulders and neck.

The steamy water relieved some of her kinks; her awkward positions in the tub added a few.

Wishing for a mammoth whirlpool spa, she made quick work of the bath, pulled herself out with considerable effort, and dried off as best she could with a large piece of linen that had the absorbency of tissue paper.

Next obstacle: choose what to wear. Staring down into the trunks, she saw multicolored piles of fussy clothing with lacy ruffles and frivolous bows. She shuddered. Sylvia Wetzel's clothing. She wouldn't touch the dratted things, let alone wear them! With perverse delight, she closed the trunks, then slipped into her own bikini briefs, underwire bra, starched petticoats, and calico docent costume.

Her eyes felt irritated, and she batted them, suspecting something was wrong with her contact lenses. The left one was particularly scratchy, and she removed it and inspected it against the candlelight.

The blasted thing had torn! So much for her cat-eyed look—at least on this subconscious level. Rummaging through her bag she had a disturbing realization. She'd been right earlier. Items *were* disappearing from its interior.

But she succeeded in finding her contact lens supplies and, after efficiently lining them atop a mahogany table, put both green lenses in their storage case and inserted her fresh violet pair. A few blinks assured her they were placed properly, and she returned the supplies to her bag.

Now. How did she look? According to the full-length oval mirror standing against the wall, fine and dandy. A bit wan, maybe. But she had her makeup kit.

Didn't she?

She stared down into her purse. Good grief, it

was decidedly less filled. What was going on?

Ah—there was the padded makeup kit. Far lighter than usual, though. She wrinkled her brows, disconcerted. Inside she found only a small bottle of Elizabeth Taylor's Passion and a square of lavender eye shadow.

Odd. Hadn't she supplied the kit better than that?

Toying with the square of lavender eye shadow, she opted against using it. Why, she wasn't sure, but when in Rome . . .

*I'm not in 1774. I'm not really here.* She had to keep reminding herself. She was Meredith Davis, in 1991. None of this was happening.

She frowned at her reflection. So why on earth did it feel so miserably real?

*Don't think about it. Just be yourself. Everything will be okay if you hold down the panic.*

She straightened her shoulders, adjusted her bra to reduce the enticing bosom display she'd dared earlier, and steeled herself for what lay ahead.

And she made up her mind. From now on, as long as this silliness lasted, she'd do exactly what she pleased and say what she wished. And she'd fight with tooth and nails if necessary to stop being bossed around and treated like a ninny with no brains. She knew she was a bred-in-the-bones controlling woman, and she fully intended to control the rest of this stupid fantasy!

The firm knocks on the door behind her were like sharp blows between her shoulder blades, and she came close to snapping to attention.

"Are you ready, Miss Wetzel?"

She scowled. Benjamin Foxworth, of course. The commanding general.

*Remember. Take charge!*

"Just a minute, please," she trilled pleasantly. Defiantly she applied a wisp of the lavender shadow on her eyelids and a splash of Passion behind her ears and on the insides of her wrists. Stuffing the strangely emptied makeup kit into her bag, she shoved the whole shebang under the bed. Later she'd find a way to get Benjamin Foxworth alone and knock his socks off by showing him some of her twentieth-century belongings. In the meantime, she'd be sweet as sugar. What possible harm could a little sweetness do?

She readjusted the bra to maximum enticement, lifted her chin, and moved with renewed confidence to open the door. And nearly lost her cool the moment she saw him. Oh dear. The man was drop-dead gorgeous. He'd changed clothes and was in burgundy now. Intoxicating burgundy.

"Follow me," he said with a dip of his head that dropped one charming black wave over his high smooth forehead.

"Gladly," she said, meaning it, though she held back, hanging on to the door. Her smile was unavoidable. Oh well, she'd planned to be disgustingly sweet.

He pushed away the wave and raised one brow. "Your rest calmed you, I see."

"Rest?" She was dropping cotton balls again. Damn.

"You didn't rest?"

"I, uh, bathed. And dressed. An hour, you said. No time . . ." Good grief, she sounded downright goofy.

"You chose not to change?"

She looked down at her calico costume, freeing herself from his captivating gaze. Decidedly a smart move, she realized at once. *He's not real, remember. Take control!* Steel returned to her backbone. "These are my only clothes."

"What of the trunks?"

She shrugged. "Not mine."

"What do you mean, not yours?"

"They're Sylvia Wetzel's, I suppose. Look, I've told you, I'm—"

*"Enough!"* He whirled her around and propelled her into the room with dizzying swiftness. She heard the door close softly, but was fully aware he stood behind her. Breathing fire, from the sound of it. Silent, not breathing at all, she battled to regain her composure. *The nerve of him! Pushing me around that way.*

"Stop this bloody nonsense, woman!" he growled, gripping her shoulders as if he planned to shake them.

She stiffened beneath his touch. He let go and stepped back with a heavy sigh. She stayed exactly where she was, mad enough to spit flames, but said nothing, waiting.

"Why are you so unreasonable?" he asked at last, the fire gone from his voice. "Are you that loath to wed my brother that you continue your pretense to be someone other than who you are?"

Meredith bit her lip. The time had come. She had him alone—no need to wait till later. But facing him, she had an immediate, wrenching twinge of regret that she was forced to add to this man's burdens in order to free herself. She knew nothing about him, and yet his burdens were a tangible presence. She sensed them hovering like demons around his wavy hair, weighing against but not bending his broad, sturdy shoulders. Instinctively she wanted to help him, not hurt him. But she must convince him who she really was. She *must*.

"I have proof of who I am," she said. It sounded like an apology.

He pushed himself away from the wall. "Then show me, please."

Strangely, her eyes misted with tears as she walked to the bed and bent down to reach under it for her bag. She should be tasting victory. He was, after all, finally willing to listen to her. But her heart was heavy, thudding as though it were pumping cement.

*Foolish to regret upsetting a phantom,* she tried to console herself as she pulled her wallet out of the bag and opened it.

It was empty.

She stared down at it, dumbfounded. Where *was* everything? Frantically she ruffled through it, shook it. Not even a speck of dust fell out.

"I've been robbed," she gasped.

Benjamin came up beside her. "Is there a problem, Miss Wetzel?"

"Everything's gone." Her shoulders sagged, and her fingers kneaded her forehead. "I . . . I don't understand."

"What's gone?"

"My I.D.s, credit cards, bills, change, all of it!"

He was silent. She felt his eyes probing the back of her bent head.

"I comprehend nothing you've spoken," he said. "Are you saying you're unable to find this proof you wish to show me?"

"It's got to be here! I've got a zillion things . . . here, I'll show you!" She grabbed for her bag and upended it in a frenzy of panic. Even before the few items fluttered to the coverlet, she knew something was horribly wrong. The bag had lost its heaviness. The only things that spilled out were a linen handkerchief, her wire-rim granny glasses minus their case, and the Timex watch.

She punched the bag, turned it inside out, shook it vigorously. She couldn't accept what she was seeing! In desperation, she plunged to her knees and groped beneath the high bed. Surely the stuff had fallen out when she'd yanked the bag up. It *had* to be under there! Fighting the darkness, she swirled her hand over the rug, reached in farther. Swirled, slapped.

Nothing.

Everything had vanished into thin air.

"No," she whimpered, cringing against the rug, hating the bag's emptiness, suddenly limp with her own emptiness.

She felt his hands around her legs, pulling her; gripping her waist, sliding her across the rug, back into the light. She didn't resist. Like a rag doll, she was devoid of bone and muscle.

And without a sliver of a brain. All she knew was that the nightmare had defeated her. *Dear God. I'm stuck in this nightmare.*

"What is it, woman? Are you not well?"

She lay prone, her face buried in her arms. "Gone," she sobbed. "Nothing's left. You . . . you'll never believe me now."

He sat beside her. His fingers stroked her back, then ran through her hair, pushing it away from her chilled cheeks. His hands warmed her, but couldn't banish the terror. It lay too deep, out of his reach.

"I'll send for a physician," she heard.

Her mind reeled out of control. She tried without success to lift her head, but could only roll it to one side. With her wet cheek pressed against the back of her hand, she opened her eyes. His face was there, blurry through her streaming tears, but so close she felt his gentling breath on her face. His soothing hand curved behind her head.

"I'll send for a physician," he repeated.

"Pl . . . please," she moaned. The growing black circle whirled, swallowed up the light, closed in.

A wisp of a thought floated by. She was passing out. The nightmare was over.

The light narrowed, until only two tiny spots of deep turquoise remained.

His eyes. She'd never forget them.

They were gone. All was black.


"Hysteria is my guess," Dr. Hughes said, turning to Benjamin. "Her pulse is slow but strong enough, and all else appears in order. I'll wait here with you till she awakes—shouldn't be long, she's mumbled some, moved a tad now and then."

The old man looked tired as he rolled down his sleeves and sat in a chair beside the bed. "What can you tell me about her, Benjamin?"

Benjamin stood against the far wall where the doctor had insisted he remain during his examination of the woman. He rubbed the tight coils at the back of his neck and frowned.

"Her name's Sylvia Wetzel, a merchant's daughter from Richmond. She gave birth to Joshua's son a few weeks ago. We brought her and the babe here today. The marriage is scheduled tomorrow—a joint decree by the fathers, you might say."

Dr. Hughes chuckled. "Joshua's been snared at last, then? Just desserts. Knew it was only a matter of time. Where is the lad, by the way? Shouldn't he be the one here worrying over his bride rather than you?"

Benjamin ran his fingers through his hair and scowled. "He's ridden off to enjoy his last night of freedom in Hanover Town, so Robert told me. Departed without a word to the rest of us, as usual. Before Miss Wetzel's sickness." He lifted a ladderback chair and placed it beside the bed, near the physician. With a worried sigh, he sat down and leaned toward the man.

"She appears sorely unbalanced, sir," he said in a low voice. "She's fighting the marriage, keeps claiming she's not Sylvia Wetzel. Her actions are most strange, near witless at times."

The physician's spectacles sparkled in the candlelight. "A sign of true intelligence, perhaps. Joshua is ill-suited to be a devoted husband, you know that well."

Benjamin's brows furrowed. "But what if she's truly deranged? The hysteria . . ."

Dr. Hughes smiled. "Too often it's a woman's final resort when she's not getting her way. Means little; I've seen it frequently. She's a healthy woman, of strong stuff, I suspect, and like all the others will be reconciled to her lot without further ado once she settles down."

"I'm not so sure. There's a difference about her. What, I can't explain. Just a . . . a difference."

Benjamin looked over at the unconscious woman. The bright coverlet was drawn to her chin. She was pale, her eyelids an unhealthy purplish hue. Tears still clung to her dark lashes like candle-caught diamonds. Her face, soft, was at peace now; her loose chestnut hair spread upon the white pillow like warm burnished silk atop a mound of snow. She wafted a haunting scent.

God, she'd been so distraught. She had unsettled him, true. But also she'd aroused his pity and concern. *"Nothing's left,"* she cried. *"You'll never believe me now."*

What had she planned to show him? His eyes alit on her emptied valise, a dark clump on the rug near his boot. He picked it up, and was puzzled by its lightness. It had held but a mere trifle of items and yet had weighed fairly heavy upon his shoulder earlier.

*"I've been robbed,"* had she said? He frowned. Who could have done such a thing? As far as he knew, only Lucy had been in the room, and the servant was as honest as she was wide. Never had he had reason to suspect her of wrongdoing. Nor any of the other members of the household, except Joshua, of course. But he'd left the house directly after going for Sukie and would have had no opportunity.

"Is this a bracelet?"

Benjamin looked up and saw what the physician held in his hands.

"She called it a 'wristwatch,' I believe. It's some kind of new timepiece."

"Timepiece? Peculiar, if so. How does it open?"

"Open? What do you mean? Here, let me see it." Confused, Benjamin reached for the object and turned it over in the palm of his hand. A black leather strap with a buckle, as he'd remembered it. But the timepiece's face was blank—no words, no numerals, no hands. Had there been a cover she'd lifted? He examined the sides, and found no hinge or clasp; pulled the stem, not unlike the one on his own pocket watch. Nothing happened. He held it to his ear. No ticking.

"Strange," he said, befuddled. "I thought . . ."

"Did she wear it like a bracelet?"

"Aye, but . . ." Benjamin stopped himself and folded his fingers around the curious item. He'd ask her about it another time. Dr. Hughes was eyeing him with suspicion. He needed to assure him *he* hadn't become deranged.

"Aye, it's but a bracelet," he said quickly, shoving it into his waistcoat pocket.

"Damned ugly one, I'd say," the old man commented, removing his spectacles and pulling out a handkerchief to wipe them. "Laura will have to instruct her about suitable fashion, I vow."

"Perhaps," Benjamin muttered, distracted. He bent and picked up the woman's few belongings that lay scattered on the rug and placed them in her satchel. The strangely wrought clasped leather case, a linen handkerchief, a pair of spectacles. He saw nothing else, and noted again what little weight they added to the once-heavy valise as he set it carefully against the bed's post.

He studied it a moment before speaking again. "Her protests were such that I believe I should postpone the wedding a day or so. I'll ride to Richmond tomorrow, discuss my concerns with Herman Wetzel."

"I know few of the Richmond folk, get there seldom. What's the man like?"

"Only met him the once, last week when he rode out to make his demands. German. Strict, I'd say; rigidly proper. Father believed him an honorable man and approved of his keen business mind. Figured his daughter was from good stock, had a strong, solid upbringing, and therefore might be the kind of woman who could keep Joshua in line. And, of course, the thought of a Foxworth male child in the household appealed to Father. He's waited long for one, as you know."

Dr. Hughes met his eyes. "Was Joshua there?"

Benjamin nodded. "And confessed he was the father, albeit not with an overabundance of joy, needless to say."

"But he's reconciled, you think?"

"Seems to be." Benjamin sighed. "But that alone concerns me. He's highly unreliable, and could have come up with some cleverness. That's why I believe I should confront Mr. Wetzel with this woman's actions, check on her identification, even bring him back with me if that should be necessary."

The physician smiled. "The woman's eye color alone should be sufficient description, I would wager. I lifted her lids when I was examining her. I've seen no other eyes of such a hue."

"Nor I," Benjamin agreed.

"Like lilacs in the rain—most unique."

*Lilacs?* He stared at the physician. "The leaves, you mean? Not the blossom, they're quite—"

"Definitely the blossom, or very near to it."

Benjamin's hands tightened. He was reluctant to pursue the matter further. The physician was old, and his eyesight as weak as the candlelight in the room. Then too, she was unconscious. That might effect some color change. He knew green when he saw it.

"How's Abraham? Cantankerous as ever?" Dr. Hughes asked. Benjamin welcomed the change of subject.

"His leg's flared up again. Perhaps you can look in on him before you leave."

"Lord, he's a bear when his rheumatism keeps him out of the saddle. I'll give him a dose of laudanum to quiet him. You have enough on your mind, Benjamin, though I sense the days he's bound to his room give you some needed peace."

Benjamin expelled a resigned sigh. "Father's often more hindrance than help when he's up and about, true. He's thoroughly disorganized and his tinkering disrupts our routine, but . . ."

"But you love him," the physician said with a smile, patting him on the knee and rising from his chair. "So do we all. Abraham Foxworth is a gentleman without parallel, but 'tis good he had the fortune to sire you, Benjamin. You alone are the reason Fox Haven is Hanover's leading plantation." He chuckled and lifted his medical bag. "Abraham's head was ever in the clouds. I'll mosey over to his room and administer an added cloud or two to provide him some relief for tonight. You stay by the lady's side, should she awaken. I'll be gone but a brief spell."

Benjamin stood and accompanied the man to the door. When he returned to the bedside, he was startled to see the woman wide-eyed, looking up at him. Awake.

"You're real, aren't you?" she asked. She lay still, her face taut with anguish.

He didn't know how to respond to her strange question. Nor how to quiet her anguish. Though he wanted to call out to Dr. Hughes, he knew the man would return soon. Why bother him? This was, after all, a Foxworth problem.

Fighting to remain calm, he sat beside her, praying she'd be sensible now that her hysteria had passed.

"I'm real, Miss Wetzel, and you're at Fox Haven. You're safe, and you should rest your fears."

She turned away from him and closed her eyes. A tear slithered down her cheek.

He reached over and wiped it away. Fresh tears rolled over his fingers. He kept his hand there, hoping to soothe her. The streaming tears were liquid warmth; the delicate skin of her cheek, cool.

Meredith felt nothing but despair. She knew. Dear God, she knew! Defying all logic, she'd been transported through time. The unreal was real.

She wasn't going to wake up in Richmond. She'd known the moment she'd opened her eyes in this candlelit room, the moment she'd heard the low voices beside her. She'd squeezed her eyes shut and lain quietly, listening to them. She'd understood little, but knew with cold certainty.

She wasn't dreaming.

Meredith Davis was in 1774, abed in an elegant house called Fox Haven, thought to be an unwed mother. Doomed to marry a colonial playboy . . .

"You weep as though your heart were broken, and it sorely troubles me. Is there some way I can comfort you?"

Benjamin's deep voice. His warm fingers stroking her cheek. *Oh, why couldn't he be the bridegroom?* She wept harder. If fate had brought her here, why had it willed her such a hopeless future?

"Shhhh." His fingers combed through her hair and pushed it away from her wet face. His gentle touches softened her despair, and she longed to lean into them. But she knew she shouldn't. Benjamin Foxworth had wonderful strength, but she couldn't be dependent on him. She'd never been dependent on anyone in her life. Only she could get herself out of this mess.

Unable to control her tears, she struggled to control her thoughts. What had she heard? The wedding was to be postponed so that Benjamin could check with Sylvia's father, maybe bring him to Fox Haven.

That could free her. A surge of hope. Once it was discovered she wasn't Sylvia Wetzel, she'd be able to leave.

And then what? What in God's name would a twentieth-century physical therapist do stranded alone in pre-Revolutionary Virginia?

Renewed despair. A torrent of tears.

She heard Benjamin speak. "Thank God you're back, sir. She's awake, but cries like a babe. She's sore disturbed."

Another's hands replaced his and were turning her shoulders, pressing against her forehead. " 'Tis but a normal reaction after hysteria. She needs sleep, a deep rest. Fetch the laudanum from my bag, Benjamin."

She looked up at the man's glimmering glasses and saw his kind face. And then Benjamin's pain-wracked face was there beside the doctor's.

"Lift her shoulders from the pillow, Benjamin. Is there water?" she heard.

Benjamin's strength surrounded her, raised her. When her head fell back, his hand cradled it and held it up. She felt the tip of a cold spoon against her quivering lips, tasted the bitter drug, and swallowed with a grimace. Benjamin held her close, and she willingly leaned into his hard chest. The doctor gave her water. It tasted sweet. Benjamin felt sweet.

She looked up into his magical eyes. He wiped away her tears. "Sleep now. All will be well," he whispered. Like a promise.

*All will be well* echoed through the fog clouding her brain. He made it sound possible.

75

# Chapter Five

Meredith paced back and forth across the dark red Tabriz rug in her room. Benjamin had been gone two full days. What in heaven's name could be delaying him so long in Richmond?

The wedding was on hold until he returned, she'd been assured, but everyone at Fox Haven continued to call her "Miss Wetzel." None of them seemed curious about Benjamin's unexpected trip to Richmond or aware that he might have any suspicions about her identity. Obviously, Benjamin kept things close to his chest, and at Fox Haven they apparently never questioned him.

The suspense was driving her batty. And not only the suspense. Her desperate situation was mind-boggling. What on God's earth was she going to do? She couldn't envision what lay ahead for her, let alone plan and prepare for it.

She paused at the window. Rivulets of rain now streaked down the glass, blurring her view of Fox Haven's side grounds. But she'd seen them off and on during the gloomy day—for all the world like a movie set of a busy colonial plantation. An army of stooped dark slaves in floppy hats and bandanas working the fields beyond the emerald lawns. Wooden plows, mules. Pigs, cows, and chickens. A nearby well; a distant windmill; a cluster of clapboard and brick buildings. Miles of stone or post-and-rail fencing stretching as far as the eye could see.

Not a movie set. Real.

Staggering. Unbelievable! She'd been zapped to 1774.

Pressing her forehead against the cold pane, she shivered. She had to come to grips with the impossible. She was uprooted from all she'd ever known or cared for. Alone. Unarmed.

Unprepared.

Smothered by layers of mysteries—too many to ponder.

Yesterday she'd been muddled from the aftereffects of whatever they'd given her to make her sleep. Today, even though her head had cleared, she still found it difficult to order her thoughts.

She was sure about only two things. She would not marry Joshua Foxworth, no matter the consequences; and from now on she'd have to be extremely careful about what she said and did.

So far at Fox Haven she had maintained a low profile. Mostly, she'd stayed sequestered in the guest room, though she had wandered through the spacious upstairs hall a bit today and had even ventured downstairs a couple of times.

She knew she needed to explore. She had to

learn everything she could as fast as possible; otherwise she'd never get control of her life again. It wasn't easy. Searching for knowledge and lying low weren't mutually compatible.

Continuing her restless pacing, Meredith once again went over the scant information she'd managed to unearth.

The family and servants she'd encountered were polite, but sadly subdued. She wondered if they were always that way.

That "curse" business kept nagging at her.

She'd met Sally Foxworth, the pretty sister of Benjamin and Joshua, who was strangely dispirited for someone in the bloom of youth—she looked to be about nineteen. And she had achieved a nodding acquaintance with prune-faced Laura Preston, the gray ghost of that awful night of her arrival. "Aunt Laura," as she had insisted she be addressed, bustled about with an amazingly high energy level. She "managed the household," she'd made patently clear to Meredith this afternoon.

Lord, she could have it. Meredith had enough on her mind without getting embroiled in a territorial conflict. Besides, she'd be leaving Fox Haven soon, and she needed to focus her own limited energies on planning how she was going to survive in an alien culture.

She had checked in on the baby, who gurgled and cooed at her from his wooden cradle like a tiny rosy-cheeked pasha packed in white down and frothy lace. Dark Lucy and light-skinned Sukie fussed over him as if he were their own. He, at least, had found a safe refuge. She was glad for him.

His eyes, she'd noted, were a dead giveaway that his father was a Foxworth. Bright turquoise.

Joshua seemed to be avoiding her, thank goodness. She hadn't seen hide nor hair of him. Nor Benjamin's wife, either.

Finding that Benjamin was married had been a blow of sorts, though Meredith was still so stunned to find herself in the eighteenth century that nothing else, including that little surprise, could make much of an impact.

But she did wonder why Benjamin's wife wasn't heading up things. No one had mentioned the woman. And yet Meredith had seen their daughter Betsy, a lovely but heart-wrenchingly despondent little girl of about five, who had some affliction she hadn't dared inquire about. Couldn't walk, evidently. She was either carried around by the servants or sat silently by herself holding a doll.

She hadn't met Benjamin's father, but she'd heard him ranting and raving a few times. Sounded crabby. He was confined to his room. Why, she didn't know.

Tired of the rug's dizzying pattern, the room's mustardy walls, and her repetitive, getting-no-where thoughts, she stepped out into the upstairs hallway.

And continued pacing.

A gruff, gravelly voice pelted her as she passed an open doorway.

" 'Tis time we meet, Miss Wetzel. Come here and let me see you."

She jumped as if he'd shot her.

"Come in, I say. You annoy me walking the hall like a caged catamount."

"I'm sorry, sir." She stood at the doorway, reluctant to enter. The man looked formidable. He was seated in a cushioned wooden chair, his quilt-covered legs propped up on a stool.

"Never apologize, my dear. Puts you on the defensive. Say, rather, 'I'm measuring the hall to determine if Fox Haven is grand enough for me.' Come in and sit a spell with me, lass. I'm lonely and ill-tempered. Need company, I do, and yours will be a tonic unless you're the simpering sort of woman who can't put two words together without fluttering a fan against her cheek."

Meredith's spirits lifted. "I've never simpered in my life, and I don't even own a fan," she said with a smile.

"Excellent!" His eyes twinkled beneath his heavy white brows. Turquoise, of course.

Boldly she walked to the chair nearest him and sat, surprisingly at ease. She, too, needed company. And information.

"I'm Abraham Foxworth, Miss Wetzel. Joshua's father."

And Benjamin's, she thought. He was a tall, muscular, handsome man—a silver-haired version of his older son. But without the sternness. She liked him right off the bat.

"I hear Dr. Hughes dosed you with the same poison he gave me. I do believe it's the only medicine he knows. Have you recovered from his so-called remedy?"

"Partially. I'm still a little confused." Boy, what an understatement!

She felt his eyes examining her. "You're older than I expected and far less buxom."

Meredith bristled. "Meaning what, sir?"

He laughed and raised a defensive hand. "Don't get your dander up—Benjamin warned me you could be fiery as the devil. I meant no offense. Please, let me start anew." He straightened in his chair and cleared his throat. "You're a lovely, mature lady who will grace Fox Haven with far more than the welcome man-child you've brought to us."

She squirmed involuntarily. "In fact," he continued, "now that I've seen you I find myself hoping Benjamin doesn't succeed in his quest for Joshua. You're better suited to be Benjamin's bride. His taste in women is like mine, and to me, you're quite—"

"What on earth are you talking about?" She leapt to her feet, her heart pounding.

"You don't know, of course." He looked up at her, so placidly she wanted to scream. "If you'll return to your seat I'll explain. I can't talk with my head cocked this way—hurts my neck."

Thunderstruck, she sat rigidly on the edge of the chair and clasped her cold hands in her lap. Her head buzzed.

"Yesterday when Benjamin arose early, he noted a letter on his desk. It had been placed there by Joshua, probably the night before. The message was brief. You should read it." He gestured behind him. "It's back there on my night table."

Meredith thought she was too frozen to move, but she managed the three steps to the table. Her fingers trembling, she reached for the folded paper. It rattled in her hands as she squinted, trying to decipher the strange script.

Fox Haven. March 23rd, 1774

To Benjamin.

I leave tonight, dear Brother, bound for our blessed Motherland, England. The Die is cast here in the Colonies, I fear. Soon the Rabble will raise Arms against all that's

Right and True, and I want to be no Part of the Turmoil. I am English and desire nothing other than to live my remaining Days in that fair, civilized Country.

As for Miss Wetzel and the Babe, I turn my Back, shirking, as I know you and Father will say, my Responsibility. So be it. Neither of you should find my Action surprising or anything but true to my Character.

I rest assured that you, Benjamin, will, as always, do what is Proper to protect the Foxworth Name.

I leave you, Father, and the others at Fox Haven my fondest Wishes for a brighter Future. May you all, in some way, find Happiness. Farewell.

> I am, dear Brother,
> The Family's Wastrel,
> Joshua

Meredith read the letter a second time, her heart lodged in her throat. What did this mean? She'd been abandoned—no, Sylvia Wetzel had been abandoned. Whatever, Joshua had flown the coop. Good riddance. Only . . . what was it Abraham Foxworth had said? *"You're better suited to be Benjamin's bride."*

She gripped the paper. What the heck was going on? Wasn't Benjamin already married? Surely colonial Virginia hadn't allowed bigamy. He was widowed, then. That explained the wife's absence.

"I'm not sure I understand," she said to the back of the man's chair. But she was afraid she did. Poor Sylvia Wetzel, who'd made the one foolish mistake of succumbing to Joshua's wily charms, had been reduced to a pawn in a game where men alone moved the pieces.

Meredith's heart sank. Good God, she'd never fit into such a society!

"Come around so I can see you. I don't relish talking to empty air."

Like Sylvia, she, too, was a pawn, so he thought. She tossed a sour face at the back of the old gentleman's head.

"What's the difference between empty air and a woman who has no say-so as to whom she's to marry?" she complained, walking around to face him. Purposely she remained standing. She wanted him to be uncomfortable.

He rested his chin on the steeple formed by his long fingers and lifted his eyes, looking thoughtful. "You'd prefer Joshua as a husband over Benjamin?"

"No . . . that is, th . . . that's beside the point," she stammered, struggling to regain the upper hand. It was womanhood in general she was defending. She had to avoid specifics. She controlled her voice, made it firm. "It's just that I resent your attitude that women have no rights in a matter of such importance to their future."

"Ah, Benjamin spoke to me of your protests. Gave him pause, you did. He's checking with Mr. Wetzel, you know. It's the other that's delaying him—having to detour to Hanover Town or Newcastle, maybe down to Norfolk to stop Joshua before he sails." He shifted his legs beneath the quilt. "Like looking for a sharp needle in a vast haystack," he said with a groan. Sweat beaded his forehead.

Concerned, Meredith moved toward him. "Are you in pain?"

83

He nodded. "Damn rheumatism."

"May I see your leg? I—I've had some experience treating rheumatism." She tried to ignore the strange look he was giving her.

"Are you into witchery, Miss Wetzel?"

She flushed. "No. I helped my grandfather through a bad siege," she lied.

"Hell, look at it then. I'd welcome your help even if you were a witch."

She pulled back the quilt. His right knee beneath his nightshirt was red and swollen. Acute osteoarthritis, she knew at once. She touched it gently. Hot. "When did you hurt your knee?" she asked.

"About five years ago. Fell from my horse. But that injury's long since healed. This is something other—old age, Dr. Hughes calls it."

She shook her head. "What has he done to relieve it?"

"Laudanum now and again. Leeches once, but they didn't help."

She cringed inwardly. Opium and bloodletting. She might as well be in the Middle Ages. Her brain raced. She didn't have any modern modalities with her, but she had her knowledge, her professional experience. She could improvise . . .

"I can help, but you must cooperate and do exactly as I say."

He smiled. "The say-so is yours, Miss Wetzel."

When Benjamin stalked into the room, Meredith was holding a hot compress around his father's knee. Her heart skipped a beat when she saw him, mud-splattered but handsome and stern as ever. Gray exhaustion shadowed his set, chiseled face. He'd been riding hard since he'd left and hadn't slept, she suspected. She quickly returned her eyes to the hotpack she'd fashioned from a piece of linen.

"Tell us your news, Benjamin," Abraham said from his chair.

She held her breath.

"Joshua sailed from Norfolk on the *Brittany* yesterday afternoon, well before I could arrive there. He'd arranged passage to England about a week ago, so I learned."

Abraham's fingers twitched, but otherwise he was impassive. "And what had Herman Wetzel to say?"

She stiffened. Here it was—what she'd been waiting for. She would be free at last. Her chest felt heavy. Dear God, where would she go?

"Mr. Wetzel is ill abed with the ague. I spoke with him briefly. This woman here, he assures me, is his daughter. Said she was highly reluctant to come and was not surprised by her inventive denials." She heard him sigh. "Had her heart set on joining a theatrical group since she was a child, he said. Has a penchant for drama, something he never allowed, of course."

Meredith's hands chilled against the hot cloth. She kept her head bowed and chewed at her lip. They couldn't be talking about her—and yet they were, or thought they were. As if she weren't present.

"Did you describe her, Benjamin?" the father asked.

"As well as I could remember. All apparently matched. Size, hair color, even the dress. He said her eyes were changeable, often picked up surrounding hues. Miss Wetzel—"

Meredith jumped. He was speaking to her. She looked up.

"Your father said he accompanied you to the oak himself—left you less than a quarter of an hour before I was due."

She shook her head and turned away from him.

"Our family's honor is at stake, and your child is a Foxworth. We must make it so in the eyes of the law. In the absence of Joshua, I will wed you tomorrow."

His voice was cold. She shuddered.

"You would marry a woman you don't even know—for *honor*?" She gasped out the words, staring at him.

"It is my duty" was all he said, and he left the room.

Meredith prepared for the wedding with weary resignation. She hadn't slept a wink, wrestling all night with her dilemma. The marriage would be a sham, couldn't be legal with a stand-in bride. But who would believe her?

She was trapped, with nowhere to turn. Under her lamentable circumstances, she should be grateful, she supposed. Her problem of where she'd go after Fox Haven had been solved. She wasn't going anywhere. And at least it wasn't Joshua she was marrying. All things considered, the situation was better than it might be. Certainly it was better for that poor baby. His real mother had abandoned him, and probably had run off to pursue her dream of stardom on the stage.

And that scoundrel Joshua. It was clear that the two had cooked up their disappearances—but the missing pieces still eluded her. Suppose she hadn't been standing at that tree. *"I'd have left it alone on the ground"* hadn't the wild-eyed woman said? What would Joshua have done then? He'd ridden up calm as a cucumber as if he'd known that some woman would be sitting in that buggy.

Meredith knitted her brows. Merely one of the mysteries. There were so many others. Why, for instance, had most of the things in her bag vanished piece by piece?

They couldn't exist in 1774, she realized.

Then how could *she*?

She groaned. That, she knew, was the biggest mystery of all. And unsolvable. She had to accept it and not waste her feeble remaining brain power thinking about it.

Picking up a brush, she stroked it through her damp hair, trying to simulate Henri's styling artistry. Without mousse and blower, she couldn't come close.

Well, anyway the baby was better off. Joshua and Sylvia would have made rotten parents. She and Benjamin would be worlds better for the child.

Benjamin. Her heart turned a somersault. He was devastatingly attractive, but cold as a stone. What kind of a husband would he be? Bossy, she'd bet.

She scowled at her reflection in the mirror. Not a lovely bride. Without makeup, her pale face was plainer than ever. Her straight, mousy hair hung as limp and lifeless as she felt. And fancy puffs of patterned gray satin didn't do a thing for her, though Sylvia Wetzel's strange eighteenth-century version of a wedding dress fit her fairly well. The woman obviously was far plumper and a good deal more bosomy. But the surplus of ruffles camouflaged Meredith's less endowed figure, and she'd tied a wide pink ribbon at her waist to give the dress some shape.

The extended-wear violet contact lenses she'd been vain enough to purchase had only a day or so of use left before she'd have to discard them. Then, with her granny glasses perched on her nose, she'd be like the old Meredith—plain Jane herself. Not likely to enchant anybody, especially a man with ice water in his veins who'd had trouble remembering what she looked like even when he'd seen her in her best makeup.

With a moan, she turned away from the mirror. Lord, in less than an hour she'd be Mrs. Benjamin Foxworth. Married to a sullen stranger. Instant mother of two children, neither her own. A player with no power in a game in which she didn't know the rules.

She wanted to cry, but had no tears left. She felt as if her insides had withered. This wedding day was light-years away from the one she'd pictured for herself. There would be no radiance. No mutual love and respect. Not a shred of romance. Just a bridegroom marrying out of duty, and a surrogate bride, ensnared in a century where she didn't belong, who had run out of options.

"Do you need he'p with yo' gown, ma'am?"

Meredith jerked alert and puckered her face. "No, thank you, Lucy," she said to the closed door.

"They'se waitin' fo' you, in Mister Abraham's room. The parson's arrived."

She tensed. Inhaling a ragged breath, she lifted her chin and pulled back her shoulders. *God help me*, she prayed, moving toward the door. The iron latch was like a lump of ice.

Lucy, standing in the hallway, beamed a snaggle-toothed smile as she handed the bride a bouquet of white lilies. "From a neighborin' plantation's greenhouse," the black woman said. Deadly appropriate, Meredith thought hazily as she wrapped her moist fingers around the long stems. She'd always associated lilies with funerals.

A misty sea of people turned their solemn faces toward her as she entered the room. One face, towering above the others, emerged clear through the mist. Her heart skipped a beat. Benjamin. Her bridegroom. Dressed in a fine suit of turquoise.

She flushed.

He watched her glide toward him. Her gown shimmered in the sunlight streaming through the windows. Her high, porcelain cheeks glowed pink; her silklike hair hung free, gleaming with strands of amber and russet that threaded through the chestnut. Her wide eyes, indeed like dewy lilacs this day, caught his and held him captive.

Benjamin clenched his hands by his sides. He must remember. She would be his wife in name only. His responsibility was but to wed her. Nothing would be altered at Fox Haven, nor in his life.

She stood before him. Her long lashes dropped, their lacy shadows caressing her cheeks. The scent of fresh lavender wafted from her creamy bared shoulders. He was conscious of a peculiar throbbing against his ribs as he moved to her side, and they turned together to face Reverend Hobson.

"Dearly beloved . . ." the parson began.

# Chapter Six

They'd moved her trunks into Benjamin's chamber. Dejected, Meredith stood in the middle of the room. Alone.

His room was like him—tall, lean, and severe. Twice the size of the guest room she'd had earlier but without a trace of softness. The floor was bare, the rigid wooden chairs were minus cushions, the walls unadorned. No ruffles hung beneath the bed's olive drab coverlet. A starkly plain khaki-colored canopy surrounded the mahogany sky-frame atop the four high posts and fell in stiff folds behind the head of the bed.

The bed.

Staring at it, she lowered herself to the hard seat of a spindle-backed chair and frowned. Olive drab and khaki. Fitting colors for a general's bed.

Only the general wouldn't be sleeping in it, he'd told her. He had moved into the adjoining room.

A mere door separated them, but its dark wood was heavy. And shut tight.

"I will not exercise my rights as a husband," he'd announced to her in a private moment after the ceremony. "You may rest your fears in that matter."

She'd studied her wine glass, not daring to meet his eyes. Possibly she should have been relieved. But she'd felt an unexpected stab of rejection.

Duty alone had caused him to marry her, of course; and he'd made clear from the beginning that he didn't find her the least bit attractive. No big surprise there. Unfortunately. She'd bitten her lip.

She knew she possessed none of the attributes that seemed to drive men wild—like her mother, for instance. Or her two sisters-in-law. Or like the women the couple of men she'd stupidly become involved with had, when the chips were down, chosen for their wives. Oh, they'd enjoyed her passion all right. But passion couldn't compete with feather-headed teasing and deep cleavage. Men wanted compliant ornaments as wives, not someone who could balance a checkbook, run a successful business, and who refused o kowtow to their every wish without a second thought. Hadn't her own sensible father married two out-and-out bimbos? His current wife was only a year older than Meredith.

Keeping her eyes on the unsipped claret, she'd suppressed the sigh that had pushed up into her throat. Benjamin Foxworth without doubt was a sensible man. And his taste in women was clearly the same as his twentieth-century brothers'.

He might be stuck with her, but he didn't want her.

Damn him anyway.

"I expect you to be a dutiful wife in all other ways, however," he'd continued in his stilted tones. "You're to assist in the rearing of your son and my daughter. And you're to help Aunt Laura with the management of the household."

Her face had grown exceedingly warm. She'd raised her head, pinning him with a challenging glare. "Is that all, sir?" she'd asked, clipping her words, but managing to avoid a salute. His jaw had tightened.

"Aye. You shall find that quite enough to fill your days I believe, Miss Wetzel."

"You may call me Mrs. Foxworth," she'd retorted and walked away from him.

What a god-awful way to start a marriage! Scowling, she leaned back, and the chair's bony spindles cut into her shoulder blades. Blast it! This room had the charm and comfort of an army barracks. Even the candlesticks and candles looked like government issue, and their flames stood stiffly erect.

She rose in a huff and kicked off the ill-fitting satin slippers that had come with the wedding dress. Tomorrow she'd insist she be moved back to the guest room or, by golly, she'd redecorate this abominable user-unfriendly bedroom!

With less care than angry frustration, she undid the numerous hooks at the back of her dress and slipped out of it with relief. Having no idea what to do with the dratted thing in the absence of closets, she draped it over a straight-backed chair. The fancy petticoats came off next and then the oversized lacy chemise. They'd been her only underclothes. Women apparently didn't wear panties in 1774, and in keeping with her pledge to be careful, Meredith had hidden her bikini briefs and push-up bra in the bottom of one of the trunks. She'd opted not to use the bone stays she'd found among Sylvia's clothing. The contraption made no sense, and how or why one wore it were matching riddles.

The soft knock on the door caught her off guard. Good grief, it was coming from his door! Naked as the day she was born, she felt a rush of panic.

"Who is it?" she asked unnecessarily, grabbing for the frilly silk robe Sylvia Wetzel had furnished. Had he changed his mind? Did that disturb or please her? She wasn't sure, and her rapid heartbeat prevented clear thinking.

"It's Benjamin, Mrs. Foxworth. My pipe was left in there on the mantel. Would you please hand it to me."

No change of mind. Tobacco was the sole attraction. She shoved her arms into the sleeves and tied the sash in a double knot around her waist.

"Where?" She saw the pipe clearly, but was stalling for time, trying to get her unruly pulse to behave itself.

"The mantel. Over the fireplace."

"Oh. Yes, I see it now. Just a moment." She sounded breathless. Damn it all, she *was* breathless.

"The pouch of tobacco also, please."

Her hand shook as she picked up the clay pipe. She scanned the mantel. No pouch.

"Only the pipe's here."

"Look in the table drawer by the bed."

Holding the pipe, she walked over to the nightstand and pulled out the drawer. Empty.

"Not there." She hated her squeaky voice.

A long pause.

"May I enter to find it?"

Clamping her teeth against her lip, she tightened the robe and walked barefoot to the door. Her villainous pulse quickened as she released the latch, opening just a gap. She stepped back.

He walked in, gave her one disinterested glance, then busied himself with his search. She did her best to ignore him but had little success. He wore a calf-length navy blue robe over his handsome, sedately ruffled white wedding shirt. Still had on the well-molded turquoise knee breeches, she'd bet, though she couldn't see them, thank heaven. They'd done squishy things to her insides most of the day. But his shiny black leather boots were quite visible as he stalked about the Spartan room.

She wondered if he slept in them.

"Here it is," he said, lifting a buff pouch from a table in the far corner and heading toward her. "Now if you'll but give me the pipe, I can take my leave."

She stood without breathing and held it out to him. His hand brushed hers as he took it, and an electrical current shot up her arm.

"What in the name of God is wrong with your toes?"

"What?"

"Your toes, Mrs. Foxworth." He was staring at her feet. Confused, she looked down.

Ten dots of red nail polish jumped to attention under his gaze.

"Uh, I painted them," she hedged, hoping nail polish had been invented.

"Highly peculiar." Uh-oh, evidently not. She squirmed her feet backwards in an attempt to hide them beneath the folds of the white robe.

The toes peeked out anyway—only inches from the toes of his boots.

He was silent. For a maddening moment, she was intensely aware of his powerful body standing so close that one small step forward from either of them would result in physical contact. She could imagine where that might lead. One thin layer of silk between her and that navy wool robe covering the most magnificently built man she'd ever seen . . .

A frisson of anticipation leapt through her. This was, after all, their wedding night. Wasn't it?

His strong chest was level with her eyes, and she watched it rise and fall beneath the snowy white ruffles of his shirt. Her breasts tingled as she imagined the heady textures of wool, linen, and hard muscles crushing against them. As other unseen parts of her stirred recklessly to life, she ached to look up into his eyes. But her own were hopelessly fastened to his chest. Not willing to be the first to move, she waited with shallow breaths for him to move.

But he walked away from her, toward the door.

Her disappointment was like a cold shower.

"I trust you find your chamber satisfactory," he said over his shoulder, not looking at her.

"No." It was out before she could stop it.

"No?" He turned. One dark eyebrow lifted toward the ceiling, but his stunned eyes were directed fully into hers.

Oh God, his eyes would undo her if she didn't fight them. The stunned look in them reminded her that he wasn't used to contradictions. Too bad. He'd have to adjust to a few. She tightened her chilled hands into fists and pressed them into the sides of the silk robe.

"This room is stark and unfriendly. Exactly like you, Benjamin. I plan to redecorate it to my own tastes, beginning tomorrow."

Her heart pounded, but she stood firm, ready to defy the angry barrage she knew was coming.

But what he threw at her wasn't anger. It was unassailable power.

"You may redecorate when I give you my permission, Mrs. Foxworth. And not before." He spun around on his heels and left her, closing the door behind him with a solid thud.

She glared at the dark oak, fuming. "We shall see about that, General Foxworth," she sputtered under her breath.

The war, she realized with a tug of perverse pleasure, had just begun.

Benjamin leaned against the closed door and commanded his body to put itself into order. Bloody hell, he'd come within a hair's breadth of embracing the woman. Far more than embracing. He'd been mad with desire for her, and would have taken her with heated ferocity had his sorely weakened conscience not pulled him away. Her slender curves beneath that silk wrapper had incited him with a fiery lust he hadn't known lay hidden within him. Not since Catherine's death had he wanted a woman the way he'd wanted Sylvia Wetzel this night.

He frowned at the pipe clutched in his hand. Dear God in heaven, she couldn't have known how the candles had made the silk transparent. How every inch of her lovely flesh had been revealed to him as if she'd stood before him without a thread of clothing.

And how the sight of that flesh had tormented him, had come close to making him forget his pledge to her that he wouldn't demand his rights as her husband.

The ache in his swollen groin raged still. He pushed away from the door with a low moan. A damnable pledge he'd made. Yet one he'd been duty bound to make considering the woman's reluctance to wed. Never had he forced himself upon an unwilling woman. Nor would he, even though that woman should be his wife.

*Especially* if she were his wife, he thought, packing tobacco into his pipe. Sylvia Wetzel was now part of the Fox Haven household. Her temperament was uneven, and she was prone to hysteria and far too quick with sharp-tongued challenges. In time, perhaps, she would become resigned to her lot as Dr. Hughes had predicted and would settle with proper docility into the orderly routine of Fox Haven. But from her unpredictable behavior thus far, he sensed that could happen only when and if she comprehended that this place and its inhabitants held no threats to her. In particular, she must feel no threat from him.

He held a long stick to a candle's flame and watched it ignite. Indeed, he must keep in mind that he'd married her for the family's honor and nothing other. Hanover Town and Newcastle provided wenches aplenty to douse his earthly needs. They'd sufficed for him well enough these past three years of his widowed loneliness. And they would continue to suffice.

As the flame touched the tamped pipe, he inhaled. The tobacco glowed red, the thin sweet smoke promising a peace of sorts. He studied the small fire at the end of the stick. It undulated seductively in the room's draft. His forehead creased.

Dear God, the woman filled his mind. She possessed a quality he didn't understand. But he'd felt it every time he'd been near her. Like a lodestone's pull on iron, she'd consistently drawn him to her.

He snuffed the flame with his fingertips and threw the stick into the dead ashes of the fireplace.

Bloody nonsense. Tomorrow afternoon he'd travel to Hanover Town. Too long a time he'd been without the solace of a woman's body. That alone must account for his dastardly confusion in her presence.

That alone.


Meredith dreamed about her Richmond physical therapy practice that night. She was instructing Mrs. Florio in gluteal squeezes to add to her home exercise regimen. Mrs. Florio's arthritic spine needed far more than the temporary relief Meredith provided with moist heat, ultrasound, electrical stimulation, and massage during the woman's twice-weekly therapy sessions. Strengthening her lax abdominal, back, leg, and thigh muscles was essential.

"Hey, this one's kinda fun," the middle-aged matron said with a giggle. Meredith, standing back and watching the fat buttocks jiggle together to her count of five, had to smile. This exercise, at least, the woman might do on a regular basis.

In the typical disorder of dreams, Mrs. Florio became sweet old Mr. Cruikshank, a post-stroke patient, and Meredith was using manual resistance to increase his weakened arm's range of motion. His determined smile warmed her.

But then, without warning, her hands were kneading the strong, healthy muscles of a much younger man's sleek, broad, athletic back. This patient had no name, and she couldn't remember why he had come to her. Apprehension gripped her. Like working in the dark, she ran her educated fingers across the hard expanse of his sinewy back, testing for trigger points, tightened fibers, strained, coiled muscles. Surely she'd made a pre-treatment evaluation. What was she checking for? The patient said nothing, wouldn't respond to her questions.

She couldn't find a clue. The man's back was anatomically perfect. Why on earth was he lying beneath her professional hands on her treatment table?

She woke up. And groaned. She knew at once who the back had belonged to and what had caused that gut-wrenching feeling of being unprepared. Hopelessly inadequate.

Blast it all! Before he had intervened, the dream had been pleasurable. Now it was a fierce reminder of all she'd lost. She'd been so content back home working with her patients, doing what she did so well and having the satisfaction of seeing their conditions improve under her competent care.

Her throat constricted. Lord, to be reduced to *this*. Abandoned in a world where her knowledge and experience were meaningless; where her strengths meant nothing. Where she'd have to dance to unfamiliar rhythms and others' tunes if she were to have a ghost of a chance to survive without going stark raving mad.

Lying in the stuffy darkness of Benjamin's hostile room, she found it difficult to see how she could help herself, let alone help anybody else. She closed her eyes, but sleep wouldn't come. Forcing her thoughts to pull away from her impossible predicament, she let the comforting memories of her former life play through her brain.

But they, too, brought concern. What was happening back there in her absence? She was listed as missing, she guessed. An unsolved riddle to the authorities, her family, and her friends. Her father would be distraught, though he was strong and his workaholic nature would alter little. Affairs at the bank would keep him busy; they had always been his prime focus. And now, of course, he had beautiful Heather to occupy any spare time he allowed himself. Oh, Jamison Davis III would be concerned and worried. He'd even miss her, God love him. But he'd survive.

Sonia Davis-Bellman-Osterlitz-Castano, her mother, would be all aflurry for a few days, Meredith figured. But she'd find solace in the sympathy offered by her new gigolo husband and her coterie of shallow friends in Malibu Beach. And—Meredith cringed at the harsh truth—she undoubtedly was basking in the "celebrity" of having a missing daughter. Sonia loved attention, herself, and little else. She'd never understood Meredith. And vice versa.

Ticking down the list—her brothers, her few close friends—she regretted the apprehension and uncertainty her disappearance must be causing them. But they, just as she had been, were active, busy people with full lives. They'd get along fine without her.

Meredith threw back the covers, sat up on the too-soft mattress, and issued a sad sigh. What a lousy thing to discover! Here she was transplanted full-blown into a new life, and in the one she'd left behind she couldn't think of a single soul who would suffer any true void because she was gone.

Except her patients. And perhaps her colleague Kay Schaefer, who'd been her mainstay at the office. But her patients would find other therapists. And talented Kay had been making noises about opening her own practice.

As for her business affairs, Meredith had kept meticulous records, left everything in apple-pie order. Nobody would get headaches from straightening out her effects.

Good grief, she'd stepped out of the twentieth century leaving hardly a ripple. Was that something to be proud of?

She wasn't sure.

Crinkling her brow, she climbed off the bed. The thing was so blasted high she had to use a bed step. She frowned back at the mattress. Feathers. She'd fully expected Benjamin Foxworth to prefer sleeping on nails.

Barefoot, she padded across the wooden floor to one of the open windows. Spring had finally arrived in 1774—with a vengeance. A heavy layer of Virginia humidity had come along with it. She found it hard to breathe.

A clock from somewhere deep in the house bonged a tinny twelve times. Midnight.

Meredith stared out into the fog-shrouded night. Dismal and gloomy, just like her thoughts. And precisely like her prospects in this godforsaken place with its dreary people.

Suddenly an eerie circle of light flickered through the fog. The back of her neck prickled. Drawing in a sharp breath, she grasped the sill.

The light wavered, then grew brighter, expanded, became phosphorescent before fizzling away into a silent white shower.

Meredith blinked. Fireworks? Did they have fireworks in colonial times? But there'd been no sound. Nor was there, to her knowledge, any occasion to celebrate.

She squinted at the dimming glow, all that remained of the ghoulish display. The dark outline of the slaves' quarters hunkered in front of it. And then, a moment before the last flicker, she saw it. Or thought she saw it.

A shadowed figure darting behind the trees, disappearing into the fog.

She shivered and dug her fingers into her suddenly cold arms. She didn't believe in ghosts. But, dear God, had she just seen one? With a tremor of alarm, she remembered Fox Haven's reputed curse.

But that was ridiculous. Someone quite alive had set off that light and run behind the trees. But who? And equally as puzzling, why?

While she pondered this newest mystery, two tiny yellow circles glimmered to life from within the slaves' quarters. Candles had been lit; the poor souls had been awakened. From the low clapboard building, a plaintive, keening wail skirled through the fog.

Meredith shuddered and turned away from the window with a troubled frown.

# Chapter Seven

"The gold brocade indeed brightens the windows, Sylvia. Though I'd truly thought Benjamin ordered the fabric for the dining room," said Sally Foxworth, sitting cross-legged on the chamber's bare floor, surrounded by bolts of gaily flowered chintz.

Meredith stepped down from the chair and looked with smug satisfaction at the newly hung draperies. Step one of Mission Face-Lift had been accomplished.

"The dining room's green damask will serve quite well enough for a while longer," she said. "This chamber's long overdue for some serious redoing. Now, what do you think of this for the coverlet?" She fluffed out the magenta velvet she'd found in an unused room down the hall.

"Perfect. And the colors of this chintz will enhance it mightily once we've sewn it into a bed skirt and canopy," the young woman said with an enthusiasm that heartened Meredith. Throughout the afternoon she'd watched Sally emerge from her shell of gloominess and become delightfully radiant. Exactly as a beautiful nineteen-year-old on the threshold of life should be, to Meredith's way of thinking.

She adjusted her granny glasses over her nose. This morning she'd had to give up her contact lenses—stranded without her supplies, the lenses now were a thing of the past. Or future? she thought wryly.

"I want piles and piles of cushions in all the colors of the rainbow, Sally. Any suggestions where I might find them?"

Sally looked thoughtful, then beamed. "The house is filled with them. We can scurry about, picking them from this room and that like gathering a bouquet of flowers."

"And rugs? My feet will be riddled with splinters if I continue walking on this awful bare floor."

"The attic!" Sally jumped up excitedly. "We have dozens of rugs rolled up there. Old Robert, Will, and Lucy will bring them down and lay them for us. I'll go fetch them."

"Hold a minute," Meredith said with a chuckle, lifting a restraining hand. "You'd better let me do it. I don't want to involve you too deeply in this little project of mine—I'm not sure how Benjamin's going to react."

Sally hesitated, a look of puzzlement tucking a pleat in her flawless forehead. "Do you mean Benjamin doesn't know you're altering his chamber?"

Meredith pressed her finger to her lips. "Our secret, Sally. I thought I'd surprise him."

"But, Sylvia." She looked worried. "I'm not sure . . . he might not . . ."

"Might not like it?" Meredith interjected, faking pained innocence as if the thought hadn't occurred to her on a minute-by-minute basis the whole day. "Why, whatever wouldn't he like about it, for heaven's sake? It's going to be much prettier, don't you agree?"

"Oh yes, *much* prettier, but . . ."

"No buts, Miss Foxworth. Now, I'm going downstairs to round up some help with the rugs. I'd love for you to stay here for the rest of the afternoon and keep me company, but I'll understand if you're skittish about lending me a hand since Benjamin hasn't given me permission."

Sally's smile had disappeared, but her navy blue eyes sparkled. Though she hadn't inherited the turquoise, she'd been blessed with an equally enchanting shade. "I'd like to stay, Sylvia. And I want to help, too. I'll start on the bed ruffles while you're gone."

"Good girl!" Meredith said with a strong nod as she left the room.


By late afternoon Benjamin's once monastic bedroom had been transformed into something between a lady's lacy chamber and a French brothel. It was worlds away from Meredith's taste—she would have preferred quieter colors and simpler lines. In particular, she loathed the garish gold and magenta ribbons she'd removed from Sylvia Wetzel's clothing to use as tie-backs for the drapes. But she wanted her message to Benjamin to be loud and clear. His heavy thumb might hold down the rest of the family; she'd be damned if *she'd* cower beneath it!

Together, she and Sally, both standing on chairs on opposite sides of the bed, were putting the finishing touches on the hastily sewn canopy.

"My brother's in for more than a tiny surprise, I wager," the ravishing young brunette said with a giggle. "He's oft said he abhors sleeping beneath ruffles and flowers."

"He's not sleeping in this room anyway, so it shouldn't matter to him one way or the other," Meredith said, stretching sideways to puff out an extra ruffle at the corner of the sky frame.

Sally's eyes widened. "He's not? But . . . I thought, since you're man and wife . . ."

"He married me out of duty, remember. He's not interested in . . . anything else." The family might as well know, she figured.

The girl fidgeted with the chintz beneath her hands. "Did you love Joshua a great deal, Sylvia?"

Meredith hesitated. The question was loaded. She sensed that Sally was disturbed about something other than her own miserable sex life, and she wanted to get to the bottom of it. She pursed her lips, planning her strategy carefully.

"No, Sally. He took advantage of me last summer after he'd plied me with too much wine. I've never been in love and would be far happier not married to anybody." Well, at least the last part was true. Ducking her head beneath the canopy, she peeked between her extended arms to check out the girl's response.

Bingo. The poignant sigh and a slight tug around her suddenly saddened eyes gave Meredith the clue she needed.

"You're in love with somebody, aren't you, Sally?"

Another sigh. "Aye," she whispered.

106

"Now, don't tell me he doesn't return your love. Lord, you must be the prettiest young lady in Hanover County, and I'd imagine he—"

"Tom loves me true," Sally interrupted softly, lowering her eyelids. Meredith saw the glint of a tear creeping from beneath the feathery black lashes.

After giving a perky bow at the end of the canopy a final adjustment, Meredith stepped off the chair. "We've finished, I believe," she said. "Come on down and let's have a little heart-to-heart talk."

Looking melancholy, Sally joined her, and they sat side by side on the wild array of multicolored cushions that Meredith, in a whimsical moment, had propped in an otherwise bare corner.

She listened to the girl's tale of woe, getting angrier by the minute. Fiercely angry. At Benjamin.

Sally was in love with Tom Morris, the twenty-year-old son of a shopkeeper in Newcastle. The two wanted to wed, but Benjamin wouldn't allow it.

"Not because he's a shopkeeper's son, mind you, Sylvia. After all, you're from a merchant's family, and Father and Benjamin thought you to be a suitable match for a Foxworth. It's because they'd earlier pledged my hand to Mr. Smithson of Goose Creek. And though Father might have relented under the pressure of my broken-hearted wails, Benjamin would never turn his back on a pledge."

Meredith covered the girl's chilled hand with her own. "Who's this Mr. Smithson?"

"A frightfully old widower," she sobbed. "He must be at least thirty-five. A friend of Benjamin's since their childhood. Wealthy, I reckon, for Goose Creek is near as grand as Fox Haven."

Her tears ran freely now, fading her dark blue eyes into a color more like prewashed denim.

"Does he have children?"

She nodded. "Six. He . . . he wants a dozen more." Her small shoulders quivered as a shudder ran through her. " 'Tis the reason he desires a young bride."

Meredith combed her fingers through the girl's raven-black waves, so like her despicable older brother's. She ached with sympathy for Sally at the same time that her chest seethed with anger toward Benjamin. Damn him! Didn't the bastard have a spot of softness in his stony heart?

"There's more than one way to skin a cat, Sally. Trust me. I'll find an out for you. Okay?"

The girl looked at her, perplexed. But a glimmer of hope surfaced in her eyes as well. "You speak peculiar English, Sylvia. Are you saying you might find some means so I don't have to marry Mr. Smithson?"

Meredith nodded with a grim smile. "Trust me, Sally."

*Too bad, Benjamin Foxworth. Your blasted control over Fox Haven, like your former bedchamber, is about to undergo a complete overhaul.*

"Ah, you work magic, my Sylvia. What's that soothing liniment you're applying to my knee?"

Meredith smiled at Abraham. "Fresh-churned butter. It was all I could find with the proper consistency for a halfway decent massage."

"Massage?"

"Therapeutic rubbing."

He chuckled. "So it's butter, is it? I'm to become airy as a puff pastry and an attraction to flies under your witchcraft?"

"Feels good, doesn't it?"

"Aye, that it does," he said with a contented sigh, settling back in his chair.

"Then don't complain," she admonished.

"Never again will a complaining mutter escape my lips, dear woman. Not unless you cease your magical rubbing."

"Oh, I'll stop all right and in just a few minutes. We must go slow at first. Your knee's a mess, and it will be a couple of weeks before you're ready for anything more strenuous than heat wraps and gentle rubs."

"But you'll have me on my feet again?"

"One of these days." She patted his calf and stood, wiping her hands with a cloth and smiling down at him. "If you behave yourself and follow my orders."

"You're bloody dogmatic, woman."

"And bloody right, Abraham Foxworth. Don't forget it."

He shook his head, but she didn't miss the twinkle in the turquoise of his hooded eyes. He harrumphed. "Poor Benjamin. Saddled to such a domineering scold of a woman."

She stiffened and flung the cloth in a wooden bucket. "Poor *Benjamin*? What about me? Sadly married for life to a man who makes Attila the Hun look like a veritable Prince Charming!"

"Oh? Do I hear the whisper of a protest from the not-so-blushing bride's corner?"

"Damn right. You should have paddled him when he was a boy. I've never known a more undisciplined tyrant."

"Undisciplined? Not my Benjamin. A tyrant he can be, true. But a benevolent one, my dear—always benevolent. And disciplined to a fault."

"To a fault," she agreed, covering Abraham's legs with the quilt and sitting again by his side. "And so far I've yet to see even the smallest touch of benevolence."

Abraham rubbed his chin and pinned her with a steady gaze. "Did he treat you roughly last eve, my dear?"

Her cheeks warmed despite her resolve to remain cool. "In a manner of speaking," she said too quickly.

He issued a low grunt and looked troubled. "That astonishes me, Sylvia. Seems highly out of character for Benjamin to act in a beastly fashion. I'll have a talk with him."

"No," she protested, unsettled by the turn the conversation had taken. "Please don't say anything to him. I'd rather tame him myself. If, indeed, he's tamable." She bit her lip. Why would she say such a blatantly improper thing to an eighteenth-century gentleman?

But Abraham, lost in thought, didn't seem to notice. His high brow creased with worry wrinkles. "He was a lamb with Catherine. I don't understand why he—"

"What happened to Catherine?" she interjected, surprised by her morbid curiosity as well as her inappropriate question.

"She died in a carriage accident three years ago. 'Twas the same accident that crippled little Betsy. A loose wheel fell off. Benjamin's ever held himself to blame."

She shuddered. "He feels to blame? Why, for heaven's sake?"

"He'd checked the wheels himself before he let Catherine take the carriage out. Going to Scotchtown, she was, to visit that poor Sallie

110

Henry. Though Sallie wasn't yet stricken back then. She and Catherine were dear friends."

Meredith filed away the Henry questions to pursue another day. At the moment, she wanted to find out more about the carriage accident. And why Benjamin felt guilt. Could that explain some of his hardness?

"Were the wheels tight when Benjamin checked them?"

"Tight as a drum, he said. He's never understood how the hub could've loosened up in such a short time."

"How short a time?"

"He'd tested them closely no more than a half-hour before Catherine and little Betsy rode away."

"Was anyone near the carriage after Benjamin's check?"

"Only Jack, the stable boy, as far as we know. But we trust Jack, and he was near as distraught as Benjamin over the accident." He shook his head, and a thick white wave tumbled over his forehead, reminding her with a pang how much this kind old gentleman resembled his hard-as-nails and far-too-handsome son. "No. 'Twasn't Jack who loosened the wheel."

"Who then?"

His distraught eyes searched hers. "No one, Sylvia. It was, perhaps, the workings of Fox Haven's blighted curse and nothing other."

"You believe in the *curse*?" She was appalled.

He sighed. "No, not in truth. But we've been plagued with so many tragedies, I have bleak days when I give the nonsense some credence."

"Curses are indeed nonsense, Abraham," she said, patting his hand and rising from the

111

chair. *Pure nonsense*, she reiterated to herself. She wished her heart would quit pounding like a jackhammer.

"I must go down for supper now, dear man," she said, her voice far calmer than she felt. "Lucy will be bringing up your tray in a little while. Meanwhile, ring the bell there if you need us for anything."

She waggled a warning finger at the old gentleman. "You're to keep your legs absolutely quiet till Will comes up later to assist you to bed. And no matter how good your knee starts to feel, you're not to try walking with or without a cane till I've given you my permission. And that won't be for at least a week, maybe longer. Do you hear me?"

"Aye, I hear thee loud and clear, Miss Captain of the Militia," he said with a disgruntled snort.

Meredith gripped the door latch and looked back with a lifted eyebrow. "Captain of the Militia?"

Abraham tossed her a winning but decidedly wry smile. "Aye, captain."

She winked at him. "Remember your captain's orders, Abraham," she said lightly and bustled from the room with an air of haughty authority.

But a deflating prick of anxiety hit her the instant she started down the stairs. Oh, oh. A general outranked a captain.

And in just a few moments she'd be having supper with the general. And his obedient staff.

Benjamin's afternoon frolic with the plump wench in Hanover Town hadn't helped. He knew it the minute his bride walked into the dining

112

room, looking fresh as a morning daisy and trim as a prized race horse.

He wanted to groan.

"Ah, there you are, Sylvia," Aunt Laura chirped. "We were about to send Lucy up for you. You've been hiding from us this entire day it seems."

"Abraham's ready for his tray," she said, ignoring Aunt Laura's comment and taking her seat at the foot of the table without a glance in Benjamin's direction.

A pair of spectacles perched atop her head. "Have you been reading, Mrs. Foxworth?" he asked as he pulled out his accustomed chair at the table's head. That she could read at all he found both unexpected and a touch satisfying.

"No, Benjamin. I've been thoroughly occupied with alterations to my chamber. And I've just come from your father's room where I applied some heat and rubbing to relieve his swollen knee."

He stared at her. She stared back at him, unmoving. Her eyes were silver in the candlelight, further unnerving him. He looked away first. The silence around the table made the air heavy. He cleared his throat and lifted his fork.

"The grace, Benjamin," Aunt Laura reminded him.

"Of course." Still holding the fork, he bowed his head and offered a few words of blessing by rote. His heart wasn't in it. The bloody thing was pumping a litany of its own.

How dare she defy him? And what in the devil was she doing to his father? The woman was disrupting Fox Haven. And she was disrupting his

113

own peace of mind to a bloody fare-thee-well!

"Did you accomplish your mission at Hanover Town this day, Benjamin?" Aunt Laura asked cheerfully after the family had been served their light supper. He'd missed the heartier midday dinner. And so, apparently, had his bride. Still, her appetite, he noted, seemed as scant as his own. She but toyed with her food. His fork weighed like iron in his hand.

"Yes and no," he answered his aunt truthfully, knowing full well she'd be shocked out of her rigid stays if she had an inkling of his true purpose for going to town. "People have politics on their minds and their tongues rather than tobacco and corn prices. It's near as bad as down in Williamsburg."

"Are we going to have a war?" Sally asked, sounding excited by the prospect.

He frowned at his sister. "I pray it doesn't come to that, Sally. And so should you. Surely the King will listen to our grievances."

"Oh, he won't," his bride piped in as if she knew what she was talking about. "Let's see. This is 1774, isn't it? I predict that by 1776 the war for independence from England will begin in earnest."

Benjamin put down his fork and glared across the table at the woman. "Are you a Sibyl as well as a Sylvia, Mrs. Foxworth?"

"Perhaps one as much as the other," she said with a damnably enigmatic smile.

"Make certain you keep your treasonous outbursts within these walls, milady. If events lead inexorably to war as you predict, the decision as to which side the Foxworths will support will be mine alone to make. And you and the others will follow my decision. In the meantime we shall all remain silent."

"Are you a Tory, Benjamin?" Her displeasure leapt like fire from her silver eyes. Two blazing torches willfully igniting his own displeasure.

Women had no heads for political matters—nor was it proper for them to question their husbands in such a fashion. This one, it seemed, thought otherwise. His scowl darkened. No, he would never be a Tory. But his sentiments one way or the other were of no concern to her.

He edged his words with ice. "I am a Virginia planter, Mrs. Foxworth, and have no interest in politics."

"Nor must any of us," Aunt Laura said in her calming voice. He smiled at her, ignoring his wife.

Or trying to. Even with the long expanse of table between them, he felt her disturbing presence. Nor would his eyes stop straying in her direction. She wore a pale blue frock of a simple style, bare of ruffles and ribbons save for a satin sash tied around her narrow waist. The rounded neckline dipped low in the current fashion, revealing the piquant tops of her small, firm breasts. They would fit comfortably in the palms of a man's large hands . . .

He pressed his own into the napkin that lay across his legs. Hard.

"Sukie told me this morn that the ghost frightened the slaves again last night," Sally said.

Benjamin turned his attention to his sister, who sat to his left. "There was fog and moist air last eve. Did you not explain to her that night gases form the apparition?"

Sally nodded. "Sukie knows that well, and she's far too sensible to have fear herself, but many of the others—"

"Are swayed by mindless superstition," Aunt Laura interrupted. "They are a silly lot."

"I saw it myself," his bride chimed in, once again drawing his eyes toward her. "I'm far from mindless, but it was a bit scary."

She looked not at all scared.

"Benjamin's correct, you know. It's but earth gases," Aunt Laura said pleasantly, as if to assure the woman.

Sylvia smiled softly, and Benjamin's mutinous heart kicked into a frisky trot. "Of course," she said agreeably to the older woman. And then she aimed her disarming smile at him. "May I be excused, Benjamin? I promised Betsy I'd tell her a bedtime story, and after that I'll hold the baby for a while. Little Philip has his days and nights mixed up, and Sukie deserves a rest."

He pushed back his chair and stood. "Your concern for the children pleases me, Mrs. Foxworth. Aye, you may be excused."

"Why, thank you, sir," she said, a mite sweeter than usual. Too sweet, he knew. He clenched his hands by his sides, watching her walk from the dining room. She held her head high, and he detected the insolent flip of her chestnut hair as she passed through the door. A silent jeer it was. Meant for him alone.

He glowered at the empty doorway. He must throw up better guards against her. She displayed an unseemly contempt for his role as her protector.

Sally, who was spirited more than customary this eve, giggled behind her hand. Aunt Laura coughed daintily behind hers.

"I find myself weary and will retire to my chamber. Have a good night, the both of you," he said brusquely and stalked out of the room.

# Chapter Eight

"What is the meaning of this travesty?" Benjamin growled as Meredith entered her bedroom later that evening.

That he was standing there had stunned her. His rage, of course, she'd expected. Eventually. Not now. She was exhausted.

She peered over her glasses at him and stood by the door for a moment, keeping a firm grip on the latch as she struggled to get a grip on herself.

"Travesty?" she croaked.

"Aye. A travesty, Mrs. Foxworth. You've turned this chamber into a looking-glass image of your frivolous imagination."

Just what she needed. Supercilious put-downs were guaranteed to clear her thoughts—and get her back up. Firmly she settled her glasses on the bridge of her nose. She closed the door with controlled calm, then walked toward him, fuming.

"I redecorated *my* chamber, Mister Foxworth. To suit *me*. I didn't design it for your cold eyes, but for my far more discerning eyes. *And* for my comfort and pleasure. Not, I assure you, for yours." She warmed to the fray. Twirling around, she stretched out her arms as if to embrace the room. "Why, it's the loveliest chamber in Fox Haven!"

The riotous mix of colors and excessive frills were atrocious, actually. Downright nauseating. She'd outdone herself redecorating the room, and for a fleeting moment wondered how she'd developed such a mean streak.

It was his fault. He brought out the worst in her.

Her steam rose. "And my imagination is *not* frivolous," she challenged him, her hands on her hips. "I was practical from the word go and scavenged about the house for discarded or otherwise unneeded materials."

"The brocade was ordered for the dining room," he snarled.

"The dining room looks perfectly fine. *This* room needed dressing up." She wished he would stop glaring at her. It only made her madder. "Why in heaven's name are you nosing around in here anyway? It's *my* room, you told me!" Her adrenaline was off and running.

He looked ready to explode. Only he didn't. Not quite. Oh, the cushion he swept off one of the ladderback chairs bounced like crazy when it struck the hideous purple-flowered carpet she'd chosen. But he folded himself down on the bared wooden seat with maddening aplomb, crossed

119

his arms over his chest, and stared at her. She found she much preferred heated glares over piercing stares. Glares she could handle. The staring unsettled her. She turned her back to him.

"Do you truly consider this chamber beautiful now?" he asked.

"I do indeed," she lied, fixing her eyes on the large painting of wood nymphs she'd recovered from a dark corner of the attic. Its heavy gilt frame, encrusted with crudely carved oak leaves and acorns, was even uglier than the scene it surrounded.

"Then you should sleep content within these walls, Mrs. Foxworth."

She was quiet, but grimaced at the painting. She'd probably have nightmares.

"I must remind you that you made your alterations without my permission," he continued. "I will not tolerate continuing insubordination such as you've demonstrated this day. You are my wife. Do you understand me?"

Rockets were firing off in her head. "Your wife or your slave?" She spat out the words, too stiff with anger to turn to face him.

"My wife, alas. A disobedient slave I could place on the market."

She closed her eyes and shivered. The man was uncivilized.

"Please leave my room," she hissed.

"No."

She whirled around. *"No?"*

He shook his head. "No. Not until you seat yourself and we have discussed my concerns in a sensible manner. Without temperament and anger, Mrs. Foxworth."

"Don't you think I have a few concerns, Mr. Know-It-All?"

His jaw twitched, but he remained calm. She desperately wanted to throw something at him, but only pillows were within reaching distance.

"I'm certain you have many concerns," he said, almost kindly, unbalancing her. "We shall discuss those also. Now be seated please." He gestured to a nearby chair overflowing with orange and pink cushions.

She had little choice. It would take a crane to lift him from his seat and a bulldozer to push him out of the room. Besides, she was limp with fatigue. Her body wasn't accustomed to wild bouts of anger. Before being zapped to the eighteenth century and finding herself beneath the heavy boots of Benjamin Foxworth, she'd prided herself on being even-tempered.

With a weary sigh of resignation, she sat. But in a chair with blue cushions, a good ten feet farther from him.

"We'll talk about your concerns first," he said.

They sped into her head from all directions. Gridlock. Most of them she couldn't possibly articulate to him. He'd think she was nuts—and they'd lock her up in some god-awful lunatic asylum.

She squeezed her hands together in her lap. Good grief, why hadn't she been more careful? She didn't have a leg to stand on in this alien world. Why on earth couldn't she just have been quiet and complacent and accepted her stupid role? At least until she'd become more established, and had learned the rules and mastered the game.

She didn't respond.

121

"Perhaps I can help you begin," he offered like a trained social worker. "You were wed against your wishes. Am I correct?"

She nodded. That was for sure.

"May I inquire what you would have preferred under your circumstances?"

Good question. But she had no answer. Staring down at her hands, she shrugged.

"An unwed mother and her bastard child have naught but bleak futures in our society. Even if you believe yourself capable of withstanding the cruelties that would be heaped upon you, have you no regard for your son?"

Her heart twisted. The baby had won her over the minute she'd seen him. Holding him this evening, playing with his tiny fingers and toes, had brought her a special contentment, unlike any she'd known, even in the twentieth century.

"I care deeply for little Philip," she said softly.

"Then I understand not why you behave as if you're unappreciative of the refuge we've provided him at Fox Haven."

Tears stung her eyes. "I am appreciative."

He was quiet for a long while. His scrutiny made her scalp tingle. She kept her head down.

"We come to one of my major concerns in that case, Mrs. Foxworth," he said, breaking the tense silence. She knew what was coming and held her breath, praying her reaction would be a mild one. Her hot temper certainly hadn't gotten her anywhere.

"Why do you battle me at every turn?"

She bit her lip before answering. "It's my nature to fight for independence," she said truthfully.

"And for control?" he asked.

"That too, I suppose." Her voice sounded strangely meek, but again she'd spoken the truth.

"The traits are unseemly in a woman."

She looked up at him then and knew immediately she'd have been better off if she hadn't. His turquoise eyes glistened with concern. And they didn't harbor a hint of accusation, despite his terse statement.

She felt weak under his gaze, and more than a little foolish for having acted so despicably. She was here. She was part of this backward century, and she had to accept it, had to adapt better. But old habits died hard. She couldn't buckle under. Not completely.

"Are they seemly traits in a man, Benjamin?"

The corners of his mouth lifted in a near smile, doing funny things to her insides. "A man's responsibility is to protect and care for his family. For their welfare alone he must rule them."

Meredith pushed her glasses to the top of her head. Seeing him too clearly wasn't in her best interests, she decided.

She waited a moment before speaking, trying to measure her words and to strike a tone that wouldn't sound combative.

"Because only you know what's best for them? Is that what you're saying?"

"That's precisely what I'm saying."

And precisely what rubbed her the wrong way. She pressed her tongue to the roof of her mouth to keep it quiet.

"It will disrupt the household mightily unless you and I can form a truce," he said after a long pause. "Do you believe that's possible?"

"A truce requires the agreement of both parties, Benjamin. And compromises, I believe—from each side."

One eyebrow shot sky high, but otherwise his face remained placid. "You're asking me to compromise?"

"Of course," she said with the sweetest smile she could muster. "If I can do it, I'm sure you can too."

Now *he* looked off balance. But she didn't dare relax. Didn't even consider it, for she hadn't won anything yet. And she wasn't likely to, if she wasn't careful.

"What would you have me compromise?" he asked.

"We could start with your manner of speaking. Personally, I prefer to be spoken *with*, not spoken *to*."

It was, apparently, a new concept. His face lost its placidity and became taut with contemplation. "I'm speaking with you now, Mrs. Foxworth."

She nodded. "Exactly. And it's far more pleasant, don't you agree?"

He almost smiled again. This time enough to make that devastating dimple appear in his strong cheek. *Both* cheeks, dear heaven. She averted her eyes so she wouldn't lose her concentration.

"You see, Benjamin, like most intelligent beings, I respond to reason, but orders turn me off."

"Turn you off?"

"Make me want to resist," she said quickly.

"I see." His fingers massaged his temple as if he had a headache, and then he shoved a stray ebony wave back off his forehead. She did her darndest not to let that charming mannerism of his distract her. "Henceforth I shall attempt to

124

phrase my wishes in a more reasonable fashion," he said at last.

"And I will respond with less resistance, I can assure you." Oh Lord, she hoped she could live up to such a promise. "Provided you're truly reasonable," she felt honor bound to add.

He frowned and rose from his chair. For a skipped heartbeat, she thought he was going to walk up to her, but he stood where he was, taking advantage of his lofty height to view her from above.

"Which leads us, I believe, to the compromise I request from you, Mrs. Foxworth."

Oh oh. Something other than listening to reason? She stood up to reduce his advantage, even considered standing on the chair to top him, but common sense prevailed.

"And that would be?" she ventured.

"That you, too, employ reason in your actions. I prefer order to chaos. My work on the plantation requires much of my time and thoughts, and a smoothly run household is essential. Aunt Laura has maintained it thus, freeing my energies for the labors I do best."

He moved one step forward. She stood her ground, as erect and tall as she could manage. His penetrating gaze played havoc with her pulse beat, but she was determined to gaze right back at him.

"I request, therefore, that you learn from her," he continued. "That you not interfere with her routine—or with mine. If you see matters that you believe need improvement, consult with me, please, before you make changes. Above all, avoid . . ." He paused and his steady gaze faltered. "Please avoid disruptive behavior," he finished, his voice strangely husky.

They stood, silent. Had she only imagined the lusty fire simmering behind those captivating turquoise eyes? Did the huskiness mean what she thought it did?

Wishful thinking, she told herself, all too aware of the effect he had on her. He'd just presented her with a long list of requests, and none of them suggested he'd changed his mind about "exercising his rights."

"Your wishes appear reasonable, Benjamin." As reasonable as could be expected, she amended to herself. "I accept my compromise."

He nodded, apparently satisfied. "If you were a man, I'd offer my hand to seal our bargain."

And since she was a woman, what then? Not even the tiniest kiss? She clamped down on the thought.

"I was taught that a lady might shake hands on appropriate occasions," she said impulsively. "Assuming, that is, that she extends her hand first," she added with a smile as she did just that.

He moved forward quickly and took her hand, encompassing it within his own. It felt more like an embrace than a firm grip, she thought as her nerve endings went haywire. No, it was a simple handshake. Nothing more.

Was it? He held on longer than necessary, true. His eyes were lit with something other than their own magical color.

But she was misinterpreting, of course. She slipped her hand away from his.

"The bargain's sealed," she said, hoping she sounded business-like rather than breathless.

"Aye," he said, all business. "Good night, Mrs. Foxworth. I hope you sleep well." His eyes focused

126

briefly on the wood nymphs behind her before he turned to leave.

"By the way," he asked from the door. "Why do you wear spectacles?"

"To see."

"For close work? Reading, sewing, and the like?"

"No. Only for distance."

"For distance?"

She nodded.

"Peculiar," he said. And he left.

He'd left, doggone it! She grabbed up a crimson pillow and threw it at the door.

It didn't even make a thump.

Meredith was the soul of discretion for almost a week. She settled into the routine of the house with an ease that surprised her. There was much to learn, so she watched before she offered assistance, making sure she didn't step on any toes. Booted or otherwise.

Aunt Laura was competence personified. Nobody could call the woman cheerful, but she was pleasant enough, and Meredith had to admit she had everything running like a well-oiled engine.

The myriad (and, to her, arcane) tasks of a colonial home were handled by a veritable army of house slaves marching to Aunt Laura's steady drumbeat. Though Meredith had been prepared to raise the roof if she spotted even a hint of mistreatment of the poor souls, she'd seen none. On the contrary, Fox Haven's labor practices were both humane and fair. No one was overworked, days off were scheduled regularly, and the distribution of labor was surprisingly equitable, even by twentieth-century standards.

According to Aunt Laura, Benjamin would have it no other way.

But, of course, he still viewed the work force as property rather than free, independent humans. That bothered Meredith, and she vowed to convince him how wrong he was.

Somehow.

Meanwhile, faced with such orderly efficiency, she might have felt superfluous. Instead, she found her days increasingly busy, and even satisfying. She continued her therapy sessions with Abraham, spent hours with little Philip, and made it her business to get better acquainted with Betsy, Benjamin's daughter. The child hid behind a wall of sad defeat that broke Meredith's heart. She'd seen only two things bring a smile to Betsy's pretty rosy lips—her rag doll Moopie and the sight of Benjamin.

Meredith was determined to expand that meager repertoire. So far she'd batted zero, but she kept trying.

April had dawned gloriously, and in the afternoon of its first day she'd requested Will to carry the girl out beneath the shade of a sycamore by a small spring-fed stream not far from the house. She sat with her there, hoping that sunlight, birdsong, and maybe a bright idea or two on her own part might bring about a breakthrough.

"It's April Fools' Day, Betsy. Do you know what that means?"

The girl shook her head.

"Well, where I come from it's a day when pranks are allowed. Funny little things, mind you. To surprise people, and make them feel a bit foolish for falling for your trickery. Can you think of someone we could unsettle a mite in the spirit of fun?"

Betsy kept her eyes on the doll lying across her fluffy pink skirt and didn't respond.

"How about you, Moopie?" Meredith bent to address the painted face of the cloth doll. "Can you think of someone?" She raised her voice to a mousy squeak. "Aunt Laura? We could tell Aunt Laura that her petticoat was showing, and then when she looked down all flustered we could shout 'April Fool!'"

The slight curving at the corner of Betsy's mouth was a heartening sign. Meredith continued. "Why, Moopie, you naughty girl," she chastised in her natural voice. "You'd have Aunt Laura swooning from embarrassment before our very eyes. Can't you think of someone stronger to unsettle?"

The squeak again. "Betsy's father would never swoon. Let's tell him *his* petticoat's showing."

It worked. The girl popped her hand to her mouth that had curved into a delightful U. Her bright blue eyes danced. "Father doesn't wear petticoats, silly Moopie," she told the doll. "He's a *man*."

"Indeed he is, Moopie," Meredith agreed. "He wears breeches and vests—"

"And buttons!" Betsy squealed excitedly, looking up at Meredith. "We'll tell him his breeches have lost a button!" Glory be, she actually giggled.

Meredith gave her a big hug. "*You'll* tell him, Betsy. Not me," she said with a chuckle. "But make sure everyone's in the room and say it loud and clear. That should give him a merry surprise."

And so should the sight of his daughter warming to a little fun, she thought with a surge of happiness.

129

After they'd laid their plans with impish glee for the pre-supper entertainment, Meredith realized she'd taken a mighty step. Seeing Betsy come out from behind that sad wall was suddenly more than a project—it was a necessity. And she was going to do everything in her power to see it happen. She wondered about the child's disability, and if perhaps she could do something for her. But she'd have to go slowly, win her confidence. And first of all, try to find out what the problem was.

"The stream looks inviting, Betsy. Why don't we take off our shoes and dangle our feet in it?"

The small oval face paled. "One of mine is sorely ugly, Miss Sylvia," she said, the light gone from her eyes.

Meredith knew she had to move cautiously. "Lord, I've seen so many ugly feet, you wouldn't believe it. I helped a physician many years, and it seemed that every one of his patients possessed at least one ugly foot. It was an epidemic of ugly feet there for a while."

Betsy looked interested. "You helped a physician?"

Meredith nodded. "He was our neighbor. He told me he'd never seen a woman who could handle ugly feet the way I did. Why, most women would swoon dead away, he said. But then, my own feet are peculiar, so that might explain it." She took off her slippers and wiggled her painted toes. "Born that way, Betsy. Have you ever seen anything like it?"

The girl was awestruck. "They're truly ugly," she gasped. "Do they hurt?"

"No. But I keep them hidden, of course, so as not to upset people. But you don't mind, do you?"

She slid over to the bank of the stream and stuck her feet into the sun-warmed water, oohing with contentment. "Now, *that's* a balm."

Out of the corner of her eye she saw Betsy wiggling forward hesitantly. Meredith didn't want to pressure her, so she waited, adding a few splashes to underline how marvelous the water felt.

"Well, maybe . . . but don't look, Miss Sylvia." Betsy set Moopie on the ground, removed her tiny pink slippers, and scooted with some awkwardness over beside Meredith.

Meredith pretended complete disinterest. "Push your frock up to your knees now. You mustn't get that pretty skirt wet," she said with nonchalance, hoping the girl wouldn't note her surreptitious glances. In her enthusiasm to try the water as Meredith was so blithely doing, Betsy didn't appear to, thank heaven. And Meredith saw enough to make a quick professional appraisal— and to start her heart singing. Drop Foot. And only the left one was afflicted. It was the result of a bad compound fracture of the leg, she guessed. Undoubtedly some nerve damage.

But treatable, thank God. Maybe not to full function, but treatable enough so that perhaps she could walk. It would take time and ingenuity. She'd have to devise a splint, to strengthen the atrophied muscles in both of the shriveled little legs that had suffered from disuse. With the combination of the girl's vibrant youth and her own talents, there was definitely hope.

Offering a silent prayer of thanks, she stashed away her happy knowledge. She'd have to start her treatments another day—when she'd truly won Betsy's trust and love. Today, they'd made their breakthrough. And it was reward enough to see the big smile on the dear child's face as she dipped her limp feet into the water.

Close beside Meredith's.

Betsy's April Fool joke on Benjamin was a rousing success. The family had never heard of such a thing, it seemed. Meredith had assumed that April Fools' Day had been around since the Year One, and, had she known it hadn't, might have thought twice before she'd risked introducing the silly practice. But the results were worth it. Sobersided Benjamin Foxworth actually blushed!

And he demonstrated he could be a good sport. He laughed heartily when he'd recovered from his initial jolt of embarrassment and realized that his daughter had been fooling him.

It was the first time she'd heard him laugh, and Meredith was struck by the deep richness of the sound. Too bad he didn't do it more often. Betsy's open radiance had triggered his good-natured response, Meredith could tell by the way he looked at the girl. Lord, his beautiful eyes were brimming with love. Magic enhancing magic. What a sight!

She figured she was smiling like a ninny herself, but no one was noticing her. Benjamin, Aunt Laura, and Sally were focused on Betsy. Aunt Laura started making noises as if she might scold the child for being too forward, but Benjamin nipped that in the bud by jumping in with his jovial: "A good prank you played on me, Betsy my love. But be wary next year on this date you call 'April Fools' Day.' Think on it, lass. I have an entire year to conjure up a merry trick to surprise a young flaxen-haired lady."

Betsy looked delighted at the prospect. "It was Miss Sylvia who told me of the custom. You must plan a trick for her, too."

She had his attention now, she knew, though she didn't dare meet his eyes. Her blasted cheeks flamed.

"That I'll do, Betsy. That I'll do," he said most pleasantly, but Meredith was acutely aware of a new spark of tension in his voice.

Aunt Laura announced it was time for supper and called for Will to carry Betsy up to her room.

"I'll carry her up myself this eve," Benjamin said, whisking the ecstatic little girl up into his arms. "The rest of you go on into the dining room and start your supper. I'll join you in a brief spell."

"But the blessing, Benjamin," Aunt Laura protested.

"You may offer it, Aunt Laura. I have another and far more important blessing to attend to for the moment." The dimples in his smiling cheeks were devastatingly deep.

Somewhat wistful, Meredith watched him leave with the child. Oh, my, she was seeing a different side of Benjamin tonight. And one she liked. A whale of a lot.

She shook her head. Drat it all, she couldn't start thinking that way. His physical charms were turn-on enough to discombobulate her. She'd be a basket case if she began finding attractive qualities in his psyche.

"Everything's arranged," Sally whispered beside her as they headed for the dining room. For a second Meredith hadn't a glimmering what the young woman was talking about.

133

"Benjamin gave me permission to visit my good friend Patsy Thurgood for two days. I'm leaving on the morrow. It's all as you recommended, Sylvia. I'm so happy I could crow!"

Meredith stopped in the doorway and pulled Sally back by her arm. Aunt Laura had bustled off to the kitchen, well out of earshot.

"Do you mean you've *done* it? *Already?* But, Sally, those were but idle suggestions I made to you. I didn't—"

Sally, undeterred, put her finger to Meredith's lips. "Your suggestions were perfect! I would never have been so clever to come up with them myself. It's all arranged, I tell you. Patsy's sneaking me out of her room tomorrow evening. Tom's to be waiting outside with two horses and our needed papers, and we'll speed like the wind to the parson in Newcastle. Once we're wed, Benjamin can do naught but accept it. It's exactly as you said, Sylvia." She threw her arms around Meredith. "I'm to marry the one I love!"

Dear God in heaven. She *had* put the idea into the girl's head—the young man's, too, she supposed—just two days ago, when she'd come upon Sally and Tom hiding out behind the stables. A moonier, more love-struck couple she'd never seen. Nor one so handsome and obviously meant for each other. It seemed perfectly reasonable at the time to suggest they take matters in their own hands.

But, oh boy, there'd be hell to pay when Benjamin found out.

She studied Sally's dancing eyes and knew at once that his disapproval didn't amount to a hill of beans. He'd know it, too, when he saw how much happier his sister was going to be when married to the man of her choice rather than the unsuitable one he'd chosen for her.

She gave the young woman a big squeeze. "Better turn down those spotlights in your eyes, Sally, or Benjamin and Aunt Laura are going to be suspicious. Save the dazzle for Tom and tomorrow night," she whispered.

Sally giggled and kissed her cheek. "You do speak peculiar English, Sylvia. But I love you anyway."

So much for discretion, Meredith tutted to herself as she took her seat at the table. And compromise. She'd opened up a wiggly can of worms for sure. Aiding and abetting an elopement. Against Benjamin's wishes.

She'd better fasten her seatbelt.

# Chapter Nine

She considered reasoning with Benjamin, but the cons kept outweighing the pros. Sally's statement that he'd never turn his back on a pledge haunted her. And the girl's conviction that he'd accept the accomplished deed was probably true.

Only Sally wouldn't be around for the fall-out. Meredith would be the one at Ground Zero.

After supper she went out to sit alone in Fox Haven's brick-walled garden to ponder her options. If she discussed this with Benjamin, she'd put Sally's future in jeopardy. If she stayed quiet, she'd be blasted to high heaven. She didn't like either option, but when she placed them side by side, Sally's future tipped the scales over her own temporary discomfort. She could withstand his tirades. Lord, she'd already put up with several. And given him as good as she got—with a few licks extra, now that she thought of it, somewhat devilishly.

"Enjoying the night air, Mrs. Foxworth?"

She nearly jumped out of her skin. "Geez!" she gasped.

"I gave you a start. Forgive me." Benjamin sat on the stone bench beside her. The thing was small, and no more than a couple of inches separated them.

Meredith contracted her elbows into her ribs and clasped her hands on her lap. Mentally she batted away the swarm of butterflies that Benjamin's unexpected presence had unleashed in her head. And in her chest and middle as well.

Good grief. Why was he here? He puffed on his pipe and was silent.

She found her voice. "You did startle me. I was deep in thought, I guess."

Stupid word selection. She hoped like mad he wouldn't follow up on the subject of her thoughts.

He didn't. "My intention was but to come out to express my gratitude."

Her brain was slow. "Gratitude?"

The sweet smoke from his pipe mingled with the heady aroma of lilacs that surrounded them. "Aye. For Betsy's bright spirits this eve. It's been long since I've seen the child so gay."

"Oh, *that*," rode out on her sigh of relief. "She's a dear girl."

"Yes."

More silence, smoke, and the scent of lilacs. Her elbows and hands relaxed, but her fingers trembled slightly as she pushed her glasses to the top of her head. She cleared her throat. "I hope to make smiles come easier for Betsy from now on. It's one of my goals." She saw no viable way to let him in on her therapeutic hopes for the girl.

"Goals? It's odd to hear a woman speak of goals."

"I would hope everyone has goals of some sort—even women, Benjamin. Maybe they couch it in different terms around you, or perhaps you've just never observed them closely enough." She tensed. Her blasted tongue wasn't doing her any favors.

Of course his eyebrow lifted, and of course he was eyeing her. She should be used to the combination by now. But she wasn't.

"You have a way of couching everything you say in different terms, Mrs. Foxworth. How do you explain that?"

"Uh, Richmond versus Hanover?" she ventured weakly.

He didn't respond.

"Different cultures," she offered with a bit more strength and without the question mark. For sure, a deeper truth than he could possibly fathom.

"Your birth document states you were born in Virginia."

"Oh, but there's Virginia and then there's Virginia," she said, realizing with discomfort that she must sound cryptic as the devil. "I mean, my parents were from Germany. And most of their friends, too," she lied.

"German was spoken in your home, then?"

"All the time." Lord, she hoped he never tested her on that. Her knowledge of German was limited to *Gesundheit, Kindergarten,* and *Volkswagen.*

Oh. And *Jawohl, Herr General,* she remembered, noting the erect posture of the stern-faced man by her side.

"The German home would explain your peculiar way with words, I suppose," he said.

138

Well, that was settled, thank heaven.

"Now, Mrs. Foxworth, might I inquire what matter of thought held you in such deep concentration before I interrupted you?"

Her heart leapt into her throat, not because of what he'd said, but the way he'd said it. The lighter tone—like small talk. And his rigid body language had softened considerably. He was working on his compromise, she figured. Attempting to talk *with* her. She was at a loss as to how to respond to his softly spoken question.

Truthfully, she decided. But only up to a point. She wouldn't betray Sally's confidence. And just maybe, if she were careful enough, she'd listen to Benjamin's side and then reason with him until she changed his mind. After all, she'd never discussed Sally with him.

"I was wondering about this Mr. Smithson you've pledged your sister to. What kind of man is he?"

"Peyton? An honorable man, he is—a longtime friend."

"How old is he?"

"But a year or so older than I. Thirty-four? Aye, his thirty-fifth birthday's in June, shortly before the planned wedding."

She looked over at him. He'd moved closer, she could have sworn, but she tried not to notice. "Sally is only nineteen, isn't she?" The needed arithmetic evaded her. Gracious. He was *really* close!

"Sixteen years is not a long span between man and woman," he said, as deft with subtraction as (*good heavens!*) distraction. His breath was soft against her face. It smelled wonderful—like fresh bay leaf, she thought fuzzily. Uh-oh. Had he placed his arm across the back of the bench?

"Peyton desires . . . many . . . children," he added, his words slow, with a telling huskiness. The sleeve of his shirt brushed across the ends of her hair, generating a tingly brand of static electricity.

"But . . ." She forgot what they were talking about. Moonlight streaked his ebony hair with silver and shadowed the strong planes of his face. What it did to his eyes was best left undescribed.

"But what, Mrs. Foxworth?" A heated whisper—grazing across her lips.

It happened so swiftly it took her breath away. His hand was behind her head, pulling her to him. More than moonlight permeated his eyes before she closed her own, with a sigh of surrender. Touch alone took charge.

His kiss was heaven—and the Fourth of July. Angel wings and fireworks all at once. Her fingers ran through his thick wavy hair, drawing him closer.

Being coy didn't occur to her. She'd seen the desire in his eyes, and felt it now in his lips, hungry upon hers; in his tongue, playing across her teeth, entering her mouth with its suggestive rhythms promising deeper explorations, an even more powerful, intimate entering.

He wanted her! Oh boy, he *really* wanted her! For sure, she was alive with want of him. Had been since the moment she'd seen him, she knew that now, when she was conscious of little else. Conscious of nothing else except him. Benjamin Foxworth. Her *husband*—holding her so close their heartbeats had mingled.

His kiss deepened, and she returned it with a fevered intensity that brought an ecstatic moan from his throat. Her own moan was an affirming echo.

"Mmmmm," he breathed as his lips left hers to trail heated kisses up her cheek, across her ear and then, with tantalizing nibbles, down to the sensitive hollow beneath her jaw. Her head fell back, but his hand was there to cradle it, his wonderful fingers threading through her hair, caressing her scalp; his lips continuing their fiery journey across throat and neck to the other side—the vulnerable hollow, athrob with pulsebeats, her jawline, then back behind her ear, over it. Lingering there till his breath and tongue had her in a frenzy of need.

She clutched his hard shoulders and heard her own ragged groan. And then his mouth crushed into hers with a passion that swept through her like wildfire.

He was magically transforming her insides into the consistency of hot, melted wax. His every movement—his embracing touches, his sizzling kisses—told her she was in the hands of a master lover. She was in his control.

And enraptured. Beyond recall.

"Dear God." It was a low rumble only, from deep in his chest.

"Hmmm?" she sighed, pressing in closer.

But she felt the wave of tension run like a twisted cord through his arms. For a moment, they held her tighter, then released their hold with a suddenness that stunned her.

Her hands were splayed against his chest, the only support that kept her from sliding off the bench. His strong heart pounded against her palms. His face was stricken.

"What's wrong?" she gasped, too limp to move.

His hands encircled hers and pulled them away from his moist shirt. He placed them on her disheveled lap and shook his head.

"Forgive me, if you can," he said with a low moan.

"Forgive you?"

"I pledged . . ." He moved away. Her startled eyes watched him in disbelief as his back stiffened. He expelled one long sigh of agony, and then he was perfectly straight, erect. Composed.

Untouchable.

She strangled her own sigh and frowned. What would an eighteenth-century lady do under such circumstances? Protest? Which way? That he'd started something or that he hadn't finished what he'd started?

She knew all too well how she felt.

Rejected, mostly, with a heavy overlapping of anger at him and at herself. Blast him and his stupid self-righteous pledge. And blast her unruly hormones for firing off that way! She envied him his quick recovery. She figured she'd ache till morning.

Well, whatever had turned him on in the first place was the big mystery. She looked up at the moon, but it was blurry. Replacing her glasses, she saw it clearly. Full.

It figured.

She stood. "Good night, Benjamin," she said, using icy formality to disguise her miserable dejection, and walked from the garden.

Watching her leave, he groaned. What had gotten into him? They'd been holding a civilized conversation, about what he couldn't recall. And then he had come unhinged. Thoroughly unhinged.

The woman worked a magic on him he'd never

encountered. Was it her wide silver eyes? The intriguing flow of her silky hair? The creamy softness of her skin?

No, there was something other. Something not visible, but sensed. An irresistible aura that drew him toward her. An unseen web of gossamer attracting him beyond reason.

Aye, beyond reason. And bloody well beyond his control. Never had he so willingly lost control. Nor with such fool-headed abandonment. The woman was not to blame—the web was of his own making, not hers. He himself had woven it. Without thought. With his own mindless desires.

He'd been so overwrought with his dastardly needs that he'd wrongly construed her struggles as eager responses. Her stunned expression, her stiff demeanor when he'd torn himself away from her, were testament that his actions this night had frightened her.

He bent to retrieve his pipe, carelessly discarded at the moment he'd discarded all sense of propriety. Its fire was dead.

His wasn't, blighted devil. His swollen groin pulsed maddeningly against his breeches. Even his damnable body would obey him no longer.

He reprimanded himself harshly. The woman who was his wife deserved far better than a husband who would force his wild lust upon her. She'd proven herself a devoted mother and a woman of reason. He alone was disrupting the calm he'd professed with such vehemence to treasure.

He alone.

*"Bloody hell!"*
Benjamin's angry roar reverberated through the house.

143

Tense, Meredith sat on the edge of her bed. She'd been downstairs at Sunday breakfast with the family when, through the dining room windows, she'd seen the express rider's approach. His knock at the front door was all she'd needed to give her a "sudden headache" as an excuse to run up to her room. Her cowardice amazed her. But she knew the message would be from Sally— Mrs. Thomas Morris, by now—and she wanted to be well out of Benjamin's throwing range when he read it.

But Fox Haven wasn't big enough. Virginia wasn't big enough. She prayed for a bolt of lightning to zap her to another century. Preferably the twentieth, but at the moment the Stone Age would suffice.

*"Who in bloody hell is responsible for this heinous turn of events?"*

She cringed. Another, more moderate, voice came muffled from the downstairs hall. Aunt Laura, probably. Trying to calm him with her Pollyanna philosophy, Meredith supposed.

*"Where in God's name is the termagant hiding?"*

Aunt Laura had fingered her? Why, the rotten biddy! She had no reason to suspect . . .

Gnawing at her lip, Meredith heard his boots on the stairs, vaulting over five steps at a time by the sound of it. She contemplated hiding under the bed, but couldn't move fast enough. The door flew open and Benjamin stormed through it. His face was livid with rage. Magenta, she thought crazily. The fire in his eyes had turned them indigo.

*Here it comes!* She steeled herself for the onslaught.

The door slammed with such force that the

wood nymphs vibrated, then crashed to the floor.

"You did this thing?" he growled. The letter was crumpled in his heavy fist.

"What thing?" she rasped.

"Put bloody ideas of mutiny into my sister's head. That's what!" He flung the wadded paper toward her. It rolled beneath the bed step where her frozen feet perched.

"Mutiny?"

"Damned right, mutiny."

God, he looked ferocious. "What on earth are you talking about?" Ignorance was worth a try.

"You know bloody well what I'm talking about, *Mrs.* Foxworth."

"I do?" A weak stall, she knew.

His glare was as deadly as an armed Uzi. "Sally was ever obedient till *you* entered this house. Aunt Laura saw you conspiring with her, putting your seditious thoughts into her head."

Wait a minute. "Aunt Laura said that?"

"She said you had your heads together Friday eve."

"And you're the one who deduced the conspiracy and sedition part—am I correct?" New strategy. Diversionary attack.

"It's true, I'm sure of it," he bellowed. But his anger level had reduced from H-bomb to A-bomb. Still dangerous.

She chose her words carefully. "Are your deductions never wrong? Is that why you're so sure of yourself all the time?"

He glowered, his rage down to something at least non-nuclear. Nothing to toy with, but she could take a stand now without risking life and limb.

Meredith stepped down to the floor and stood

stalwart against the bed. "Did it never occur to you, Mr. Foxworth, that Sally should have been consulted before you offered her hand to a man near twice her age?"

A low roar erupted from his throat. She waited for it to develop into another string of fierce words. When it didn't, she braced herself and continued. "That's your trouble, Benjamin. You're so busy being sure you know what's best for somebody that you forget important things such as that person's wishes in the matter."

"A suitable marriage for a young woman is far too vital a matter to leave to her silly wishes," he snarled.

"Even when that young woman is deeply in love with another, far more suitable man?"

"What has love to do with marriage?"

"I should think everything."

"Balderdash! Had you not interfered, Sally would have been content with Peyton Smithson. As mistress of Goose Creek, she'd soon have forgotten her transitory affection for Tom Morris."

"Your friend Peyton Smithson would have kept Sally barefoot and pregnant—he wants a brood mare, for heaven's sake. Is that the future you truly wish for a sensitive, delightful girl like your sister—a brood mare for a man she cares nothing for?"

His face was growing magenta again. She went on quickly. "Did you ever see the two of them together, Benjamin?"

"Sally and Tom? Of course not. She was not allowed to see him—he was ordered to stay away from Fox Haven."

She laughed dryly. "Your orders fell on deaf ears. A pair of attractive ears, I might add. Tom was here regularly, I suspect. I ran into them behind the stables last week."

There went the roar again. Meredith was determined to finish. "Their love is deep, Benjamin, and far from transitory. Tom is a fine young man who will take splendid care of Sally. Instead of raging like a lion you should be cheering with happiness for your sister."

He didn't look in the mood to cheer. "You dared to override my wishes for Sally—my honorable pledge to a friend—by assisting in her elopement?"

Damn him. He wouldn't listen to reason. She elevated her chin and looked him straight in the eyes. "I didn't assist. The plans were their own, but the suggestion was indeed mine. And I'm glad I made it, you stone-hearted paragon of propriety. You care for nothing but your own blasted peace of mind." She sneered, her anger rising to fever pitch. "Honor? Ha! I spit on your twisted sense of honor. You revere your stupid pledges over everything else—including those you profess to love and protect. And a broken pledge matters more to you than a broken heart. I find that disgusting!"

Stiff with fury, he took two long strides across the room, stopping directly in front of her. His pinched tone was venomous. "You attack my honor, woman. A man speaking the vile words you've just uttered would die."

She stood defiant. "Challenge me, then. A duel at dawn? I welcome it! Pistols, Mr. Foxworth. I warn you—I'm a helluva shot!"

He grabbed her shoulders and shook her. "Hold your vicious tongue, woman!"

Her eyes were afire, steaming her glasses. She didn't give a damn. "Go right ahead—strike me!

**147**

Isn't that what your kind does to women who dare to question your grand and glorious superiority?"

His fingers dug into her arms. "You are a sharp-tongued harridan," he gnarled through clenched teeth.

"And you are an uncivilized beast who hides behind fancy clothing and a thin shield of false honor," she snapped back.

"Cease, you ungrateful wench! I brought you into this home out of the honor you deign to spit on."

"And see what a rotten marriage results from honor alone? Maybe that should tell you something!"

He released his hold. Without stepping back, he pressed the heel of his hand to his forehead and issued a weary sigh. "You defy understanding."

She rubbed her sore arms through the thin linen of her sleeves. "That makes two of us." Her sudden tears surprised her. She flung her hopelessly misted glasses across the bed and wiped her eyes with her fingers. "Blast you, you've reduced me to *this*."

"I refuse to apologize."

"I don't expect you to, nor should you expect an apology from me." Her tears wouldn't stop. Hating her display of weakness, she turned her face away from him.

His hand cupped her chin and lifted it less than gently, forcing her head toward him again. Braced between his fingers and thumb, her chin was immobile and resisted the efforts of her neck muscles to wrest away from him.

Refusing to look into his face, she closed her eyes. Her cheeks were soaked; she could feel the tears dribbling through his fingers, down to her chest, between her breasts.

"What am I to do with you?" he asked with a troubled groan.

She frowned, keeping her eyes shut tight. She wasn't about to answer that. Other than "leave me alone" she couldn't think of an even halfway sensible response.

"You are my wife."

She sniffled. Her stupid nose was running. "In name only, according to your high-and-mighty decree."

"My decree? Made, I assure you, for your comfort, not mine."

Her eyes popped open. Mistake. Would she never learn? "My *comfort*?"

"Aye. I believed it essential that you held no fear of me."

God, he was earnest. She didn't know whether to laugh or cry. Since she was already crying, she left it at that.

"Because you've demonstrated you're fearless and consider me a man without honor, it would serve you right if I broke yet another pledge this day."

No you don't, Buster. "Take your hands off me!" she exploded. His hands weren't on her, she suddenly realized. He'd released her chin ages ago.

He frowned and pushed that damnable wave of his off his forehead. "I have no interest in forcing myself upon you."

"Well, that's one thing we can agree on at least," she said, moving to one side. Wrong side. The bed step was in her way. She kicked it away and walked around Benjamin, over to a chair. She didn't sit, but stood looking at it, her back turned to him.

"I'll have no man who would take a woman out of spite or in anger," she said firmly. "Your pledge to me is no different from the one you made about Sally. They were both in *your* interest, for *your* convenience. Sally was a prize you could offer a friend. I'm a woman you married out of some insane sense of duty. It's as simple as that."

"I see nothing simple about either of my pledges—and neither were made in my interest but in the interest of others."

"Well, the Sally one wasn't in *her* interest, Benjamin, you must see that now. I'll grant you that Peyton Smithson's interest would have been served had your pledge been carried out. But I'll grant you nothing else." She scowled at the hideous puce and purple cushions on the chair.

"And what of my pledge to you?" It sounded as if he'd leaned back against the bed. She heard it squish.

"That one was *totally* in your interest." She bit her lip. "You have no desire to be my husband."

"Do you believe I have no desire for you?"

She turned around with a huffy snort, glaring at him. "Why should you? I'm not exactly Marilyn Monroe."

"Who?"

"Forget it." She plopped down on the chair. The cushions were so high her feet couldn't reach the floor.

With his stolid frame propped against the bed's side, his arms across his chest, he stood quiet and looked ill at ease. She suspected he was itching for his pipe.

"I fear you misinterpreted the purpose of my pledge," he said at last, his voice extremely low. "I'm a man with normal appetites. I chose separate beds for us because I assumed you would prefer such an arrangement."

She couldn't believe they were carrying on this conversation. She wished he'd just get the hell out. "You never asked me one way or the other," she said, bone weary.

Eyebrow up; penetrating stare. The combination had lost its magic for her.

"How would you have answered?" he asked.

"I have no idea." She wiped her cheeks with her fingertips. Her tears had dried up along with the rest of her.

He began pacing the room. "This is ridiculous!" He appeared thoroughly exasperated.

"I fully agree." She avoided watching him. His buff pants, she knew well enough, were molded to him. His white open-necked shirt had wreaked havoc on her at the breakfast table. Black chest hairs had curled tauntingly over the V.

She shoved away the disturbing memory and concentrated instead on the gold brocade draperies and their riotous tie-backs. Sunlight streamed through the paned windows.

"Mrs. Foxworth?" She jerked upright. Good grief, how long had he been standing there beside her? She lifted her eyes.

"You've unbalanced me this day, given me much to ponder," he said. His face, though bathed in sunlight, was darkly troubled. A wave of compassion shoved against her heart. What had she done? Or what on earth had he thought she'd done?

Meredith stood slowly, her knees as unsteady as her mind. She had no idea how she was going to do it; she knew only that she must do something to relieve this latest burden she herself had heaped on him. She faced him, reached for his arms, and looked deeply into his turquoise eyes.

"Benjamin, your persuasions are as they should be; my own, however, are as deep and unassailable as yours—and undoubtedly appear very strange to you, coming from a woman."

She paused, knowing she was treading on dangerous ground. Taking a deep breath, she went ahead cautiously. "I am what I am, just as you are what you are. It will ever be that way, and we both must be aware we cannot change the other."

Her legs were poor supports. She held tighter to his arms.

"I believe it's time for me to make a pledge to you," she continued, her voice more trembly than she wished. Despite her intense discomfort, she tried hard to use his vocabulary. "Though I'm not likely to ever become a docile wife, I promise henceforth to strive with all my power not to undermine your authority at Fox Haven."

She could say nothing more. It was, she believed—prayed—enough. She lowered her eyes, acutely conscious of his strong pulse pumping beneath her fingers.

"You have formidable power, Mrs. Foxworth. Your pledge comes to me bolstered by a strength I find assuring—and comforting. I thank you."

She should release him now. Only she couldn't, not until the numbness left her legs. Nor could she allow herself to look back up into his eyes. Whatever they might hold, they were likely to weaken her even further.

He released his own arms. They slipped away

from her grasp so smoothly—so rapidly—she might have collapsed at his feet. Only he didn't let that happen. His arms suddenly were around her, crushing her to him.

He held her head to his chest. His powerful heart hammered against her ear. Slowly, with one sturdy, gently persuasive finger, he lifted her chin.

"I deeply desire to make you truly my wife," he whispered low, and his wonderful lips met hers.

# Chapter Ten

Meredith experienced total meltdown. Instantly. He was unleashed power, burning strength, fiery passion, and more. Resisting never once crossed her mind. Quite the opposite. She knew from the moment of his first blazing kiss that they were at long last completely together, in perfect unison, hell-bent for paradise this time. Boundless desire alone was their tyrant. She became liquid fire beneath his fevered touches, his heated lips. He was everywhere—and everything. Nothing else mattered but Benjamin, his scorching hunger for her and hers for him.

Clasped together, frenzied mouth against frenzied mouth, roused body melded to roused body, they slid to the floor. Clothes—so many of them—were between them, she fretted through the scarlet haze that had taken over her mind. No problem.

His deft hand was under her skirt, working its way upward with tantalizing swiftness, discovering her conveniently uncovered bottom. And his talented fingers, *oh Lord, yes!* had found the throbbing spot that ached for him . . . for *him*. Like a gifted virtuoso, he was transforming her into a pliable instrument of wild desire. She writhed beneath him, sinuous with her need that only he could fill.

She might have heard a rip of cloth—possibly more than one—and gasped with pleasure as the welcoming hot waves of his luscious mouth fell upon her bared breast, circling the hardening tip, drawing it in, suckling. Pure sensation took charge. She groaned, grasped his head, thrust her fingers through his thick, rich hair. Her thighs spread to his magical strumming; she felt herself swelling beneath his touches, slickening with want. As he raised his head and moved over her, she arched to him, opened to him with her strangled plea for release.

His beautiful face was taut with passion, his gemstone eyes locked into hers, blazing—liquid, near green with their fire. And then, with a jagged moan of ecstasy, he entered her with his magnificent, throbbing fullness. With his ultimate promise—the glorious promise of coming fulfillment for them both. His kiss was deep, his hands holding her head, his fingers threading through her hair. Their tongues parried in a rapturous duel, mingled with a joined rhythm matching the steadily increasing rhythm of their joined bodies. Her nails dug into his hard shoulders, squeezed, held tight.

He carried her with him masterfully. Higher. Expandingly higher until the spreading rush of climactic fire released her in an explosive fireburst of sublime completion.

*Ohhh . . .* was her only thought. *Oh, indeed,* like a heartfelt breath of deep satisfaction. She lay limp beneath him, their bodies bonded, moist; their hearts beating a wild cadence, taking far longer than the rest of them to be calmed by the bliss of contented peace.

Wrapped together, neither moved for a long while. Euphoria, like a soothing cloud, enveloped them. His soft breath caressed her ear. Their hearts, at last, slowing—in perfect harmony.

Lifting his head, he gazed down upon her with a smile of pleasure that matched her own. He patted light kisses on each of her eyes, the tip of her nose, and, with lingering warmth, upon her lips.

"You're a treasure," he said with a sigh.

"You, too," she whispered, aware she'd never been more content. Lord, he was wonderful. Who would have dreamed an eighteenth-century Virginia gentleman would have that kind of skill in the art of loving? No wonder the era was considered Virginia's Golden Age.

This first time they'd come together in a maddened frenzy of overcharged impatience, neither willing to prolong the exquisite agonies. Yet he'd taken her to heights she'd never reached—a satisfaction beyond any she'd known. What wonders lay ahead for them?

She smiled into his enchanting eyes, feeling her wee pulse of gleeful anticipation palpitate against his magical rod of pleasure, at rest now within her, its powerful potential leashed—waiting. All at once she knew with joyous certainty. Her future in this world of the past was splendidly bright.

She wiggled slightly and reached up to push the tumbled black waves from his strong forehead.

"With that kind of authority, Benjamin, I'll never battle," she murmured.

He chuckled, tweaking her ear. "Good," he said. He rolled to his side, taking her with him, keeping her firm within his embrace.

"I've wanted you from the moment I saw you," he said, fingering the ends of her hair.

"I find that hard to believe." She nuzzled happily into his hard, broad shoulder—she couldn't imagine where his shirt had gone.

"God's truth." He brought her face up to his and looked into her eyes with such earnestness she found herself almost believing him. Why not? He made her feel beautiful, that was all that mattered.

"Why do your eyes change from color to color?" he asked playfully.

"What color are they now?"

"Silver."

"Do you like them that way?"

"Aye—the best of all, I vow." His lips brushed across her lashes.

"Then I'll keep them that very color," she said with a big smile. Not that she had much choice. But she did so relish his calling her nondescript gray eyes silver.

"You can change them at will?" He looked puzzled.

"Not any more," she said honestly. "They're stuck at silver now—you turned them that way," she added with only a tiny twist of the truth.

"I think I've wed a sorceress," he grunted, sounding downright pleased as he hugged her close, nestling his chin at the top of her head.

157

She snuggled into his dark, silky chest hair, savoring the sweet mingled odor of their spent passion.

Spent but far from insolvent. His fingers were moving suggestively down the flesh of her back, down the opened gap of her dress—the hooks had been ripped apart earlier, she realized without a trace of concern. His hand maneuvered beneath the bunched cloth, found her bare buttocks, and pulled her to him.

A wave of renewed desire surged within her, and she nibbled her way provocatively through the nest of matted hair on his chest till she uncovered the soft, flat button of his nipple with her lips, teasing it with naughty licks and kisses. He groaned, and she felt his arousal harden against her ripening center. They would savor each other slowly this time, she pledged, moving her mouth with titillating precision up to his shoulder, his neck, his ear . . .

The sharp knock at the door was a rude interruption. They both jolted, stiffened. She sat up quickly. With a low moan of agony, he did likewise, but far more slowly.

"Who is it?" he barked hoarsely.

"Aunt Laura, Benjamin," came the stilted reply. Passion disappeared in a poof. "Is everything all right in there?"

He scowled at the door and didn't respond. The man was stark naked. Even his boots had been cast aside—heaven only knew when and how. Meredith reached down for the tattered remnants of her bodice, trying to bring a semblance of covering about her.

"You haven't hurt her, have you, Benjamin?"

He lifted a questioning eyebrow at Meredith.

She stifled her laugh behind her hand and shook her head.

"No, Aunt Laura. We're but discussing the matter—attempting to come to some, uh, agreement." He smiled devilishly; his dimples winked at her.

"Well, our midday dinner is about to be served. You two should come down to the table now."

Again the questioning eyebrow. Meredith shook her head vigorously.

"Go on without us," he said, not taking his dancing eyes off her. "Neither of us at the moment have any appetite . . . for food."

"Very well," Aunt Laura said primly. Her clicking footsteps grew fainter as she walked down the hall and descended the stairs.

They sat quietly, their eyes locked in a mutual twinkle.

"Our appetites are for something far more delicious than food, Aunt Laura," he said low as he scooted over to Meredith.

"I bow to your authority," she said wickedly. "But will you have me on this rough carpet again, Mr. Foxworth? With yards of tattered linen chaffing between us?"

He shoved the loose shreds of cloth away from her shoulders and cupped his hands over her breasts, his thumbs flicking lightly across the tips. "No, Mrs. Foxworth. I order you to stand and rid yourself of the useless frock immediately."

"Unless you stop what you're doing, I won't be able to stand," she protested mildly, pressing her erect nipples against his thumbs.

"Then I shall stop," he said with a winning grin, pulling away his hands. "Now stand and disrobe for me." His general's tones were a light-hearted mockery of the real thing.

159

"In broad daylight, Mr. Foxworth?" she asked with feigned modesty as she scrambled to her feet.

"Bloody right in broad daylight," he replied with a big smile, staying seated on the riotous purple carpet, his chin resting on his knees, and watching her with avid interest.

"Your command is my wish," she said with a giggle, tearing away what was left of the fluffy lavender dress and the petticoats beneath and stepping daintily aside from the mussed pile of cloth.

His eyes sparkled with the sunbeams that bathed the room and with his own smoldering inner fire. They burned across her flesh from tip to toe. He appeared absolutely enchanted, making her feel like a genuine Venus.

He rose, a gloriously nude Atlas, and walked toward her. They stood, not touching, gazing into each other's eyes. A frisson of electricity tingled between them.

"That frock was far too large for you anyway, Mrs. Foxworth. I shall replace it with a new one," he said. His eyes were promising something else entirely.

"All of the clothes in my trunk are a bit too large," she said, quite fluttery. Mesmerized.

"I shall replace them all in that case," he replied in a hoarse whisper, closing in. He swept her up into his arms and carried her to the tall bed, placing her down gently onto the magenta velvet coverlet. She sank into the feathers as his long, hard body slid up over her.

"I much prefer you bare, however," he said seductively, his hands gliding with fluid ease down the curves of her hips. "This time we proceed far slower, my treasure," he whispered as he teased his lips across hers.

Oh my. Her own idea . . . exactly.

Without fanfare, Benjamin moved back into his refurbished chamber that night—to sleep with his wife. Happily exhausted, they lay in the moon-washed darkness, semi-entwined on the big bed.

"I insist we make a few improvements," he announced lightly, his arm beneath her shoulders, his fingers playing with her ear.

"Improvements?" Good grief, how would one go about improving perfection? Meredith wasn't sure her energy level was up to it.

"There are far too many ruffles and bows overhead. I'll never be able to sleep," he complained.

She smiled into his chest. "Oh? You're planning to sleep?" she teased, though the thought of sleep had some definite appeal.

"Aye . . . eventually," he chuckled. His hand caressed her arm. "But the bows and ruffles must go tomorrow, Mrs. Foxworth. Some of the damnable cushions, too—and those bloody wood nymphs can cavort midst their trees upstairs in the attic where they bloody well belong."

Meredith suppressed her giggle. "There's a lovely painting up there of horned satyrs romping about with nubile forest maidens wearing nothing but gauzy ribbons. I'll replace the wood nymphs with that one." Impishly she laced her words with giddy enthusiasm.

She could almost hear the rustle of his brows pulling together. "No, Treasure." She loved the name he'd chosen for her in this passionate day of discovery. She hoped it would stick. It made her feel like something of special value. "Sylvia," even today, would have jarred—reminded her all too well that she was an impostor.

"*No?*" She felt obligated to protest, though the satyr painting was ten times worse than the wood nymphs. Matter of principle, she decided.

He tapped her elbow. "No indeed. This room is mine now, too. That satyr painting is atrocious—it would interfere with my digestion."

The man had taste, apparently. But she'd be doggoned if she'd let him revert the place back to a barracks. Bargaining time, she figured.

She lifted her head and ran her finger back and forth across his enchantingly full bottom lip. "Tell you what, Benjamin. We'll compromise—I'll agree to no pictures, removal of one-third of the pillows and all of the bows from the canopy. But the ruffles remain intact. Reasonable?"

"What of the sickening ribbons holding back the drapes?"

She worked at a put-upon sigh. "Must they go, too?"

He nodded, but his lips curved in a soft smile. She fingered the dimples in his cheeks. "You'll find a roll of plain gold braiding up in the attic, Treasure."

"Agreed," she said, returning his smile. She wished she'd found the gold braiding in the first place.

He cleared his throat. "Then, too, some of the colors in here—"

"Are perfectly horrible," she interjected with a laugh. "Benjamin, I purposely messed up this room just to rattle your cage. Believe me, it's not to my taste either, the way it is."

"Rattle my cage?"

She planted a light kiss on his raised eyebrow.

"A quaint Richmond term—'to upset you,' should I say?"

"I'll never understand you," he said with a deep laugh, wrapping his arms about her and rolling her up so that she lay atop him. The long, hard expanse of his muscular body lying supine beneath her was a decided distraction, making topics like redecorating a room of no further interest whatsoever.

"What's to understand?" she asked, pushing up on his shoulders and sliding her knees down on either side of his hips, centering herself precisely where she knew he wanted her—or would very shortly.

She held his arms down, massaging his biceps and watching his face tighten with the tell-tale tension of rising passion. His fabulous black-lashed eyes widened, then narrowed, as she moved her hands to his broad, sinewy shoulders and began kneading deep therapeutic circles with her thumbs and fingers. Without releasing his eyes, holding him captive below with her knees, she shifted her hips upward slightly to accommodate his growing arousal, but maintaining the sensual contact.

"Like that?" she purred, gently massaging the tender area behind his ears while she undulated ever so lightly over his hardening shaft.

He nodded, his breaths shallow now. "You have talented hands, Treasure," he groaned.

"Only my hands?" she challenged, lowering the upper part of her anatomy so that the swollen tips of her breasts brushed tauntingly over his chest.

With a lusty moan he threw his arms around her and rolled her over on her back. "Lord, woman! You'll drive me berserk," he gasped explosively into her neck.

And, with fiery gusto, proceeded to drive her berserk.

"The roaring lion appeared uncommonly tamed this morn," Abraham Foxworth said with a sly smile to his therapist.

Meredith kept her eyes on his butter-smeared knee beneath her fingers. No hiding the instant flush on her cheeks, she knew.

"Was he, now? I didn't see him." She hadn't. He'd risen before dawn. His days routinely began abominably early. And though she'd been a bit put out when she'd awakened to find him gone—without, as far as she knew, even a parting salute—she was inwardly too serene to let a little thing like that bother her.

Abraham went on amiably, "Benjamin and I had breakfast together here in my room. We do that on occasion—when I'm awake before sunrise, and we have matters of import to discuss. He was mellow as a lamb, but ate like a steed who'd run a frisky race." His eyes prickled her with their twinkles.

She ignored his naughtiness. "You discussed matters of import? Like Sally, for instance?"

"Aye, this morning it was sweet Sally on our minds—or on mine, at least," he added with a chuckle. "I'm content with her running off, by the way. Benjamin will be, too, once he sees the good sense of her action—and how happy she is with that Morris lad."

"My thoughts all along," she said with a sigh. "I prompted her to do what she did, I suppose. Benjamin was rightfully furious with me."

"And that he was, that he was. For a while there I feared Fox Haven's roof was endangered. Sour Laura fretted that you might be at greater risk than the building's structure, but I assured her that wasn't the case."

She goosed his calf. "Oh you did, did you? At least Aunt Laura shows some compassion—can't say the same for you, Crabby Appleton."

He chuckled. "Sour Laura is woefully unaware of the normal frictions twixt husband and wife, and how marital wars can become something quite other with but the flutter of a lovely eyelash."

That hadn't been the scenario at all, but Meredith wasn't in the mood to quibble. "Why on earth do you call that kind lady 'sour Laura'?" she inquired as if she hadn't thought it a few times herself.

"Because she is, alas. Not her fault, poor woman. 'Tis the hand life dealt her—doomed to spinsterhood, she was, from the day she took in her first breath through those tight, priggish lips."

"Abraham, you're awful!" she chastised.

"Speaking the truth only, my dear. God knows, she inherited none of her mother's grace and beauty as did my fair Emily—my wife was her younger sister, I assume you're aware. I've always said Laura got her looks and temperament from her father—a humorless man, he was, prone to biblical quotes, with a gaunt, lanky body and the ugliest countenance God ever put on a man."

Meredith puckered her face. "You men are all alike," she scoffed. "Beauty's only skin deep, you know—it's what's underneath a woman that should count, but you're all so hooked on exteriors you're blinded to anything else. I sympathize with poor Aunt Laura. I'm another one who took after her father instead of her mother, and though Father's handsome for a man, his attributes hardly come off as ravishing in a female."

Abraham's eyebrow rose. "Wherever did you get the notion you resemble your father? You're not one whit like Herman Wetzel, my dear Sylvia. I've suspected from the first time you walked into this room that you'd inherited the man's keen mind and good sense. But he's stocky as a fence post with a round face the color of a beet—no offense to your father, mind you, I liked the man. But I see nothing of his physical characteristics in you."

Oh oh. She'd been so wrapped up in defending Laura Preston and plain women in general that she'd forgotten she was supposed to be Sylvia Wetzel. Her spirits plunged. Her whole sheltered life at Fox Haven was based on that one deception—even, dear God, her marriage to Benjamin. *Especially* that, for he'd never have felt obligated to marry her otherwise. One visit to this house by Herman Wetzel and her flimsy cover would be blown sky high! And then what would become of her?

She wiped the butter off her hands and tried to wipe the disturbing thoughts away from her mind. "Well, I don't look like my mother, either. I must be a throwback to another generation."

"Has anyone commented on your innovative use of our English tongue, young lady? 'Throwback' is it now?" he chortled.

"It's the German influence," she said quickly, hoping that rickety excuse would continue to hold. She wished to high heaven she could watch her words with more care.

It was time, she believed, to change the subject. She buried her concerns under a hastily donned professional demeanor. "Now, Mr. Foxworth. I've placated you enough with heat wraps and soothing rubs. You've improved to the point I can start some strengthening exercises. You won't like them, I can assure you, but I don't want to hear any grousing from you."

He scowled, but didn't protest as she gingerly lifted his leg and began a few passive resistance movements to start the slow process of getting his quadriceps and hamstrings stronger.

"Relax," she scolded. "I'll do the work for now. Later on you'll have to do most of it yourself, according to my instructions. That is, you'll obey me if you want to keep this knee from flaring up so blasted often."

The old gentleman groused, of course. She'd expected it. But he cooperated, bless him. When she finished, she patted his shin bone and covered his leg with the quilt.

"Where'd you learn such bedevilment, woman? Torturing a man to the limit and holding out promises that the nonsense will have him on his feet again," he grumbled.

She smiled at him and busied herself gathering up her primitive therapy supplies and tossing them into a bucket. "Be patient, Abraham, and you just might be in for a pleasant surprise."

"Did you study under a witch?"

"Several of them," she said with a laugh and an inner apology to the outstanding physical therapy faculty at the Medical College of Virginia.

He shook his head and started to pursue the matter. But Aunt Laura intervened, popping into the room with Abraham's dinner tray. She looked questioningly at Meredith and the bucket of rags. Her nose wrinkled. "There's the distinct odor of butter in this room," she sniffed. "Have you been eating between meals, Abraham? And what?"

Though her pinched face was directed toward the old gentleman, her next words, Meredith knew, were directed to her. "No one should be sneaking in extra food for you, Abraham. You know Dr. Hughes doesn't want you growing fat while you're confined and doing naught but sitting all day."

"He's been eating nothing but crow, Aunt Laura," Meredith said with a softening smile. "I've been rubbing his sore knee with butter—it relieves his pain."

Laura Preston eyed Meredith as if she thought she'd lost her sanity. And, even worse, as if she'd suspected as much all along. Meredith felt a tiny chill. The woman, despite her calm, charming manner most of the time, obviously didn't like her. She felt threatened, maybe. Meredith filed away the information—she'd bend over backwards to alleviate the woman's concerns. After all, Laura evidently had run the house to Benjamin's and Abraham's complete satisfaction before Meredith came upon the scene. She'd have to be careful not to rock her boat by interfering.

"Here's your dinner, Abraham," Aunt Laura said, turning her full attention to the man. "Your daily ration of black pudding should please you this day. Lucy's made a fresh batch for you and she tells me the ingredients were especially fine this time."

"Black pudding? What's that?" Meredith asked without thinking. A greasy, sausage-like black blob sat on a small plate of its own beside

Abraham's dinner plate filled with more normal-looking food. Thank heaven they hadn't served her the stuff.

"A concoction that only Abraham demands, Sylvia," the woman said, back to her charming self. " 'Tis sometimes called blood pudding, for fresh animal blood is mixed with the suet, marrow, and groats, or hog pudding because it's encased in hog entrails."

Yuck. Meredith's stomach churned.

" 'Tis the secret of my robust health, Sylvia," Abraham said with a gleam in his beautiful eyes so like Benjamin's. "Black pudding every day keeps the bloody physicians out of thine way, my grandfather ever said, and the man fathered children till he was seventy—lived past ninety."

"Our dinner awaits us downstairs, Sylvia," Aunt Laura said, turning to Meredith and heading for the door. "Benjamin won't be joining us this afternoon. He's making his call to Peyton Smithson, to inform him, of course, of Sally's rash behavior."

Meredith's heart tugged with a pull of sympathy for Benjamin. His day wouldn't be a pleasant one.

After ensuring that Abraham was set up properly to eat his meal, she kissed him lightly on his forehead. "Enjoy," she said, trying not to think about that awful black pudding, and followed Aunt Laura down the stairs.

"Benjamin's mood will be dark this eve," the woman said, a whisper of warning in her voice. "You might wish to move back into your former chamber—until, that is, he's reconciled to Sally's scandalous imprudence."

No way, foolish woman. "As a dutiful wife I must adjust to Benjamin's moods, Aunt Laura,"

Meredith said lightly. "Perhaps I can find the means to soothe him."

Indeed, she thought with a secret smile, she suspected she could.

# Chapter Eleven

Benjamin didn't make it home for supper that night. Meredith might have been concerned, but she'd been so occupied in redoing their chamber that time had slipped away unnoticed. It was well past ten o'clock, and she was perched on tiptoe on a chair putting the finishing touches on the new softly draped canopy when he at last arrived.

He stopped in the doorway. She looked back over her shoulder, her heart kicking into a merry canter. God, he was gorgeous. But she couldn't get a bead on his mood. His eyes made a quick survey of the radically changed decor. This time, she hoped fervently, he'd approve of what she'd done.

"Welcome home," she said with a tentative brightness.

He nodded, came into the room, and closed the door quietly behind him. "Is this chamber furnished to your taste now, Mrs. Foxworth?" he asked, maddeningly noncommittal as to how he liked it. His eyebrow was lifted, of course.

She raised one of her own. "What do you think?" Two could play the same game, she figured.

"I think it's more conducive to restful sleep," he responded, his dimples at a reassuring depth.

Relieved, she stepped down from the chair.

"I'm sorry you removed the purple carpet, however," he complained with a wily grin. "I'd grown uncommonly fond of it."

She worked at a coy pout. "But, Benjamin, I thought this subdued dusky rose and gold pattern a far better match with my other changes, and it's much . . . softer," she added, a touch devilishly.

He nodded, undeniable agreement dancing from his eyes. She held on to the back of the chair, restraining her impulse to run into his arms.

Though his mood appeared anything but dark—defying, certainly, Aunt Laura's prediction—instinct told her that he should make the first move. Patience on her part was definitely indicated. And some ladylike propriety, too. She was beginning to feel very eighteenth centuryish.

Good thing. With a twinge of foreboding, she sensed now the undercurrent of tension that lay coiled within him. It had been there all along, but, as usual, his dazzling effect on her had fouled up her awareness. Meredith realized with a pang that she knew little about this man and what made him tick.

Apprehensively she watched him walk over to a tall chest, swing open one of its doors, and pull out a bottle of brandy and two rounded goblets.

"You'll join me in some liquid refreshment, I trust, Mrs. Foxworth?" Placing the glasses on the nightstand, he unstoppered the bottle and poured a goodly amount of amber liquid into each of the goblets. He stood there, his back turned to her, apparently waiting for her to come over.

She did, feeling a bit wobbly. "Something wrong?" she asked.

He shook his head. "No, Treasure. But the day was wearying." His using that marvelous term of endearment heartened her. Whatever was eating him, at least maybe this go-around she wasn't the problem.

He lifted one of the goblets and handed it to her. Raising the other, he clinked it lightly against hers and impaled her with his deep turquoise eyes, warming her to the tips of her toes. "Here's to dusky rose and gold, Treasure, and to our chamber which you've converted into a haven of comfort."

"I'll drink to that," she said, awash with pleasure. With their gazes fastened in a warm embrace, they each took a sip of brandy.

His hand gently circled her upper arm, and he led her to a sedately cushioned chair. She sat with renewed ease on the single dusky rose pillow. Benjamin pulled over the one ladderback she'd intelligently left bare and folded his long frame down on it with a sigh. He sat across from her, their knees almost touching.

"Was your encounter with Mr. Smithson terrible?" she inquired. He needed to talk, she could tell.

His long finger traced slowly around the rim of his goblet. "Not in truth. Peyton was disappointed, of course, but he recovered quickly. Surprised me, actually. Said damsels aplenty awaited in neighboring plantations. Though none were as fair as Sally, he avowed, many of them showed genuine promise as adequate vessels for a tribe of children."

She opted to remain silent. Something else was bothering Benjamin, then. What? She tightened her hold on the glass to keep it from sliding out from her suddenly moist fingers.

He lifted his eyes and his brows pulled together. "What I must say to you is woefully difficult for me," he said.

She braced herself. Good grief, what on earth . . .

"I was abominable yesterday. Can you forgive me?"

Abominable? He had to be kidding.

"Forgive you?" she asked, puzzled.

He studied his brandy. "On my long ride back from Goose Creek, I had much time to ponder through my troubled thoughts. You were right, Mrs. Foxworth. I indeed should have cheered for Sally's happiness rather than roared like a lion."

Dumbfounded, she waited for him to say something else. But he was quiet. That was all of it? Her forehead crinkled. "What are you saying, Benjamin?"

He cleared his throat. "That I had erred in forcing my pledge to Peyton on Sally in the first place—and I sorely erred in lashing out at you who had only demonstrated the good sense to see what my stubborn pride had blinded me to."

Meredith squirmed uncomfortably on the cushion. "I interfered, Benjamin. Don't punish yourself needlessly—and please, for God's sake don't make me sound like a saint or something."

He raised his eyes to her again, and she couldn't read them, mainly because her brain had turned to mush. But his deep voice went on, weighted with suffering. "It was dastardly wrong of me to attack you with such vehemence, Treasure. I apologize."

She stared at him. Lord, admitting such simple things as an error in judgment and a perfectly normal blow-up of temper was "woefully difficult" for him?

Suddenly the incredible span of more than two hundred years that stretched between them loomed as a formidable barrier. She might never understand him, really.

Nor, she supposed, would he ever truly understand her.

They'd each been shaped by cultures and societies that were as different as night and day—one no better than the other, she hastened to remind herself. She'd long ago come to the conclusion that the highly touted progress of the nineteenth and twentieth centuries hadn't done much for human nature. Indeed, it too often had encouraged some of its worst characteristics. She'd come to that realization way back in her other life. And now, seeing this wonderful, decent man agonizing over something most people would have shrugged off with a "Boy, I sure goofed—must've had my head on crooked" jarred her.

But Benjamin, the dear soul, needed comfort and reassurance. She could only be herself. She prayed that would be enough.

"Good grief, Benjamin. I wasn't exactly quiet myself. If you start apologizing, I'll have to throw in one or two apologies of my own, for heaven's sake—and that's no easier for me than it is for you. Can't we just call it a draw . . . all's well that end's well, that sort of thing?"

175

His eyebrow jumped up. "I'm prepared to make a pledge never to strike out at you in anger again."

"Don't you dare make such a pledge," she exclaimed with a laugh. "With our track record, you'll be hard put to keep it, anyway."

"Track record?"

She squiggled her mouth. "Let me start over—with our volatile personalities, it's hard to believe we won't have clashes ahead. Over something or other. Please don't make a pledge I don't even want you to make."

He looked very serious, so she continued, aiming for a most endearing smile. "Besides, Benjamin, making up can be the best part of any good argument."

His smile burst forth at last—radiantly. She took a big gulp of her brandy.

"You are a treasure," he said, reaching for her hand.

A warming rainbow-tinged bubble expanded in her chest. The brandy wasn't causing it, she knew, but something else entirely.

Dear God, she was falling in love with this man—head over heels, completely, deeply and irretrievably in love.

Not wise, Meredith, she warned herself. None of this could last. They were of two vastly different times—she didn't even belong here. Like those contents of her bag that had slowly vanished piece by piece, she might be destined to disappear. Lord, she might be whisked away in the first thunderstorm of the season.

The thought struck her as downright depressing.

But he had lifted her glasses off her nose and was removing the goblet from her hand, setting

176

it on the floor beside his. And there he was on his knees before her, pulling her toward him. Depression didn't have a chance.

"Come to me, Treasure," he said in something between a husky command and a whispered promise. Held within his embrace, feeling his dexterous fingers behind her back free the tiny hooks of her dress one by one, she was content to know she was indeed here at this moment. Definitely here. With him.

His soft lips, sweet with brandy, greeted hers with an invitation she accepted with undeniable pleasure. Wrapped in his arms, she slid—floated—to her knees, and pressed her body close to his. He slipped her dress from her shoulders and followed its downward flow with his superb hands, his delicious lips.

"We must put to test the carpet you've selected to ensure it's truly a satisfactory substitute," he said, quite sensibly, as he eased her to her back, disrobing her along the way as if the great quantities of billowing cloth were nothing but wisps of air.

The carpet would be more than satisfactory, she was certain, succumbing with avid delight to the flames of desire that engulfed her. With Benjamin, under his skillful, fiery touches, even a bed of nails beneath them would swiftly become a nest of warm feathers.

Beyond their open window, in the moist midnight fog of the Hanover spring, an eerie white light sizzled to life, spread into a ghostly brightness, then faded silently into the darkness.

Locked in their own separate world, neither Meredith nor Benjamin took note of the strange event.

\*    \*    \*

April flowed on a bower of fragrant blossoms into May. Meredith flowed happily right along with it. The previous month, indeed, had been a time of discovery, settling in . . . almost heaven, she thought as she smiled contentedly at the wooden butter churn between her knees.

On this Monday, the second of May, she sat on the back steps of Fox Haven involved in the quaint chore of transforming cream into butter. It was labor intensive as the devil, but required little brain power. So she put her arms in automatic drive and let her mind churn away on more interesting subjects.

Like this past weekend, for example, when Benjamin had invited her to accompany him to Newcastle to visit Sally. He'd wanted to make his peace with his sister—and there was the matter of her dowry. Benjamin was a generous man. He'd given the young couple fifty acres of prime land on the Pamunkey River near Newcastle, a herd of cattle, and silver enough to make their eyes sparkle. Not that they weren't sparkling like diamonds already. The pair clearly was on Cloud Nine!

As she and Benjamin had prepared to depart on Friday afternoon, he'd demonstrated delight at discovering that his wife could ride. Meredith grinned at the memory. Naturally, he'd disapproved of her sitting astride the horse and frowned mightily upon her riding costume.

"Sitting astride's the way I learned, Benjamin," she'd protested when he'd demanded she ride sidesaddle. "Would you have me slipping off the side of the blasted saddle in the name of propriety, for heaven's sake?"

He'd relented, but insisted she return to the

house to change into a proper dress before they would start their journey. Her riding habit was a pair of buckskin knee breeches and a white linen balloon-sleeved shirt she'd "bought" from Jack the stable hand by bartering her leather shoulder bag. Jack had coveted the bag, and she'd considered it absolutely useless since most of its contents had vanished into the ether of time.

She'd sat stubbornly astride the fine black horse and glowered at Benjamin. He, of course, was comfortably dressed in buckskin knee breeches and a white balloon-sleeved shirt.

"I'll change into a dress the same minute you don one of the ridiculous things, Mr. Foxworth," she'd snapped. "If you expect me to ride fifteen miles bare-bottomed on a saddle, you've got rocks in your head."

He'd smiled—despite himself, she'd suspected. "If you'd sit sidesaddle as a proper lady should, Mrs. Foxworth, your bare bottom would be seated on dress rather than saddle."

"Riding sidesaddle I'd be bare-bottomed on the ground in less than five minutes!" she'd exploded.

She'd gotten her way. But only after assuring Benjamin she had suitable frocks stuffed in her saddlebag. She'd promised him she would change her clothes in the woods outside Newcastle and ride into town perched properly sideways. But at a slow walk, she'd told him, in no uncertain terms.

Remembering the happy resolution of that little scene, Meredith's lips softened into a serene curve.

The costume change in the woods had delayed their arrival at Sally's an hour or so, as it turned

179

out. Pine needles, too, could become like warm feathers in short order, they'd discovered with delight.

She squirmed on the step and continued her endless pumping of the churn. And sighed with contentment. Life in colonial Virginia was immensely pleasurable, she thought with deep satisfaction. Churning butter, maybe, wasn't any great joy—but almost everything else had exceeded her expectations.

Benjamin, of course, had eased her adjustment to all the differences. Lord, he couldn't know how much he'd helped. It surprised her, even. But she'd never felt better or more eager to face— and conquer—any and all obstacles. Having a lover who made her think she was the most desirable creature in the world was a wonderful new experience.

She realized that her former life, where she'd complacently thought she had the tiger by the tail, had suffered from a great big void. No Benjamin. With him around, any era—past or future—would be more than acceptable. Perfect, actually.

Her arm muscles were sore, but she resisted resting. This butter-making job had to be done. Aunt Laura had assigned her the task this morning, saying Lucy was needed for washing linens. A number of the house servants had taken to their beds with a mild fever running rampant through the slave quarters, she'd explained, and Meredith had taken on this new chore with the enthusiasm of ignorance.

She wiped the perspiration from her forehead with the back of her hand and resumed pumping. Butter took one heck of a long time to become butter.

180

Oh Lord, with her occupied this way, Abraham was going to be crotchety as the devil. She'd begun allowing him to walk an hour or so a day with his cane for the past week, but she'd given him strict orders. Either she or Will was to be at his side, and he was restricted to the upstairs hall. Today Will was busy helping with the laundry. She'd have to check in on Abraham later and unruffle him as best she could. But for the time being, she was cast in the role of a dairy maid. Physical therapy would have to wait.

Surrogate motherhood, too, she thought with a frown. Doggone it, she missed little Philip. She'd had to relinquish her customary two hours with him this afternoon because of the servant shortage. Aunt Laura had assured her that Sukie was taking good care of the infant. "He did well enough these past three days without you, Sylvia," she'd said with a hint of disapproval. The woman had resented Benjamin taking her to Newcastle, she figured.

But she was glad she'd gone. Sally looked wonderful. Meredith chuckled, recalling that the young woman also appeared to be decidedly pregnant. Only the tiniest bit of thickening around her middle, but sufficient evidence—along with that Mona Lisa smile—for Meredith to know that Sally hadn't gotten that way on her wedding night. Just one more piece of evidence—as if any were needed—that Sally had done the right thing by marrying the man she loved.

If Benjamin noticed his sister's budding condition, he hadn't said a word. And Meredith had learned to keep her mouth shut about certain things. Most of the time.

Sukie walked around the corner of the house,

a basket of wet linens in her arms.

"Is Philip sleeping?" Meredith asked, surprised to see the pretty young mulatto out hanging laundry. She'd understood that Sukie was to be in the nursery this afternoon.

"Sleeping like a lamb, Miz Sylvia," Sukie assured her. "Lucy tells me I'se needed for th' washin', what with the babe he bein' so content in his cradle for th' while."

Meredith nodded, but was suddenly aware of a prickle of uneasiness. Nothing she could put her finger on, but she felt a strong need to look in on the tyke. Well, the cream was almost thick— for the past few minutes she'd had to shove the paddle with some amount of force through the mess rather than idly pumping.

"I believe I'll go peek in on him," she said, releasing the paddle and rising with some difficulty off the step. Her muscles had kinked into permanent sit-knots, she realized with a groan, rubbing the small of her sore back with her even sorer hands. "I've missed the little rascal, and the butter's near set, or whatever you call it when it's almost ready."

Later, she would wonder about the way she'd hurried into the house. Motherly intuition? A goading premonition from out of the blue? *Something* had sent her scurrying back to the nursery.

She heard Philip's terrifying throttled whimpers the moment she entered the room. With her heart in her throat, she rushed to the cradle.

He was choking! Dear God, a loose ribbon from the crib's side had tightened around his neck! His cherub face was distorted, turning blue. Meredith frantically disentangled the twisted ribbon and without hesitation pressed her mouth over the baby's little nose and purplish lips and expelled light puffs of breath, tapping his wee chest in the life-giving rhythms she'd been taught.

*Please, God, please . . .*

Philip fidgeted fretfully beneath her, then expelled a soft but heartening sob into her mouth. She raised her head, and he bellowed out a full-blown cry that brought tears of joy to her eyes.

She pulled the red-faced squalling infant up into her arms and held him close, patting his tiny back. "It's all right, it's all right," she blubbered over and over. Trembling, she sat with him on the small rocker and cradled him against her. Her tears streamed unabated, dampening Philip's lacy blue bonnet.

"Lawsy, Miz Sylvia! What's all dis uproar in here?" Lucy ran into the nursery, her wide, dark face drawn with anxiety.

Meredith cuddled the now-contented baby against her breast and scrunched to wipe her tear-soaked neck and jaw with her shoulder. Philip hiccuped, and she kissed the warm sweet curve of his blessedly rosy cheek.

"He was strangling, Lucy. The ribbon . . ." She could barely speak, weak from the awful terror of the past minutes and now, thank heaven, from relief.

Lucy stared down into the cradle, perplexed. "But we'd removed all dose ribbons jes like you'd asked us to, Miz Sylvia. 'Member that day—weeks ago it was—when you carried on so 'bout the ribbons being needless frills and a true danger to th' babe, you said." She looked at Meredith, her black eyes rounded with distress.

"We's took 'em every one away that very day,

Miz Sylvia, I swears to good Jesus we did. Where'd dis ribbon come from?"

An icy chill ran up Meredith's spine. "I don't know, Lucy. I only know it came close to . . ." She couldn't continue. Burying her face in the child's bonnet, she began to weep again.

Lucy came and patted her back. "He's fine now, Miz Sylvia. We can thank the blessed God in th' heavens dat you found him when you did."

Meredith sniffled and looked up into the woman's warm face. She nodded. "Thank God," she agreed.

For a long time, she sat in the nursery with little Philip, who fell blissfully asleep in her arms. The chair whispered its sweet lullaby as she rocked back and forth. Thinking. Puzzled, disturbing thoughts.

Who at Fox Haven had tied that deadly red ribbon to the side of Philip's cradle?

"It was no accident, Benjamin," she said later that afternoon when he bounded into the nursery out of breath, his heart heavy with worry.

Word had spread quickly to the fields where he'd been working with his men—there'd been "a near terrible accident," he was told. "But th' Miz Sylvia she saved the babe. By the grace of God she ran in before th' dastardly ribbon had . . ."

He'd made a mad dash for the house, not waiting for Will to finish his alarming message. His wife needed him—something had happened to her beloved babe!

But all looked tranquil when he entered the room. She was silhouetted against the golden sunlight beaming in through the windows, a lovely picture of serene motherhood—his treasure of a wife, rocking her sleeping child.

He ran to her and knelt before her. "Dear God, is all well? I heard there was an accident, that—"

And she interrupted him with those words that pierced like ice into his soul. "It was no accident, Benjamin."

A fresh tear slithered down her streaked cheeks. He wiped it away with his fingertips, fraught with concern for her, for the babe—deeply disturbed by the implications of what she'd said.

"What are you saying, my Treasure?" he asked, low.

Her voice came muffled through the tears that clogged her throat as she explained about the small bow-ribbons that Lucy and Sukie had used to decorate the cradle, how she'd had all of them removed weeks ago, fearing they posed a risk to the child who had grown far more active in the past month.

"And yet someone placed one there today, Benjamin—not a small bow, but a long ribbon that became entwined around Philip's little neck like a noose. Had I not happened to look in on him . . ." She shook her head, inhaling a quivery sob.

Benjamin enveloped the two of them in his arms, offering his comfort. But he felt no comfort himself—only a dark cloud of heavy gloom.

Once again, a babe at Fox Haven had lain in the ever-ravenous jaws of death.

This one, at least, had been snatched away before the jaws had clamped shut. But there had been so many others not so lucky. His heart twisted in sorrow. He pressed his face into his wife's neck so that she couldn't see the torment in his eyes.

So very many little ones the Foxworths had lost.

Five younger brothers had gone before his mother's untimely death. Two sons of his own—torn from him before they'd reached their first year. All of them found dead in their cradles, taken in their sleep without warning. Robust, healthy, growing . . . and then—dead, as if their tiny glowing lights had been snuffed by a phantom's hand.

Those tragedies, coupled with a long line of other mysterious events, had given rise to the whispered rumors of Fox Haven's curse. And now he had the added burden of a new mystery. His wife believed that someone in this house might have purposely placed that ribbon in Philip's crib.

Dear God, who amongst them would have done such a thing?

He must assure this tormented woman in his arms, whether she was right in her suspicions or not—and bloody hell, he prayed with all his heart she wasn't—he must let her know he would do all in his power to keep the babe safe.

"What you've said troubles me deeply, Treasure," he said, pushing her silky hair away from her tear-slickened cheek. "We shall move Philip's nursery to the room adjoining our chamber. He'll be safer near to us."

"And I'll watch everyone like a hawk," she sniffled, managing a small smile. "Until we discover who the culprit is, I can't trust anyone, Benjamin." Looking far calmer, she gave him a quick kiss on his nose. "Except you, Love. I trust you, and Abraham. But not another soul."

He hugged her close, feeling better himself. This wife of his, indeed, was a special woman.

A treasure.

Meredith snuggled her face into the warm hollow of Benjamin's strong shoulder. He'd brought her comfort, assurance. Somehow, together, they would get to the bottom of this mystery.

Together, she knew, they could do almost anything.

The gentle knock on the nursery door jarred her a little, but with Benjamin there with her, she relaxed immediately. "Thank you," she whispered in his ear. "All will be well," she added as a promise of her own.

After pecking a warming kiss on her forehead, he rose and went to the door.

"There be guests here, Mistuh Benjamin, up in Mistuh Abraham's room. He says you're to come there at once," she heard Lucy say in a low voice.

"Who's here, Lucy?"

"A Mistuh Herman Wetzel, he says, and a young lady is with him, sir."

Meredith froze.

# Chapter Twelve

Benjamin looked back at Meredith. "Your father's here, Treasure. You'll want to come with me, of course—and bring the babe." He was walking toward her, reaching for her arm. Smiling, dear God.

She couldn't move. Her world had splintered into a billion pieces—all of them stabbing into her heart.

This, then, was how it was going to end. Her refuge at Fox Haven was over. And the sharpest, bitterest pain of all—in just a few moments Benjamin would be gone from her. Forever.

She found herself standing. He'd gotten her to her feet, she guessed. She must weigh a ton—there was that much heaviness in her. Couldn't he feel the difference? Couldn't he see, for heaven's sake? She was dazed, walking as if in a trance. Not a drop of blood was in her face; all of it had settled in her feet, like congealed lead.

And yet she was climbing the stairs beside him, his hand warm on her numbed elbow. Temporarily warm. One minute from now and he, too, would be ice cold. Toward her. With just one knock on a door, the stairs of Fox Haven had become the steps to a scaffold. The guillotine awaited her up there.

They entered Abraham's room. She saw the woman first—the wild-eyed woman from Richmond who had dropped Philip into her arms. Sylvia Wetzel. Philip's real mother. And soon to replace her as Benjamin's wife.

Meredith stood paralyzed in the doorway, and let Benjamin walk in ahead of her. If she'd had a grain of sanity left, she knew she would be rushing to Sylvia, handing her the baby, and running straight out of the room, down the stairs, and away from Fox Haven. Standing there waiting for the ax to fall had to be pure insanity. But she stood.

"There's a—uh—problem, it appears, Benjamin," Abraham said from his chair. He was pale and agitated.

Little wonder, Meredith thought. She felt disembodied, as if she were up on the ceiling hovering over this scene. She looked down on herself—she was like a stiff statue of a mother holding her child, leaning against the doorjamb, white as a ghost and cold as marble. Benjamin, tall and dark, splendid even in his work clothes, stood in the middle of the room, his booted legs spread.

The stocky German merchant, his round face beet-red as Abraham had described, nervously turning his brimmed hat in his hands. Stooped. Pensive.

# Thomasina Ring

The young woman—dumpling plump, curly blond hair wisping around her picture-pretty face. Bosomy. Luscious. Shyly standing behind her tense father, peering over his shoulder.

All of them, including Abraham, were focused on Benjamin. Words were being spoken. She couldn't hear them. Wouldn't.

Didn't have to.

Like a film gone haywire, the scene's frames tilted, jerked, moved in slow motion, sped ahead in a blur. The soundtrack was garbled.

"In Williamsburg we found Sylvia . . . a troupe of players . . . to an actor . . . Kitty paid . . . feared curse . . . apologies . . . too late."

*Too late.*

Meredith was back against the doorjamb, its edge cutting sharply into her shoulder blades. All eyes in the room were now on her. *His* eyes, stunned, questioning. She cringed, whimpered, then stumbled forward. Some external force was moving her, for nothing alive enough to create motion remained inside her. She handed the baby to Benjamin, turned, and fled down the long hallway to her room.

Or to what had been her room.

She had nowhere else to go.

She lay on the bed staring at the ceiling for what could have been five minutes—or hours. Time no longer had meaning. *Time.* She shivered. Time was her fierce captor. It had imprisoned her here—tortured her with frivolous hopes. Cruelly whispered to her that she could make a difference. Could make the lame walk, soothe a tormented spirit, give love—and find it.

And now her captor, Time, had torn her away, but had left her in this era that was not her own to fend for herself. She wasn't sure she could. Not now. Not after Benjamin.

He walked into the room and closed the door behind him. She sat up quickly, clasped her icy hands together, and waited. She knew she should search for her calico docent costume and Capezios and leave at once. But she sat on the edge of the bed instead. And waited.

"Who are you?" he asked her.

"Meredith Davis."

"So you told me on the road from Richmond. I wouldn't listen to you then. I shall listen now." His sigh was long and weary as he sat on the bare ladderback chair a good twelve feet away from her. "Please tell me everything, Miss Davis."

She shook her head. "If I speak the truth, you won't believe me, Benjamin. I'm far too drained and emptied now to fabricate anything for you. Let's just leave it at that."

"We'll *not* leave it at that," he said through clenched teeth. "I will hear your truth."

"No."

He stared at her. His turquoise eyes held numerous warring elements—doubt, anger, strained patience, confusion. She saw no hope for her in them. Only further despair.

"I should leave Fox Haven, now," she said, her voice quivery. "I don't belong here. Please leave me alone, Benjamin."

"Where do you belong?"

"Richmond, I suppose." She concentrated on her clasped hands. Her knuckles were white. Yes, Richmond was as good as anywhere. She'd have to find work. Doing what, dear God?

"You *suppose*?"

"That's what I said." She realized the sun was still shining brightly outside. It hadn't been hours, then. But the lapsed time since the Wetzels' arrival made little difference, one way or the other.

"You have no home, Miss Davis?"

"I did . . . once." This was torture, damnit! Why didn't he just go on downstairs and marry Sylvia Wetzel?

"When?"

She looked up at him and shook her head. He couldn't know what he was asking.

"I asked you *when*, woman. Answer me!" he shouted angrily.

That did it! Blast it all—he was *angry*. She pulled back her shoulders. Damn it to hell. She bit out her words. "The year was 1991, Mr. Foxworth. The twentieth century, I'll have you know. Now just put that in your colonial clay pipe and smoke it!"

He was quiet. Too quiet. She shook like an aspen leaf.

"You said you were too tired to fabricate," he said at last, his anger gone, but his voice heavy—almost ponderous.

"I'm not fabricating, Benjamin! I told you, didn't I? You won't believe me. You *can't*, for God's sake!" Tears pricked her eyes, and she looked away, feeling desolate. "Nobody here could believe me," she groaned softly.

He placed his hands on his knees and rose slowly, walked toward her, standing close. She kept her head bent. His eyes were boring into her skull.

"You're right, Miss Davis. No one could believe what you've just told me. I recommend that you tell me the truth about yourself."

She'd gone this far; there was no turning back. Survival no longer seemed important. The most important thing in the world at the moment was to convince this man—this man who had so thoroughly stolen her heart but could never be hers now—that she was who she was. He *had* to believe her.

"I've spoken the truth. I'm from the twentieth century—the future, Benjamin. I didn't choose to come here. It was a bolt of lightning, I think. I don't know . . ."

"You're determined to continue in this vein?" He sounded tired.

She grasped for straws. "Listen to me, Benjamin! Listen! I was a docent—a hostess, guide—at St. John's Church in Richmond. It was the 216th anniversary of Virginia's Second Convention. A reenactment of that great event—it will happen next March, I guess—when your neighbor Patrick Henry stated—states—words that rang or will ring through history. 'Give me liberty or give me death.' It inspired the country, and was one of the many things that led to the American Revolution."

"The Revolution?"

"Yes, doggone it—it's coming, Benjamin. And it's successful, though it takes a few years. Where I come from, Virginia's a state. One of fifty in what's known as the United States of America that stretches to the Pacific Ocean and into it. Hawaii is part of the country now—"

"You're extremely inventive," he interrupted with obvious impatience.

"Listen to me, please!" she shouted. "Then do with me what you will," she added, lower, plaintive now. Her brain raced . . . where should she begin? What would get through to him?

"George Washington will be the country's first president. You know him, don't you? He lives up at Mount Vernon. Patrick Henry will be Virginia's first governor." She was drawing blanks. What else? What else? "In the 1860s, there will be a terrible Civil War—North against South. The South loses, and slavery will be a thing of the past."

"I'll hear no more, woman. Desist!"

She was growing desperate. How could she reach him? "Benjamin, my world was so very different from this one. Richmond was a huge metropolis—Virginia's capital. There were buildings that reached high in the sky. Industry beyond your imaginings. A network of paved roads. I drove a car—a metal horseless carriage, if you will—that could go more than ninety miles per hour, though I seldom went over sixty. A trip from Richmond to Hanover would have taken only twenty minutes or so instead of the four hours you're accustomed to. Airplanes soared through the sky. Big metal birds with engines that carried more than two hundred people. Last year I flew to California, it's a large state way out on the West Coast of the United States. Over three thousand miles. It took me only five hours . . ."

It wasn't working. He had turned his back, had slapped his hands to his ears.

Frantically, she ventured down another path. "I wore little disks in my eyes that corrected my vision without spectacles—they were called contact lenses. I had two pair, Benjamin. One was green, the other was violet."

She saw his shoulders tense. His hands went down, but one pushed back through his hair first. Maybe she'd found the ticket. Something he could relate to. Something he'd seen.

Encouraged, she went on. "When I arrived here, and I didn't even know where I was, mind you—let alone *when*—I had a bag filled with wonders from the future. Don't you remember it? It was heavy at first. But it kept emptying on me in a weird fashion, piece by piece, though I wasn't aware of it at first. I had a wristwatch. It told the time. You saw it, Benjamin, looked at it closely. It disappeared, along with everything else. But you saw it."

He turned around then, with a curious look on his face. "The wristwatch?"

She nodded. "Don't you remember? Timex? Quartz? The second hand that swept around . . ."

But he wasn't listening to her. He'd run to his trunk and was rummaging through it, pulling out the handsome burgundy waistcoat he'd worn that terrifying night when she'd discovered she was a time traveler.

"I have it," he said low, almost breathlessly. "It had fallen on the floor. I'd planned to ask you about it, but it truly slipped my mind. The face had vanished, I didn't understand . . . here!"

He brought her Timex to her. His hand shook slightly, and hers was absolutely spastic as he handed it to her. He was right. The face had disappeared, and the workings, too, she figured. But he had seen it . . . he remembered.

She closed her hand over the watch and held it like a talisman.

"Like almost everything else I had with me, this too faded away. I've reasoned they all disappeared because they hadn't been invented yet, didn't belong here. Perhaps I'll fade, too. Lord knows, I should—and I want to, desperately, though I'd hate to end up in some no-man's-land between eras. So far, though, I appear stuck here. And you know as well as I that I don't belong here."

"You would disappear?"

"Gladly."

He went back to the chair and sat slowly. He rubbed his hands across his eyes, appeared to be in deep distress.

Lord, she should have known he couldn't handle this. What had she done?

"Nothing in my life has prepared me for the truths you profess to speak, Miss Davis. And yet I find myself believing you, though my believing makes me wonder about my own sanity."

She was afraid to say anything. His words brought her a tenuous thread of hope. If Benjamin knew, believed, somehow she could go on with her life and face whatever lay ahead.

"Since the day I met you in Richmond, you've presented me with a staggering array of puzzle pieces," he said, massaging his temples with his long fingers. "I lacked the imagination to fit them into such a picture as you've described. I either ignored them or blithely assembled them into a pattern I could understand."

She felt like crying, but she wouldn't let herself. "No one could expect you to think right off the bat that I had dropped in from the twentieth century," she offered.

"Your peculiar English alone should have made me more curious." His voice was distant as if he were talking to himself. Maybe he was.

A tear slid down her cheek. She wiped it away hurriedly and fought to keep control of herself. "Benjamin, I don't know any more than you why I'm here. But if you believe me, that's all I could ask for, under the circumstances. And I'm sorry I've had to dissemble, hide behind deception, pretend to be someone I wasn't—but I was so lost, so confused—"

"You tried to tell me, Miss Davis."

"Only at first. When I thought my options had run out, I went along with everyone's assumptions that I was . . ." She couldn't say the woman's name.

And dear God, that woman was in this house. Waiting for him.

"I had nowhere to go," she ended feebly.

"My father wants you to stay at Fox Haven."

She stared at him, dumbfounded. "What on earth are you saying?" Stay here? Under the same roof with Benjamin and his new bride? She'd be better off begging on the streets of Richmond.

"Father and I talked awhile after Mr. Wetzel left. He expressed concern about you—sensed that only desperate circumstances could have forced you to accept the role of another. He's grown fond of you. He told me to tell you that you have a home here—if you want it."

Abraham's concern touched her. But what Benjamin had left unsaid cut painfully deep. His *father* was concerned, his father had grown fond of her— had offered her a home. Not one word about what Benjamin might think on the subject.

She shook her head. "No, Benjamin. I shall leave immediately."

He continued as if she hadn't spoken. "The information brought to us this day nullifies our marriage, of course. But Father suggests you remain as governess to Betsy and Philip and as Aunt Laura's assistant—he considers your contributions to the household valuable. We would pay you wages, Miss Davis. You may wish to think over the matter."

"You must be out of your mind," she blurted out. "I can't possibly stay here. Not now, not with . . ." Her words dangled in the air. She left them there.

But he wouldn't cooperate. "Not with what?"

Damnit, was he that dense? Or was he torturing her this way on purpose?

"Good grief, Benjamin. Don't make me say it."

He sat forward in the chair and studied her intently. "We are offering you a refuge, Miss Davis. From what you've told me this afternoon, I should think it would be welcomed by you."

She pinned him with a piercing glare. "Perhaps you should consider how much this stupid proposition would be welcomed by Sylvia Wetzel."

"What has Sylvia Wetzel to do with what we're discussing?"

The man was stark, raving crazy! "She's Philip's mother, for crying out loud. Your new bride-to-be, Benjamin. Don't you think she'd resent a usurper—"

"What on God's earth are you talking about, woman?" He looked as aghast as she felt.

The stiff wind that had held her erect collapsed. Everything inside her collapsed along with it. Nothing was making sense. She was unable to think, let alone speak.

"Did you not hear a word of Mr. Wetzel's?" he asked.

She shook her head. "I couldn't . . . I knew . . ."

His deep sigh stopped her. "Sylvia Wetzel ran off to Williamsburg, joined a troupe of players, and has married an actor. She has no interest in

Philip, nor I assure you, is she any bride-to-be of mine."

"But the woman with Mr. Wetzel . . ." Now she was thoroughly confused.

"Is Kitty somebody, naught but a Richmond tavern wench. Sylvia had paid her—with Joshua's money, of course—to bring the babe to Hanover."

Meredith couldn't digest any of what she was hearing. "She thrust Philip into my arms. Why?"

He frowned and pushed his fingers through his hair. "The woman had heard rumors of Fox Haven's curse, became frightened, and had second thoughts. She was sorely chagrined as she related to us that when she saw you . . ."

Meredith expelled a sigh of her own. Benjamin continued to explain. How Mr. and Mrs. Wetzel had been startled to discover Sylvia in Williamsburg on a recent trip they'd made to the town. How the unrepentant Sylvia had confessed her sly trickery . . . told them of bribing Kitty with silver and lies. How Mr. Wetzel, on a hunch of his own, had found Kitty still in Richmond and had brought her to Fox Haven to back up his painful story. And how the Wetzels were returning to Germany and believed their grandson should remain with the Foxworths where the child would have a proper birthright.

On one level she heard all of Benjamin's incredible words, but on another her mind was galloping at full speed in varying directions. Could she stay at Fox Haven, after all? *Should* she? True, she had fit in here, had made herself useful. Abraham was improving daily. She'd made inroads with Betsy and planned to begin her therapy soon. Philip had become so special to her . . . and today she'd had reason to suspect he needed her care more than ever.

But she'd played her role here under the pretense of being Benjamin's wife. Could she, as a hired hand, have even a chance of continuing successfully without the unspoken power that the status as a family member had given her?

And could she, dear heaven, be in daily contact with this man who had been her husband without dying a little every time she saw him? "Nullifies our marriage," he'd said as easily as if he'd said, "Rain prevents our taking a stroll." She knew what a nullified marriage meant to a proper eighteenth-century gentleman. Separate rooms, separate beds.

And, clearly, the whole idea didn't disturb him one bit—probably pleased him. After all, he couldn't have wanted to marry her in the first place. That truth she had to accept. Somehow.

"Can you consider our offer now, Miss Davis?" he prompted her, jolting her away from her depressing thoughts.

Lord, how she hated the way he spoke her name with such cold formality. *New rules, Meredith,* she reminded herself, cringing inside.

But he was waiting for her response. And once again she was left with a poor selection of choices. She could either sign on as a housemaid in Fox Haven or panhandle down in Richmond. One was likely to be intolerable—but the other was downright frightening.

"I have little choice," she said honestly. "I'll stay here at Fox Haven. Only I wonder how we'll handle this time problem—none of the others should have to come to grips with my . . . strangeness."

That was not her biggest concern, by a long shot. But her worries about life without Benjamin's lovemaking wasn't something she believed she should even try to articulate to him. He'd never understand.

"Father will be pleased that you're staying."

*But what of you, Benjamin?* she wanted to cry out.

He knitted his brows and leaned back in the chair. "As for the time problem, as you call it, I see no need to disclose that. We'll have to fabricate a story, of course—something plausible that would be acceptable to them. The other shall remain a tightly held secret between the two of us."

And that would be the only thing held tightly between them. One blasted secret.

He went on, very businesslike. She had fled from an intolerable situation as a governess, he would tell them. Had been desperate, destitute. Feared for her life, for her employer had been an abusive tyrant who threatened her daily. She had only happened to be at the oak that day in Richmond. Hungry, cold, without means of support. Kitty's actions had been a salvation, like a wand of magic. And with no other option, Meredith had grasped it as a drowning man would grasp for a piece of floating jetsam.

But she'd done it only after trying with fervor to deny that she deserved salvation, he continued, for her nature was to be honest. When no one would listen to her pleas, she had accepted at last—but not without true misgivings—the solution that had been offered to her.

"God, Benjamin, that makes me sound like some goody-goody heroine out of Dickens or something."

He ignored her comment and stood once again, starting for the door. "My belongings will be removed from this chamber within the hour, Miss Davis. Philip's nursery is being set up in the adjoining room as we discussed earlier. I shall go to Father now and inform him that you have agreed to stay."

So sad she ached, she sat quietly on the edge of the bed and watched him open the door.

He paused, then stopped and turned to her. Her heart skipped a beat. Was he at last going to say something to soften her misery? "I shall miss you" would be comforting. "I too am pleased you will be staying with us" might even give her a lift.

"Colonel Washington is truly to be the first president?" he offered instead. "Had I been asked to predict, I would have thought it might be Tom Jefferson."

She wanted to cry. "Jefferson will be the third president," she managed to say.

"I see," he said, leaving her then. The door shut tight.

Now she could cry.

And she did. The wrenching, desolate cry of unmitigated heartbreak.

# Chapter Thirteen

So, she wasn't supposed to eat? Big deal.

Virginia's House of Burgesses had declared the first day of June a day of fasting, humiliation, and prayer to demonstrate the colony's sympathy and support for faraway Boston, where Britain had closed the harbor. The Massachusetts port town, the Mother Country had decreed, would remain shut off from trade until full reimbursement had been received for the tea dumped into the harbor during Boston's "tea party" the previous December.

To Meredith, fasting, humiliation, and prayer had become old hat—and it didn't have a thing to do with the growing revolutionary fever in the colonies. After all, she knew how all of that was going to turn out, anyway.

But her own future was a blank. And she was

hard-pressed to see anything close to a satisfactory resolution ahead. Ever. She was "making do," and that was about it.

But today, at least, things would be a little better. With the fast in effect, she wouldn't have to sit at the same table with Benjamin and pretend to eat. The dinners and suppers for the past month had been brutal torture.

She sat to his left now—Aunt Laura Preston had returned to the foot of the table where she "properly belonged," as she'd told Meredith. Abraham, who'd long ago relegated head-of-the-household status to Benjamin and was up and about at last, sat happily during the dreary meals to Benjamin's right.

The elder gentleman and Miss Preston (as the woman had requested Meredith to address her since her demotion) pretty much carried the conversation ball. Benjamin interjected an "aye" or a "truly interesting" now and then. Meredith nodded a lot and tried to keep her stiff upper lip curved into a pleasant smile.

But eating more than a few bites was out of the question. Benjamin's appetite, she'd noted, was that of a healthy, robust man without a worry on his mind. That didn't help things a blasted bit.

Had she not had the breakfasts, where Benjamin was never present except on Sundays, she figured she'd have died of starvation by now. As it was, she'd gotten down to skin and bones and had had to alter all of the smaller-sized dresses that he'd bought for her.

Back earlier, before her world had fallen apart.

So today she'd tightened her sash around her diminishing waist and had done without even breakfast. She hadn't missed it. Food, along with almost everything else, had lost its appeal.

With Philip strapped to her back in a soft sling she'd fashioned, she dropped in on Jess, Fox Haven's black cobbler, on the afternoon of the fast to see how he was progressing with the special shoes she'd asked him to make for Betsy.

"They's comin' along dandy, Miz Meredith," he told her with his toothy grin. "I'se workin' on 'em ev'nings,'fore I goes t'bed. Mistuh Benjamin he gives me plenty work for th' days."

"No hurry, Jess. Betsy won't need them before September, when the weather turns a bit cooler."

She didn't add that she figured it would be at least that long before she'd have the child ready for the serious part of her therapy. Betsy was still reluctant to let Meredith too near her foot, so things were going slower than she'd hoped earlier. The sudden change of her position from stepmother to governess had taken its toll, and she was finding it harder now to get close to the girl.

Oh well, she had time. Nothing but time—an endless stretch of it ahead.

"They's soft as a fawn's belly and'll have soles good 'n firm like yo' ordered for that po' child," Jess said with pride. "She's only had slippers befo' this, what wit' her not needin' anythin' mo' sturdy."

Meredith ignored his unspoken question as to why Betsy should have something sturdier all of a sudden.

"Remember, they're to be a surprise for her, and I don't want anyone else to know," she reminded him. She certainly didn't want Benjamin aware of her plans. He'd either disapprove out of hand or, if he should become unnaturally reasonable and let her go ahead with them, he might expect miracles she couldn't produce. Heaven only knew if she'd have Betsy walking some day. But the last thing she wanted to do was to hold out hope and then dash it. There'd been enough hope-dashing at Fox Haven recently.

Smiling up from his cobbler's bench, Jess assured her he'd keep the shoe project a secret and returned his attention to the leather boots he was making for Benjamin. Handsome boots, she couldn't help but notice. Rich cordovan. Was it just her imagination, or was he dressing a little fancier these days? She didn't even want to think what that might mean. That's all she needed—Benjamin Bachelor on the loose among the Hanover party circuit.

"Are you married, Jess?" she asked to change the course of her thoughts.

"Yes'm, to sweet Verna. Mistuh Benjamin he lets us slaves marry and keeps the fam'lies together too, he does. Not like most masters."

Chalk up one for Benjamin. But this whole problem of slavery nettled her constantly.

"Do you have children?"

"Yes'm—two fine boys runnin' wild back in the quarters an' one risin' like yeast dough now in its mama's oven."

Meredith smiled. "Are you happy at Fox Haven, Jess?" she felt compelled to ask.

"Most time, ma'am." His awl stopped a moment and he looked up. "We's treated well here, and th' master he be a good man. But th' place has spooks that oft' times scares us near white."

She wrinkled her brow. "The ghost you mean?"

"Yes'm," he said, looking down at the boot under his wide, strong hand.

"That's no ghost, Jess. I've seen it myself. A real person's doing it, I'm sure of it, though I have no idea who, how, or why. Don't let it scare you; that's just what the rascal wants."

He raised his eyes. "You believe that, Miz Meredith?"

She nodded. "And you must believe it, too. And tell all the others they mustn't be scared."

His trusting look heartened her. Maybe, just maybe, she could put this ghost business to rest.

"Tell you what, Jess," she said, a prickle of excitement animating her for the first time in weeks. "Next time that old ghost comes to call on you folks, do me a favor. Even if your knees are shaking, all of you should go stand at the windows and laugh as if it's the funniest thing you've ever seen. Laugh and laugh till you make a wonderful roar. Whoever's doing this silly thing should be in for a mighty surprise. And I'll bet the ghost will stop appearing—just like that!"

It would work. She knew it would.

"Miz Meredith, is yo' sure?" He wanted to be convinced, she could tell.

"Bet your boots and all you can make I'm sure," she said to the cobbler with a big smile, but crossing her fingers behind her back. God, she'd better be right, or she'd have a hard time staying on the good side of these sweet, worthy people. Suddenly she saw a number of innovative ways in which she could possibly help them—a school for the children, some adult education programs. And, she prayed, she would see them given their freedom one of these days.

Big orders, maybe. But if she played her cards right, it could all be possible. She needed things—lots of things—to keep herself occupied.

Surely she'd been brought here for something other than pining away over a silly broken heart.

After Jess promised her he'd at least discuss her suggestion with the other slaves, she left him and his orderly workshop, trading its vintage colonial smells of fine leather and human sweat for the outdoor, equally vintage aromas of sun-warmed dirt, manure, and banks of blooming flowers.

Her short visit with the cobbler had lifted her spirits, she realized with a surge of pleasure. No more gloomy Gus, she commanded herself. She *did* have a future here. She *could* make a difference.

Lord, she was even hungry! But she'd do her bit for the Revolution and wait till tomorrow to eat. After all, never in her wildest dreams could she envision herself in a position to take a stand against British tyranny!

Her head was in some cloud of her own making when she almost collided with Aunt Laura—Miss Preston, she reminded herself—who was heading with dispatch toward the grist mill.

"I'm taking Abraham's dinner to him—Benjamin's ordered that he must eat to maintain his strength," the woman said in her usual polite but keep-your-distance manner. "He says the elderly, children and slaves are not to participate in the fast."

The food beneath its linen covering smelled heavenly. Meredith's stomach growled.

"Good sense on Benjamin's part," she said, reluctantly admitting to herself that this day's order by the commanding general indeed did make good sense. "Is Abraham in the grist mill? Would you like for me to carry his dinner to him, Miss Preston? I'd love to see him." She would. He had to be nagged constantly about doing his leg-strengthening exercises. Like so many of her patients, now that the pain was gone he considered himself healed. Only compliance with her instructions would lessen the chances of a new flare-up of his knee.

"No, I've come this far, might as well go the rest of the way. The Lord only knows what he's up to out there."

"May I accompany you?" Meredith asked. Now she was curious, too. What new devilment was the unpredictable Abraham generating? Since he'd become mobile, he'd wreaked havoc with Benjamin's well-run plantation. Last week he'd "improved" the well with a new rope pulley for the bucket. It took Benjamin and six slaves three hours to get the thing into workable condition. And his "repair" of the windmill had put it out of commission for four days.

She'd come to the conclusion that she hadn't done Benjamin much of a favor by getting Abraham back on his feet. But she wasn't into worrying about favors for stick-in-the-mud Benjamin these days. The important thing was that Abraham was happy as a lark with his tinkering. And she was going to keep him that way, come hell or high water.

This time the old gentleman was using his questionable talents on the inner workings of the grist mill. Meredith couldn't believe her eyes when she walked inside. He'd completely dismantled the wooden gear assembly, and the big toothed wheels lay scattered around him on the stone floor like giant puzzle pieces.

The three slaves he'd enlisted from Benjamin for the day's project stood behind him, shaking their heads in a forlorn way.

"Abraham, what madness have you perpetrated here?" Laura Preston exclaimed, a look of dismay on her face as she surveyed the shambles before her.

Meredith stood by the back door of the mill, somewhat amused by the scene. So he'd disemboweled the thing. He'd wanted to be useful, and feeling useful was important to everybody. She was confident that superefficient Benjamin could get it back together before they ran out of flour.

But Miss Preston wasn't as charitable. She scolded Abraham left and right. The man didn't seem to pay a bit of attention to her harangues.

"The gears needed adjusting, Sour Laura," he said. "The way they were, the millstones might have met and sparked a fire." He scratched his head, still charmingly full of silver waves. "At the moment I'm having some difficulty remembering which one goes where, but by nightfall we'll have it all together."

Miss Preston snorted a disbelieving huff and stepped over a wheel to place the dinner tray on a brick window ledge.

"Your dinner's there, Abraham," she said. "Benjamin insists you eat this day, and I've brought hefty rations for your men, too—though the black pudding's only for you, remember."

The old man didn't look interested in food. He looked even less interested in Laura Preston. And Meredith had a jolt of insight. Good heavens, why hadn't she seen it earlier? Laura was carrying a torch for Abraham Foxworth—had probably been hankering for him since she was a young woman and had first come into this home of her sister's.

When her sister had died, undoubtedly she'd thought Abraham would turn to her. But he hadn't. And for all these years the woman had served and waited. To no avail. And now look at her. Stiff and proper as the devil. A gray bitterness in her eyes when she looked at the man.

Was that what unrequited love did to a woman in the eighteenth century?

Meredith shivered. Dear God, would she turn into a Laura Preston? *No.* She wouldn't let herself! She'd save her wages and get far away from this place as soon as she could.

The next thing that happened truly astonished Meredith. Laura focused sharply on the array of gear wheels at her feet and began snapping orders to the black men standing haplessly behind Abraham.

"This one goes up there on the top," she said with crispness. "This one and this belong on that second level yon." She pointed the toe of her shoe to two separated by some distance. "And these other two fit one on top of the other at the bottom."

The woman was a mechanical wizard! Too bad she'd been born in the wrong century. With that kind of aptitude for spatial relationships, she would have been a candidate for chief engineer of a top-notch manufacturing firm a couple of hundred years later.

The black men hustled, hoisting the heavy wheels and placing them as Laura had directed. Within minutes, it seemed, the puzzle pieces had been fit into their proper working order. The grist mill would be operational without Benjamin's even knowing of his father's latest folly.

Abraham let all the flurry behind him continue without notice. He'd lifted the linen and was inspecting the food that had been brought out to them. He showed not a sign of gratitude for the amazing work Laura Preston had just performed. Meredith groaned inside. Despite the love she felt for the old gentleman, she could see how unfeeling the typical man of this century was toward the fine work that an intelligent woman could do.

Blasted chauvinists! All of them. She wrinkled her nose in distaste.

"That's not tight enough, Seth," Laura said to one of the slaves. Meredith watched with amazement as the woman grabbed the man's wrenchlike tool from his hand and shoved him aside. Single-handedly Laura Preston turned the big wooden bolt to fasten the drive shaft to her own satisfaction.

She was strong, too, Meredith remarked to herself. She'd never noticed before how large Laura's hands were, and her grip was a true surprise. Maybe, she thought wryly, the woman could have qualified as a stevedore if she hadn't landed that engineering position.

Powered by the stream outside, the gear wheels began to turn. Laura made a quick inspection of the millstones. "The buhrstones are a proper distance and will not spark now, Abraham. Indeed, I doubt if they ever would have," she added with a sniff.

Abraham had called over the men and was busily distributing the food. He didn't say a word.

"We should return to the house, Miss Davis," the

gaunt woman grumbled, bustling past her at the door and walking out into the sunshine. Meredith, with renewed respect—and pity—for plain-faced Laura Preston, followed. But the hard bitterness in Laura's smoky eyes deeply disturbed her. It was as if the woman's soul had withered and died. Meredith's backbone felt a chilling shiver. No! She wouldn't allow herself to become like that!

"I find it passing strange that you insist on carrying around that poor child on your back like a sack of flour," Miss Preston said to Meredith as they walked toward the house.

"He likes it," she responded simply. And he was safer, she added to herself. Weeks ago she'd decided she could trust Sukie and Lucy—their love for Philip was nearly as strong as her own. But until she found out who had placed that ribbon in the cradle, she was determined to keep the child under close watch. She'd even moved his cradle beside her bed to protect him during the long, lonely nights.

Laura humphed but said nothing further on the subject. What she did say, however, sent Meredith's tenuous airy spirits into a nose dive.

"We might have a proper wedding in the near future, Miss Davis. Benjamin's resumed his visits to Patricia Smithson of late. He had shown his intentions toward her before that, uh, highly unfortunate Joshua-Sylvia episode."

"Oh?" Meredith managed to keep the trembling out of her voice and hoped like the dickens her face didn't reflect her inner turmoil.

"Aye. It's an ideal match, and the lovely damsel dotes on him."

No surprise there. Who in her right mind wouldn't?

213

As they rounded the corner of the house, a horse-driven two-wheeled gig was pulling up to the front entrance. A tall blond man was at the reins. Beside him sat a gorgeous young woman in a daffodil-yellow dress with hair as golden as the June sunbeams.

"Why it's the Smithsons themselves," Laura trilled happily, running ahead. "Will!" she shouted through the open door of Fox Haven. "Go fetch Benjamin from the fields. Tell him a pair of truly special guests has come to call."

The woman turned then to the buggy, her ordinarily rigid face abloom with a gracious smile of welcome.

Meredith had stopped dead in her tracks. Moving back into the shadows of the house, she thought for a wild second that she might crumple down into the bushes. But she sidled away slowly instead—toward the rear entrance.

Benjamin wouldn't let her off as easily as that. The man had developed a sadistic streak, Meredith thought gloomily as she sat in the garden with him and his blasted guests. He'd insisted she join them "to meet my good friend Peyton and his charming sister."

He'd introduced her as "a woman of superior education who we've been fortunate to employ as governess and household assistant." Not a word, of course, about their brief, aborted marriage. Surely the Smithsons had heard about it, though perhaps they hadn't made the connection between her and the here-today-gone-tomorrow Sylvia Wetzel.

They'd been served some god-awful variety of home-grown tea. No food, naturally. The

Smithsons, like Benjamin and Meredith, were complying with the fast. The colonial Barbie doll across from her even had a starlike patch on her dainty left cheek—"the Whig side," as she'd chimed in her saccharin-sweet silver-toned bell of a voice.

Meredith felt about as glamorous as Miss Marple. Her plain gray dress had the charm of a burlap sack. She had on her granny glasses, and her once-attractive blunt cut had grown limp and straggly, hanging now almost to her scrawny shoulders. She kept a frozen smile plastered on her face; but her insides had gathered into one giant black frown.

"Governor Dunmore's dissolving the House of Burgesses hasn't deterred our representatives, I'm pleased to report. They're meeting in a Williamsburg tavern and issuing resolutions like barrages of cannon shot," said Peyton Smithson, sitting on the bench across from her as stiff and erect as a telephone pole.

The man was quite handsome, not at all what Meredith had expected. She'd pictured him as short and pudgy, with a lascivious leer in his eyes. Instead, he cut a fine figure. Colonial Virginia obviously had produced more than its share of hunks. She couldn't help but wonder what had happened in the 200-year interim before her birth. Definitely a watering down of genes, she figured.

Oh well, Sally was still better off with her equally handsome Tom. Peyton Smithson was far too old for her.

The conversation went on around her. She felt as if she'd been plopped down in the middle of a costumed movie set—a film about pre-Revolutionary Virginia. The dialogue went according to script. The defunct Burgesses—now formed as the Virginia Association—had issued calls for an annual general congress of representatives from all the colonies and a boycott of the East India Company. That sort of thing, on and on, straight out of the history books.

She wasn't interested in any of it, so relegated herself to a minor, non-speaking role. And kept her eyes off Benjamin Foxworth. That left only two to look at, and one of those set her teeth on edge.

Patricia Smithson. Damn her for her ripe perfection. Not a hair out of place, not a blemish to be seen. Meredith found herself wishing the young woman would suddenly sprout a wart on her upturned nose. But her witchery, unfortunately, was limited to more narrow powers, like physical therapy, she lamented. Patricia Smithson remained absolutely perfect. And her large sky-blue eyes tilted toward Benjamin with a frequency that made Meredith want to throw up.

Whether he was returning the glances with equal fervor, she wasn't about to investigate. That would have involved her looking over at him. No way. *Feeling* his presence was torture enough.

"And what do you think about that, Miss Davis?" Good God, he was addressing her! She'd didn't have a clue what they'd been talking about.

"Uh, I'm sure it's a good idea," she said, hoping they hadn't been discussing a way to assassinate King George. "But the teapot's empty, Mr. Foxworth," she exclaimed with more distress than such a minor problem called for. "I'll scurry back to the house to replenish it."

Anything to get away from this impossible situation, she thought with near panic as she rose and picked up the teapot. Nobody interfered with her mission, and she hurried into the house as fast as her numbed legs would carry her.

Benjamin was relieved to see her go. Bloody hell, he'd been foolish to invite her to have tea with them. Didn't he know full well that her presence ever brought him torment? He'd undoubtedly been a distracted host. His eyes, like undisciplined stallions without restraint, persisted in stampeding in her direction whenever he was around her.

She'd grown a touch wan recently, giving her porcelain skin a translucent, ethereal quality like that of the finest English china. She'd become more beautiful to him with each passing day. Her silver eyes beneath their strange spectacles were oval lodestones that drew him into their depths. Her gleaming chestnut hair flowed with magnificent freedom.

Sedately proper, she held her lithe body erect at all times with a bravery that only he knew required the strength of a dozen men. Having her near without touching her was bloody difficult for him. And yet, he had no option. His mind told him over and over that the woman could never be his. Time itself would ever stand between them—she was a fairy sprite from the future, destined to vanish without warning. He, a mere creature of this solid world he'd been born into, must finish out his length of time on this separate plane where she could never belong.

His senses and every atom of his body taunted him with other messages, however. He would never forget the silken feel of her beneath him, the fiery passion of her wonderful body. However long his days on this mortal coil, he'd never forget her, and he'd never cease wanting her.

Dear God, she was unhappy, he knew, but he could think of naught he could do to make her otherwise—no true comfort he could offer her. If he took her to him as he so desperately desired, only he would be comforted. Her heart and soul would always reside elsewhere—a place where he could never go. And only her return to her strange world of the future would truly bring her the comfort she desired and so richly deserved. He knew no way to work such magic for her.

"Your new retainer is a lovely woman, Benjamin," Peyton said, yanking Benjamin's mind back into the garden and to his woefully ignored duties as a host.

"Aye, we were fortunate to find her. She's excellent with the children," he responded, adjusting his position on the stone bench.

Patricia chirped in with her unpleasantly high voice that had ever grated on Benjamin's nerves, "She has little fashion, however, Benjamin. You should furnish her with a new wardrobe and have Miss Laura instruct her in arranging her hair in a more modish style. And the spectacles—" she said with a pucker of her undersized nose "—must she wear them all the time?"

No, Miss Pouty Smithson. She doesn't wear them to bed. God in heaven, he must cease such tormenting thoughts!

He ignored the silly girl's question and returned to the topic of politics, addressing himself primarily to his old friend, but uncomfortably aware of the young woman seated beside Peyton. Patricia, he knew, was considered the prize belle in Hanover County, now that Sally was married.

He glanced at her, and his heart sank. Indeed a prize. Plump and ripe for the picking. And his but for the asking. His, if he wanted, for a suitable, proper marriage to end his widowed loneliness.

But frivolous Patricia Smithson could never be enough for him now—would never fill his loneliness.

Only Meredith Davis could do that.

A deep sadness permeated his soul. His destiny was sealed. He would live out his days forever alone.

"I'll carry the teapot out to the garden, Miss Davis. I've been remiss sitting in here working on my accounts rather than visiting with our guests," Laura Preston said, rising from her chair and replacing the quill pen to its holder. A large ledger lay open on the table.

"Give them my apologies for not returning," Meredith said, restraining her sigh of relief. "I must see to Philip. Sukie should be through with his feeding now."

Laura left her alone, and she dropped wearily into the wooden chair the woman had just vacated. The seat was still warm. Telling herself she should go on upstairs, she leaned her elbows on the table instead and rested her chin in the cup of her hands. She needed a moment to compose herself and put some starch into her bones if she could.

Idly her gaze drifted across the neatly scripted lines of the ledger book. Like everything else Laura Preston did, her household account book was in perfect order. She'd just begun her June entries, and already a number of items had been listed. *Bal. as of 31st May, 1774—30 £/ 7s/ 5d* was at the top. Meredith knew little of the current money, but thought it meant thirty pounds sterling, seven shillings, and five pence. What all that amounted to, she had no idea. She received twenty-five shillings a week—probably a mere pittance.

Below that was the entry: *Rec. from B. Foxworth, 1st June, 1774—500 £.* Wow! It seemed a hefty sum. Maintaining a house like Fox Haven was a pretty expensive proposition, obviously.

Curious, she looked at the expenses so far for June.

*20 lb. West Indies Sugar—25s.* Well, she knew now what her worth was equivalent to. Twenty blasted pounds of sugar!

*Bolt of Dimity Cloth—7s/6d.*

The items continued in the spidery script—nearly everything in shillings and pence, piddling amounts considering the allowance. But they'd add up, she guessed, in the course of a month. And all of them were for household expenses only—imported foodstuffs, cloth, tableware.

*Set of Silver Serving Spoons (2 pcs.)* registered in at 1£/8s. A true expense, relatively speaking.

The entry below startled Meredith. *Fr. Cards—50 £.* Fifty big ones for a deck of cards? French? Lord, was Laura into dirty postcards?

Curious, she flipped the pages back to May. Again, the balance entry was across the top, and the monthly receipt from Benjamin of five hundred pounds duly recorded.

She scanned the expenses quickly. Another entry stood out as an unusually expensive item: *Fr. Sticks—50£.*

Sticks? Made of gold, maybe? And that "Fr." again. What on earth could that be but French?

Fried? Frigate? Frog? Her mind searched for a clue. None of it made any sense.

She quickly turned to April. To March. To February. Each had a fifty-pound expense—and each included the mysterious "Fr." *Fr. Cndl.; Fr. Lgt.; Fr. Env.*

Meredith stared at the pages, befuddled. Was Laura squirreling away fifty pounds sterling every month? Or was she truly spending that kind of money on sticks, cards, and envelopes, of all things?

Did Benjamin ever check the account book?

Reminding herself that none of this was any of her business, she turned the pages back to June and positioned the book as she had found it. But her brow remained knotted with concern. Something was amiss here—she felt it in the pit of her empty stomach.

She sighed and pushed her troublesome hair behind her ears. As she started to leave the room, motion outside the window caught her attention.

Good. The Smithsons were leaving. Laura stood beside Benjamin, seeing them off. Naturally, he helped the nasty little canary-clad bimbo up into the buggy they called a "chair." And of course he bowed politely. But good grief, did he have to bend over with such grace and kiss her stupid hand that way?

Meredith had never realized that a stab into an already shriveled heart could hurt so much.

# Chapter Fourteen

She had figured out a way to make a whirl-pool tank. Well, a close approximation, anyway. Constructing it was simple enough—or so she'd thought this late-June morning when she'd started on the blame thing.

Now, standing in the neck of the stream she'd picked as the ideal spot for her primitive Jacuzzi, she wasn't so sure. The afternoon sun was hot as blazes, and she'd already spent several hours calf-deep in the water relocating rocks to dam off the small circular area.

She'd skipped dinner and had made certain Philip and Betsy were happily occupied and in safe hands while she carried out her project. Straightening up and pressing her hands against her back, she puffed out a sigh of exhaustion. She'd piled hundreds of rocks, and from the looks of it, she had hundreds more to go.

"What in the name of God are you doing, Miss Davis?"

Turning around quickly, she shaded her eyes and saw Benjamin, astride his horse on the stream's bank, scowling at her. His all-time favorite expression. Drat! She'd hoped he wouldn't find out about this—not, at least, until her whirlpool was operational. While her mind raced to form the just-right words, she bent to lift another rock from the stream's bottom and tossed it on the half-finished dam. Only then did she answer him.

"I'm making a little pool of churning water, Benjamin. It's something I believe both Abraham and Betsy will enjoy—it'll help relax their tight leg muscles."

He dismounted, tethered the black steed to a tree, and walked to the stream. Though she continued stacking rocks, she knew all too well what kind of picture he made standing up there. Handsome as the devil in his buff work knickers, black boots, and loose white shirt.

And, of course, his damnable eyebrow would be cocked.

"Why didn't you ask for help? I'd have loaned you men. This appears a mighty task for a frail woman."

That frail business rankled. She moved three dripping rocks over to her dam in quick succession before she dared speak.

"Not a mighty task at all, as you see," she said, injecting an ease into her voice she didn't feel. "Time-consuming, but not difficult." God, she looked a mess. She'd bundled up the full skirt of her plainest gray work dress into knots above the sides of her knees. She was barefooted, naturally, and drenched—as much from perspiration as from the stream's tepid water. Unlike him, she was not a pretty picture.

"How will it work?" He seemed halfway interested.

She paused and wiped her forehead with the back of her hand to push the straggles of damp hair away from her eyes. She'd removed her water-splattered glasses long ago, placing them out of harm's way up on the bank.

"The stream's good and swift—by damming up this small corner here to reverse the flow, I'm hoping to create enough of a whirlpool to get the effect I want," she told him.

"And that effect would be to relax tight muscles?"

She nodded and transferred a few more rocks.

"Here, I'll help. You'll still be at that beyond supper at the pace you're going, and your flesh has shrunk enough around your bones as it is."

He didn't have to mention it. She knew she was about as curvy and appealing as an anorexic these days. And, good grief, she certainly didn't want him down there in the stream with her! But, contrary as the dickens, as usual, he was there in a matter of moments, his boots and shirt cast off and his knickers shoved above his knees.

"These bigger boulders on the side will shore up your dam far more efficiently," he said, lifting one that must have weighed a ton and placing it in a gaping hole she hadn't had time to fill. The well-developed muscles in his shoulders and back didn't even make a ripple under the strain. She tried to concentrate on rocks.

"Did you learn to do this in the twentieth century?" he asked as he reached back for another Gibraltar-size boulder.

In pitiful contrast to what he was doing, she was contributing mere marbles to the dam. "Not really—I'm improvising. Back there we had big tubs for therapeutic use. It was far easier. All we had to do was fill them with water and plug them into the wall, and an electric motor did the rest."

"Plug? Electric motor?"

She attempted to explain electricity and modern motors, but she knew little about either and did a miserable job of it, she feared. Nevertheless, he was fascinated. Now she wished she'd gone to engineering school.

"The future appears to hold true wonders. I trust mankind thus blessed with such miracles will have solved most of his woes," he said, closing yet another gap in the dam.

She leaned back against the stream's bank. Lord, he'd have the dam finished in less than ten minutes, the way he was going. Her measly rocks weren't even needed. Well, that was fine and dandy with her. She was exhausted.

"That depends on what kind of woes you're talking about, Benjamin," she ventured. She couldn't believe it. He was actually *conversing* with her! More than a word or two at a time, at that. She lost her train of thought.

"Well, sickness for one."

She smiled. Thank heaven. Something she was better versed on than electricity. She filled him in on medical progress and the increased life expectancy, taking some shortcuts along the way. She didn't want to overwhelm him.

And she kept her eyes off his splendid bare torso as much as possible. Atlas had come to her rescue. Just knowing that was sufficient distraction, she told herself; watching him would likely overwhelm *her*.

"And wars? Have they found a method to secure peace among men at last?" he asked.

Meredith shook her head. "Afraid not," she said, sorry she couldn't report otherwise. As she recited the long list of all the bloody wars she could remember since 1774, she could tell she'd depressed him.

But suddenly, swirls of warm water began to caress her lower legs. "Hot damn, Benjamin! I think it's going to work!" she exclaimed joyfully.

He looked down at the churning pool and came so close to smiling that his dimples showed. She'd nearly forgotten their devastating effect on her. She held on to the bank to keep from sliding down into the water.

"Only a little more shoring and I think you'll have your improvised whirlpool, Miss Davis," he said, reaching for another boulder. The circling water foamed delightfully around his strong calves. She knew better than to notice. But she did.

"There! It's completed, I believe," he announced with triumph, brushing his hands against his tightly molded breeches and wading in her direction. She pressed against the wet bank behind her. He kept his distance, however—no big surprise, she realized, accepting the let-down with an unspoken "what's new?" She relaxed her hold on the bank. He settled his too-attractive buns against it, properly situating himself at least a foot away from her, and studied the results of their joint effort with something that looked for all the world like admiration. Her heart flipped a lopsided somersault.

"That truly looks therapeutic," he compli-mented her. Having grown unaccustomed to his compliments of late, she didn't know how to respond.

"We can use it only in the summer months, of course," she informed him—needlessly, she knew. "But both Abraham and Betsy will find some relief in it, I believe."

He was silent for a moment, his face shadowed. "Betsy's foot will ever be useless, Dr. Hughes tells us. But some enjoyment for her in the water would be a good thing."

She didn't dare contradict Dr. Hughes's prog-nosis. Time alone would tell. *Blasted time.*

"Your descriptions of the wars ahead and the mighty weapons to be developed give me cause to lament, Miss Davis. Here, where we have so little progress, as you know it, each new discov-ery brings wonder and hope to us that life will be better for those who follow us."

She risked a sideways glance at him. He was concentrating on the water and looked far too sober.

"Life will be better, Benjamin. For each new generation," she offered. "But I've come to the conclusion that mankind itself doesn't change a whole lot. Deep down the same motivations drive us all, whatever our era. Some needs are basic to human nature, I guess. Survival, of course, is the foremost need. Food and water, shelter, protection of our loved ones, continuation of the species, that sort of thing."

"But each society, depending on how available or plentiful the resources, dictates acceptable and unacceptable ways to satisfy those needs, isn't that true?" He sounded awfully serious. The conversation was getting pretty deep. But at least they were having one. And the subject was interesting.

"I think you're right, Benjamin." She chewed at her lip. "Customs and conventions change."

"And the customs and conventions you knew were very different from the ones that form our society here, weren't they?"

She nodded. "Very different. But the basics for a good life were the same—treat others as you'd like to be treated, keep your hands off what belongs to someone else, share if you have more than enough to fill your own needs. Know, respect, and love yourself so that you can know, respect, and love other people."

He was quiet for a while. She pondered what she'd said—there must be many more things she could have mentioned, but she couldn't think of them at the moment.

"Admirable qualities for any time, I vow," he said at last. "Straight from the Bible except that last part. Shakespeare, I believe. 'Know thyself and to thine own self be true.'"

"Both the Bible and Shakespeare were alive and well in 1991," she said with a smile.

"Then perhaps there's hope for the world, after all," he said with an answering smile, pushing away from the bank. "I've enjoyed this talk with you, Miss Davis. It's rare to speak of such matters with a woman."

He was, she saw, ready to leave. And so was she. She glanced quickly around to find the best exit from the stream.

He'd already scaled the bank. "Over here," he pointed to his right toward a lower section and knelt, stretching out his hand. "Give me your hand and I'll assist you up," he said.

Why she didn't accept his offer, she never knew. Ingrained stubbornness, probably. Or a determination to show him she could manage beautifully on her own.

She grabbed for a sassafras branch to pull herself out under her own power. And failed miserably. The weak bush tore loose from the wet soil, and she splashed back into the stream, fanny first. Totally without grace.

"Damn!" she spluttered. She'd been soaked enough earlier; now she was sopping. Her skirt, its knots having come untied somehow, floated like a water-logged sail around her. The stony bottom of the stream chafed her bare rump.

He'd jumped down beside her before she knew what was happening.

"Did you hurt yourself?" he asked, bending over to help her to her feet.

"Only my pride," she said with complete honesty, struggling to keep upright in the bubbling water. The full skirt dragged her awkwardly from side to side. She attempted to push it down, while trying to get a firm foothold—somewhere.

Standing behind her, he placed his strong hands under her armpits to hoist her to her feet. He almost made it, and would have if the stream bottom hadn't been so all-fired slippery and a particularly frisky whirlpool swirl hadn't come along at that very second.

The combination buffeted her back against him, and then he, too, was suddenly sitting on the stony bottom. But Meredith realized with startling awareness that she now was firmly seated on *him*.

For her, the contact was a textbook example of electricity in action. The seductive motions of the water lapping across her nether regions added high-voltage amperes that sent tingly charges through all her circuits.

But she was sure he felt none of that. He would be on his feet immediately, getting both of them to shore as easily as he'd moved boulders for the dam.

Only he wasn't moving. Momentarily nonplussed, she guessed. That his arms had circled in a protective clasp beneath her breasts during the fall kept her from making the first move, even if she had wanted to. She didn't, not really, though it occurred to her that she should. His rock-hard chest pressed against her back, the beat of his strong heart reverberating like low thunder within her own chest.

Good grief, this situation was fast becoming unbearable! She *had* to get away from him—she'd lost all sense of reality. The man considered her a bloody nuisance, he didn't have the tiniest spark of interest in her unendowed stick of a body, he . . .

Was groaning in her ear, for goodness sake! His lips were trailing heated kisses down her neck, across each of her shoulders, then following the moist paths opening to him as her thin, water-slick sleeves slid compliantly down her arms.

No question what he had on his mind. Her own had taken on the swirling pattern of the riotous water. His hands were cupping her bared breasts, fondling them. Her nipples hardened, swelled to his touch. The rest of her softened, becoming fluid and decidedly catching fire.

His intense fire was anything but soft. His powerful arousal throbbing against her naked bottom was beautifully positioned beneath the very spot that ached the most for him.

"Good God, woman," he moaned, swiftly maneuvering her around to face him. Holding her so tight she could barely breathe, he crushed his lips to hers with a fevered intensity that made breathing seem suddenly far less essential for survival than what he was offering her.

Her legs spread over his hips and embraced him as she felt the driven urgency of his hand between them freeing buttons—freeing him. With the galvanizing speed and force of a blazing spear of lightning, he thrust inside her, pervaded her with his magnificent presence—his wild need for her filling her, rushing forward, crashing headlong into her unleashed, incredibly wild need for him.

Frenzied, she rode him like the unbridled stallion he was, and his hands, gripping into her buttocks, fiercely guided her faster, harder, deeper. Unrelenting.

Wonderful.

Her ecstatic cry burst muffled against the distended cords of his neck. She clung to him and bit into his shoulder as they both exploded in accelerating convulsive waves of turbulent release.

They sat, intertwined, locked together for a long spell of time. She had no idea how long—time had lost any significance.

Her thoughts whirled in the same sensual rhythms as the sun-warmed water that swirled around their joined bodies—disconnected thoughts, swimming through her head. He had wanted her. They had coupled like a pair of sex-starved animals—driven by some shared force stronger than either of them. How had it happened? Who cared how? He had wanted her—with an unrestrained fervor that had surpassed even her mad, overpowering wanting for him. Dear God, he had truly wanted her.

She smiled into the silky wet hairs of his glorious chest, and listened with complete contentment to the resonant hoofbeats of his heart growing steadily slower, softer.

Growing more distant? His arms holding her clasped to him denied that. So did his lips upon her hair, his gentling breath against her ear.

Perhaps they could stay this way forever. Why not? Stay just like this, nestled together forever in their private whirlpool, freed of everything that threatened to separate them—freed even of time itself.

She should have known better. Time, like the big red sun dipping westward, moved onward. And their brief magical interlude was coming to a close. He gently lifted her off him, and she stood slowly, managing to maintain her balance despite her weakened knees.

As he rose to his feet, he turned his back to button his breeches. She squirmed her sleeves up over her shoulders, adjusted her low-cut bodice. Nothing had been torn this time, amazingly enough. Except for the wet dress clinging to her slender frame, she was modestly attired once again.

Neither had spoken a word since the frenzied beginning—nothing other than his moaned "Dear God, woman." She prayed that his first words to her wouldn't be the same. Their connotation would be far different now, and regrets from him at this point she couldn't handle.

But as if on cue, he said exactly that. "Dear God, woman," and turned to her, his beautiful turquoise eyes filled with remorse.

She stiffened, her nails cut into her palms as she tightened her hands by her sides. "If you dare to tell me you're sorry, I may start screaming, Benjamin Foxworth," she said sharply.

Up went the eyebrow, back went that blasted ebony wave from his forehead.

"Can you truly believe I didn't want that as much as you did?" she continued. "Didn't you *feel* me, for God's sake? As hungry as you—just as needy. Don't you dare start in on your eighteenth-century male hangups that only men need this—this transcending act of pleasure. Women, I'll have you know, need it equally as much and enjoy it a whale of a lot!"

There. She'd said it. Screamed it, actually. She took in a deep breath.

He looked shaken to his boots—if he'd had them on.

"But we're not married, Miss Davis."

"*Miss Davis?*" she exploded. "After what just happened, I believe my given name would be far more appropriate. *Meredith*, Benjamin. For crying out loud, at least call me Meredith!" "Treasure," she knew, was forever relegated to the past.

He stared at her, apparently too stunned to speak.

She glared at him. And had plenty to say. "And what on earth has marriage got to do with it? You wanted me at that moment, and I sure as heck wanted you. We're neither of us wide-eyed innocents—and it's not as if we hadn't known each other pretty damn well before this afternoon!"

Tears stung her eyes. She blinked them back and whirled around, headed for the bank. Though she tried for assured strides, she had to settle for something closer to a clumsy waddle. The whirlpool wasn't conducive to dramatic exits.

But she successfully scrambled up the side. Firm ground helped. She found her glasses and put them on. Seeing everything clearly helped, too.

Feeling stronger, she brushed at the bottoms of her muddy feet and donned her leather work slippers. Her heart was going a mile a minute and had lodged primarily in her throat, but she wasn't going to let a little thing like that deter her.

Benjamin Foxworth needed some straightening out. He *had* to understand her—only he knew of her crazy predicament. Surely, he could become her friend, if nothing else. She desperately needed someone in this alien world she could be herself with. Having to fit into the confining mold of another century one hundred percent of the time would drive her batty!

"I'll never understand you," he said, affirming her worst fears. He'd joined her on the bank, stood about ten feet away from her, and was pulling on his boots.

"Maybe I'm asking the impossible, Benjamin. But it would sure help me immensely if you'd give it a try."

He sat back on a boulder and rubbed his knees with his hands, looking thoughtful. "Your angry outburst surprised me—and your words stunned me mightily. The conventions of your era indeed appear far distant from those of mine. That a woman would speak openingly of such matters—"

"Is quite ordinary where I come from," she finished for him. "And I wasn't angry, Benjamin. Frustrated is a better word." She sat on a boulder a few feet from him. The physical distance was essential, she believed. Right now, she wanted only the attention of his mind—for the peace and comfort of her own.

"Look, Benjamin, during my generation women had come a long way toward something resembling equality," she began. "Since I was shaped by my generation, as you were by your own, you can only understand what makes me tick if you know how things were for me."

It seemed terribly important to her. Benjamin perhaps could be a lifeline for her—never a husband, of course; possibly never even a lover again. But he could help her, was in a position to grease the skids for her adjustments while she was stranded back here. If, after this, he would treat her as a person of intelligence and ability, she'd have won a tremendous victory.

"We have a couple of hours before we need return to the house for supper, Meredith, and our clothing should be dry by then. I would like to understand you, and will admit I'm deeply curious about your twentieth century. Please tell me what 'makes you tick,' as you so charmingly put it."

She smiled, her spirits soaring with hope. He'd called her Meredith for the first time. He wanted to understand her. He'd even said "charmingly," for heaven's sake—charm, she knew, was definitely her weak suit.

He was willing to listen to her. And she began, talking on and on, touching on as many subjects as leaped to her mind. Women's lib, of course; changed attitudes toward sexual roles and behavior; birth control; the lamentable decline of families. She was careful to include the bad as well as the good.

He interrupted her only occasionally—when her vocabulary befuddled him or, more often, with a discerning remark or question demonstrating he was quick-witted and resilient about accepting facts that had to be mind-boggling for him. And most importantly, demonstrating that he was truly interested.

She diverged from the changed sexual patterns per se and filled him in on women's roles in the workplace—how one by one the former male-only bastions had crumbled. Women as police, as fire fighters, engineers, astronauts (she had to explain that one). Senators, doctors, lawyers, judges. Even in combat.

And she told him of her own profession as a physical therapist—more female than male, true—but she wanted him to know how important it had been to her, how she'd run her own practice. That her life, once, had had direction and meaning.

"So that's the way you got Father on his feet again? Physical therapy?" he asked with a smile.

She nodded. And then realized that dusk had nearly fallen. Their two hours were up. She was tired, hoarse from all the unaccustomed talking. But she felt as if a boulder as big as the one she was seated on had been lifted from her shoulders.

Benjamin, she believed, would now accept her on her own ground. At long last, maybe, they could be friends.

"You've provided me with much to ponder," he said, standing and giving that devilishly rebellious wave a futile push backward. "We should return to the house now, I'll ride you back on Midnight. And, Meredith—" he paused, and looked almost tentative "—I truly hope we can have further talks as we've had today. You do need a friend while you're in this foreign land. I would like to be that friend."

She was so happy she wanted to shout hallelujah. "I'd like that very much, Benjamin," she said instead, quite subdued, but glowing like a halogen headlight set on high beam.

"Could it be possible that you might disappear as quickly as you appeared?" he asked out of nowhere.

She shrugged. "Who knows?" And driven by an impish impulse as much as by her high spirits, she folded down the thumb and first finger of her right hand and raised the three remaining fingers toward him, feigning amazement. "Why, look at that! I think I'm already beginning to disappear—piece by piece it'll be, I guess."

His beautiful eyes registered such shock and dismay that she quickly lifted her other fingers. "Only kidding," she said with a laugh and ran over to the horse.

Oh, but that dismay she'd seen boosted her spirits into the stratosphere. She'd be foolish to read into it anything more than he just might miss her a little bit if she got whisked away.

That knowledge alone was something to cheer about.

# Chapter Fifteen

Meredith found much to cheer about in the following weeks. Most of it centered around Benjamin, of course. He'd lost his stuffiness around her. Boy, had he lost it! In little ways—and in big ways. The whole household must have noticed it. They all had followed his lead and addressed her as Meredith now, and even Laura Preston had removed a few bricks from her fortresslike demeanor toward her.

She was far from "family"—she'd never be that. But her status in the group had risen a notch. The renewed respect shown her was tangible—and gratifying. That her opinions were solicited on matters now and again was downright euphoria! Dinners and suppers were no longer miserable affairs but congenial get-togethers. In the changed atmosphere, Meredith's appetite had returned with a bang, and she added some meat to her bones. In all the right places, according to Benjamin.

Remembering his ego-boosting remark earlier this evening, she smiled, nuzzling into the hollow of his wonderful shoulder. He was asleep, and she'd have to waken him soon so that he could return to his chamber. No one was aware of his nightly visits to her bed. They'd been discreet and careful as the dickens.

This lovely state of affairs hadn't popped into full bloom immediately after the whirlpool afternoon. It had been a gradual process—perfectly platonic conversations between new friends in the garden, library, and parlor leading, without either of them fully realizing it, to what she now knew had been inevitable from the beginning.

After all, their history together hadn't been a sterling example of banked fires remaining banked for long. Noble intentions were one thing; the volatile chemistry between them was something else entirely.

She sighed happily. Indeed, Benjamin had taken to twentieth-century freer ways with ease. With unabashed zest, actually. But they both knew that the rest of their Fox Haven world would be shocked beyond measure—and highly disapproving.

Except Abraham, maybe. But they weren't about to test him.

Meredith tried not to let herself wonder how long they could continue this way. They were dancing on a thin tightrope, and it could snap beneath them without warning.

Occasionally they spoke of it. Benjamin was always the one to broach the subject. He "worried for her," he'd say. Or "we shouldn't be doing this, Meredith—it isn't fair to you."

She'd assure him that she considered it quite fair indeed. Which she did. But she never told him why.

Oh God, she loved this man deeply, with every fiber of her body, mind, heart, and soul. He was everything she'd ever longed for—more, for how could she have ever envisioned Benjamin?

And her love for him kept growing, with each passing day and night. But that had to remain forever her secret, the only thing she couldn't share with him. Letting him in on her true feelings would be laying needless guilt on him and would undoubtedly ruin everything. He'd accepted her on the terms she'd laid out that spectacular afternoon of the whirlpool. She'd come to him from an open culture where women were more free, more in tune with their physical needs.

Lord, he couldn't imagine how hung up she'd really been back there. A prude, actually, compared to the Cosmo life a lot of her peers had led. Her need for a man had taken a back seat, way behind her need to advance her career and to prove to the world at large and her family in particular that she could make her own way, independently.

But that had been before Benjamin. He'd knocked her for a loop from the beginning. Far more, she realized now, than the incredible zapping that had transplanted her to this era.

She'd never tire of him. She reveled in his courage and strength, adored his sensitivity, his intelligence, his devotion to duty and responsibility. He had her respect; and, though he'd never know it, her undying love.

For whatever time allowed them, she had this— his physical presence, his desire. That was enough, she told herself. She couldn't expect more from him. He was human; she was available and willing. She wouldn't kid herself. Too much separated them.

At the moment, she had two things going for her: proximity and unlimited tales of the future. Benjamin's curiosity was as boundless as his libido. He loved hearing about life in the twentieth century. She felt a bit like Scheherazade and hoped she could keep him fascinated for a thousand and one nights.

But she was, after all, Meredith Davis. He'd tire of her sooner or later and go on to greener pastures. Patricia Smithson appeared to be on hold for the moment, but the little snit was out there, waiting with her curly blond locks securely in place for his "intentions" to be declared.

Meredith grimaced. She was merely a hired hand—a woman, literally, without a country, let alone a birthright. Eighteenth-century gentlemen didn't dally long with women beneath their station. They married proper damsels with pedigrees.

Lord, she was playing with fire, she knew. Suppose she got pregnant? She tensed. Good grief, she had to put that out of her mind.

She'd been lucky so far, hadn't she? Her periods had come with blessed regularity, thank heaven. Perhaps all those years she'd been on birth control pills had had a cumulative effect. Maybe she'd never needed the blasted things at all, and had a fertility problem of some kind. Oh well, she shrugged inwardly, fertility definitely wasn't a desirable commodity under these circumstances.

The grandfather clock downstairs clanged its muffled twelve bells. She wiggled away from him and removed his arm from her hip.

"Benjamin," she whispered, bending to kiss the pulsebeat at his temple. "It's midnight."

He moaned, reaching for her.

"No you don't," she said with a light chuckle as she pushed him away, wishing she wasn't so doggone responsible.

His brows pulled together and his eyelids fluttered open. Her heart went crazy—it always did when he unveiled those heavily lashed turquoise marvels. "Midnight already?" he protested with a sleep-fuzzed groan. "And I've slept away the whole bloody evening?"

"Not all of it, Mr. Foxworth," she said, keeping her voice light. "Or have you forgotten?"

His lips curled, and his dimples deepened. "Never forget," he mumbled, snuggling forward.

One of them had to be sensible. It was her turn, she guessed.

"Away with you now," she objected, wondering where she'd dredged up such strength of will. For sure, it wasn't what she wanted to say—or do. "It's *midnight*, Benjamin."

The sudden bright light glowing through the window announced something else. Not dawn, she knew at once. She gasped and sat up quickly.

"Look! It's the ghost again!"

He was slower to react, but sat up beside her. And frowned. "Night gases, Meredith. Not a ghost."

She jumped off the bed and ran to the window. "Come here and look at it, Benjamin. I know it's no ghost, but I doubt if it's gases, either. Someone's doing it, I'm sure of it—to scare the slaves, I believe."

He was beside her in an instant. Standing together, they watched the glow expand, grow white, and fizzle away in a spray of silent sparks.

Even without her glasses she could discern the tall, lean shadow ducking behind the fog-shrouded trees. Benjamin had twenty-twenty vision; surely he'd seen it, too. And more clearly.

"There! Did you see that shadowy figure?" she whispered, pointing.

"Aye."

She looked up at him. He was fully awake now. Intense. The furrow between his brows etched deep.

And then she heard it. A ripple of laughter at first, two ripples, three, four—until it had built into a huge wave of rich, gloriously rich and decidedly raucous laughter.

They'd done it!

Ecstatic, she threw her arms around Benjamin. "They did it!" she exclaimed, hugging him tight. "God love them, they stood up to the rascal!"

He looked stunned, puzzled. "What?"

"The slaves *laughed*. Don't you see? Whoever's doing this will stop it when no one is scared by the ghost. Like I told Jess—"

"You suggested they laugh, Meredith?"

He'd turned to her, was studying her with an expression she couldn't interpret.

"Beats wailing any day," she said, studying him right back. Good grief, was she going to have to convince him? Some of her joy diminished.

He was silent as he kept staring at her—incredibly serious.

"It might work, Benjamin. It's worth a try, don't you think?" Now he had her sounding tentative. She held her breath.

And he expelled his. In one beautiful groan. "God, you're a treasure," he said low as he drew her to him.

He didn't get away until well after two that morning.

The ghost didn't return. Foggy, humid nights came and went during July, but on none of them did the apparition appear.

Meredith was amazed it had been as easy as that. She'd expected that at least several episodes of the slaves' brave laughter would be required before the perpetrator got discouraged.

But once had done it. The fields of Fox Haven now rang daily with the dusky, full-throated songs of the workers. She'd never heard them sing before—it was a lovely counterpoint to the music that filled her own life these bright summer days.

Someone on the plantation, however, wasn't sharing in all these good vibes. Who? she asked herself again and again. Who among them had wanted the slaves unhappy and disturbed? Who had it in for the Foxworths and Fox Haven? That ghost business, had it gone on much longer, was sure to have caused serious problems. Slave insurrections weren't common in eighteenth-century Virginia—but they did happen, she knew.

Well, whoever the villain was, he'd had his dirty plans shot to high heaven now. Wouldn't that person react in some way? If nothing else, one would think he'd be sporting a hound-dog expression.

No one within the household appeared any different from before. Meredith asked Benjamin if he'd noted any changes in any of his men workers.

"No," he told her. "The slaves, of course, are far more cheerful and light-hearted these days, thanks to your creative solution. My white men are few—only a dozen are left now, but none of them gave any credence to the ghost from its beginning, and I've seen no change of manner in any of them."

Mulling over what he'd said, she sipped the before-supper claret they were sharing alone in the parlor.

"When did the ghost begin appearing?" she asked.

"Six years ago was the first, to my knowledge." He frowned. "Though it had never occurred before, I was truly convinced it was a combination of earth gases—a natural phenomenon caused by moist air, fog, and our nearness to the Newfound River." He chuckled lightly. "Your 1991 scientists would laugh at such a simpleton theory, I vow."

"On the contrary, they'd probably applaud you for arriving at such a sensible conclusion," she said with a smile. "Weird phenomena like that occur in nature all the time—in swamps, for instance. They would consider you inspired for chalking it up to gases rather than hanging garlic on the door to ward off evil spirits."

"But in this instance, I was wrong, Meredith. It never occurred to me to be suspicious of someone."

Well, she loved him for his trusting nature— along with a billion or so other wonderful characteristics. "Maybe it took an objective outsider, viewing with fresh if somewhat nearsighted eyes, to hit on something between ghost and gases."

"And that something places a rogue in our midst."

Meredith nodded, accepting his offer of more claret. "So it appears." She hesitated a moment. "Benjamin, I know you don't like to talk about it—but what were some of the events other than the ghost that made people think Fox Haven was cursed?"

His jaw tightened and his brows lowered. The charming ebony wave got its push-back. "Deaths, I suppose, Meredith. But death is a frequent visitor to every home."

She hated to do it, but she felt compelled to pursue the subject. "What kind of deaths? How many?"

"My mother and father lost four young sons in a span of four years, from 1747 to 1750, and yet another in 1756. All of the babes had seemed healthy and robust, but died without sickness or warning within a year of their birth—asleep in their cradles. The sorrow was too heavy for my mother, who took ill and died in 1757 when she was but thirty-three."

"And you were how old then?"

"Sixteen. Joshua was twelve, and Sally, the only daughter their marriage was blessed with, was but two."

Meredith's heart wept. Such a long list of tragedies! She'd read enough history to know the hardships of the colonial era. But this . . . this wasn't dusty knowledge from the past. This was real!

He wasn't through. "You might as well hear of the others," he said, finishing off his wine and lifting the crystal decanter to refill his glass. His strong hand trembled slightly. She shook her head when he asked with a raised eyebrow and a gesture with the decanter if she'd like her own glass topped.

"My wife and I lost our two sons, who were taken much like my young brothers in their early months—in 1766 and 1768. The ghost appeared first on the night of the second boy's funeral. Catherine ever felt it was little Timothy's bright spirit reluctant to leave us."

Meredith chewed at her lip, striving to keep her tears back.

"Betsy, thank God, lived and has thrived," he continued. "Though she's lame as a result of the same carriage accident that—that took away my wife." The final part of his statement was a wrenching choked whisper.

She sat quietly, afraid to speak. Abraham had told her of Benjamin's blaming himself for the accident. She wanted so to convince him he wasn't at fault—couldn't be—but her words, she knew, would be futile.

He rubbed his forehead, then straightened in his chair. "Seven male babes and two young women, Meredith, were taken away from us. A little girl was made lame. The numbers are truly great— a mighty toll, though many other families have borne sufferings as mighty. It was, I believe, the ghost that gave Fox Haven its damnable reputation as being cursed."

God, she ached to run over to him and wrap her arms around him; to soothe his tormented brow and kiss away his misery. But she didn't dare, not here in the parlor. Laura or Lucy would be coming in at any minute to call them in to supper.

"I'm sorry, Benjamin," she said, feeling woefully inadequate.

His smile was weak, but at least he offered her one. "If the ghost indeed has been put to rest, perhaps we're at last freed of the curse business, as you call it."

"When we find who caused it," she reminded him. "Your overseer—Peter, is it? Do you trust him?"

"With my life," he stated firmly. "He's been with us since I was a wee lad—and though he's more than sixty, he's got the brawn and strength of a man half his age."

"And your other men? Do you have doubts about any of them?"

He shook his head. "Far too loyal each of them have been over the years for me to have doubts—they are more like brothers to me than Joshua ever was. Peter and the other eleven stayed, when the remainder of our servants abandoned Fox Haven for 'safer' havens."

But somebody around here hated Fox Haven, she wanted to tell him. And she might have said just that, only Laura Preston swept into the parlor to announce supper.

Later, she figured. She should sift through the dreadful information he'd given her this evening before she brought up the subject with him again. Was there a pattern to any of it? Could it be possible that any of the tragedies he'd recounted might, like the ghost, have had a human hand behind them?

The thought gave her goosebumps. Such evil was inconceivable to her. And yet, little Philip's frightening brush with death had been no accident. He was a male Foxworth babe, and he, too, could have been "taken away from them" asleep in his cradle.

But who among them, dear God, was insane enough to do such a thing? Mysteries weren't her cup of tea—she knew next to nothing about criminal minds, especially demented criminal minds. Where on earth should she start her investigation, if, indeed, she should undertake such a thing?

*Motive and opportunity*, she suddenly remembered from somewhere. Lie low and search for the one sick individual who had both.

Abraham was ill. At first he'd seemed simply "off his feed." His appetite had diminished. But it grew worse. He'd lost interest in taking on new projects—napped off and on during the days, and stayed in his room far more than usual. Meredith became increasingly concerned. He had no fever, and his knee was unswollen and didn't appear to bother him. But something was wrong. And whatever it was, it was sapping the life out of him.

"Do you have any pain?" she asked him. He'd chosen to stay in bed this bright August day. Truly unusual. And she'd come up to stay with him for a while, to keep him company and to help him if she possibly could.

"My stomach cramps now and again. Nothing serious, I vow," he said.

But he wasn't himself. The twinkle was gone from his eyes. In fact, his eyes were puffy, the lids inflamed.

"Anything other than the stomach, Abraham?"

"My bloody mouth is tender."

"Your mouth?"

He spread his lips. His gums were red and swollen. She felt helpless. She knew nothing about dentistry, other than she'd avoided it as much as possible. Yet she couldn't let this man waste away before her eyes.

"Has the mouth been tender all along?" she inquired.

"No. That affliction struck me but today. The stomach began giving me trouble a day or so ago. My Emily went like this years ago when she was in her prime. I'm old, Meredith. My days are near over, I fear."

"Nonsense, you silly man. What are you? Fifty-five? Sixty?"

"Fifty-seven last February. Not likely to see sixty the way I feel—do I look sixty to you, woman?" The snippet of his former crustiness gave her encouragement.

She smiled down at him. "If I hadn't known your eldest son was thirty-three, I would've sworn on a stack of Bibles that you were no more than forty a week or so ago. Now, with you low like this, I might have guessed—oh, fifty?"

He chuckled dryly. "You lie, Meredith Davis. But you lie with good intentions. I forgive you."

His dinner tray sat untouched on the night table. "Could I convince you to eat a mite? Whatever you're battling, you need your strength. And more positive thinking, Abraham Foxworth. You'll beat this, I know you will. Why, think of all the wonders out there on the Fox Haven grounds that require your talents. I'm not sure we could get along without you." She meant it, doggone it. She wanted him well.

She lifted the tray and removed its linen cloth. "Something here should sound good to you—let's see, there's beef collops with Lucy's special onion sauce, chicken pudding, asparagus dressed the

Spanish way with oil and garlic, just like you love it, and minted peas."

He grimaced as she listed each of the items. She'd opted not to mention the ever-present obnoxious black pudding on his tray. Lord, that was enough to make anybody sick!

"How about the chicken soup? It's still steamy and looks hearty."

He gave her a halfway nod. "I'll have a spoon or two of the soup," he said.

She ladled it herself into his mouth and saw to it that he consumed more than two spoonfuls. Chicken soup worked magic—everyone knew that.

"Is my black pudding there, Meredith?"

"Why, no," she lied. "I believe they forgot it this afternoon." She covered the tray quickly. Good grief, his cramping stomach didn't need that heavy rotten stuff today!

"Then I think I've had enough, dear woman. I'll sleep awhile now." His swollen eyelids had already closed, and within seconds he was sound asleep.

Meredith sat with him for a while, deeply disturbed. His lethargy had begun only about a week ago—now he'd developed cramps, puffy eyes, and sore gums. The symptoms were beyond her, but "old age" didn't come on like that. Not at fifty-seven, for heaven's sake. He'd said his wife "went like this."

Something peculiar was going on. What?

Her brows pulled together, and she lifted the linen and examined the dinner tray. Everything on it was part of the same meal they would all be eating in a short while. Everything but one item.

The untouched blob of black pudding lay curled like a sickening grin. Only Abraham ate that awful mess, and only Abraham was ill.

Dear God! Was he being poisoned?

Ridiculous, she told herself. She was becoming absolutely paranoid.

But she couldn't shake off the wild suspicion. Well, blast it all, she could just test it! What harm could it do? Wrapping the greasy sausage in a handkerchief, she stuck it in the pocket of her apron. Leaving pale Abraham, still in his seemingly peaceful sleep, she hurried to her room.

Though she came perilously close to throwing up in the process, she managed to gag down every disgusting bite of his foul black pudding.

She'd do it for several days, she decided. And no matter what, she'd see to it that Abraham never ate it again—poisoned or not, the concoction had to be loaded with cholesterol and couldn't be good for him.

But she'd make certain that others in the house would assume he was continuing to eat his "elixir of youth" right on schedule.

She drank a cup of water quickly to wash down this first test of her admittedly madcap theory.

# Chapter Sixteen

Within three days, Meredith felt as if she'd been run over by a truck. And Abraham was up and spry as a colt—demanding his daily ration of black pudding. He couldn't have it, she told him. "And that's that!"

"And why the hell not, Captain Davis? It's what makes me appear but forty. Do you want me to wither away and grow old before your very eyes?"

This was going to be tricky, she knew. And her stomach was so queasy she wasn't in any condition to conjure up much cleverness. But she was determined.

"Tell you what, Abraham. Don't eat that blasted stuff for four weeks—only a short month, I'm asking of you. That pudding is way too greasy to have any benefit to you, believe me. If you indeed start withering, I'll reconsider my order."

It was a long shot, but she needed more time.

He harrumphed and kicked his legs petulantly beneath the whirlpool's water. "You'll be the death of me, woman," he grumbled.

"Merrie's right, I vow, Grandpapa," Betsy obligingly trilled, adding a few splashes of her own. "Father's ever told you the pudding was bad for you. He's never touched it himself, you know, and he's youthful looking though he's truly advanced in years."

Meredith would have laughed if she hadn't felt so rotten. She'd thought about canceling the pair's water therapy session today, but her sense of duty prevailed. They did so love their time in the whirlpool, and Abraham had already missed a number of sessions while he'd been ill.

"One measly month, Abraham. Agreed?" she prodded him.

"I reckon, woman," he grunted. "But if I wrinkle up like a dried plum I'll hold you responsible."

"It's a deal," Meredith said, continuing her massage of Betsy's legs beneath the water. The girl had begun letting her do this a week or so ago, and they'd started some simple exercises. "To wake up all the sleeping princesses inside," Meredith had offered as a fanciful reason that had appealed to Betsy.

It had felt so good from the beginning that the child now automatically scooted over next to her as soon as they were seated in the stream. "The princesses have fallen sleep again, Merrie," she'd say, nudging her frail little legs toward her. It seemed that the awkward movements were getting stronger and a bit more controlled each day. Still too early to tell, and certainly too early to start making promises to anyone. The more difficult parts of the therapy lay ahead, but Meredith was encouraged.

She had made matching bathing costumes for Abraham, Betsy, and herself—brightly colored dimity creations that would have been considered modest even by Victorian standards. Nevertheless, she knew that the concept of the attire, as well as the activity, was strange to the Fox Haven population. Laura Preston had been "scandalized" at the whole idea of the trio "bathing together," but she'd ceased her grumbles when Benjamin had told her in no uncertain terms that "warm spring water is known to have healthful benefits" and recommended the woman try it herself. She wouldn't, no surprise, being far too rigid for "such nonsense," as she'd called it, but at least she'd stopped carping.

Oh Lord, if *this* scandalized the woman, what on earth would she do if she knew what was really going on under her roof? Meredith didn't want to think about it. Not today, when it took most of her energy just to sit upright in the water. All she wanted to do was sleep. Was her malady the proof she needed that someone had been trying to poison Abraham? Or had he simply had a virus of some kind, and she'd caught it from him?

She didn't dare eat any more of the pudding, and she'd informed Laura and the kitchen staff that Abraham wouldn't be needing his special dish for a while "because he tells me he's lost his taste for it," she'd lied.

They'd thrown away today's portion, but she'd secretly retrieved it and sneaked it upstairs to her chamber.

Not, of course, to test it on herself again—she wasn't stupid. She had hit on another, safer plan.

After collecting a colony of ants, she'd found a small box, punched holes in its top, and set inside it some dirt, the ants—and the black pudding. The insects had swarmed over the fat sausage immediately. She'd hidden the box under her bed.

Now, all she had to do was wait. If the ants were thriving tomorrow, she could forget about the whole troublesome conspiracy theory. And probably develop stomach cramps and sore gums from some eighteenth-century version of the forty-eight-hour flu.

And if they were dead?

Her dizzy head wasn't up to thinking through the implications of that. Though the "opportunity" would be narrowed down to the ten or so members of the kitchen staff, the "motive" would still be far from being established.

Patrick Henry was downstairs!

Meredith threw on her prettiest lawn dress, feeling more energetic than she had all day. After returning from the whirlpool, she'd collapsed on her bed, thinking seriously about dying.

But then Benjamin had knocked lightly on her door. "A gentleman is downstairs whom I believe you'd like to meet, Meredith," his polite and formal voice had come to her through the heavy oak. The sun was still shining—he never entered her room in daylight.

"Gentleman?" she'd asked, trying to hold back the groan.

"Our neighbor from Scotchtown has come to call—Mr. Henry, Meredith. We're in the parlor, if you'd like to join us."

Of course, he knew she'd be ecstatic. She'd made no secret of her admiration for the man.

But today, of all days! People should be at their best when they were about to meet a legendary hero. She wasn't in great shape at all.

"I'll be right down," she'd said, hoping her hesitancy didn't show. She didn't want Benjamin to know she was under the weather—and she certainly didn't want him to know about her black pudding strategy until she had more definitive information than she now had.

"Are you not feeling well?"

Damn. Sometimes his acute senses were a pain.

"I'm fine, Benjamin. I was just napping, so my head's not on straight yet."

He'd chuckled. "Well, straighten it as best you can and come on down."

She'd smiled despite herself as the sound of his booted footsteps diminished down the hallway. And her lethargy had lifted. After all, this was a special occasion, and she wasn't about to miss it!

Her body wasn't as strong as her spirits, she found as she bounded from the bed a bit too swiftly. A wave of nausea stopped her momentarily, and she held on to one of the sturdy bed posts for support. When the unsettling sensation passed, she shook her head to banish the cobwebs.

Reaching for the lavender frock—Benjamin's favorite, he'd told her once—she gave her stomach a brisk order to behave itself. She desperately hoped she wouldn't throw up on the parlor rug.

Her enthusiasm easily won out over such misgivings, however. Giving herself a quick once-over in the tall looking glass, she pinched her wan cheeks into a Lancôme-like rosiness, brushed the tangles out of her hair, and, with a steadying breath, hurried downstairs.

To meet one of her longtime heroes.

Patrick Henry and Benjamin stood as she entered the parlor. The heady combination of both of them in the same room made her flutter inside.

The introductions were brief, and she took her seat beside Laura—prim and sedate in her smoky gray as usual—on the cushioned settle. Benjamin brought her a glass of sherry before returning to his chair.

He and the Patriot were drinking rum, she saw. Her stomach churned miserably. She wouldn't touch the sherry, she knew, wishing the age were enlightened enough that she could've asked for a stomach-settling Coke or ginger ale.

"Patrick was just telling us he's been elected as one of Virginia's representatives to the Continental Congress," Benjamin said to start the conversational ball rolling. "He'll be leaving for Philadelphia later this month."

"How very exciting," she said, sounding about as intelligent as Patricia Smithson, she feared. But what else dare she say? She knew precisely what was going to happen there—the cast of luminaries who'd be present, who'd do what, say what. Under the circumstances, though, she was reduced to the ladylike vapid "how very exciting."

Abraham breezed into the room, without his cane, she noted with a scolding glance in his direction. He gave her one of his "I don't need it all the time, Captain" expressions and greeted the honored guest with a handshake and an ebullient welcome.

While Benjamin repeated the Continental Congress information for Abraham's benefit, Meredith concentrated on Patrick Henry. Tall and lanky, just as she'd expected. He had a loose-boned country-boy appearance, with rustic clothing to match—a homespun hunting shirt, buckskin breeches, and worn, dusty boots. Such was his frequent attire, she'd read. Though an uncommon man, he relished dressing like this—for he represented and spoke for the common men, he often said.

His thinning coppery red hair was tied back in a queue. His clear blue eyes were by far the most arresting feature of his long, angular face. She was fascinated by them. They radiated sharp intelligence and, she noted with a tug of surprised pleasure, a decided sparkle of humor.

"You'll have many halfway patriots to contend with up there, I wager, Patrick," Abraham said. "They'll want to kiss the King's pompous arse (Laura gasped) even while his army's muskets are aimed at their wool-filled heads."

"Aye," he responded with a deep chuckle. "Many still hang on with futility to the frayed hope that Britain will redress our grievances. I have no such hope."

His voice was richer than she'd imagined. She wished he'd stand up and deliver a spellbinding speech. But he didn't, of course. The men carried on their three-way conversation in a low-key, amiable fashion. Laura, sitting stiff as a board, and a now considerably more relaxed Meredith—holding her unsipped sherry—remained properly quiet.

"I stopped by Goose Creek on my way back from Williamsburg," Patrick said, changing the course of the discussion from political to downright disturbing. Meredith came close to spilling her wine. "Peyton Smithson said to tell you they're awaiting with impatience for you to visit them, Benjamin."

She steadied her glass with both hands. "I'll make note of the message," was all he said. Lord knew what his body language was saying. She kept her eyes off him.

"And how is your wife, Patrick?" Laura asked. The unexpected sound of her voice made Meredith jump slightly.

"Not well, Miss Preston," he responded. His eyes clouded and his shoulders sagged. "Her malady worsens with each passing day, and at times we must restrain her for her own safety. 'Tis a heavy cross for all of us to bear at Scotchtown, but I would willingly bear weights far heavier if only we could bring our poor Sallie back to us with the gay spirits she blessed us with before."

Meredith remembered something about his first wife having gone insane. Legend had it that she'd had to be confined to Scotchtown's basement, attended by someone at all times and restrained in a "strait dress" to prevent her from committing suicide.

Dear heaven, that was happening *now*!

"This sad subject brings me to the reason for my visit today, Benjamin," Patrick said, leaning forward in his chair. "My mother and sister Annie Christian, with her children, have come to Scotchtown for refuge from the western lands where there's renewed Indian unrest," he continued. "Annie's husband, William Christian, has been called to serve Governor Dunmore in his war against the tribes. Mother and Annie will be at Scotchtown to care for Sallie and my six children while I'm in Philadelphia this fall, but Pennsylvania's truly a far distance—

and I fear my absence may extend well beyond a month."

He put down his glass and rubbed his long hands together. "I would be beholden if you'd ride over to look in on them occasionally—to ensure that they're faring as well as these burdensome times allow."

Benjamin assured him he would, and Meredith made a mental note to figure out a way to accompany him as often as possible. Though she knew there would be little she could do to stop the progression of Sallie Henry's illness, she might be able to alleviate some of the woman's distress— and that of Patrick's family.

It would be but a small contribution, but she'd be honored to do what she could to assist those so beloved by this fine man who was about to cut a wide swath through history.

As Patrick Henry prepared to take his leave, Meredith could hold her tongue no longer— though she measured her words carefully.

"The two Adams gentlemen from Massachusetts—their names are Samuel and John, I believe—should be valuable allies for you, Mr. Henry. And I vow you should beware of machinations by the likes of Mr. Galloway of Pennsylvania."

She couldn't change the course of history, but she didn't see any harm in preparing him a bit for coming events.

"I'm honored to accept the advice of such a lovely lady, Miss Davis," he said with a warm smile, bowing to brush his lips across her hand. It was far better than an autograph, she decided, thrilled to the tips of her toes.

"However do you know of these men, Meredith?" Abraham asked, obviously taken aback. Her heart sank.

"Miss Davis devours the *Gazette* when we're fortunate enough to receive a copy, haven't you noticed, Father?" Benjamin jumped to her rescue. And he cleverly maneuvered the tall Patriot toward the front door to abort further questions.

The two men, both heroes in her book—though the taller, darker one was far more than that—left the parlor.

Before Meredith could assimilate the relief she felt, Laura Preston's next words to Abraham alarmed her considerably.

"What's this most recent madness of yours that I hear from Meredith, Abraham? Have you truly lost your taste for your black pudding?"

Meredith flushed and tried to catch the old gentleman's eyes. His eyebrow shot up; she held her breath.

"I'm but briefly dissatisfied with it, Sour Laura. A month only perhaps, and then I'll be ready for more, I wager."

She exhaled her *whew*, hoping like the dickens the woman didn't notice. If she did, she paid it no heed but walked ramrod straight toward the kitchen. Only then did Meredith give crotchety old Abraham his overdue kiss on the cheek.

And she suddenly felt better than she had for days.

As Benjamin was leaving her chamber that night, he wrinkled his beautiful nose and sniffed. "An unpleasant odor appears to hover within these walls this eve," he said from the door.

Oh oh. She knew precisely what the source

was—that abominable pudding she'd hidden beneath her bed. She'd been aware of the smell herself, but had prayed he'd be too otherwise occupied to notice it. She'd doused herself with a lavish amount of lavender as a precaution.

"Must be the chamberpot," she offered as a logical excuse, long ago rid of the embarrassment she'd experienced over the primitive toilet facilities. "I'll see that they clean it more thoroughly tomorrow."

He nodded, apparently placated, and left her then. But not without a great dimpled smile for her and a whispered "Sleep well, Treasure."

She sighed contentedly and snuggled back into the feather mattress. Lord, he'd started calling her "Treasure" again. Her world, despite its current invasion by the stink of rotting sausage, was indeed a thing of beauty.

Benjamin walked down the long hallway to his chamber. His mind was filled with thoughts of the woman he'd just left. She was truly wondrous, and with her he came as close to heaven as mortals were allowed. More than his physical body had been enwrapped by her. His heart sang in her presence—his very soul adored her.

Perhaps only a transient sprite from another world could have entered him this way—enchanted him beyond all sense and reason. Dear God in heaven, if only he could keep her near to him forever.

Unlikely, he knew, as the familiar despair and torment of such thoughts bedeviled him once again. He could never burden her with the avowal of his growing love for her. She would demand her release from such foolishness—tell him "in no uncertain terms" as she would undoubtedly phrase it—that their moments together were but woefully temporary. She longed to be back among her own. Would gladly disappear from him if she but had the magic to do so.

And that was his burden. To bear alone.

When he entered his candlelit chamber, he was startled to see Aunt Laura, sitting poised and stiff in a chair, waiting for him. A sharp stab of guilt accompanied his astonishment.

"You're returning late to your chamber, Benjamin," she announced.

"And you're retiring late yourself," he responded, closing the door behind him, struggling for a semblance of composure. "To what do I owe the honor of your company at this hour, dear Aunt?"

He was afraid he knew.

"I believe you know," she said coldly, affirming his fears.

"No," he lied, lowering himself into a chair with weariness. "Perhaps you should tell me."

"Your regular visits to that sinful woman's chamber have not gone unnoticed by me, Benjamin. God in his wisdom forbids fornication—and I too forbid such actions in my house." She held a large Bible in her hand, thumping its black cover as she spoke.

"This is not your house, Aunt Laura. We've offered you a home here for many years—but the house, I must remind you, is the property of the Foxworths. What transpires beneath this roof is of no concern to you."

Her thick hands gripped the book in her lap. "When the devil himself takes up residence, it must be the concern of all of us. God smites those who disobey his Commandments. Never forget that, my nephew. You profess to care for those dependent upon you, and yet, by your sins you expose us all to the wrath of a vengeful God."

He was silent. Anger like bile rose in his throat.

"I must remind *you*, Benjamin," she continued, her voice steady, strong. "Fox Haven has been struck by enough tragedies that the fear of God should be well entrenched in your soul."

"I shall never accept your twisted beliefs that any of our sufferings were brought about by the punishing hands of God," he snarled. "No sins have been committed in this house that would justify the deaths of babes and innocent women!"

"Until now, perhaps." She stood. "God is all-wise and can see into the future. He has smitten this house in the past as a warning to you, mark my words. You've not heeded those warnings but have listened to none but Satan with his vile messages of carnal lust. If you choose to continue down this path of sin, I tremble to consider what travails are ahead for us."

"Leave my chamber at once," he growled.

"Think on my words and beware," she said and walked with purposeful strides from the room, holding the Bible before her as though its light would guide and protect her through the darkened hallway.

Benjamin lowered his head and clamped the heels of his hands against his temples.

Dear God in heaven, would he have to give up Meredith now? *Could* he? Never had he been presented with such a trial to test his strength.

With a heavy sigh, he stood and pounded his fist against the oak door. He held no credence for Aunt Laura's rigid, self-righteous interpretations of the Scriptures. God was just and would never view what existed between him and Meredith as sinful. He himself must have sent her here for some purpose neither of them could yet have knowledge of. He had smiled on them and in His omniscience would have expected and welcomed their stolen moments of pleasure.

But Aunt Laura knew of them, dear Jesus, and would continue her tormenting harangues. There would be no peace at Fox Haven until he ceased his visits to Meredith's chamber.

Far worse—unless he complied with his aunt's demands, he knew the woman would see to it that Meredith would have no peace.

His heart cried out in anguish. He could not allow Meredith to suffer thus.

For the first time since he was a wee lad, Benjamin Foxworth wept.

# Chapter Seventeen

The ants died. Every single one of them. Meredith peered down into the foul-smelling box, reluctant to believe the evidence staring her straight in the eyes. But knowing she had to believe it.

Someone in this house had tried to poison Abraham Foxworth. And the field of suspects had narrowed considerably. Fewer than a dozen women were involved in food preparation at Fox Haven.

One of them was a murderess.

Reeling from the blow of this awful knowledge, Meredith replaced the top on the box and shoved it under the bed. Lord, how she wished she could deep-six the reeking sausage, its retinue of tiny corpses, and, most of all, the implications this held for Fox Haven.

But she'd have to share her terrible discovery with Benjamin. Tonight, she'd bring out Exhibit

A, and together they'd devise a careful strategy to find the culprit.

She shouldn't venture alone down this dangerous road she'd taken any longer. Wild suspicions were one thing; hard evidence required extreme caution—and the able assistance of the strongest person she knew. This information was going to upset him, and she hated that part of it, but they had to move quickly.

With such an ominous beginning, Meredith should have known that this day held evil portents. And they met her the instant she arrived downstairs.

"I must talk with you, Meredith," Benjamin said with grave seriousness as she descended the last step.

That he'd been standing down there in the entry hall had surprised her. Ordinarily by this hour of the morning he would've long been out in the fields. The heavy tone of his voice sent a warning prickle up her spine.

"In the parlor," he said with a nod in that direction.

She followed him, gnawing at her lip. Her chest felt as if a chunk of ice had lodged up next to her heart.

"We must end our clandestine meetings," he said with a quiet simplicity that defied the noisy turmoil he'd unleashed in her head. As well as the rest of her.

"Why?"

"I have many reasons. Suffice it to say my conscience will allow me to use you no longer in a fashion that men in this era reserve for trollops."

That stung. She winced as if he'd slapped her.

"I know you're no trollop, Meredith," he added quickly, but it didn't help. Her nausea had returned in full force.

"But because there can never be anything more than what we've had between us," he continued, his words ripping into her, "I believe for the good of us both—and for the sanctity of this home—that we cease . . . that we return to the more sensible status of friendship alone."

She swallowed hard. He'd grown tired of her. She'd known it was bound to happen. But later. Not, dear heaven, now.

Not ever, she might have even dared to hope in the rapture of his embraces.

Foolish. When in God's name had she become so foolish? And so blasted vulnerable?

His eyes were lusterless and ringed with shadows, indicating he'd had little sleep. Wrestling with his conscience? Or just steeling himself for breaking this news to her gently—and without, of course, a scene.

He hated scenes.

And for a chilling second she hated him.

"Friendship alone is quite sufficient for me, Benjamin," she heard herself say as if she meant it. He'd accepted her twentieth-century hype about her being a free-thinking woman, and, by God, she'd hide her hurt from him if it was the last thing she did!

"I knew you would feel that way, Meredith." He pulled out his watch and looked at it, and frowned. "I must see to the fields now, if you'll excuse me?"

She nodded, an army of emotions battling

behind her easy-come easy-go facade—the facade she was determined to maintain until he got out of this room.

Lord, then she didn't know what she'd do.

But after he left, she stood exactly where she was and didn't do much of anything.

What *could* she do? Nothing, from crying hysterically to throwing a handful of porcelain objects, was going to make her feel any better.

She tightened her lips. Well, she'd just have to get used to walking around with a deadened heart. And she might as well start practicing.

The walk to the dining room for her solitary breakfast seemed to take an uncannily long time. Zombies moved slowly, she realized. And they ached all over one heck of a lot.

Not until she was pouring herself a cup of coffee did she remember the dead ants upstairs. She paused, then returned the silver pitcher to its candle-heated trivet. No denying it, she'd still have to tell Benjamin—her *friend*, she thought with a grimace. She'd do it tonight, in the parlor, library, or garden. It didn't matter where.

She sat down with her coffee, taking nothing else from the buffet that had been set out for her.

He must be told what she'd discovered. Somehow, the two of them would have to work together to eliminate this terrifying danger to Fox Haven.

One big tear dropped into the steaming coffee, startling her. Deadened hearts could cry? Quickly she pushed her fingers up beneath her glasses, wiped her cheeks, and patted her eyes dry. Her desolation was too deep for tears, she told herself restraightening her glasses.

And then she attempted valiantly to put her

frozen mind to work scheduling her day ahead
as if it were a day like all others.

Benjamin wasn't at the supper table that evening.

"He'll not return till near mid-morning tomorrow, he advised me," Laura Preston announced
with an air of self-importance as she took her
place at the head of the table in Benjamin's customary seat.

"And where did he go without telling the rest of
us, Sour Laura?" Abraham asked, disgruntled.

Meredith was too numb for disgruntlement.
She sat placidly, keeping her fevered emotions
concealed behind her composed surface.

"He went to Goose Creek to pay his woefully
tardy respects to the Smithsons," the woman
said. "We shall bow our heads together, please.
In Benjamin's absence I'll present our grace to
the good Lord." Her sonorous blessing was more
like a sermon, continuing nearly long enough to
qualify as one and covering bases far removed
from food.

Meredith, distracted by this latest bombshell
that had shattered into bits what was left of
her broken heart, heard little of it. Well, he'd
certainly wasted no time in getting on with his
life. And she needed desperately to talk with him
tonight about the attempted poisoning. But his
priorities obviously lay elsewhere. She'd have to
continue searching for Fox Haven's mad woman
by herself.

The task, she'd found today, wasn't going to be a
simple one. The sun-filled kitchen was seemingly
a place of love and light and squeaky-clean industry. Merry camaraderie prevailed along with the

outstanding efficiency she'd long noted. Sweet, dependable Lucy was head honcho and supervised the staff so well it was hard to imagine that a drop of anything could get into a dish that she didn't know about. And yet, Meredith's instincts assured her that Lucy could never be the guilty party.

Meredith, with Philip on her lap most of the time, had spent a number of hours with the cooks under the pretense of "learning more about how you delightful people present us with such an endless array of lovely dishes." She'd studied each radiant face, each pair of wide, innocent-appearing eyes for a clue—had listened to their cheerful banter till her ears felt clogged with sugar-loaded syrup.

Nothing. If the murderess was among them, she was clever as the devil. But Meredith was determined to find her.

"That's quite enough praying, for God's sake, Sour Laura," Abraham interrupted the woman's pious ramblings with an impatient grumble. "The food's growing cold."

Meredith, jarred from her private thoughts, lifted her head.

" . . . we make our humble pleas in the name of Your blessed Son, our Savior. Amen," Laura stated firmly.

"A-*men*!" Abraham echoed with obvious relief, reaching for the platter of ham. "The wages of sin may be death, woman, but the wages of starvation are equally high."

Meredith took only a small serving of a couple of items. If either of her dining partners noticed, no comment was made. Laura appeared at peace with her orderly and now thoroughly blessed world. Abraham was intent on satisfying his healthy appetite. He'd been busy all day improving the stables. Jack had complained to Meredith that he'd rehinged the doors so that they opened the wrong way. Meredith had suggested that Jack correct the error quietly the following day.

"I suspect our Benjamin will have happy news to convey to us on the morrow upon his return," Laura contributed as she sliced off a dainty portion of ham for herself. " 'Tis past time he bring into our home a proper bride."

Meredith felt as if the woman's sharp knife had twisted into her breast.

"Not that simpering Patricia Smithson, I pray," Abraham scoffed, reaching for his wine. "She's naught but puff paste."

"He's highly taken with her, I vow," Laura said in her most pleasant voice. "She's everything a gentleman could wish for."

So true. Damnit.

"I've ever prided Benjamin on his level-headedness, woman. I wager you're wrong this time. He's far too intelligent to wed the likes of Miss Smithson—he prefers substance to froth," Abraham said.

Meredith knew better. Poor old man, he lived in such a dream world and harbored silly delusions about his own son.

Laura changed the subject, thank heaven. But unfortunately she seemed bent on pulling Meredith into the table chatter. "Lucy tells me you're interested in learning the ways of the kitchen," she said to her.

Meredith held on to her heavy fork, hoping she was keeping it steady. "There's much I need to learn," she responded, with more truth than the woman could imagine. She tried to sift through

273

her gloom to find a credible way she could pry without showing her hand. "The staff is extremely competent—have they all been here for a long while?"

Laura nodded. "Aye. Most of them since before my own arrival. And that's been, let me think . . ." She paused, looked toward Abraham as though she needed him to help her remember. "Why, I've been here nearly twenty-eight years, haven't I?"

"Seems more like fifty," Abraham commented under his breath.

Meredith was struck again at his rudeness toward the woman.

But Laura ignored him and changed the subject again—to a primarily one-sided discussion of the rising costs of imported foodstuffs and the need to stock up great supplies in light of the coming embargo on imports she feared was in the offing.

As soon as she could without revealing her anxiety to get away, Meredith excused herself with forced gaiety "to spend some time with Betsy upstairs before the child's bedtime."

Abraham's eyes were on her, but she refused to meet them. He sensed she was suffering, she could tell. God love him. Only he had the sensitivity to suspect that all wasn't well with her. But he couldn't help.

Too bad Benjamin hadn't inherited his father's keen ability to see through her brittle shell of false confidence.

What a weird thought to have, she told herself as she climbed the stairs. Good grief, she *wanted* Benjamin unaware of how he'd hurt her. If he knew how she truly felt, his indifference would be a hundred times more painful. Unbearable.

After a brief recounting of Goldilocks and the Three Bears to Betsy and a command performance of Cinderella, Meredith left the delighted child and checked in on Philip. The infant slept peacefully in his cradle. Reliable Sukie, too, was asleep in her bed beside him in the nursery.

At last, Meredith was free to enter her own, adjoining room and to shed the facade she'd hidden behind since Benjamin's words to her that morning. Her pent-up agonies rushed forth all at once—bitterness, confusion, anger, desolation. Despair. She threw herself across the big, empty bed and, with profound relief, succumbed to the body-wracking, soul-wrenching sobs she'd held inside for too long.

Meredith moved through the golden light of August much like a small, blinded fish swimming without direction or purpose far beneath a sparkling surface. The light and warmth above never touched her—and she had neither desire nor interest in venturing upward. Ice and darkness had become her internal environment.

Externally, she maintained a life-goes-on-unchanged aspect. Fooling everyone, she hoped. Work was her salvation. She plunged into her usual and new, self-imposed tasks with energetic zeal—continuing the increasingly strenuous therapy sessions with Abraham and Betsy; caring for and keeping a watchful eye over Philip; planning for the racially integrated school program she wanted to initiate for the plantation's children; and, of course, warily searching for the demented individual who threatened Fox Haven.

That last task was proving stubbornly elusive. No one appeared to harbor hatred for the Foxworths or their home. At times, she found herself actually believing that an evil ghost might be the culprit after all.

Nonsense, she would remind herself. But faced with nothing but innocent, motiveless people day in and day out, she couldn't help but entertain such thoughts occasionally.

Benjamin had kept his distance, and she never had a moment alone with him. So she'd continued in her futile search without his help or knowledge.

He hadn't returned from Goose Creek with any announcement indicating he intended to wed Patricia Smithson. Meredith should have been relieved, but she wasn't. Such an announcement was inevitably coming, she knew. Sooner or later. She almost wished for sooner. It was like waiting for the second boot to fall. And keeping herself toughened enough not to wince when it did drop was a full-time job.

Indeed, she'd succeeded fairly well at suppressing her thoughts of Benjamin during the busy days. She kept them padlocked in a top-secret compartment in the back of her brain. If one of them dared to seep through a suddenly opened crack, she'd push it back quickly and seal up the traitorous crack at once.

But during the nights when she was alone, the padlock slid away and the compartment opened wide, flooding her with memories and fathomless longings. She hated the nights.

On August's last day, she dropped in on Jess the cobbler to see if Betsy's shoes were nearing completion. The girl was ready for them, Meredith believed.

"They's done, Miz Meredith. Finished 'em last eve, I did," Jess said proudly, lifting them for her inspection.

They were perfect. Soft, suedelike buff high-tops, their tiny soles sturdy. He'd strung the pink ribbons she'd furnished through the eyelets.

"Were you able to devise the special cuff and leather strip I requested?" she asked.

"Yes'm, leastways I hopes these'll do." He handed her a long piece of leather, cut precisely to the measurements she'd given him, and a small circled band of buff-colored felt punched with holes around the end. She fingered the cuff— soft, pliable—and gave it a little tug between her hands; it had the exact stretchiness she wanted. Jess had come up with dandy equivalents of a toe sling and an elastic bandage!

Meredith beamed for the first time in weeks.

"Lord, you're wonderful, Jess!" she exclaimed, giving him a big hug. Tears of joy brightened her eyes.

"I'se happy you so happy, Miz Meredith. Makin' these pretty shoes for little Miz Betsy was 'deed a pleasure."

Meredith put her finger to her lips. "Remember, now, this is our secret—yours, mine, Betsy's, and but a few others in the house, like Lucy, Sukie, and Will. Promise?"

His smile widened and he nodded. "Even my sweet Verna don't know of 'em."

She borrowed a bucket from Jess and placed the shoes, leather strip, and cuff inside. Then she took off her white apron and placed it atop to hide her precious merchandise. Flushed with enthusiasm, her mind racing with plans and hopeful possibilities, she headed for the house.

And bumped right into Benjamin Foxworth who stood like an oak tree square in her path.

"Good grief!" she spluttered, backing away and rubbing her nose. It had banged into his rock-hard chest. An oak tree would have been more yielding.

"I'm sorry, Meredith. I truly thought you saw me." He made no move to reach out to steady her. Thank God. But he didn't retreat, either.

She did, three or four steps. Her heart was acting crazy. She adjusted her glasses, elevated her chin, and focused on his right ear. "You could have moved, Benjamin. My mind was elsewhere."

"I repeat my apology."

She shrugged and started to walk around him. With a worried glance at the bucket in her hand, she saw with satisfaction that her apron still covered Betsy's shoes.

"Don't rush off," he said. "I was looking for you—I have a favor to request."

"Oh?" She paused and looked back. Ear, she reminded herself. Look only at his ear.

"I'm riding to Scotchtown this afternoon. Patrick's wife, I've heard, is in sore distress. I thought, perhaps, you might know some way to provide her relief. Would you accompany me, Meredith?"

God, she was torn. She'd been wanting to do this very thing. But to go with Benjamin? They hadn't had a private moment together since that miserable morning weeks ago—he'd been avoiding her like the plague. To be alone with him now, even for such a short journey—could she stand it?

"Will has agreed to join us," he said as if he could read her thoughts.

"Why, of course I'll accompany you," she said, keeping her sigh of relief to herself. "I've hoped since I heard of her malady that I might see her—I've had little experience in such cases, but I'd like to help if I could."

He looked down at the bucket. "When can you be ready? We should depart as soon as possible."

"Let me run these berries into the house," she said quickly, swinging the bucket and herself away from him. "Be just a minute," she tossed back over her shoulder as she scurried up the path toward the rear entrance.

Good grief. Every curl, curve, and scallop of that right ear was etched into her brain.

Better that than those turquoise eyes, she reminded herself.

# Chapter Eighteen

Meredith had visited Scotchtown numerous times in her former life. But never had she seen it like this. Oh, the house looked the same—large, white, and imposing. But its setting was completely different. Situated in the center of a courtyard, the place was surrounded by numerous smaller buildings.

"That's Patrick's law office, there's the schoolhouse, their plantation store, the blacksmith shop, tanyard, ash house, wash house," Benjamin told her, pointing to the structures one by one as they made their approach. "The slaves' cabins are out behind, and their mill's a half-mile back, down by the Newfound."

She nodded, taking it all in, getting that familiar twinge of wonder. *This is now. It's the way things really were—but it's now.*

"Fox Haven's far grander, Benjamin," was what she said, again with wonder. "Oddly enough, according to the history books, Scotchtown was Hanover's largest and most prestigious plantation."

So much for the experts.

"But we don't have Patrick Henry," he said with a smile. Explaining in six simple words why historians sometimes made mistakes.

Benjamin's dimpled smile wreaked havoc with her composure. She forced her concentration back on the house.

Gentle, quiet Will took their horses back to the stables, and she walked beside Benjamin to the front door. The pretty, gray-haired woman who greeted them wasn't a docent, as on all her previous visits. She was Sarah Winston Henry, Meredith knew right away. Patrick's mother. A lively, intelligent woman, according to reports—though at the moment she seemed quite distressed.

"Thank God you're here, Benjamin," she said with an undercurrent of hopeful expectation that unsettled Meredith. "And is this the woman you've told us of? Welcome to Scotchtown, Miss Davis. Benjamin speaks highly of your abilities with the ill. We're sore in need of you this day."

Meredith shot Benjamin a look of alarm. *Abilities with the ill?* What kind of advance billing had he given her? She prayed she could live up to it. His poised confidence as he led her into the house upset her further. What in the name of God had he gotten her into?

"Poor Sallie's downstairs, Miss Davis. Annie's with her now, and two of the slaves. Please follow me," Mrs. Henry said.

Meredith felt as unsure of her legs as of her capabilities. Glancing back at Benjamin, she attempted to telegraph her apprehension. He nodded with complacent assurance and sat on a pine settle in the entry hall, leaving her to her own inadequate devices. Furious with him, but more concerned at the moment about what she'd find down in the basement—and what, if anything, she could do for the woman interred there—she followed Sarah Henry down the gloomy stairs.

The basement was far from a dungeon. Mostly above ground, it had high windows that admitted bright streams of daylight. But the floor was hard, red-brown dirt instead of brick, and the musty earth smells were those of an open grave. Meredith shivered. She'd been down here before on tours and had always shivered. But this time was different. This time the narrow cot wouldn't be empty. This time . . .

Ducking her head, she followed Mrs. Henry through the low, narrow door into the small room occupied by Patrick's wife.

She didn't see her at first. A slender young woman in a blue dress and two large black women were huddled over by the wall, struggling with something. *Someone.* Grunts of effort fused with a spine-tingling staccato of throttled gasps.

Meredith moved forward slowly.

"Miss Davis is here, Annie," she heard.

"Thank God," said the woman in blue, acknowledging her presence with voice only. Her body remained hovered over the cot, her arms tensed, straining against their burden.

Filled with dread, Meredith drew closer and saw Sallie Henry for the first time. Dear heaven, she was in a manic seizure! Already restrained in a crude gray rope-entwined wrapper, she was arched and writhing beneath the hands of her valiant attendants; her slight frame, twisting in violent spasms, nearly levitated above the cot.

Hazy instructions from past teachers sped into Meredith's mind, then became clear and commanding.

"Fetch a big tub of hot water!" she shouted back to Mrs. Henry as she ran to brace the stricken woman's head. "And linens—large linens, please!"

While waiting for the water to be brought, she supported the tormented woman's head and smoothed her contorted forehead. Soon a flurry of motion and low voices to her left told her the tub had arrived. "Here, hold her head like this," she told Patrick Henry's mother, who'd run to her side. Grabbing for the stack of linens held out to her by a frightened young red-haired girl, Meredith plunged the cloths into the steaming water.

The heat bit at her arms and hands as she frantically searched for the largest piece of linen, unraveled it, and pulled it dripping from the tub. After fiercely wringing the cloth, she folded it in half as she ran back to the cot.

"Wrap her, wrap her," she ordered, shoving Annie and one of the blacks out of her way, then proceeded to wrap the flailing woman herself. *Be careful about hot spots . . . avoid blistering her skin. There, it's around her.*

"Quick! Hand me a quilt!" she exclaimed. Someone thrust one toward her, and she covered the woman, encased now like a mummy in the wet, hot sheet.

Gradually, Sallie Henry's paroxysms diminished to tremors and, at long last, ceased completely. The small lump of her body beneath its wrappings visibly sagged, relaxed. Her eyelids fluttered, she moaned. And then she was quiet.

Asleep.

Meredith pushed her glasses up to the top of her head and looked down through tear-misted eyes at the woman.

She was frail, but beautiful. Like a dark-haired angel. Her flawless skin, so wan, stretched like translucent parchment over the delicate bone structure of her now-peaceful face. Only the deep gray shadows circling her closed eyes betrayed her recent journey into hell itself.

"She will rest now, I believe," Meredith said softly.

The group around her was silent. She felt their gazes and looked about her, self-conscious now.

"Thank you, Miss Davis," Mrs. Henry said in an awed whisper.

Meredith's throat ached with tears, her heart ached with frustration. She could do nothing more to relieve the distress of this stricken woman. And yet . . . oh, God . . . so many ways to help her existed in the world she'd known. Methods she knew little about, true. But even had she been a neurologist or psychiatrist in that world, she'd still be reduced to this in 1774 . . . heated wraps to quiet the torment.

"Does she have attacks like this often?" she asked.

Mrs. Henry shook her head. "Only occasionally. This day's was indeed the worst . . . ," her voice lowered, came choked, " . . . thus far."

They knew, then. Death itself lurked in this basement—Meredith felt its dark presence. But

284

she felt some other things as well. The dank air of the small room stirred with them: courage; dedicated devotion; love; and a brave, resigned acceptance of the inevitable.

She'd felt these things, had seen them at work in the eyes of distraught families in dimly lit intensive-care waiting rooms. The Henrys wore clothes far different—they stood clasped together now in an environment worlds away from the antiseptic impersonality of a twentieth-century hospital where medical marvels existed, but still too often failed.

And yet, these people before her displayed the strength of the human spirit as magnificently as those she'd observed, respected, and admired in her own time. Perhaps more so. For their resources were few, their lives more constricted, their hopes and expectations not nearly so high . . .

Sadly she turned away from them. She'd done all she could. "The wet linen should be removed in ten minutes or so, before it chills down. And she'll require dry clothes then, of course. I'm . . . I'm sorry I can't do more."

"But you've helped so greatly, Miss Davis," Annie Christian said. "We're beholden." The pretty young brown-haired woman, near Meredith's age and almost exactly the same height, came over to her and embraced her warmly. Their tear-streamed cheeks touched.

From the far corner of the room, Benjamin watched Meredith as she met and talked quietly with the family. He'd carried the tub of hot water down for Mrs. Henry and had stayed to offer his assistance.

But he'd not been needed—not with Meredith here. Meredith. So capable and competent, so quick, so strong, so . . . caring. A thousand more wonderful adjectives sprung to his mind to describe her. But none of them were sufficient. She was, truly, a woman without parallel in this time and, he was certain, in any time.

His heart quickened, and he ordered it to steady itself. Bloody hell, he'd successfully avoided her as much as possible this past month to keep his own resolve strong. He had suffered. But she'd obviously thrived without him, had never been more energetic nor more alive.

She needed him not. Would never need him. And that, for her, was as it should be. And as it should be for him, too, he reminded himself. Their destinies were forever separate. Why couldn't he accept that?

He knew he must.

Wearily he pushed away from the dirt wall. As he emerged from the shadows, he saw her body tense, the startled look in her eyes. She hadn't known he was down here. Hadn't wanted him to be here.

"I should return you to Fox Haven," he said, low.

She nodded, appearing sorely tired. Her hands and arms were still reddened from the scalding water she'd used to quiet Sallie, and her lovely chestnut hair clung in damp strands to her flushed tear-streaked cheeks.

She'd never looked more beautiful to him.

Patrick's oldest daughter, Patsy, a maturing girl of thirteen or fourteen, gave Meredith an emotional hug of gratitude, as did Sarah Henry and Annie Christian. They addressed her as Meredith now, Benjamin noted as they made their farewells. She'd made her mark on the Henry family as he'd known she would.

He held her elbow lightly to assist her up the stairs.

Dear God, she'd made an indelible mark on him.

"Benjamin, please don't fly around Hanover County telling everybody I'm a miracle worker," she complained as they rode back to Fox Haven. "A sickness like Sallie's is beyond me, and so is almost anything else you might set me up for, from small pox to the bubonic plague."

"You helped," he said, as sure of himself as always.

"Barely. Lord, what I did was so basic and primitive, I can't believe that Dr. Hughes himself doesn't know about it."

"Apparently not."

She fumed for a while, but was too exhausted to put her heart into it. Will, with Benjamin's permission, had left them behind. He'd needed to get back to finish his chores. So she was alone with Benjamin—if being in a forest with ten zillion trees and an equal number of birds, deer, wild turkeys, foxes, bears, and snakes could be considered alone.

None of them were likely to pounce on her, and cold-hearted Mr. Upright Benjamin was the unlikeliest of all. If he tried, she'd give him hell. That "trollop" business still stung. Besides, he was all but engaged to Miss 1774 Virginia.

Without Will, though, she could speak more freely and use her once-normal vocabulary without double-checking constantly. And that, all by itself, was a relief. So what if she befuddled Benjamin? Pleasing him wasn't high on her priority list any more.

They rode in silence for a while. Sometimes, when the path was narrow, they went single file with Benjamin behind "to protect you" he said. Sir Galahad to your rescue, ma'am, she thought wryly.

But now the road had widened, and he came up beside her.

"What's wrong with Sallie?" she asked.

"She went mad shortly after the birth of their youngest child."

"How many children?"

"Six, I believe."

"Post-partum depression, probably—advanced now to the point of no return." She sighed. "Lord, Benjamin, they have myriad ways to treat that in 1991."

"Big fat deal," he said, surprising her. "We're in 1774."

"You don't have to remind me," she responded curtly.

They were both quiet for a half-mile or so.

"Laura tells me you're marrying Patricia Smithson soon," she heard herself say, both startled by and angry with herself. Well, why not say it? They were supposed to be friends, weren't they?

His expression didn't change. "Aunt Laura is wrong," was all he said.

"Oh? The belle turned you down, Benjamin? Amazing!" Her sarcasm disgusted her, but this information was, for sure, amazing.

"She might well have; I don't know. I didn't ask her, nor do I have intentions to do so. Ever."

"Ever?" She ignored the relief washing over her, admonishing herself to keep in mind that colonial Virginia was undoubtedly loaded with nubile maidens.

"I never intend to marry again, Meredith. My decision on that is final." His tone was frosty. She glanced at him. Face frozen, too. Was he going to become a monk or something?

She changed the subject to a topic far more important—one she'd waited nearly a month for an opportunity to bring up with him. Well, the time had come. Tardy, she knew, but that hadn't been her fault, and she was tired of wrestling with this dilemma all alone. It was, in reality, *his* problem.

"Someone at Fox Haven tried to poison Abraham a few weeks ago," she blurted out, suddenly anxious and well aware that they only had a mile or so of privacy ahead of them.

He pulled his horse to a stop. "What are you saying?" he asked.

She halted also, turning her horse to face him. She told him everything she knew on the subject—Abraham's illness, her suspicions about the black pudding, her unwise testing of it herself, the ants . . . and that she had no idea who'd done it.

"Bloody hell," he groaned more than said when she'd finished.

"My sentiments exactly, Benjamin. I've watched, I've searched, I've tried, God knows, to find a clue. But it's all been a dead end. Whoever did this hates Fox Haven and the Foxworths.

I truly believe it's the same person responsible for your so-called curse—possibly every terrible tragedy you've had! Who inside your home is full of such hatred, Benjamin?"

He shook his head. She'd stunned him, she could tell. Upset him even more than she'd feared. But his response wasn't reassuring.

"These times are harder than yours, Meredith. We have no pills, no magic machines to perceive and heal such as you're accustomed to. Death and illness are constant visitors to our homes. While you're here with us, you must understand that truth."

He didn't believe her! "But the pudding, Benjamin—the dead ants!" she protested, spluttering. She was desperate. "Can't you see?"

His eyes seared into her, so deeply she lost her breath. She'd let her defenses down, forgotten their power over her.

"Your words about the black pudding indeed give me concern," he said. "Please continue your surveillance—and please, for God's sake, see that Father doesn't begin eating the foul concoction again. I also shall be watchful and wary. Should your suspicions be correct—about the poisoning, at least—the culprit must be found."

She grasped the reins. Was that enough? Shouldn't he say something about their cooperating in this venture? *Talking* with each other about it, if nothing else? Were they to continue months on end without matching notes, ideas, discoveries—if any?

He continued, answering her unasked questions. "From time to time, we must find private moments to discuss any clues that either of us might come upon. I suggest we resume taking

our before-supper claret together in the parlor—
provided, of course, you have no objections."

She nodded her agreement, saying nothing further, and they started back toward Fox Haven.

Thank heaven. Her shoulders felt as if a ton had
been lifted from them. No longer would she have
to struggle alone to solve this terrifying mystery.
Lord, she hadn't realized how the weight of that
burden had nearly done her in.

But she hadn't realized, either, how difficult
it would be to sit across from Benjamin in the
parlor for an interminable half-hour night after
night. She drank too much claret every time and
inevitably went in to supper half looped. Neither
of them ever had much to say—and absolutely
nothing to report. Fox Haven appeared to be in
a state of peace. Everyone remained healthy, and
the household ran smoothly and on schedule.

No bumps in the night; no eerie cackles from the
attic; not even an evil glint in one shifty eye could
be discerned. No ripple of anything disturbed the
plantation's placid surface. Indeed, all seemed not
only quiet but downright copacetic.

But not with Meredith. Though she, too, kept
a placid surface, she was a roiling mess inside.
Especially during these before-supper sessions
with Benjamin.

"Father hasn't begun demanding his black
pudding, I trust," he said to her one evening
in late September.

"No. I've convinced him he looks younger without it. Just between you and me, I think he always
despised the stuff."

Benjamin refilled her glass. She was determined
to sip the wine slowly—she had enough problems

without becoming a lush. Maybe she should suggest they switch to lemonade if they kept having these futile meetings.

"The kitchen staff continues content, do you believe?" he asked.

"Perfectly."

"I've visited them in their quarters off and on, and held conversations with them all and with their families. None of them demonstrate any signs of resentment or animosity—quite the contrary, I'd say."

"I know."

She also knew that Benjamin was growing more certain by the hour that she'd overreacted in the pudding episode. Sometimes she wondered if he might be right. But there had been that ghost business, too. And all those awful tragedies of the past—though Benjamin seemed adamantly opposed to making any connection between those events and the "current dilemma," as he called it.

"Aunt Laura tells me you go to Scotchtown one afternoon a week," he said. They'd already exhausted the subject at hand, she figured. "You don't ride alone, I trust."

"Will rides with me."

"How is Sallie?"

"Not well. I sit with her an hour or so to give the family and servants a respite, but can do little else for them. They use the heat wraps now to reduce her manic periods."

"Is she ever lucid?"

Meredith shook her head. "She says nothing while I'm there, and they tell me she hasn't spoken in more than a month. It's one of the saddest things I've ever seen, Benjamin. Her eyes are clear and beautiful, but vacant of all life. It's as though her very soul as well as her mind has been locked away from the rest of us." She wiped away the tears—they always came when she thought about Sallie Henry.

He was looking at her strangely. She averted her eyes and took a big gulp of claret.

"I appreciate your going there, Meredith. Representing us, so to speak. The harvesting has required my full attention, but I did promise Patrick I'd drop in on them occasionally."

"They're all fine—particularly the tribe of children. Annie misses William, but he writes her often and he appears to be under no threat of danger currently. Patrick writes less often, but of course you and I know he'll do just dandy up there." She'd told Benjamin all she could remember about the First Continental Congress—that last night he'd come to her bed. That final night . . .

She finished off her claret.

"And your little school? Are your students progressing satisfactorily in their lessons?" he asked, offering her more wine, which she refused.

Meredith smiled—here was a subject she could really warm up to. "It's amazing—I don't know much about teaching the three R's, but those kids soak up whatever I give them as fast as I can dish it out. They're all bright—but Betsy, I'll have you know, is the brightest of them all."

His proud-papa smile nearly made her lose her cool. As usual, it was those damnable dimples.

"Uh, I believe you'll have to hire a tutor for all of them soon," she continued, hanging on to what composure she had left. "They'll be beyond their teacher in short order."

Lucy interrupted them to say that supper was on the table. Laura never came into the parlor when Benjamin and Meredith were there together these days, not even to announce supper. Meredith hadn't noticed the change until this evening. She filed away that little piece of information in her slightly wine-clouded head. Maybe she should mention it to Benjamin tomorrow night.

# Chapter Nineteen

But she didn't. The business about Laura's changed supper-announcing pattern completely slipped her mind. After all, her observation was hardly noteworthy, as she'd told herself (upon more sober reflection) on the very night she'd made it.

Then, too, she was busy as all get-out. With her care-taking responsibilities with Philip and Betsy, her continuing therapy with Betsy, her constant nagging of Abraham to do his exercises, her regular chores assigned by Laura, her weekly visits to Scotchtown, and her daily two-hour school sessions with the plantation's children, she had little time for anything else.

Including futile longings for Benjamin.

And her worries about some imminent danger to Fox Haven lessened with each passing day.

The whole plantation seemed to purr like a contented kitten. Though Meredith was far from purring, she was lulled into a kind of peaceful acceptance. She'd been a bit paranoid earlier, she decided at last, and felt somewhat silly.

Certainly, she never had anything new to report about her poisoning theory during her "private moments" with Benjamin before supper in the parlor, and he didn't either. So they talked about other things—mostly small talk, she'd categorize it. And she wondered, after a while, why he even continued the sessions. They'd become part of his routine, she gathered. She couldn't think of any other reason. Good grief, all they did was sit like a couple of stumps at least ten feet from each other chatting about this and that.

But she wasn't about to suggest they stop the meetings. Benjamin was the only one she could be herself with, and she needed his friendship, limited as it was.

Of course she kept eye contact to a minimum, and a twenty-foot distance might have made her more comfortable.

In mid-October, he surprised her by announcing he would take the whole family—"including you, of course"—to Newcastle for the County Fair.

She was ready for a break in the daily routine, and she accepted with enthusiasm.

Betsy was ecstatic and Abraham was "agreeable," though he fussed when she told him he'd have to carry his cane.

Laura begged off, saying she was "behind in registering my accounts." That seemed hard to believe, but no one pressed her, so they left her to spend the couple of days alone. Meredith figured that Laura would welcome the solitude, for a change.

They departed early on a perfect Indian-summer morning with the dew still glistening on the brilliant reds and golds of the fall foliage. Collars of wispy haze floated about the dark trunks of the tallest trees; the air was redolent with the autumn aromas of apples and crisping leaves.

Will drove the large two-horse coach, brought out only for the most special occasions, Meredith supposed, since she'd never seen it in action before. With him rode Abraham, Betsy, Lucy, Sukie, old Robert, Jack, and little Philip. Philip, on Sukie's lap, was sitting up now—his round turquoise eyes full of wonder, all four of his tiny white teeth shining wetly when he smiled.

Which he did a lot. He loved the bouncing coach.

Benjamin and Meredith rode on either side of the carriage on separate horses. Their pace would be slow, so she rode sidesaddle, properly attired in brown muslin dress, white apron, and a frilly white cap placed ladylike atop her head. No reason to try to buck the system this time, she decided. Besides, pants on a lady were out of the question for the 1774 Hanover County Fair. And there'd be no costume-changing opportunities today.

Memories of her earlier trip to Newcastle kept surfacing, but she shoved them back where they belonged—under completed business.

Or tried to.

It took them nearly three hours to get there. No more than fifteen miles, she guessed, but they went at a leisurely rate. They had to, what with the rutty road and frequent "rest" stops. Spirits remained high, however—particularly in the carriage.

Meredith's mood wasn't lofty, but she was determined to enjoy the rare outing.

Benjamin's attitude was hard for her to gauge one way or the other. He seemed stuck on dour. Like every other day.

Sally and Tom Morris were meeting them at the fair site, and the Fox Haven entourage would be staying overnight with the young couple. Meredith looked forward to seeing the pair again. She loved "happy endings," and even sharing vicarious ones was better than having none at all.

When they arrived at the open field where the fair was already in full swing, Meredith blinked in astonishment. So many people! After seven months, she'd nearly forgotten what a crowd looked like. And, of course, never had she seen anything resembling the scene before her.

The parking lot was nearly full, she noted with amusement as she and Benjamin tethered their horses to a tree on the periphery of the pandemonium. Will brought the carriage to a halt nearby. Around them stood a wide variety of conveyances and animals—from rickety two-wheeled carts to grand coaches, from sway-backed mules to handsome steeds. The crowd, she saw, would be a mixed social bag of hard-scrabble farmers and the plantation gentry.

Democracy in action. She smiled.

Benjamin lifted Betsy up to ride on his broad shoulders. The fair-haired girl was aglow with excitement, her cheeks as rosy as her pretty muslin dress.

After reaching back in the carriage for

Abraham's cane and placing it firmly into his hand, ignoring his grumbles, Meredith hoisted Philip into her arms and ran forward to walk with Benjamin and Betsy.

"You have new shoes, I see," she heard him say to his daughter as she came up alongside them.

Meredith had hoped they'd remain a secret a while longer, but she'd known he'd be bound to see them eventually. She kept quiet.

"Merrie had them made for me—aren't they beautiful?" Betsy said, holding out her feet proudly from her perch on his shoulders. The buff shoes sported rose-colored laces to match her frock, only the left one had a leather strip attached to the eyelet at the base of her big toe, running at a diagonal up the leg and attached to the felt cuff below her knee.

"Indeed they are," he said, patting both shoes and fluffing the girl's skirt down to a more proper length. He'd thrown Meredith a questioning look in the process.

She stared straight ahead.

"The shoes are castles for the sleeping princesses," Betsy continued brightly. "More lie asleep in the left one, so we've built stronger ramparts for that castle."

Uncomfortably aware that her cheeks were flushing, Meredith shifted plump Philip's weight in her arms. He babbled merrily and drooled profusely.

Benjamin said nothing further about the shoes, and almost immediately the four of them were swept up into the rowdy confusion of the County Fair.

A twenty-ring circus, she decided. Something for everyone—though some of the pursuits, she quickly determined, were better observed than participated in. The greased pig chase, for example, which was causing great hilarity and a chorus of squeals in a far corner of the field.

Some events she preferred not even to observe—like the bloody cockfight she came close to investigating, attracted by the noisy ring of excited people. When she realized what held their attention, she turned away, wrinkling her nose in disgust.

"A vile activity not approved of by many even back here in these unenlightened times," Benjamin muttered to her under his breath.

Had she detected a hint of mockery in his tone? Enough, she judged, to warrant a snappy comeback. "But practiced with gusto all the same, that's apparent," she retorted.

"We've given up gladiators and feeding Christians to lions," he said.

"Well, bully for you!" she sniffed, unable to resist a small smile. If he reciprocated the smile, she wasn't about to look up at him to check.

They paused and looked around for their stragglers and found them happily occupied. Abraham had met a jolly group of old acquaintances and was deeply involved in a horseshoes-like game called quoits. His cane was hanging from a maple limb. Lucy, Sukie, Jack, and Will had joined a merry circle of servants dancing and clapping to the frenzied rhythms of three fiddlers. Old Robert, in the company of an equally stooped black man, had retired to the shade of a flaming chestnut tree and a game of checkers.

That left Meredith and Benjamin, with the delighted children, to explore on their own. The going was slow, because Benjamin seemed to know everybody in Virginia—and she was convinced the whole colony was here.

Hanover's October horse race was a popular one, she'd heard. It was scheduled for this afternoon, and Benjamin had entered his Midnight. Jack, who was light as a jockey, would ride him.

Meredith was introduced to so many people she lost track of their names, though Randolph, Carter, Lee, and Byrd rang bells in her head. She curtsied till her knees hurt.

A thoroughly nauseating number of peaches-and-cream maidens fluttered their eyelashes at Benjamin while he made the requisite introductions of Fox Haven's "governess." Philip spit up on the frothy pink dress of one ravishing brunette who insisted on holding him—to demonstrate her maternal instincts to Benjamin, Meredith figured sourly. Philip's reaction had been perfect, she thought gleefully as she accepted him back with an apologetic smile.

They watched the livestock and poultry judging, and she, Benjamin, and Betsy applauded the winning hog—all 1,500 pounds of him. Philip had fallen asleep in her arms by that time.

"Look, Father!" Betsy squealed, pointing to a sheet strung up between two oaks off to the side of the field. A large tent stood behind. "That sign says 'SEE' and 'FIRE.' What does the rest of it say?"

Benjamin congratulated her on her progress in reading, then read off the long, convoluted side-show sign.

"See the magic fire device that ignites with but a single motion! This phenomenon, brought to you at great expense from the fabled country of France, will amaze and delight one and all.

301

Demonstrations every hour, provided a group of at least 50 men, women and children are gathered inside. Entrance fee—25 shillings per head. Full refund shall be presented should performance be canceled or fail to enchant. The fabulous Doctor Le Feu from Paris demonstrates and provides illuminating lecture."

"Can we see it, please, Father?" the girl asked excitedly.

"Betsy, twenty-five shillings is rather dear," Meredith interjected. Good grief, one entry ticket would buy twenty pounds of sugar—or her services for a blasted week!

Benjamin pulled out his watch. "I believe we can manage the extravagance this once, Meredith," he said, then looked up with a warm smile at his daughter. "Aye, love, we'll come back for the next demonstration at noon—we have about forty minutes to wait."

Meredith shrugged. She'd been overridden. They'd go in and see a primitive kitchen match of some kind, she supposed.

"I've spotted Sally and Tom at last, I vow," Benjamin said, nodding toward a grove of trees in the distance.

As they turned to head in that direction, a scarecrow of a woman dressed in what looked like burlap sacking ran up to them. " 'Tis *you*," she said to Meredith, her bony finger pointing straight at her nose, her narrowed milky-blue eyes impaling her.

Meredith, startled, jumped back and leaned against Benjamin for support.

"Be gone with you, Mad Millie," Benjamin said with a kindness that further astonished Meredith. "Here, woman, good health to you." His arm reached around Meredith and she heard the sound of coins clinking into the woman's pocket. That he placed both of his hands on Meredith's shoulders to steady her could have been considered a touch of comfort.

But the woman's eyes held her captive, and she felt strangely alone.

Mad Millie shook her head, and her long strings of dull, gray-black hair rattled like dried weeds.

"I must talk with thee, winged sparrow from another world. My stone hath spoken, and you must hear its message for thee."

Meredith trembled. Benjamin's hands pressed tighter. Betsy giggled. "Have no fear, Merrie. Mad Millie is harmless—she's only a pretend witch."

Meredith wasn't sure. She looked like the genuine article to her, and she'd already pegged Meredith as being "from another world." She backed further against Benjamin, holding Philip close.

"Listen well," the woman said, never releasing Meredith's eyes. "You are a child of destiny, here for a purpose. The stone says you must make certain the tall man in mourner's black is at the church on the hill. Only then, winged sparrow, shall you be released to be where you truly belong. Only then . . ."

She ended with a cackle of laughter. Meredith wasn't amused. She was paralyzed with terror.

Benjamin's hands gripped her stiff shoulders firmly, but they'd grown suddenly cold as ice.

"She heard your message, Millie," he said in a husky whisper.

She'd heard it all right—it was etched deep into

**303**

the hard granite her brain had become. But she didn't understand a word of it.

"I wish thee well," said the witch with a nod of her head as she backed away from them. Meredith saw a flash, like lightning, leap from the woman's strange milky eyes before she turned and disappeared in a throng of people.

"Good grief," Meredith said with a gasp.

"Betsy spoke with wisdom, Meredith. She's but a pretend witch," Benjamin said, releasing her shoulders and patting her arms with reassuring gentleness.

"Of course," she said, swallowing hard. And breathing for the first time since the woman had appeared. Not good, deep breaths. Shallow, rather tremulous ones.

Mad Millie's eerie words had nipped at the edge of Meredith's earlier enchantment with the County Fair. The mingled aromas of sizzling sausages, barbecue smoke, livestock, and human sweat she'd found rather charming before. Now they bit sharply at her nose. The fiddles, singing, and cheerful voices had become strident noises; the merry hordes of people, oppressive.

Seeing Sally and Tom helped to push down her uneasiness. Sally had ballooned into full pregnancy, and to Meredith she looked like a beautiful, contented saint. She gave her a hearty hug after depositing the sleeping Philip in Benjamin's arms.

Tom reached up for radiant Betsy and swung her around a couple of times with youthful exuberance before settling her carefully on the ground beneath the sycamore. The light falling on the smiling faces around Meredith was as golden as the leaves above.

She was conscious of shadows, though—dark, chilling ones inside her. The witch's prophesy had unnerved her. *"Only then shall you be released to be where you truly belong,"* she'd said. So she was to return to the twentieth century after all? Provided, that is, that she got some man to the church on time—or something to that effect.

Pure garbage, of course. Then why on earth couldn't she forget it?

Benjamin was looking at her. Shadows appeared to have deepened his expression, invaded his eyes. But that was possibly caused by shading from the sycamore's leaves.

"I promised Betsy we'd visit the 'amazing fire demonstration.' Would you two like to join us?" he asked Sally and Tom.

They demurred, saying they'd already seen it and had found it "truly amazing" and worth every shilling.

"I'll hold Philip while you're in there, Meredith," Sally offered with a smile, reaching up toward Benjamin for the baby. "I'm sore in need of practice."

"His wrappings will need changing should he awaken," Meredith told her as she placed the small bag of baby supplies on the ground beside Sally. "That'll provide you some *advanced* experience."

With Betsy astride Benjamin's shoulders, the three of them headed for the sideshow tent.

As she'd predicted, the "fire device" was indeed a primitive match. The buildup and extravagant showmanship of Dr. Le Feu had the audience's anticipation level somewhere beyond the ozone.

Even she got caught up in the excitement—until he brought out the "miracle invention for one and all to see." Then she felt mostly smug amusement. It was a small envelope of rough paper, coated with phosphorus, according to the "doctor's" lecture. Splinters of sulfur-tipped wood would be drawn through the envelope's fold.

And *voilà!* An instant tiny flame!

"Zuitable for lighting ze pipe, ze candle, ze hearth's logs," enthused Dr. Le Feu in his studied accent.

He held up the burning envelope with small metal tongs like a victory torch. The audience ooohed with wonder, then applauded and cheered.

Meredith stared at the flame, gripped with a strange sense of *déjà vu*. It spread, grew white, then disappeared in a small shower of silent sparks.

Had it been lit in fog instead of the diffused sunlight of the crowded tent, it would have looked for all the world like . . .

Dear God, the Fox Haven ghost?

Despite peculiar prophesies and matches that turned into pseudo-ghosts, Meredith found herself shaking off the gloomy foreboding that had threatened to ruin her day.

Who could remain down amid such gaiety and excitement? The Fox Haven group gathered with Sally and Tom to watch the afternoon horse races. Jack, unfortunately, had consumed an unwise quantity of rum and was in no condition to ride Midnight.

Benjamin seemed more amused than vexed. He'd ride himself, he said good-naturedly, but advised his father not to place any wagers on Midnight—"what with the added weight, the steed is likely to finish last."

Abraham didn't listen, of course. Meredith saw him put a hefty bet of ten pounds on his son's horse.

Benjamin won by two lengths. Watching his splendid form, low over the sleek animal as if the two were melded into one ultrasmooth machine of speed, Meredith was overwhelmed with a surge of something perilously close to ecstasy.

Was he perfect at *everything*?

She sobered a moment as the crowd about her cheered the champion. Yes, he was indeed perfect.

She joined in the cheering, as gleeful as the next person. But her whole heart wasn't in it. Part of it ached with longing for what could never be— the tall, dark, glorious champion of Hanover, who would never be hers.

Fireworks lit the early autumn darkness as a fitting closing salute to the colorful day. It was a relatively pitiful fireworks display as far as Meredith was concerned—reverse rockets riding on ropes strung between trees, designed to climb but often getting stuck midway and exploding too early; a ground setup of revolving stars that didn't revolve and only distantly resembled stars; a sudden volley of noise, flame, and smoke when a too-eager assistant lit a whole pile of pyrotechnics at once, nearly setting himself and the whole forest ablaze.

But Betsy's bright eyes of wonder were worth the price of admission. Meredith held her close, deciding that beauty was in the eye of the beholder. She stopped making comparisons between this and the Fourth of July celebrations she'd seen and settled back to enjoy the magic of pre-Revolutionary fireworks.

As the Fox Haven group headed for their carriage, Benjamin came up beside Meredith. Betsy, with the smile of a blessed angel on her peaceful face, was asleep in his arms.

"Will you be able to help her walk?" he asked in a low voice so that none of the others would hear.

Meredith bit her lip. "I truly don't know. There's been some progress, but it depends on the extent of nerve damage . . ."

She met his eyes, and wished she hadn't. They always muddled her brain. But she'd seen the unspoken hope there. "I'll do all I can, Benjamin. She mustn't know what I'm aiming for—I couldn't bear it if she had high expectations and I should fail her."

Nor could she bear to dash *his* hopes, but she left that unsaid.

"I thank you for trying, Meredith," he said softly and looked away.

# Chapter Twenty

Nothing was quite the same after their return to Fox Haven. Meredith tried to put her finger on what caused the difference and could only come to the conclusion that the change was inside her and nowhere else. Quite simply, she was tired of being an outsider, permanently resigned to a secondary role. She was tired of observing from the wings rather than being in the middle of the action where she could have some influence.

She liked to be *in charge*, blast it! Well, maybe not in charge of everything; that hadn't been in the realm of possibility even back in 1991. But she desperately missed feeling that she had a modicum of control over her immediate surroundings. That was the big rub here—having to march most of the time to others' drumbeats. Lord, if it weren't for Betsy, Abraham, and her "students" in the schoolroom, she'd truly be in the doldrums. At least with them she had a purpose and could be of some use.

Winter had settled in, so schedules and activities had altered somewhat. Benjamin was freed from the fields now, but he remained absent from the house as many hours as before. "Winter's chores require time and attention," he'd explained at supper one night. So she figured he spent his days repairing fences, sheds, and whatnot. And he'd done a dandy job of designing an extension to her little schoolhouse and supervising the crew of men who'd finished and furnished it in two short days.

He traveled about Hanover often, too. "To keep current on political matters," he'd told her. She tried not to think he might be visiting one or more of the county's many comely and hot-to-trot damsels. She didn't believe that silliness he'd said about never marrying again. Highly unlikely, considering the pool of choices out there available to him. And highly unnatural, too, considering his overcharged libido. But she tried not to think about that, either.

She'd have to give him credit—he did return from his journeys well-versed in the turbulent political events of the day and frequently told the family the latest news at the supper table.

"Patrick's enrolled a number of young men into a volunteer company of militia prepared for any and every emergency," he told them one night in mid-November. "He met with them at Smith's Tavern last week and fired them up with a spirited speech that had them shouting to the rafters, so I hear—ready to defend their rights. In their hunting shirts and armed with tomahawks and short carbines, they're prepared to fight the mighty British army if need be. And they'll succeed, I wager."

Meredith nodded. She knew that the Hanover Volunteers would be the first Virginia independent military group to be enlisted after the next Continental Congress.

"Success appears highly improbable against Great Britain's fleets and armies, considering this bare, infant country's woeful lack of ammunition, arms, warships, or the wherewithal to purchase them," Abraham scoffed, playing the role of doubting Thomas tonight.

"Ah, but Patrick has a response to that very argument," Benjamin said. "Last evening I attended a meeting of neighbors over at Plain Dealing, Samuel Overton's home. Similar questions were raised to Patrick, and he's firm in the belief that other countries like France, and maybe Holland and Spain, will come to our relief."

Her own relief at the moment was that he'd been at Colonel Overton's home last evening. She'd fretted the night away wondering where in blazes he'd gone.

Samuel Overton wasn't blessed with any marriageable daughters.

Riding back from Scotchtown with Will the following afternoon, Meredith thought over the short conversation she'd just had with Patrick Henry. He'd approached her after she'd left his wife's side and was preparing to leave.

"May I speak a few moments with you, Miss Davis?" he'd asked.

Naturally, she'd agreed and followed him into his small office. Primarily, he'd wished to express his gratitude for her "kind services to my family in this time of distress." And then he'd surprised her by praising her advice to him before he'd left for Philadelphia. "By God, you were right," he'd exclaimed. "Without the two Adams gentlemen, I truly doubt we would have accomplished anything of worth—and Mr. Galloway came close to dismantling it all before we'd adjourned."

She could only smile, not sure what, if anything, she should say in response.

He'd shaken his head. "Our declaration of rights, lists of grievances, and mighty resolves will all come to naught—they'll be received like waste paper in England, mark my words. In the end, we must fight."

"Of course," she'd agreed.

His fiery blue eyes studied her. "You, a woman of intelligence, can see what few if any of my fellow Virginia delegates will acknowledge. All save Colonel Washington and I returned home complacently assured that our points would carry and that Britain 'will give up her foolish project,' as Richard Henry Lee said upon our departure. Washington himself harbors hope that the non-exportation resolve, if nothing else, will force them to yield to us."

His hands had gripped the sides of his chair. "I have no such hopes," he'd said with more fervor than sadness.

"And you, after all is said and done, will be exactly right," she'd assured him before she could stop herself.

Now, astride the gray horse riding beside silent Will, Meredith pulled the wool cloak closer around her. The air was cold and smelled of snow. She frowned. Dear God, was she doomed to stay forever in what could only be for her a halfway world where she was so . . . so *disconnected*?

She could watch from the sidelines, offer a careful word or two of advice now and then, but she could never be an integral part of this world. It was like being a full-time tourist, for heaven's sake. She hadn't yet—could never—become a native. She didn't belong here.

The distant memory of a witch's words slid into her mind. *Only then shall you be released to be where you truly belong. Only then . . .*

Was there hope for her? A flake of snow landed on her nose and she quickly pulled the cloak's hood over her head.

*In the spring that will be like winter . . .*

Well, not until spring, she guessed, simultaneously kicking herself mentally for taking any stock at all in Mad Millie's prophesy.

But why not? Good, she thought, straightening her shoulders. By spring there'd be a tutor to replace her in the schoolhouse. And by spring Betsy could well be running through the flowers. The girl had come amazingly far and would, Meredith hoped, be walking unassisted by Christmas. If all went according to plan, that would be Benjamin's Christmas present from her and Betsy.

And by spring, no one here would need her any longer. All she had to do was find a tall man in mourning clothes who should go to a church on a hill somewhere, and she'd be returned at last to her own time.

She sighed. In the long run, that was the only place she figured she might truly belong.

When she arrived at Fox Haven, the house was abuzz with the happy news. Sally had given birth to a fine baby boy the day before. His name, according to the message, was Davis Foxworth Morris.

*Davis!* Sally had honored her in this special way? Meredith was touched, and deeply pleased.

"The babe, it appears, has come unduly early," Laura Preston said to her with a heaviness that gave Meredith pause. "I do pray it will survive."

"But the message states he's weighty and strong," Meredith protested. She decided quickly not to pursue the obvious—the babe was full term. Laura, perhaps, would prefer it be thought of as premature. No matter. Her own elevated spirits would need more than Laura's misguided propriety to be deflated.

"Mr. Benjamin awaits you in the parlor, Miz Meredith," Lucy announced as she entered the pantry.

Laura Preston twirled away from her, her bulky skirts creating a cold wind that brushed across Meredith's slippers. "I must see how the supper is progressing," the woman said brusquely as she headed toward the kitchen.

Meredith's brows pulled together. Something was bugging Laura this evening. What, for heaven's sake? Tonight, for once, Fox Haven had a reason to celebrate.

"You've heard our happy news, I trust," she said to Benjamin as she entered the parlor for their routine half-hour of claret and empty chatter.

"Aye," he responded with a far wider smile than was his habit. He stood until she was seated, then took his customary chair ten feet away. "The chosen name pleased you, I vow?"

"I'm truly honored," she said, folding her hands primly on her lap. "It provides me . . . Lord, I don't know how to say it, Benjamin . . . but it gives me a *connection* here—with this time, this family. It means a lot to me."

"Claret?" he asked as usual.

"Let's have rum tonight," she said impulsively. "I'm in the mood to celebrate."

"Would you prefer champagne?"

"*Champagne?* Do you really have champagne?" she nearly squealed. "That doesn't sound at all colonial to me, somehow. Back home we assumed you folks mostly imbibed quaint drinks like syllabub."

He chuckled. "Not only do we have it, but I've iced a bottle for this special occasion. 'Snowed,' perchance, would be a more appropriate term, since that's what I used."

Meredith laughed, then watched the moist, heavy snowflakes outside pelt the dark window while he went about opening the champagne. A cheerful image of the room's fire danced upon the night-blackened panes.

She heard the soft explosion as the cork popped, but purposely kept her eyes averted from him as long as possible. Looking at Benjamin still made her insides all squishy. It did seem that by now she'd be over such adolescent non—

"I believe a toast is in order," he said, handing her a tall fluted glass.

She stood with a soft smile, facing him. The brass buttons on his charcoal gray waistcoat had an eagle design. She concentrated on eagles.

He spoke. "To Davis Foxworth Morris—may his days be long and fruitful."

She nodded and lifted her glass to his. Their fingers brushed—the sensation, for Meredith, bearing the wallop of a full magnum of champagne. She withdrew quickly

315

and took a sip. The bubbles kissed her nose.

They returned to their seats. Ten blessed feet apart, thank heaven. Now she could breathe—and speak normally, she hoped.

"Laura seems disturbed this evening, Benjamin. I suspect she doesn't approve of Sally's baby having such an early birthday."

He didn't smile. "Aunt Laura has little understanding of earthly desires—believes we all should strive for sainthood as she does."

"Oh?" Why did that surprise her? Lord, she'd seen Laura poring over her Bible often enough. She knew that the woman was rigid and prudish and had a self-righteous streak. No, it wasn't *what* he'd said, but the way he'd said it.

Benjamin's voice had been filled with bitterness. Going against her own rules, Meredith studied his face intently. Oh my, definitely bitter. And now, under her scrutiny, he looked uncomfortable as the dickens. He cleared his throat and stiffened up in his chair.

And suddenly she knew. Or thought she knew. Was it possible that Laura had raked him over the coals because of *her*? Had that been the reason he . . .

Nonsense. He'd simply grown tired of her. But he had said *"for the sanctity of this home"* on that terrible morning. *Sanctity?* That didn't even sound like him.

She dropped her eyelids, sipped her champagne, frowned at the busy flowers on the navy blue carpet that lay between them.

And waited for him to say something.

But he didn't, so she spoke up at last. She might as well get to the bottom of this, but she'd venture cautiously.

"Laura's always treated me extremely well, Benjamin. Not warmly, to be sure, but then warmth isn't one of her strong points."

"I've watched for signs of friction between you two and gratefully have observed none. I'm relieved you've verified my observations."

"Friction?" she asked, determined to follow this troublesome avenue until she got an answer one way or the other. "Why on earth would you expect friction between us?"

He pushed back that beautifully stubborn wave. "The usual reason, I suppose—two women beneath the same roof—that sort of thing." The final part of his statement came slightly swallowed.

She looked at him, puzzled.

"Laura and I are hardly on equal footing under this roof, Benjamin. She's chatelaine of Fox Haven, I'm but a hired hand."

His jaw tightened and that one highly mobile eyebrow shot up toward the plaster-medallioned ceiling.

"Do you consider yourself but a hired hand here, Meredith?"

"Why, of course," she said, expelling a light chuckle. "Good grief, that's what I am, after all."

He closed his eyes for a moment, then let out a ragged kind of sigh. "Hired hands seldom have children in the family named for them—that alone should convince you we consider you more than . . . more than that."

His hesitancy was unlike him. And his kind words made a funny little thrill run up her backbone. But what did "we" consider her then?

Wait a minute. They were straying from the subject.

"Back to Laura, Benjamin. She'd have us all strive for sainthood, do you think?" She'd made it light, purely conversational. But she'd made a direct hit, she could tell. He put down his glass and rubbed his hands together.

"She believes in hellfire and damnation and a God who punishes with vengeance those who trespass against his Commandments."

"Well, I'll be damned," she said with a low gasp.

Her exclamation hung in the air, and so did her gasp. Good God, Laura *was* the reason Benjamin had dumped her! She'd learned somehow about his visits to her room and had given him hell. So, couldn't he at least have leveled with her on that morning instead of handing out all that sanctimonious nonsense? Making her feel like dirt or worse—and miserably unwanted?

Benjamin's distraught eyes searching hers left no doubt—he knew that she now understood exactly what had happened.

"Thank God she hasn't preached to you," he said, only a shade above a whisper.

She shook her head. "But she has to you, I gather."

He nodded but once. "Aye, she did."

Meredith made a face. "And you believed her? That vengeance stuff, I mean."

"No."

"They why did you let her influence you, Benjamin?"

He stood, walked to the fireplace, and grasped the mantel. "To spare you. She'd have persisted, Meredith—would've started ranting and railing at you next. You would have had no peace. I couldn't bear having you subjected to her tirades."

He'd been *protecting* her? He'd put her through the torment of these past months in order to protect her? From what? *Tirades?*

Hogwash. He'd been protecting that all-fired-so-important peace of his home! That's all he cared about.

She was ready to chew nails.

"Why on earth didn't you tell me what was going on?" she asked, edging her words with acid.

"I deemed it better for your peace of mind that you didn't know of Aunt Laura's displeasure with—"

"My peace of mind?" she snapped, jumping to her feet. "Ignorance is bliss, I suppose you believe, Mr. Know-It-All. Good grief! Didn't it once occur to you that *I* should have known we'd been found out? Where in heaven's name is your brain?"

She'd kept her voice low, but she'd managed to give her outburst the same devastating force as a resounding shout. And she'd jolted him, too. His widened eyes held equal quantities of shock and confusion. Both only added to her anger. Lord, she would never understand the workings of a colonial mind—*this* colonial mind, in particular.

"Benjamin, you kept me in the dark, blast it all. Can you possibly believe I was better off working in this house day after day stupidly ignorant that Laura considers me a sinful scarlet woman? How do you think I could have defended myself if she'd lit into me? You fed me to the wolves, damn you!"

"But she didn't—"

"Big fat deal! What's the difference? You should have prepared me, don't you see that?"

She couldn't tell if he saw it or not. She'd turned away from him and plopped down on her

319

chair with an exasperated huff. But this time, by God, she wouldn't cry. Though she wanted to—mightily.

"I never considered that side of it, Meredith. I'd wanted only to ensure your peace—"

"The peace of Fox Haven, Benjamin," she interjected coldly. "That's your number-one priority. And it appears this time you achieved it—though you sure trampled on me in the process."

"That's an unfair judgment," he said, beginning to sound a bit irritated himself.

Excellent. She was ready for a battle royal.

Only she didn't get it. He walked back to his chair and sat quietly. Crumpled, actually, though even a crumpled Benjamin still held the sturdy elegance that a top-grade military officer would die for.

"I made an error, I see that now," he admitted with a heavy sigh. "I apologize."

She blinked, and her anger dissolved. Something had to replace it to keep her glued together. In the absence of anything better, she held to the sides of the chair.

"The peace of Fox Haven is indeed important to me," he said. "My responsibilities and sense of duty have ever been clearly directed toward that goal. But my motivations have a far greater depth than you suggest, Meredith."

He paused. She waited. "The many inhabitants of this plantation are all, in varying degrees, dependent upon me," he continued, his voice low, but steady and firm. "My greatest responsibility, my strongest duty—my driving force, if you will—is to strive to achieve for each of them an opportunity to live as happily as possible."

"A noble undertaking," she said without sarcasm. "But a heavy load for one man, I'd say, considering you must deal with such a disparate population."

He nodded. "Oft times I must weigh my actions and decisions and can accomplish perhaps only an inadequate balance." His earnest, troubled gaze penetrated clear through her. She was incapable of releasing herself—she could only listen.

"In this particular matter," he continued, "I knew that only my ceasing to visit your chamber would placate Aunt Laura; and knowing her deeply ingrained penchant for maintaining stability within the home, I was convinced she'd never confront you on the subject. From what you've told me this evening, I assume my conviction was correct."

Still fastened to his gaze, she shook her head. "She never said one word to me, nor gave me even the tiniest hint that she considered me . . . despicable and sinful."

She lowered her eyes. Good grief, Laura was quite an actress! That realization gave Meredith a peculiar sense of unease.

"My intent, believe me, Meredith, was but to free you from the discomfort she might well have heaped upon you. But I see now to my chagrin that by not informing you I indeed left you woefully unprepared and possibly perplexed."

Boy, he could say that again! But she found herself doing some repeating of her own instead.

"I'll reiterate what I told you a few months ago, Benjamin. This business of assuming that only you must decide what's best for people doesn't always work—at least it sure as heck doesn't work well with me."

She pinned him with a look she knew embodied both indignation and her fervent plea. "In the future, for God's sake, treat me as if I have a sliver of a brain. From now on, I beg you to *discuss* with me matters that have relevance to me—good Lord, is that too much to ask?"

Evidently not, thank heaven. "I so pledge," he said, his deep, rich voice warming her, but giving her chill bumps, too. "I was remiss in not recalling your own strong nature, your courage, your ability to discern with wisdom. As long as we're graced with your presence here among us, I give you my heartfelt pledge to strive henceforth for complete openness with you in all matters that might concern you."

He'd imbued his words with the solemn weight of an oath, but they'd made her suddenly light, practically buoyant. Well, that was settled once and for all. Maybe. Sometime during their conversation, she'd released her grip on the chair's arm. And now she was completely relaxed, downright contented. The tension in the room had vanished without a trace—he felt it too, she could see.

Their smiles met like a warm handshake midway across the flowered carpet.

Benjamin walked over to refill her champagne glass, then returned to top his own and sat back in his chair. He stretched his legs out before him, reveling in his comforting awareness that he'd gained renewed understanding of and friendship with this woman.

Ah, he relished her company. She unbalanced him, true. But, given time enough, eventually he might comprehend what "made her tick," as she'd say. *Given time enough.* Damn, how he hated that word "time."

"You know, despite everything I feel pity for Laura," she said in quiet tones. "Life's given her a bad rap, Benjamin. She's woefully unfulfilled—that's what's made her such a prude. And Abraham really treats her badly. Sometimes I'd like to kick him in the seat of his pants."

He had to smile. He did so enjoy her fresh way with the language. "It's an old habit with him," he said. "Started back when she first moved in with us. She's accustomed to his ways with her, I vow."

"Well, I feel sorry for her, anyway. Lord, anybody could see she'd had her frilly cap set for him once—too bad he never saw beyond the 'sour' image he gave her. They might have gotten along quite well, the two of them."

Benjamin couldn't hide his astonishment. He'd never thought of such a thing—Aunt Laura and *Father*? What a ridiculous idea . . .

"What a wild picture you've conjured!" he exclaimed with a laugh. "A greater mismatch I can't imagine—besides, Father's discerning eyes for beauty would never have allowed him to consider marrying her."

He'd made a mistake, he knew immediately. Her eyes sparked like primed flintstones, and she stiffened upright in her chair. What in God's name had he done now to arouse her anger? Wary, he watched her, waiting for her outburst—for whatever it was, she was certain to tell him. But she was quiet, and her anger faded as quickly as it had come—or seemed to. Replaced by what, he wasn't sure. But he felt its coolness, its distance, as she calmly placed her glass on the table beside her, folded her hands in the lap of her brown skirt, and appeared intent on a spot of wall above his right ear.

The tenuous camaraderie they'd achieved had been torn asunder, and he regretted the loss.

"I said something to upset you, I fear, Meredith," he offered, determined to maintain his pledge of openness, and to make amends if he could.

"Why on earth would I be upset?" Now she was the one closing up like a clam.

"I don't know why—but you are, aren't you?"

"Of course not."

His right ear prickled. That spot on the wall must have a hole bored into it by now. He resisted the impulse to look behind him to see what held her attention.

*Come back*, he wanted to plead to her. Her friendship was too important to him. Though his very soul cried out for far more than friendship, that was all they could have. He'd resigned himself to that truth. But as long as this very special, beautiful woman was on this plane of time with him, he *must* have her friendship.

What was it he'd said? Something about Aunt Laura and Father being a mismatch. Was Meredith so protective of his aunt that a few foolish words about the woman's obvious lack of feminine charms would anger her, would distance her from him this way?

Odd. He'd never realized that Meredith would feel protective of Aunt Laura. Though he shouldn't be surprised, he supposed. It was Meredith's nature to be protective of everyone—to a fault, as a matter of fact, much like himself.

But Aunt Laura? She despised Meredith—had called her a "sinful woman." How well his aunt must have hidden her hatred and disgust for Meredith that she would now react thus . . .

*How well Aunt Laura must have hidden her hatred.* Benjamin tensed, and felt a cold band tighten around his chest. Possibly he groaned. Meredith leaned forward, her large silver eyes no longer holding anger or distance, but alarm.

"What's wrong, Benjamin?"

He didn't know himself. He shook his head. Before he could respond—though he had no idea what he might have said—Lucy swept into the room to announce that supper was prepared.

Benjamin and Meredith stood in unison. Befuddlement clouded her lovely face. "I believe you've just had a thought you should share with me," she mumbled out of the side of her mouth as they headed for the dining room.

"In time, perhaps," he mumbled back. " 'Tis naught of importance."

Was it? *Of course I'm wrong. Such a thought is impossible!*

# Chapter Twenty-One

Laura Preston attended a church meeting at a neighboring plantation a couple of weeks before Christmas—and got snowbound. Her half-day trip turned into a three-day absence from Fox Haven.

"She'll probably never venture anywhere again after this," Abraham said with a wicked chuckle on the first night of the blizzard. "She'll be as sour as an unripe persimmon by the time she returns."

"I didn't know she ever ventured anywhere— she hasn't since I've been here," Meredith said, passing the basket of warm biscuits to Benjamin. The woman's announcement this morning that she was planning this short trip had taken Meredith by surprise.

"Ordinarily it would take a team of wild horses to budge her from the property. This time it took but news of a rare visit by some renowned

New Light minister to Priscilla Lewis's home," Abraham explained. "Sour Laura wouldn't have missed him for all the sugar in the West Indies, so she proclaimed."

"Is Laura a New Light?" she asked with interest. They were such gentle folk as she recalled.

Abraham shook his head. "Not in truth. She harbors rigid beliefs of her own—hasn't found a group that agrees with her yet, as far as I know."

"Poor Laura," she said with a sigh of pity. "And now she's stuck there at the Lewis's—for how long do you suppose?"

"Spring would be soon enough for me," Abraham said gleefully. "But 'tis the Lewis family I sympathize with—they're burdened with a house full of Bible-toting guests and a garrulous preacher. I wager the lot of them will have their fill of sermons and praying before the storm stops. And poor God—they'll weary Him enough that He'll probably curtail His plans for a mighty blizzard and send out a thawing sun early on the morrow to release them, and Himself as well."

"Abraham, you're awful," she chastised, but couldn't resist smiling. Lord, it was a relief to be free of Laura for one evening. Since she'd learned that the woman considered her "fallen," she'd been uncomfortable as the dickens around her.

The air definitely was lighter around the supper table tonight without the Gray Presence. Almost festive. Even Benjamin seemed uncommonly relaxed.

He was. But he didn't like the turns his thoughts kept taking. Aunt Laura wasn't here, but Meredith decidedly was. He was acutely conscious of her sitting there only an arm's length away from him.

Her familiar haunting **scent**—roses? lilacs? could it be both?—flooded **his brain** with memories he'd determined to keep **safely** under lock and key.

Tonight he was unable to push them back. But he knew he must.

His father was no help—excusing himself early, claiming "heavy snows bring out the bear in me, I vow. All I want to do is hibernate." And he blithely left the two of them alone in an awkward silence.

"Well, I should retire early myself," Meredith said, starting to rise. "It's been a long day, and tomorrow could be longer since I'll have to fill in for Laura if she doesn't return."

"Please stay awhile," he heard himself say. Had he lost his senses?

She was standing, her delicate fingers pressing into the edge of the mahogany table. "Stay? At the table, you mean?"

He stood. "No, we've both finished supper." *Let her go!* He ignored his own warning. It was, perhaps, the candlelight's play on her magical hair that drove him to such reckless behavior. "The parlor, perhaps? For brandy and a few hands of piquet? Unless you have need to be with Philip or Betsy, that is?"

He felt as if his speech stumbled like that of an untutored lad's.

"They're both asleep," she said, looking a bit hesitant, but then her face brightened. "Piquet does sounds like fun, Benjamin. Last time we played I whipped you good—won the equivalent of a full week's wages, if you remember."

Bless her. Her spirited enthusiasm for gaming had jostled him back to a semblance of his normal composure. Of course, he thought with a surge of steadying relief as he followed her into the parlor, it was but her lively companionship he craved on this snowbound evening.

"Now we shall see whose wit and skill prevail, milady," he said, dealing the cards and picking up his hand. "Aha! Methinks tonight you'll not be so successful as the last time—better be chary with your wagers."

"Never," she said with a giggle. "A shilling a point as always. I'm building my nest egg for a future of riches."

And she was indeed. She accumulated twenty-five points within fifteen minutes—and another twenty-five before the big case clock in the corner had ticked away fifteen more.

"You'd have me bankrupt in an hour, woman," he complained with a laugh, folding his cards and raising his hands in surrender. He walked over to the mantel for his pipe. "You've bested me, and I crown you victor. Lady Luck smiles on you tonight."

"Wit and skill," she reminded him with a sly grin. "And you may crown me with fifty shillings, kind sir."

He lifted his eyebrow and smiled. "I trust my signed note of debt will suffice till the morrow. My pockets are bereft of shillings—for such a sum I'd have to retire to my office and plunder my safe." He didn't want to retire anywhere. The evening was still young, and he hoped to savor these precious moments of her company as long as possible. After lighting his pipe, he pulled out the brandy and poured a moderate amount in two goblets.

"The note's not necessary," she said as he placed the goblets before her on the game table. "Your word's enough—though you may expect some nagging from me if my hefty winnings aren't forthcoming by noon tomorrow."

He moved his chair over to the side of the table, reversed it, and straddled the seat, leaning his arms across the back. "I thank you for the warning, Miss Davis," he said, his smile easy, relaxed. "You shall have your money before noon, for my ears dislike the ravages of a scold's tongue."

"It's a deal," she said, lifting her glass and taking a small sip of brandy. Her pert nose wrinkled. "Lord, that first taste always bites back and burns like liquid fire."

Apt term, he thought. "But it becomes smooth and sweet before the glass is emptied." He kept his voice light, determined to maintain a purely social exchange.

It wasn't working. The flesh of her creamy shoulders against the deep burgundy velvet of her gown's sleeves looked maddeningly smooth and sweet. And the liquid fire within him had nothing to do with the brandy.

He cleared his throat and adjusted his posture slightly.

She'd pushed her spectacles atop her head, and her silver eyes widened. She frowned. "Hn-huh, Benjamin. You're thinking dangerous thoughts. I'd better call it a night." She pushed herself away from the table and stood.

He rose slowly and stepped back from his chair. "Am I as transparent as that to you?" he asked quietly. "I've tried with all my might to convince myself I had but platonic sociability on my mind."

"Your eyes were sending far different messages," she said. "Unwise ones, Benjamin, under our circumstances. Would you have us be a couple of mice playing while the cat's away?" Her fingers trembled slightly as she reached up for her spectacles and removed them, folding them and holding them tightly in her hand.

The trembling touched him. She was as uncomfortable as he was.

"We're far from mice," he said, working around the huskiness in his throat.

She didn't respond, but her expression told him what her unspoken words didn't. She didn't agree—was embarrassed . . . pained? He'd destroyed the lightness they'd achieved this evening. The tension between them crackled like the pine logs blazing in the hearth.

"I'm sorry, Meredith," he groaned and turned toward the game table, splayed his hands against its polished wood for support. "I've missed you sorely these lonely months, but I have no right to have these feelings for you."

"Your feelings of physical desire are perfectly natural," she said, her voice strangely tight. "I'm female, here, available and we're essentially alone. No need to berate yourself for behaving normally."

He looked at her then and wished immediately he hadn't. Their gazes locked, and he knew he was lost. Openness. He'd pledged openness. "Do you truly believe that my only feelings for you are those of physical desire, Meredith?"

A whisper of astonishment brushed across her silver eyes before they narrowed slightly. "I'm not stupid. What else could they possibly be?"

"More than I have deemed wise to admit even to myself," he said, low. After inhaling deeply, he reached for the back of the chair beside him, keeping his gaze fastened on hers.

"You've invaded my heart and very soul. You've filled my thoughts day and night with desperate longings to have you by my side forever. Yet I know full well that you'd be gone from here—from me—if you had your choice . . . I know that I long for what can never be."

He'd said it. At long last, he'd said it. His words lay suspended upon the heavy silence that had fallen between them. His eyes, he knew, exposed his love for her. They, perhaps more than anything he could have spoken, revealed what his aching heart was crying out to her.

"Dear God in heaven," she said with a tiny gasp. She closed her eyes, and her fingers dug into the sides of her skirt. Though she wavered slightly, he didn't dare move forward to steady her.

"I regret burdening you thus, my forbidden treasure," he found the strength to say, though his voice was as weak as his legs had become. He held tightly to the back of the chair and looked away from her.

"Burden?" he heard. He nodded, combed his fingers through his hair, stared at the scattered cards upon the game table, and felt miserable.

But she'd come up beside him, was standing so near that the heat of her body warmed his rigid flesh—her lilac-rose scent dizzied his lowered head.

"Should hearing such words from the man she loves with all her heart ever be considered a burden to any woman, Benjamin?"

He lifted his eyes. Tears were streaming from hers, but she was smiling—radiantly.

His chest pounded, and he heard his own gasp. "You love me?"

"Of course," she whispered. "But I never dreamed you . . ."

His lips captured her unfinished sentence as his arms crushed her to him. She loved him! His thundering heart roared its chorus of ecstasy over and over. She loved him! She loved him!

And he loved her, oh God, he loved her. This treasure of a woman beneath his fevered kisses . . . this wonderfully responsive treasure, melting into him within his embrace, filling him with blazing fires only she could quench.

Only she . . .

"I love you, I love you, I love you," he moaned into her ear, lifting her to him, holding her tight against his swelling, pervasive need for her. He could feel her perfect breasts through velvet, wool, and linen, suffusing the flesh of his chest with twin flames of desire. Her lips, her tongue, her moans signaled her fiery love. *Her love!* With the driven fervor of his whole heart he accepted her signals and responded.

Melded together, they drifted down as one to the carpet. Though his fingers wanted to linger upon her silky thighs, to savor the smooth firmness of this gateway to the paradise she offered him, her writhing urgency, as great as his, propelled them upward—to the soft, pulsing mound that awaited his touches. Wondrous tiny folds of heated satin, slickening beneath his fingers with the sweet nectar of her want. Her magical center athrob, pleading for him as her lips upon his pleaded.

She moaned, arched to him, opened to him, and all thoughts of lingering fled. His unleashed hardened shaft needed no guidance, and slid with ease within the sublime warmth—within the throbbing velvety tightness, the yielding walls of its true home.

*Home.* She was his home, his welcoming home. Dear God, he loved her.

Meredith pulled him deeper inside her. Her heart sang with the rapture of ecstasy. She encircled him with her passion-driven body as her undying love encircled his spirit. *He loved her!* They were one now, would be forever one.

This was where she belonged. She knew it now. She belonged *here*, with *him*.

Oh, and how beautifully he filled her—fulfilled her.

*Oh!* The magic spred, grew as their joined rhythms quickened. Until, *oh, Benjamin, YES!* . . . the promised starburst. His warm seed exploded within her like a flood of blessings. Her answering spasms received them with encompassing love.

His glorious lips fell upon hers; a benediction affirming what his body had so splendidly proclaimed. He loved her.

But he whispered it, too. "I love you, Treasure."

She sighed with the bliss of perfect contentment and looked up into his magnificent eyes.

"I love you, Benjamin," she whispered back.

It was a December midnight, a fierce snowstorm raged beyond the windows. But here, in this candlelit parlor with Benjamin, Meredith felt the renewal of spring and saw rainbows.

Abraham knew. She saw it in his twinkling eyes the following morning. Why, the clever old rascal. He'd wanted this from the beginning, had seen what neither she nor Benjamin had been able to see, blinded as they'd been by their stubborn misperceptions.

Words weren't needed. Their glowing faces were patent evidence. And Benjamin couldn't keep his hands off her. Oh, just a touch now and then, on her shoulder or elbow or the back of her neck. She didn't mind the tiniest bit. Her own hands refused to stay put with any kind of propriety. That they both at last had discovered true love was quite apparent. Even to a simpleton—and Abraham was far from a simpleton.

"I see a Fox Haven wedding in the offing, I vow," he said with decided satisfaction.

Benjamin looked over at her, his eyebrow raised, of course. She blushed like a giddy girl as she nodded happily.

"Aye, Father. You see extremely well," he said.

Lord, they were to be married! For real, this time. For real and forever.

"Alas, the snow that has made possible this blessed turn of events will prevent the Reverend Hobson from coming this day. We must wait, I fear, for the conjugal knot to be tied," said Abraham without a trace of disgruntlement, let alone fear. He went to the window. "At least fortune smiles upon us, for we're freed of Sour Laura's pompous presence for the duration of this storm," he added with a chuckle.

It was, indeed, a storm. The world outside was blanketed with white—the heavy wind-driven snow, the sky, and the earth were merged into one solid mass of roiling whiteness. The relentless gale roared against the frosted panes, but the large rooms of Fox Haven remained cozy and warm. And not from the log fires alone. The sunshine of their love filled the rooms today.

Meredith joined Abraham by the window. A twinge of concern intruded on her euphoria. "It's terrible out there—the drifts have nearly topped the fenceposts. Are the slaves, the servants, warm enough and well supplied?"

"Aye," Benjamin said, coming up behind her and squeezing her shoulders. "Our people will be well, their homes are snug and their supplies of wood and food bountiful. Worry not, my treasured one."

"And the livestock, Benjamin?" She turned in his arms, and he kissed the crease out of her brow.

"Penned and sturdy," he said with a loving smile. "If this continues, I'll have to ride out and furnish them with additional fodder, but for the nonce they're safe—as are we all."

She started to protest his even thinking about venturing out in such frightening weather, but Abraham interrupted with a protest of his own. "You two are sweating up the panes," he pretended to fuss, smearing the weather-fogged glass with his hand. "Away with you both now and leave an old man in peace."

"I should go into the kitchen and do some supervising," Meredith said with a laugh, tweaking the man's elbow. She elevated her nose and screwed up her face as if she'd sucked on a lemon. "I'm to be Laura today, it appears."

Abraham gave her a hearty embrace. "Never, my love, could you bear the slightest resemblance to Sour Laura."

"Unhand my woman," Benjamin said playfully, pulling her toward him. "I found her first, dear Father."

"And waited an insufferably long time to claim her, I'd say," the old man chastised him with a merry half-growl. "Jumping Jehoshaphat, Benjamin, I've had serious doubts about your sanity these past months. You're lucky as the devil she wasn't swept away from you before your very eyes."

Meredith felt Benjamin's fingers tighten around her arms. "I don't sweep away easily," she said quickly, attempting a cocky cheerfulness to quiet the ripple of tension in his beautiful jaw.

But her own buoyancy had dropped considerably. She *had* been swept away with unsettling ease. Once. But never again, she pleaded to the heavens. *Please, dear God—don't ever, ever sweep me away from Benjamin!*

She looked deeply into his troubled eyes and shook her head. "I shall never leave you," she whispered, only to him.

"Never," came his low groan, and he wrapped his arms about her, holding her so close she felt, once again, totally secure.

" 'Scuse me, ma'am. Miz Betsy, she wants to talk with you," Sukie interrupted. Meredith pulled away from Benjamin with a start.

"Is she all right?" she asked the smiling mulatto, who had lowered her eyes, but her pinkened cheeks were a dead giveaway that she'd seen the governness in her master's arms.

"She's fine, ma'am, but impatient this morn 'bout somethin'. I told her I'd fetch you."

"I'd better run up," Meredith said to Benjamin, giving his fingers a quick squeeze. She nodded toward Abraham. "Excuse me, please?"

"Begone, my lovely," the old man grunted with a flip of his hand. "Benjamin sorely needs a respite—he appears a tad feverish, he does."

337

She winked at them both and hurried from the room.

Betsy looked more than impatient. The girl was awhirl with excitement.

"I can't wait till Christmas day to show Father, Merrie. I just can't!" she exclaimed. "That's two whole weeks away, and look—just look at me!"

Meredith closed the door, crossed her arms, and leaned against the paneling. "I'm looking," she said calmly, though her heart was pumping at an ungodly rate.

Betsy was standing. She'd been doing that for weeks. And she'd even walked, miles maybe, in this very room—but only with Meredith's assistance.

"Now stay over there, Merrie. And watch. Just watch."

Betsy, dressed like a princess in white muslin, held on to the bedpost with one hand, her little body standing stiffly erect. Meredith's fingers dug into her own arms, and she waited. She watched without breathing—alert, ready to dash to the girl's side should she start to fall.

Betsy let go of the bedpost, wobbled slightly, and extended her arms sideways for balance as she'd been taught.

Meredith tensed.

The girl took one step, two, paused a moment, stood steady. She smiled and lifted her head high. The small buff boots moved forward. Three, four, five, six, *seven*! Meredith relaxed and picked up the count for her.

"Eight, nine, ten, eleven, twelve . . . oh, *Betsy*!" she squealed, jubilant, falling to her knees and holding out her arms. Betsy walked right into them.

"Lord, this *is* Christmas!" Meredith exclaimed, weeping with joy and hugging the girl close.

"All the princesses woke up," the girl said, beaming.

"Indeed they did—twelve, more than twelve, wonderful steps you took. I'm so proud of you!" She kissed the child's flushed cheek and wiped the tears away from her own.

"I took fifteen earlier," Betsy said proudly. "When no one was looking."

"But you might have fallen, love."

"I did, but it didn't hurt. And I got right back up."

Meredith hugged her again, then stood and gave the girl's little rump a pat. "Want to do a few more?"

Betsy nodded with enthusiasm, then turned around, took a deep, steadying breath, and walked over to the bed.

This time, Meredith watched her with a therapist's eyes. Before, she realized, she'd observed through those of a loving mother. The girl's gait, though a bit hesitant, was nearly perfect. Only the slightest limp—the left foot would require further strengthening.

But her balance was excellent, her posture terrific.

Betsy was walking!

"May I show Father now, Merrie? May I?"

She smiled at the girl. "Yes, Betsy. Christmas has truly come early this year, I believe."

Benjamin wept. Abraham, too. Lucy, Sukie, Will, old Robert, the whole kitchen staff joined in—and Meredith, of course.

# Thomasina Ring

Only Betsy was dry-eyed, but she sparkled and her face outshone a June day's sun.

Benjamin, glowing with pride and thanksgiving, lifted his daughter and clasped her in an exuberant bear hug. He was speechless, but his smiles and his tears said it all.

The jubilant group sighed, applauded, and did some hugging of their own.

Meredith thought her heart might burst right on the spot. It was that full of happiness, rejoicing— and love.

"Merrie taught me, Father. It's our Christmas gift to you, but we couldn't wait."

Benjamin, holding the girl to him, lifted his eyes toward Meredith and looked at her over the blond curls of his daughter. His tear-bright gaze was an endearing caress.

"Meredith herself is a precious gift, Betsy," he said with an adoring reverence, keeping her locked in the embrace of his turquoise eyes. "She's truly a gift from heaven—for us all."

# Chapter Twenty-Two

Laura Preston was not pleased. She returned from her three-day snowstorm captivity in a foul mood. The nonstop praying in the company of fellow God-fearing souls obviously had put her in the dumps.

Even Betsy's walking couldn't bring a smile to her pursed lips. "God works in mysterious ways," was all she said, then turned her back on the puzzled child and went to see to the laundry.

The news of Meredith's and Benjamin's betrothal pushed her into a veritable snit. "God sees all. Mark my words," she'd pronounced, her narrow face pinched with foreboding—referring, apparently, to the fact that Benjamin had moved into Meredith's chamber before the nuptials.

And she didn't attend their Christmas Eve wedding, held in Fox Haven's parlor. Claiming a headache, she'd remained upstairs in her room with the door closed.

As the weeks progressed, she moved like a solemn dark cloud through the house's sunny merriment. Fortunately, her gloom didn't dampen anybody else's spirits.

Indeed, life was far too sweet at Fox Haven these days for even Laura Preston's notably increased sourness to spoil the happiest Christmas and New Year's season the plantation had seen in years, possible ever.

Meredith Foxworth savored her first colonial Christmas. All of it was enchanting—the pine and cedar boughs in the parlor (she'd hoped for a candlelit tree, but found they hadn't become a custom yet); the wonderful aromas of ginger, cinnamon, and nutmeg wafting from the busy kitchen; the exchange of simple gifts among the family; the open house for the slaves and servants on Christmas Day when Benjamin, before the days of Santa Claus, proved to be one nevertheless.

He gave to Peter, the overseer, and to each of his eleven loyal men ten-acre plots on the outskirts of Fox Haven. To his more than one hundred slaves and their families, he gave small amounts of cash and something of inestimable value—their papers of freedom.

The latter was a gift to Meredith, he'd told her, and to himself, he'd added with a smile, "for I'm woefully tired of hearing your endless nagging on the subject."

They'd be paid regular wages from now on, he'd explained to his people, but they were free to leave Fox Haven whenever they desired "without fear and with my blessings."

Only two left—a young couple who planned to make their way west "beyond the blue mountains." They got their blessings, a pair of fine horses and added supplies as well.

The others decided to stay "for th' while, Mistuh Benjamin." They had liked their work and his ways with them, Jess the cobbler told him as their selected representative. But wages would make a "mighty diff'rence"—and they accepted their "wondrous freedom" with an understanding of new responsibilities and challenges, with thankful hearts and with "our heads lifted to the skies."

Oh, it was a very merry Christmas! And that evening, when the family gathered around the harpsichord for an old-fashioned hymn sing, Meredith found herself caroling "Joy to the World!" with special fervor. (She shouldn't have been surprised, but she was. Benjamin played the harpsichord. Beautifully, of course.)

But Laura remained glum. She grew increasingly nasty, in fact—especially toward Meredith.

"Good grief, she's a growly bear," Meredith complained to Benjamin with a sigh of exasperation as they retired to their chamber after supper one night in mid-January. "What on earth's the matter with her?"

"All the happiness around here, I guess." His brows pulled together. "Peculiar, though; one would think it would be contagious, at least eventually."

"She's had a lifetime to build up her immunity," Meredith said. "At least her dislike of me is out in the open now. You heard her tonight, Benjamin— that's only a sampling of the way she snipes at me day after day. I've been careful all along not to encroach on her territory, but I truly believe she's despised me since the day I arrived—and she sure as heck lets it hang out these days."

She walked to her dressing table and lovingly fingered the silver brush and hand mirror he'd given her for Christmas. The gift had been a special one, but it had been the accompanying note that had sent her already-soaring spirits up to the stars: *"For my treasure of a wife—remember, my love, as this brush strokes through your gleaming chestnut hair that my fingers are longing to be there in its stead; and as this mirror gazes upon your radiant, beautiful face, my jealous eyes are aching with desire to gaze upon you—alone."*

Lord, he might never know how those few words had wiped away the last remnants of her doubts about her physical charms. To him, her mousy brown hair was "gleaming chestnut"—her plain, nondescript face was "radiant, beautiful." Her slender body he'd told her numerous times was "dynamite" (she'd taught him the word in a different context entirely). He'd convinced her— he truly considered her the most beautiful woman in the world. She smiled to herself. Oh boy, with him she felt like Helen of Troy!

" . . . disturbed me." Uh-oh, he was talking to her, and she'd been so lost in her own rhapsodies she'd tuned him out.

She looked up. "What disturbed you, Benjamin? Sorry, sweetheart, I wasn't listening."

"Aunt Laura's ability to hide her true feelings for you, Treasure. Those months I'd 'left you in the dark,' as you termed it, you had no suspicions she felt the way she did, did you?"

She shook her head and frowned. "No . . . it dawned on me that she was quite an actress. It gave me a twinge of uneasiness, but I was uneasy about so many things in those days that I didn't think anything further about it."

His brows lowered and he looked contemplative. "I'd felt uneasy, too, but pushed it out of my mind. The paths my thoughts took . . ." He scowled. "Impossible thoughts, Treasure."

She looked at him intently and knew immediately what paths his thoughts had taken. Something cold gripped the pit of her stomach.

"Indeed impossible, Benjamin," she said. "Laura hates me, but Fox Haven and the Foxworth family are her life, for heaven's sake."

He didn't respond, but continued to look contemplative, the long fingers of one of his hands kneading deep circles at his temple.

The pit of her stomach was still on ice, but common sense told her she had to speak up. "Look, sweetheart, nothing's gone awry at Fox Haven since the so-called poisoning of Abraham's black pudding. That could've been a bug, a virus—the ague, or whatever you'd call it. Why, the obnoxious greasy stuff alone is sickening enough to cause those peculiar symptoms Abraham and I had. I overreacted, was paranoid . . ."

Darn it, it was hard to communicate at times.

"Benjamin, the notorious Fox Haven curse came about because of unconnected events. They had to have been, just as you always believed. That ghost business, now, is the only thing we know that had a human hand behind it, and that's over and done with. The only thing I can figure is that somebody got hold of Dr. Le Feu's 'magic fire device' somehow and had a little fun there for a while."

345

She sucked in a breath. "Benjamin! Was that fire thing from *France*?"

He looked puzzled. "I believe so. Why?"

"I saw Laura's account books one day last summer. There was a fifty-pound item nearly every month for weird things I didn't understand. The entries stuck out like a sore thumb because of the expense—and all of them were prefaced by the letters 'F r.' "

She was pacing the room now, gnawing at a finger. "I can't remember all of it—but there were 'cards' one month, 'sticks' another. 'Envelopes,' I think, once. Anyway, they each had 'F r' in front of them. All I could figure was 'French,' but that made little sense to me."

"Fifty pounds for cards, sticks, and *envelopes*?" He sounded aghast.

She nodded and sat in a chair close to him. "Do you ever check the household account books?"

"Not for years—Laura's an excellent manager. She's frugal, drives a mighty bargain, and has a balance left every month from the allowance I've given her."

Meredith squiggled her brows. "Five hundred pounds is a hefty monthly allowance. I don't know the money equivalents, but I'll bet that translates to rich living for a household in *any* time. Most of the items listed in the book are for relatively piddling amounts—except those peculiar 'F r' things."

His thumb ran back and forth across his full lower lip and his eyes held the glaze of deep thought. "I'll check the books on the morrow, Treasure. What you've told me is troubling."

"Benjamin, I can't bear to think what I'm thinking. Dr. Le Feu's fire device burned, sparked, and sputtered exactly like the ghost, or would have looked the same if it had been lit in fog. Is it possible that Laura had ordered them from France? That *Laura* could have caused the . . ."

He placed his finger across her lips. "We'll find out, Treasure. I can't bear what I'm thinking, either."

Oh dear, he was all burdened-looking again. She felt pretty disturbed herself—but he needed her comforting now.

She leaned over and pushed the ebony wave back off his forehead, rubbed her hand over his tensed jaw, and held it there. "We'll get to the bottom of this together, my love," she whispered. "Together I know we can do anything—all will be well."

Yes, it would be. She *had* to believe that.

He covered her hand with his and wrapped it tight. His eyes looked deeply into hers.

"I love you, Treasure," he said.

Now that's comfort, she thought, leaning closer and throwing her free arm around his neck. "And I love you, Benjamin Foxworth."

She kissed the dimple the moment it appeared, then slid her lips to the soft curve of his mouth.

He pulled her to his lap, and burdens and disturbed feelings didn't have a ghost of a chance to compete.


The attic was frigid. Meredith drew the wool shawl closer about her shoulders, and blew on her hands, and rubbed them together. She squinted through the dusky gloom of the cluttered space. Somewhere in all this jumble there should be a suitable painting for the guest chamber.

She was in a redecorating mood this afternoon, and Benjamin had given her *carte blanche* to make any changes she wished. He would be occupied out in the grist mill all day, he'd told her. Abraham had adjusted the chutes and sifter the day before "for swifter operation."

Now nothing was operating.

She smiled at the familiar painting of cavorting wood nymphs, but kicked back her devilish urge to rehang the blasted thing. Spotting another group of frames against a far wall, she hurried over to see if something among them might be more appropriate for the guest chamber. It sorely needed some "warming up."

And so did she. Her breaths were visible puffs of frosty white clouds.

An old domed wooden trunk caught her eye. Neat black lettering on its side announced "Preston—Personal Goods."

Padlocked, of course. Knowing she shouldn't, but too curious not to, Meredith knelt and fingered the icy lock. It fell open with only the weakest of pulls.

Good grief. Dare she? It wouldn't be proper to snoop . . .

But . . . A shivery tingle ran up her arms. Laura *was* a mystery, and both Benjamin and she had expressed dreadful suspicions that neither had dared to explore fully. She frowned at the trunk, wrestling with her conscience. This cache of Laura's prized mementos could provide some needed insight into her personality.

Oh, what harm would there be in just a little peek? Holding her breath, she slipped away the padlock and opened the lid.

The thing was nearly empty. Meredith leaned over and peered into the dark interior. An unpleasant musty odor—like rotted, long-dead flowers—assaulted her nose. Several neat squares of needlework lay across the bottom. Old-fashioned samplers, by the looks of them.

As she lifted one of the squares to examine it closer, she realized with astonishment that the pieces of needlework had been placed to cover additional objects. Quickly shoving aside the samplers, she saw two small tin boxes, one round, one rectangular. Such a meager assortment of mementos . . . Meredith felt a wrenching tug of pity for Laura Preston. And miserably ashamed of herself for meddling.

But as she reached for the needlework pieces, hoping she could arrange them as they'd been, a thin beam of dust-moted sunlight from the attic's tall casement window fell on the trunk's bottom. Her hand stopped. *What on . . .*

Across the splintery wood was an ominous scrawl of large blood-red painted letters.

*The wages of sin are DEATH!*

Meredith shuddered. Sickened, she couldn't help but ponder, truly troubled now. What were in those tin boxes?

She was almost afraid to look. But she'd gone this far . . . With caution, she pulled out the round one and lifted the lid, scrunching her eyes and tensing her head back in case something horrific jumped out.

Powder? Her brows crinkled. Metal-gray granules of some sort. Reluctantly, she sniffed the strange contents. Garlicy. Puzzled, she re-covered the tin and replaced it on the trunk's bottom and lifted out the rectangular box. Warily she pried off its lid.

Her heart leapt into her throat.

*Dear God, no!* A small stack of folded white paper sheets lay inside—atop them, a pair of tiny metal tongs. She recognized what she was seeing at once. Dr. Le Feu's primitive matches!

Stunned, Meredith sat back hard on the dusty, cold planked floor. She covered her mouth and closed her eyes. Her brain whirled. *Find Benjamin! Go get Benjamin!* were her only thoughts. Frantically, her fingers shaking convulsively, she closed the tin, dropped it into the trunk, threw the needlework haphazardly over the bottom, and slammed the lid shut.

Somehow she got to her feet, and held to the wall to steady herself.

*Get Benjamin!*

She turned quickly, started to run.

And stopped with a strangled gasp.

Laura Preston stood before her, stolid as a gray block of stone.

"You are a woman of Satan," the stone hissed.

Meredith recoiled.

"The wages of sin are death," came the grisly whisper from the woman. With gray-cloaked arms outstretched, her long fingers gnarled into taut claws, she moved toward Meredith.

Panic gripped her. The woman was demented! Numbed with terror, she forced herself into action—*get around her! run like the devil! scream for help!*

She ducked sideways, sped with maddened fury across the attic floor toward the narrow stairs, opened her mouth to . . .

A bony hand from behind clamped fiercely against her teeth, aborting her scream, cramming her throat, choking her. Her head, her arms, her body were brutally wrenched backward. Gagged mute, feverishly struggling against the steely vise-like hold around her chest, she felt herself being dragged across the uneven planked flooring.

She kicked wildly, dug her teeth hard into the clasping hand. To no avail. Like an avenging Fury, Laura, with the strength of iron, held her captive. Helpless.

Beyond panic, beyond fright, Meredith battled for breath within the cruel muzzle jammed against her nose and mouth. A sharp, wrenching pain struck her back as she was shoved with force against the wall. The gripping hand left her face.

As Meredith gasped for air, Laura stuffed a huge wad of rancid cloth into her mouth. Her throat rebelled, convulsed by gags of nausea. And then the woman moved like lightning. With biting strands of rough rope, she trussed her stunned prisoner from shoulders to feet and propped her in a cramped sitting position back against the wall.

Laura hovered over Meredith, and stuck her hate-contorted face directly before her terror-filled eyes.

"You like the others must die," the woman spat.

Half-conscious, weakened with pain and fear, Meredith struggled against the ropes, fought against the choking cloth. Her nose was free; at least she could partially breathe.

But how long, dear heaven? How long? *Benjamin! Please come, Benjamin!* her mind screamed.

Laura walked over to the trunk and raised its lid. Her movements were slow now, studied. Her

venomous gray face had relaxed and was almost
placid. She had her victim, Meredith realized as
she watched the woman with frozen dread. My
God, she would prolong the agony . . . she was
insane, criminally insane . . .

Again, Meredith's brain reverberated with her
silent screams for Benjamin. He *must* come . . .
she *couldn't* die.

But Benjamin was far away, back in the grist
mill . . .

"You have violated my trunk, much as you
have continually violated God's Commandments
beneath this roof," Laura said, her dulled voice
coming almost sweet, pleasant.

Meredith shivered beneath the cutting ropes
that bound her.

"You have seen the arsenic, and therefore know
how my sister, a sinful woman like you, received
her punishment. There would have been others . . . many others, but . . ." Her words drifted
off, as though she were in a trance of melancholy.

She turned to Meredith. "For Catherine, I chose
a swifter death, of course. Her sins were not so
great, for her first-born came not early. But, like
Emily and you, she encouraged the carnal lust of
her husband, and she, too, had to suffer. The men
of Fox Haven require protection from their own
base, evil needs. God so directed me."

Meredith grunted her protests, and felt her bile
rise against the gagging cloth. The woman gathered a stack of old *Virginia Gazettes* in her arms
and walked toward her. She continued talking,
dear God. "Betsy should have died then, for my
message had been clear that she would grow to
be like her mother, but He in His wisdom spared

her." A brief frown clouded her otherwise beatific face. "Her lameness I believed would lead her into a life of righteousness, so her recovery confused me woefully at first. But then I learned that you, a handmaiden of the devil, had a role in that recovery."

She wadded the newspapers and placed them in balled piles around Meredith. "Of all the babes born to Foxworths after I came as God's messenger to Fox Haven, only Sally was to be allowed to live, I was told. She would be left to me as a daughter to rear in my holy light—but she, too, deceived me. With your assistance, I might add."

The woman's chilling revelations gripped Meredith with horror. *She* had killed all those innocent infants? *She* had poisoned her sister? Had attempted to poison Abraham? Had loosened the hub of the carriage wheel to cause Catherine's death and Betsy's years of lameness?

This madwoman had been under this roof for twenty-eight years, wreaking unspeakable tragedies . . . in the name of *God*, for heaven's sake!

Meredith shook her head violently, straining against the ropes. Tears of frustration, of anger, of terror gushed from her eyes.

Laura walked back to the trunk and lifted out the rectangular tin box. "Now God's voice comes clear to me. Fox Haven itself shall burn, and all those who reside within it. I shall be spared, and Benjamin, for I need his protection for my future work. Out of these ashes he and I shall rebuild a home—a sanctuary of holiness, forever without sin."

She lit one of the primitive matches and held it with the metal tongs before her. It glowed yellow, then white upon her smiling face—the twisted, black smile of evil incarnate. She lowered the flame to the edge of a high clump of newspapers near Meredith's bound feet.

"But *you* shall endure the greatest suffering of all those doomed ones within these desecrated walls of Fox Haven, for God decrees that your sinful body must burn slowly, with consummate searing pain. As did your sisters—the satanic witches of Salem."

Meredith stared with frozen terror as a serpent-thin tongue of orange fire reached for her shoes, coiled forward to lick its fiery threat across the leather soles. She cringed backward, but the relentless flame followed, fanned into wrathful fury by the weak stirrings of her frantic movements.

Stinging heat struck her feet, surrounded her ankles.

A harsh cackle of laughter bombarded her ears. The sharp point of a gray shoe kicked aside the burning paper. "*Slowly* it must be, impatient fire!" the raspy voice above her snarled.

The blazing ball of paper was shoved up against the hem of Meredith's rope-wrapped woolen skirt. Acrid smoke rose as the dark material smoldered, then burst into scarlet flames at the hem.

Meredith's groan of alarmed despair vibrated soundlessly against the foul rag clogging her throat. Searing pain ran an agonizing path up the side of her leg. She tried to writhe away from the rising flames.

Futile! *My God, I'm to be burned alive.* She clamped her eyes shut, prayed for darkness, prayed for Benjamin.

But she found only the awful glare of deadly orange against her closed eyelids, only the roaring sound of the coming firestorm . . . only the hot, scalding pain tearing into her leg.

A wild series of fierce strokes suddenly pounded against the pain. She heard low grunts. A confused flurry of noises . . .

Meredith felt the release of darkness at last.

And nothing more.

Benjamin fought the angry flames with the heavy rug, furiously beating them away from his captive wife, then smothering them into smoky, powerless defeat.

"My Treasure!" he called out, falling to his knees beside her and lifting her limp, trussed body into his arms. He yanked the filthy, jamming cloth from her mouth, buried his face in hers, and held her close.

His heart hammered against his ribs. She was so still . . . too still. In the name of God, *no!* Had he arrived too late?

A low sob rammed into his throat as he looked down upon her. Her peaceful face was streaked with soot and drying tears, her long lashes lay quiet—shadowed diamond-tipped crescents against her mottled cheeks.

No movement, no breath. *No!*

She moaned. Moaned! *She's alive!* He gathered her to him and sobbed openly into her damp hair. "Thank you, God," he breathed, his heart full of overwhelming gratefulness, his eyes swimming with tears.

"Benjamin?" Her voice was thin, weak.

"Aye, Treasure. I'm here . . . you'll be all right, my love." He gazed down into her stunned eyes, and saw relief and love flow across the tear-brightened silver. He kissed her fevered brow, pushed back the chestnut strands that clung to her temples, cradled her head, and drew her face to his beating chest.

"Who did this terrible thing to you, Meredith?" he asked, nearly choking on the words. He would kill the culprit—with his bare hands he would kill whoever had tried to take his beloved wife from him.

A stealthy movement to his right caught his attention. He turned his head quickly.

*"Aunt Laura?"* he gasped, tightening his hold on Meredith.

And then he knew. Even before she lit the white flame and held it high, he knew. The tall woman standing silhouetted against the casement window was a crazed murderess.

Aunt Laura was the Curse of Fox Haven.

With a gentleness that defied his rampaging thoughts, he settled his bound wife softly back against the paneled wall. Only when he was assured she was as comfortable as possible did he leap to his feet and storm in rage toward his aunt.

"Stand back, Benjamin!" she ordered, the sparking paper held aloft with the tongs in her steady hand. "The wages of sin are death."

Without pause, he reached out for her stiff arm and forced it sideways until the tongs dropped from her hand and clattered to the floor. The flaming envelope fluttered downward, landing atop a crumpled newspaper. Quickly he stomped the fire out with his boot.

He released the woman and stood facing her, trying to understand. "Why, Aunt Laura?" he asked with a mournful groan.

Venom flashed from her narrowed gray eyes. She stood rigidly erect, lifted her head, and glared at him.

"Fox Haven must be cleansed of its vile sins. Only fire now can cleanse us all, for we bear the taint of endless transgressions against the Word of—"

"Stop it!" he shouted. "You're mad, woman!"

He moved toward her, attempting to inject a calming tone into his voice. "We must put you in restraints, Aunt Laura. We'll send for Dr. Hughes. Perhaps we can find help for your troubled spirits, put to rest your . . ."

She shook her head and stepped backward. "Come no closer, Benjamin," she warned, holding her hands out before her. He stopped, waiting with alert wariness.

" 'Tis not I but you who needs help," she continued. "Lust must be banished from your soul. Of all the Foxworth men, only you, Benjamin, are worthy of salvation. I've long known that Joshua, unrepentant, is destined to burn in the eternal fires of hell. Abraham, too, is without hope. But for you it's not too late. You must see the light, Benjamin. Join me in destroying this house of iniquity. Only then will you—"

"You're sorely ill, Aunt Laura." He walked toward her and reached out his arm. "Please come downstairs with me now, and we'll find peace for you."

She jumped back. "Never!" she screamed, batting away his hands. "There can be no peace until we cleanse this house and your soul. This evil woman who has ensnared you must die— you must be free of her!"

357

"This woman is my wife, and I love her with all my heart," he said through clenched teeth. Desperate, he moved in closer, tensing his hands to restrain his insane aunt.

Her face twisted with crazed hatred as she recoiled from him. "All is lost, sinner!" she spat out. Then, driven by the swift frenzy of madness, she ripped herself from his grasp and turned from him and ran.

Flinging open the casement, she jumped to the sill, teetered precariously.

"Aunt Laura!" Frantic, Benjamin reached out to pull her back into the room.

But she was gone, plunging headlong through the gray void with an ear-piercing shriek. From far below came a distant, bone-jarring thud.

Benjamin stood still, dazed with horror. A cold wind whistled through the empty casement and bit at his stunned, frozen face.

An eerie quiet descended upon the attic. And then, from behind him, came a whimper of pain.

*Meredith!* He ran to her and wrapped his arms around her trembling body.

"Dear God," she moaned.

"Dear God," he echoed with a throttled sigh, holding her tight.

# Chapter Twenty-Three

They buried Laura Preston's broken body in a far corner of the family cemetery on the following day. Reverend Hobson read the prescribed verses, and those gathered around the open grave bowed their heads in solemn prayer for the demented soul who had wished them all dead.

Meredith clutched Benjamin's hand and wept. She held Philip in her left arm, and the child, seeming to sense the melancholy of those he loved, held his little arms close about her neck and planted his cherubic face deep into the wool cloak around her shoulder.

Betsy, standing pensively on the other side of her father, gripped the fingers of his right hand. Meredith felt a flush of warmth as she noted how he drew the girl closer to him and engulfed her small hand within the comforting nest of his own.

Abraham stood slightly apart from them, his lined face pale. The icy wind ruffled the thick waves of his white hair and reddened his nose. His eyes watered, but not from tears.

Mr. and Mrs. Lewis stood beside him. At news of Laura's death, they'd ridden at once to Fox Haven.

"She grew sore distressed those snowbound days in our home and gave us much worry," they'd told the Foxworths. "It was as though our simple prayers nettled rather than comforted her. The New Light minister spoke messages far too gentle, she complained—and she objected with bitter displeasure that the married couples among us shared the warmth of conjugal beds."

Benjamin had shaken his head sadly. "Aunt Laura frowned upon earthly love, understood it not. And her love for God became naught but a distorted sickness that wreaked hatred—and death. May God forgive her . . . I'm unsure that I can ever do so."

"Nor I," Abraham had agreed with a desolate sigh.

Meredith, distressed, had studied their stricken faces—the dull cast in their matching turquoise eyes. "We must find forgiveness in our hearts," she'd said at last to them. "Laura's wrongs can never be righted, but if we harbor hatred, she will have won a terrible victory over us, and we can't allow that."

Benjamin had walked to her side, put his strong arm around her shoulders, and pulled her to him. "You speak wisely, Treasure," he'd whispered into her hair. "But had those dire premonitions not driven me to the attic—if she'd succeeded in harming you, I . . ."

"I'm all right," she'd said quickly, reassuring him once again that her burns had been only minor. The flesh of her leg was reddened still, but early applications of snow had stopped the stinging pain. She could expect some peeling ahead, but her wounds were hardly serious.

The outer ones, anyway. The bitter inner wounds that all of them had suffered would take far longer to heal. But the love shared within their small circle would sustain them and provide them strength, she knew that with all her heart.

And their nightmare was over. Fox Haven's curse had been laid to rest at last.

As they walked away from the grave—filled now with frosted rust-brown soil, a fresh pine bough lying atop—a thin ray of sunshine broke through an opening in the bleak gray winter sky. A small patch of bright blue appeared above them.

"A good omen, I vow," Meredith said, pausing on the snow-covered hill, her face upturned.

The others stopped and looked up. "Aye," they agreed in unison. Their smiles were as weak as the sun's ray, but they were, indeed, smiles.

Heartened, Meredith reached for Benjamin's hand, and the Foxworths headed for home.

A somber pall lay over Fox Haven for weeks. Steps were softer, and laughter, when it came, was subdued. Evil had stalked these halls for nearly three decades, and the realization brought deep pain to family and servants alike.

No one could fully understand. How could the woman have been in their midst for so long without any of them being suspicious? How had she fooled them so? How could they have prevented the horrendous things she'd done?

Early on, Meredith sensed a need to encourage open discussion. She wasn't sure if their reticence to speak up was an eighteenth-century way or a Foxworth way.

No matter. Keeping this kind of trauma bottled up inside, with each person wrestling with it alone, wasn't healthy. And so she saw to it that the subject of Laura Preston was brought up frequently in the kitchen, the nurseries, the parlor, and the dining room.

"It's called post-trauma stress," she'd explained to Benjamin in privacy a day after the funeral. "All of us, even Betsy, must deal with it openly and together. Talk it to death, in other words. Only then can we come to grips with this thing—understand it, if possible, and rid ourselves of deep-seated guilt, which each of us feels in some way or another."

He'd bowed to her "twentieth-century advantages in such matters," and cooperated wholeheartedly.

In mid-February, another sadness struck the family. News of Sallie Henry's death reached Fox Haven.

"The poor woman is released from her sad tortures at last," Abraham said that evening in the parlor where he'd joined Benjamin and Meredith for their before-supper claret. But tonight they all three had chosen something stronger—rum.

"It appears that there are madnesses of varying sorts," the old man continued with a shake of his head. "Sallie's affliction destroyed only herself. Laura's, on the other hand, was bent on destroying others . . . until the end."

Meredith agreed with a nod. "They were indeed different," she said, arranging her thoughts with care so that she'd speak her opinions in ways acceptable to Abraham's eighteenth-century mind. "Sallie was badly depressed—an imbalance within the workings of her brain and body that came on quickly and could do naught but run its dastardly course. Laura's mania was sporadic— came about only occasionally. And she remained clever throughout, even when besieged by her inner devils. I believe that's how she kept her madness hidden for so long."

"What drove her, do you think?" Abraham asked.

"Many things, probably," she responded. "Her father was gloomy and strict, you told me once. Quoted from the Bible all the time. That might have planted the seed of her deranged religious fervor."

"He was Emily's father, too. He had no such effect on her," Abraham reminded her.

"Emily was younger, and prettier. Laura, being the eldest, possibly bore the brunt of her father's lectures and harangues. And then, life, as you've mentioned, dealt Laura a bad hand. She was unfulfilled as far as earthly love was concerned—and, eventually, all that got twisted in her mind, too."

Benjamin spoke up. "Considering her penchant for banishing sin, I can't help but wonder how philandering Joshua escaped being poisoned or garrotted by her."

"I think Joshua had two things going for him," she said with a small smile. "He did all his philandering off the premises—away from Fox Haven. It was her home she wanted to protect, to keep pure. Then, too, she blamed the women for encouraging the men."

Benjamin frowned. "When I think now of the danger you were in from the minute you walked through our doors, I'm deeply tormented."

He indeed looked tormented, and she couldn't have that. "Rid yourself of that guilt right now, Benjamin Foxworth. How could you have known of any danger then? My arrival—and all the weird circumstances that ensued—sure as heck brought things to a head, but those swift happenings kept her off balance, too. And she didn't succeed in even one of her sick plans after I came."

Meredith hesitated. That sounded terribly self-serving somehow. She'd fumbled around in the dark like the rest of them—had ignored evidence that stared her straight in the face.

She bit her lip. "We were just plain lucky she didn't succeed," she admitted. "She had me fooled as much as the rest of you."

"We have much to be thankful for," Abraham said.

All nodded, and they sipped their rum in silence for a while.

And so it went. Gradually, with such conversations, the pall over Fox Haven lifted. Together, they had pushed it away, and light and sparkle and laughter returned to the plantation.

The coming arrival of spring would be especially welcome this year, Meredith believed. This spring would mark the true end of their terrible winter and bring to them its eternal promise of renewal of life.

Her heart fluttered with warm anticipation. Glory be, she held that renewal within her even now! She was pregnant. This blissful state of affairs had begun sometime around Christmas, she'd figured.

Benjamin was ecstatic, and so was she. The whole household was, in fact. This was one special secret they couldn't keep to themselves—so they'd announced it right away, long before it was the custom to do so in proper Virginia homes in 1775.

Ah, spring, she thought with a contented smile.

But spring was slow to come that year. Despite the glorious warmth within Fox Haven, winter held its icy grip far longer than usual in Hanover County. During March there were a few bright springlike days, just enough to bring out the buds on the fruit trees. But then heavy frost descended with a vengeance, and worries abounded that the crops would be sorely affected this year.

"This spring is woefully like winter," Abraham complained at the supper table one night.

Meredith felt a stab of apprehension. *"In the spring that will be like winter,"* rang its taunting chorus through her brain. She kept her eyes lowered, and prayed that Benjamin wouldn't remember Mad Millie's silly prophesy.

So much was perfect now. She had to get over these occasional thoughts that all was *too* perfect—that it couldn't possibly last. But the anniversary of her arrival was coming up, and it was hard to shake the terrible premonitions.

She prayed fervently, with every atom of her being. *Please, God, let me stay here. Please don't send me back.*

Abraham's next words struck her with a paralysis of fear.

365

"Patrick is sore distraught since Sallie's death, so I've heard. He sits forlorn in his office and has lost interest in other matters. Hanover's elected him and John Syme to represent us at the Second Virginia Convention that's meeting in Richmond later this month, but 'tis said he won't attend."

"But he *must*," she blurted out. Her heart and mind were shouting disturbing messages of their own. Patrick Henry was tall, and now he would be wearing mourning clothes. He *had* to be at St. John's on the 23rd. Dear God, *St. John's*—the church on the hill! That's what the place was called, even. It wouldn't get its name of St. John's until 1828 or so.

She felt a cold shiver. Was that why she was here? To ensure that Patrick Henry delivered his "Liberty or Death" speech to spark the fires of revolution? Was it her duty to ensure that history unfold as it must?

Her eyes met Benjamin's over the candle's flame between them. His thoughts were as hers, she knew at once. She felt a sense of panic, and deep despair. She shook her head, tried to tell him with her eyes. *No, I won't do it, Benjamin. I'll never leave you. I'll be sent back "where I belong" if I do this thing. I won't. I won't!*

The troubled light suffusing the turquoise orbs across from her told her he wasn't comforted. He had remembered Mad Millie's words, then. They'd never spoken of them—now, she supposed, they would have to discuss them.

Abraham interrupted her depressing thoughts. "And why must Patrick be there, may I ask? We'd like him there, of course, for his fiery tongue oft helps clear muddled heads, and many remain muddled on the issue at hand. But if he's lost his fire, he can be of no use. You speak with such vehemence, Meredith. Why do you believe Patrick must be at this Convention?"

She hedged. "Was I vehement? Sorry, I didn't realize it. It was just a shock to me, I guess. He's always been so interested, such a leader, and it's hard to imagine his not being there in the forefront of things, that's all."

The handsome old gentleman seemed satisfied with her response and went on to other subjects.

But she dreaded the days ahead. Could she turn her back on history? Could she ignore a heavy duty like this—a responsibility greater than any she'd ever been presented with—because she feared a witch's stupid prophesy? Because she believed her own happiness could be at stake?

But, heaven help her, she didn't *want* to return "where she belonged!" She wanted to stay right here at Fox Haven and live the rest of her days in the arms of Benjamin Foxworth.

So there.

The pressure grew. A messenger from Scotchtown arrived on Friday, the 17th of March. Patrick Henry wished to speak with Mrs. Benjamin Foxworth. Would she honor him with a visit on the following afternoon?

"Of course I must go," Meredith told Benjamin that night in their chamber. "Maybe I can talk some sense into his head."

"But then you'd be making 'certain the tall man in mourner's black is at the church on the hill in the spring that will be like winter,' " he protested, quoting Mad Millie verbatim.

She attempted a scoff. "Not really making *certain*, Benjamin. Just giving him a little push in the right direction. Besides, surely you don't take any stock in that woman's prophesy, do you? *Speaking stones*, for heaven's sake! You know that's nonsense."

She was trying to convince herself as much as Benjamin, but he didn't have to know that.

Somehow, she believed she'd be all right as long as she didn't go to Richmond—as long as she wasn't in the exact spot where she'd been a year ago.

He looked glum—and determined. "I take stock in anything that threatens to separate us, Treasure. You're dearer to me than life, and you're carrying within you our child—our future. I'll battle the heavens themselves if I must to keep you by my side."

Well, they were in complete agreement on that. She'd battle heaven, hell, and everything in between to stay beside him. Only deep down she knew that their combined battles might not be enough if Fate and Time willed otherwise. They wouldn't dare tear them apart now, not after all they'd been through, not after they'd found this perfect love. Fate and Time wouldn't *dare* do such a thing to them!

Would they?

She pulled her brows together. "I'm wrestling with this dilemma as much as you are, Benjamin. The thought of ever being swept away from you is too frightening to even consider. I'd die without you. Pure and simple, I'd die if I woke up one day back in the twentieth century. I could never belong there now. This is my home—*you're* my home."

She was teary-eyed again, doggone it. She took off her glasses and wiped them dry with her handkerchief, then placed them on the table beside her.

Concentrate on something else, she ordered herself. Something practical. Her glasses, for example. Of course she was going to remain here with him. She *must!* Then she should be practical and begin planning for her future—*here*.

She should wean herself from her glasses. Lord, it was a wonder they hadn't been broken by now, considering everything they'd been through. Someday they were bound to get damaged or lost, and then what? Few, if any, people in these parts wore spectacles for distance. And they'd be hard if not impossible to replace. Fortunately, she wasn't terribly myopic. She could get along passably well without them. She decided she'd start practicing.

Benjamin's worried look brought her back to the far more serious problem at hand. "Don't you understand why I'm concerned, Meredith?" he asked. "If you go to Patrick, you'll surely try to persuade him to go to Richmond. And he's likely to listen to you; he admires you, you know. Thinks you're uncannily wise for a woman."

She lifted an eyebrow and issued a tiny snort. He chuckled, then grew serious again.

"We can't take the risk of your getting involved," he continued, his beautiful face dark with concern. "I don't believe in speaking stones any more than you do, but Mad Millie's words haunt me. And they're ringing truer every day. It's a cold spring, Patrick's in mourning, the Convention's being held in the church on the—"

"I know, I know," she interjected with a sigh. "And I should stay far away from the whole thing in case the rest of her prophesy should be true. But—" She frowned. "—but what if he doesn't go? What if he doesn't give that speech?"

"The Revolution will happen anyway, I wager. Maybe not on the same schedule you read about or with Patrick Henry as one of its leading lights, but it will happen nevertheless."

Her frown deepened. "But history wouldn't unfold as it's supposed to. And in 1991 there wouldn't have been a reenactment at St. John's, and I wouldn't have been a docent, and then I wouldn't be here." She shook her head. "It's all so confusing, Benjamin. But when all's said and done, I feel duty-bound to—"

"Your duty's first and foremost to remain here at Fox Haven with those who love you," he broke in sensibly.

"And with those I love," she said softly. She met his gaze, looking deeply into his eyes. "Benjamin, your sense of duty and responsibility is as great as mine. What would you do if you were in my place?"

He took a long, mournful breath. She saw his jaw tense. "I would do my best to convince Patrick Henry to go to Richmond and deliver the speech that will make him immortal," he said with a heavy sadness that brought new tears to her eyes.

And she knew what she had to do. She crossed the first two fingers of both her hands and held them up. "Wish me luck then, my love. I'll do that very thing tomorrow. Let's pray that Fate and Time aren't as frivolous as I've sometimes thought and that they know where I truly belong."

"You belong here, Treasure."

With a smile, she stood and walked over to him, sat firmly on his lap, and wrapped her arms around his neck. "I know that and you know that, Benjamin Foxworth. Now if Fate and Time just have it all straight, we're home free!"

"I hope they're watching," he said, drawing her close. "But I'm going with you to Scotchtown tomorrow anyway. If they sweep you away, they'll have to sweep me along with you."

# Chapter Twenty-Four

Patrick Henry wasn't cooperative. He had no interest in attending the Convention, he told them.

"With Sallie gone, I find she's taken my spirit with her," he said.

"But Sallie's been truly gone for a year or more, Patrick," Meredith said in her most reasoning tones. "We all lament her recent passing, but we must think of her as freed at last from the tortures of her illness."

He sat lower in his chair, furrowed his brow, seemed distracted. "I've heard those very sentiments many times these past weeks. They bring me no solace."

Glancing across at Benjamin, she saw him shrug his shoulders. She straightened her own and decided to try a different tack.

"Virginia needs you, Patrick. Indeed, *America* needs you. Haven't you said 'the distinctions

between Virginians, Pennsylvanians, New York-
ers, and New ·Englanders are no more'? That
you're 'not a Virginian, but an American'?"

He lifted his eyes and stared at her intently.
"How do you know these words? I spoke them
at the Continental Congress in Philadelphia last
September, true. But the proceedings were to be
held secret."

She felt her cheeks warm. Uh-oh, she'd goofed.
"I don't know where I heard them . . . maybe I
just imagined them." She squirmed, groping for
the just-right phrasing to express herself. She had
his undivided attention now, at least. "But what
I heard or imagined is beside the point, isn't it?
If you feel that way, surely you understand the
importance of being in Richmond next week and
using your talents to convince the undecided.
Virginia needs a militia to defend itself. This
colony must lead, inspire—and so must you. We
need you there to state our cause, Patrick."

He rubbed his chin and moved up a little in his
chair. "I don't know, Meredith. My light died with
Sallie. Others will have to lead and inspire."

*"Who,* for heaven's sake?" she protested, growing desperate. "Jefferson? He's relatively young,
unseasoned, and he writes better than he speaks.
Washington? He's a leader, I grant you, but fairly
taciturn, I understand. Certainly he's not known
for firing up men with words."

Her mind raced. Who else was on his side?
"Thomas Nelson of York County will support you,
like Jefferson and Washington, but he's old—not
much of a speaker." She was grasping for straws.
She knew little about Thomas Nelson, but older
actors usually played him at the reenactment, and
his one speech was brief. "And Richard Henry Lee

has come around to your way of thinking, I understand—but he'd never have the same impact with the masses as you could."

Benjamin broke his silence. "You do believe we need to form a militia for our defense, don't you, Patrick?" he offered.

"Aye, Britain has its mighty fleets and armies covering our waters and darkening our land. What means this martial array if its purpose be not to force us to submission?"

Meredith's heart skipped a beat. He'd just uttered nearly the exact words of a portion of the great speech he must deliver next week. She threw Benjamin a glance of deep gratitude. Of course! Here was a surefire way they could stir Patrick into action.

"And what have we to oppose them? Shall we try argument?" she asked, using the best bait she knew—his own soon-to-be-immortal words.

Patrick Henry expelled a protesting grunt. "We have been trying that for the last ten years."

"Have we anything new to offer upon the subject?" she inquired, quoting the text she knew so well.

"Nothing. We have held the subject up in every light of which it is capable; but it has been all in vain," he answered compliantly—to the letter, in fact.

He was despondent still, but she was encouraged. Thinking quickly, she deleted a few lines and jumped ahead a bit.

"Let us not, I beseech you, sir, deceive ourselves any longer," she said earnestly, continuing her ploy of using his own words.

"We have done everything that could be done

to avert the storm which is now coming on," he responded on cue.

She leaned forward. "But when shall we be stronger? Will it be the next week, or the next year?"

"Will it be when we are totally disarmed, and when a British guard shall be stationed in every house?" he followed up, exactly as he should— would. A spark of fire leapt from his blue eyes. Excited, she ventured toward the end of his speech.

"The war is inevitable," she said.

"And let it come! I repeat it, let it come!" The black bombazine mourning cloth draped about his high-backed wooden chair fluttered from the force of his agitated movements. He'd come back to life!

"But many gentlemen are crying 'peace, peace,' " she admonished softly, paraphrasing only slightly.

"There is no peace. The war is actually begun. The next gale that sweeps from the north will bring to our ears the clash of resounding arms!" he shouted, truly on fire now. She smiled, and waited.

"Our brethren are already in the field!" he added with fervor. "Why stand we here idle?"

His words resounded through the small office. He sat silently, his fiery eyes widened with surprise.

*"Why stand we here idle?"* he repeated with a low groan.

And then he unfolded his lean, black-garbed body from his chair and stood tall above them. "Aye, I shall go to Richmond," he said.

Meredith breathed a sigh of relief and looked at Benjamin. He smiled and gave her a nod of congratulation.

"But may I ask an additional favor of you, my friends?" Patrick said. Meredith tensed. "Today you have renewed my spirit, but tomorrow or the next day I might falter beneath the heavy burden of my sadness. I need you two with me to keep my fires kindled. Dear ones, I beseech you, accompany me to Richmond. I must depart early on Monday morn. Can you find it possible to favor me in this way?"

*No! Not Richmond!* She searched Benjamin's eyes, and knew her face had paled.

Silence lay thick over the room. From outside the office, the dulled chirp of a sparrow cut through the silence, startling Meredith. Her taut body jerked. And then the bird flew like a tiny dark shadow by the small-paned window across from her. *Winged sparrow.* Her hands were cold. She gripped them together.

"What think you, Meredith?" Benjamin asked, barely above a whisper.

Her voice quavered. "Is there no one else, Patrick?" she asked.

"None I know of," he responded, his long face drawn. "My courage is diminished, my sense of direction sorely weakened. It's as though my mast has toppled and my sails have furled. You and Benjamin alone appear able to provide a support upon which I might cling and perchance once again catch the wind to . . ." He turned away from them, lifted his hands to his bowed head, and buried his face in them.

"Ne'er have I looked to others in such a manner. But in this instance, I need you. Our future country needs you," he cried out plaintively.

That did it, of course. Though tears filled her eyes and clogged her throat, she heard her congested words tremble through the room.

"We shall accompany you, Patrick."

Benjamin was quiet, but with two long strides was standing before her. He pulled her to her feet and into his arms.

"The whole Foxworth family will accompany you, Patrick," he said, his deep voice laden with emotion. "We shall leave none of our loved ones behind as we embark on this momentous journey."

Meredith clung to him. Tight.

Snow was falling when the small caravan left Hanover County early on Monday morning. Despite the weather, the mood in the Fox Haven carriage was bright and festive. The unscheduled visit to Richmond was viewed as a special treat, and none of the coach's occupants were aware that Benjamin and Meredith felt otherwise.

Abraham sat cockily in the "driver's seat." His passengers were Betsy, little Philip, Lucy, Sukie, Will, and sweet old Robert. Benjamin, astride Midnight, and Jack, on Croesus, rode beside the carriage.

Meredith accompanied Patrick Henry in his one-horse gig that led the way. She kept up a sprightly stream of chatter, though her heart wasn't in it. Was she, dear Lord, never to see Fox Haven again? Was she heading toward an appointment with destiny that her heart and soul and body were dreadfully loath to keep?

Benjamin, bless him, had convinced himself that by keeping his small circle of loved ones together, physically touching during Patrick's speech on Thursday, that one of two things would happen—either Meredith would not be swept from their midst or they'd all be swept into the future with her.

He was prepared, he'd told her. "Far better that I and the others adapt to the strange world of the future than our having to adapt to this world made unbearably bleak and empty by your absence from us," he'd said.

She wished she could be equally convinced that his strategy would work. She longed to stay here, of course. That was by far the preferred scenario, for all of them. But if she had to return to the twentieth century, she definitely wanted the beloved Fox Haven contingent to be there with her. And Benjamin, please, dear God, especially Benjamin!

Abraham, the children, and the servants would be in for a whopping big surprise, she thought with an inward smile. And so would modern-day Richmond if the little group of befuddled colonial time travelers should appear suddenly in the vestibule of St. John's church.

But their love was strong enough to handle anything the twentieth century might dish out. She was sure of that. Together they could handle anything. But God forbid, should they be parted . . .

She shuddered and shoved away the despairing thought. After sending up yet another fervent silent prayer, she turned to Patrick to continue her efforts to restore his revolutionary fever to high pitch. And, along the way, shamelessly fed him line after line of his own speech to spark his motivation.

When they arrived in Richmond, they were greeted by a cleared sky and brilliant sunshine. But the brisk wind remained that of winter.

Church Hill—so desolate but a year ago—was bustling with activity. More than a hundred men mingled in small groups, the air astir with their talk and their spirited gesticulations. Here were assembled all of Virginia's great leaders of the time. A thrill of excitement ran through Meredith's deep sense of personal gloom and doom.

Standing somewhere among that throng were George Washington, Thomas Jefferson, George Mason, George Wythe . . . Peyton Randolph, she supposed, Edmund Pendleton, Benjamin Harrison . . .

But she had no way to identify any of them. And there wasn't time for introductions. The church's bell began to peal, and the delegates, one by one, started for the door.

"Run on in, Patrick, and take your seat. I'll leave your gig and horse here, and we'll await you down at Shockhoe's tavern as we've arranged," she said to him.

He looked reluctant. "Nothing of import will be done today. Perhaps I'll wait till the morrow's session—"

"Nonsense!" she remonstrated. "Your work begins today. You need to get a feel for sentiments—identify and encourage your allies, defang your opposition, that sort of thing."

"'Defang'?" he chortled. "An appropriate term, perhaps, for serpents there be aplenty here." He nodded his head toward a stocky bewigged gentleman preparing to enter the church. "Mr. Robert Carter Nicholas, for one."

Meredith eyed the pompous aristocrat, dressed to the nines in crimson and purple. His loyalties were to Britain, and she knew he'd abandon Virginia for his "homeland" once the die was cast for revolution.

"He won't win, Patrick. You will. Now get in there and start giving them hell!"

His smile was weak, but he jumped from the gig. "I'll meet you all in the tavern after adjournment," was all he said.

She watched his tall, black-cloaked figure walked stalwartly toward the church. A small huddle of townspeople standing by the door let out with a ringing cheer when they spotted him.

"Pah-trick! Here comes our Pah-trick!" she heard them shout.

His head raised a notch and he stopped to shake their hands before entering the church.

Benjamin, on foot now, came up beside her. She smiled wistfully at him and took his offered hand.

"He'll be all right, I believe," she said as she stepped from the gig.

"Aye, and so shall we, Treasure," he said with assuring confidence.

"I pray you are right," she whispered, her eyes filling with tears as she reached up to give him a quick kiss on his lips.

Arm in arm, they walked back to join their loved ones and together they all headed down the windswept hill to Shockhoe's tavern.

And Meredith and Benjamin began their three-day vigil of hope—and of dread.

Their accommodations at the tavern were far from five-star. All ten of the Fox Haven group were housed in one room about half the size of the master bedchamber back home.

No one complained—not even Abraham. The packed little town was alive with excitement over the momentous proceedings under way up at the Church on the Hill, and he and the servants and children alike were delighted they'd been brought to be a part of it.

Never dreaming, any of them, that Meredith and Benjamin were taut with anxiety. They kept it hidden, and both of them worked overtime to act as lighthearted as the next person.

"Lord, we're a great team, you and I," she told him in a rare moment of privacy late on Wednesday evening. The others were asleep on their pallets or cots in the tavern's upstairs room, and she and Benjamin had opted to take a midnight stroll down by the James. Both knew they'd neither one be able to sleep this night.

This last night together? She gripped his hand.

"A truly great team," he agreed. The near-full moon bathed his splendid face. She couldn't keep her eyes off him, and his own eyes seemed to be having similar difficulties staying off her.

"Maybe we'd better sit a spell," she said with a small laugh, pulling him to a soft spot of ground beneath a huge sycamore. "Our unguided feet are apt to stumble over something at the rate we're going."

The night was far from balmy, but the wind had died. Spring was in the air. Only a kiss away, she decided. She gave it a try, and it worked.

"Ah," she sighed, snuggling within the warmth of his arms, inhaling the comforting scents of wool, leather, and Benjamin. The moonlit James lapped against the rocky shore nearby. The river's rapids—the legendary "falls"—were a muffled roar behind a far bend.

"You've worked wonders with Patrick, Treasure. And with the family, too. History might thank you for the former, but my own heart is filled with gratitude and love for that latter miracle. How you've kept them content and happy these past hectic days I'll never know—never once have you 'lost your cool,' as you'd phrase it."

She laughed, throatily this time. "Watch your language, my favorite colonial gentleman," she chided him. "Far better that I start spouting words like 'vouchsafe' and 'forsooth' than your picking up my vocabulary."

"I'll need a 'crash course' in proper speech if tomorrow afternoon we land together in your time," he said lightly, but his arms tensed around her tighter, telling her his thoughts weren't light at all.

"Oh? 'Crash course,' is it now?" she teased, determined not to reveal her own heavy fears. "I vow you've learned enough twentieth-century jargon already—when we get back to Fox Haven I'll have to brainwash you."

*When we get back to Fox Haven.* Oh God, let that happen!

"And anyway, Benjamin, you've been a wonder worker with Patrick and the family far more than I have. My own sense of responsibility and duty pales in comparison with yours—and I used to think I was a world-class champion."

"You *are* a world-class champion," he said huskily, lifting her chin and staring down into her eyes.

"Then we're indeed a perfect team," she whispered with a smile, awaiting his kiss.

It came. Far warmer than spring. Summer. The blazing heat of summer.

"God, I've missed you," he groaned into her ear.

"Me too," she mumbled into his lips, drawing him close.

And their private moon-speckled spot of ground beneath the sycamore on the banks of the James quickly became an obliging bed of warm feathers.

Tonight was theirs.

Willingly, she forgot about tomorrow.

# Chapter Twenty-Five

Thursday, March 23rd, 1775, dawned gloriously. Spring, at last, had come to Virginia.

"It's not like winter at all," Meredith said with a surge of hope to Benjamin as they breakfasted downstairs in the crowded tavern. Dare she consider this pleasant turn in the weather a promising omen? Finally, something wasn't following Mad Millie's bleak prophesy—was it, maybe, the awaited breakthrough?

The family and servants had left them "to walk down by the river this fine day." All of them were walking now—even little Philip, though his steps were tottery and he required a watchful eye and frequent carrying. Abraham had left his cane behind, Meredith noted, but she hadn't said a word about it to him. He'd been a dear these past few months, had done his leg exercises regularly with the weights she'd devised out of bags of buckshot—and without a quibble.

Oh, let Abraham do as he would today, she'd decided. Chances were he truly didn't need the cane all the time now. But she'd watch him . . .

She stiffened. *If* she were allowed to continue . . .

Benjamin, alert as usual to even the slightest shift in her moods, lifted his beautiful eyebrow. "All will be well, Meredith," he said softly, reaching across to cover her hand with his. "The weather change alone seals my conviction we've worried for naught. See, Mad Millie's words ring not so infallible now."

"But this *is* the anniversary of my arrival," she heard herself blurt out with a catch in her voice. Lord, she wanted so to hang on to hope. "It's as though events are closing in on us, becoming a complete circle."

"*We're* a complete circle, Treasure. We must have faith."

She nodded, but bit her lip. "And pray, love. God, how I'm praying!"

"And I also," he said with a melancholy smile and a squeeze of her hand.

She sipped the last of her now-tepid coffee, then squinted across the room. Determined to learn to fend without her glasses, she'd left them behind at Fox Haven. So far, she'd managed beautifully. The project had given her a needed distraction and seemed such a positive move for her, especially now. She was preparing herself for her future—*here*.

Where she belonged. Right?

Right.

As her gaze wandered around the room, she struggled to relax. Had she and Benjamin gathered about them every possible weapon? She listed them all in her mind—love, faith, prayer, heartfelt hope fortified with positive thinking. Had they overlooked something?

She noted Patrick Henry sitting at a table against a far corner, talking animatedly with George Washington and Thomas Jefferson. It had become old hat by now, finding herself in the company of such notables. She'd met most of the delegates, including the two illustrious gentlemen over there with Patrick—had *spoken* with them, for heaven's sake. Oh, and quite demurely and eighteenth-century properly, too.

*See, Fate and Time, I'm behaving myself. I'll do fine back here . . . please leave me be. I've done what I've believed you wanted from me. Reward me. Reward Benjamin . . .*

But despite everything, the afternoon loomed ahead of her like a huge, dark wall. And she couldn't see beyond it. Even with her glasses she wouldn't have had the power to see beyond it.

She returned her attention to Benjamin. He was clear, perfectly focused. Oh my, how she loved him! She blinked away her tears and smiled bravely.

And in a flash remembered one additional weapon she'd almost forgotten. She reached for it, even as she reached out for his arm.

"We must have courage, love. Yours is so wonderfully strong it strengthens my own," she said with an earnestness that firmed her voice and her resolve.

He leaned across the table and kissed her forehead. Not a proper eighteenth-century gesture in public, she was sure, but decidedly a comforting one.

Their smiles met in a warm, tender embrace. Yes, they were well-armed, girded now for the battle ahead.

Let it come.

Like that life-changing afternoon the year before, this one, too, got off to a rotten start.

Patrick Henry dropped down into the doldrums again, and Abraham, cranky as the devil suddenly, decided he'd nap rather than join the rest of them on their "pilgrimage" to Church Hill. As it turned out, Patrick was easier to manage than Abraham. Meredith appealed to the woeful patriot's pride; told him simply (and truthfully) that he had the power within him to achieve immortality.

She wasn't gentle, didn't mince words. "Do it, by God. Go up there and speak with your tongue of fire. You've been given a rare gift, Patrick. Use it this day, or you'll never forgive yourself—nor will any of the rest of us forgive you!"

He looked momentarily shocked, but recovered quickly. He took her hand and bent over to graze a kiss across it. When he straightened, a tear glinted from the corner of his eye, but he managed a big smile.

"I'll give them hell, as you'd say, Meredith Foxworth. I'm beholden to you."

"As you should be, Mr. Henry," she retorted, her own smile cutting through her pretense of haughtiness. "Now begone with you," she added with a wink. "And, Patrick—good luck, dear man."

*Good luck to us all*, she pleaded to herself.

But Abraham wasn't nearly so malleable.

"Damn it, woman, I need my rest," he grumbled.

"You're coming with us, Father, and that's an end to it," Benjamin insisted. "We're not leaving you back here."

Meredith hated those words . . . *"an end to it,"* *"not leaving you back here."* But she was silent.

"And why is my presence on that bloody hill so urgent, may I ask?" Abraham mumbled, disgruntled.

"Patrick's speaking, they tell me. Surely you want to be there," Benjamin said, attempting reason.

"What can we hear? The church will be fully packed with delegates, and we'll not be allowed inside." He looked immovable.

"The windows will be open, Father. The churchyard's filling already with townspeople. 'Tis a historic moment, I vow. We must hurry to secure a place near the building."

She'd told Benjamin the exact spot where they should stand. The north end, where the future vestibule would be. They'd both decided to face this final, great challenge head on. To keep their end of the frightening "bargain"—if, indeed, that's what it was—with their love held high, gleaming in the sunlight like a polished shield.

The old man relented at last, but his crustiness remained intact. "Marriage to this woman has but added to your tyrannical ways, Benjamin," he snorted. "I'd had hopes she would have mellowed you."

"I need more time to work that kind of miracle," Meredith said with a chuckle. *Years and years of time*, she pleaded. *Forever, preferably.*

388

But bless Abraham for this newest distraction—and bless the rest of them, too. Seeing that all their charges were fed, packed, and in the carriage had kept her and Benjamin so occupied that their apprehensions had to take a back seat in the order of things.

Until they reached the top of the hill.

"Here's where I landed," she said to him out of the corner of her mouth so that none of the others would hear. They were standing side by side, and she was holding Philip in her arms. The toddler was blissfully asleep.

They'd maneuvered around gigs, carriages, and horses and elbowed their way through knots of spectators already stationed near the opened windows of the tiny church.

"Over here," he said to the others in their small group, motioning with his head for them to join him and Meredith.

"That window yon's far better, I vow," spoke up Abraham, heading off in a different direction.

"*Here*," Benjamin demanded. Scowling, the old man complied.

Betsy, her face brighter than the warm sun, ran up beside her father and held his hand. The servants gathered close around them.

The meeting inside had already begun—and the spectators outside grew silent, intent. A prayer by the Reverend Miles Selden was being intoned. Meredith, her heart hammering, offered a silent one of her own.

As the delegates discussed a noncontroversial resolution expressing gratitude to the Island of Jamaica for something or other, Betsy grew restless.

"Must we stand here, Father? The men use big words I know not."

"She's tired, I fear," Meredith whispered to him.

Benjamin reached down for his daughter and lifted her up to his shoulders. "Wait, love," he told her. "You might find it more interesting in but a short while."

Oh, she might at that, Meredith thought. A low growl of thunder in the northwest sky sent a shiver of alarm through her and she pressed closer to Benjamin. He put his arm around her.

"All of you hold hands," he ordered Abraham and the five servants. "And move in a mite here. We must all be touching."

"Balderdash," Abraham scoffed. "Have you taken leave of your senses, Benjamin?"

"Do as I say, Father." There was no doubting it, Benjamin meant business. Abraham made a face, but did as he was told. He put a protective arm around old Robert, who looped his withered hand around Will's forearm, who grasped Jack's wrist, who put his short, burly arm across Lucy's fat shoulders, who held on to Sukie's hand, who reached across Meredith and Benjamin to grip Betsy's hand.

Betsy, from her lofty seat astride her father's neck, reached back for Abraham's free hand, and their circle was complete.

Lord, they'd walk through fire for Benjamin, she thought. And so would she.

But then she heard Patrick Henry offer his anticipated resolution to establish a "well-regulated militia." It was a resounding call to arms.

The sky responded with an ominous roll of thunder. Their small circle tightened slightly. Meredith leaned into Benjamin's strength, and prayed. She closed her eyes.

The debate was stormy. The spectators around them grew rowdy, issuing catcalls at the "timid gentlemen" who spoke in opposition to the resolution, cheering Richard Henry Lee, Jefferson, Washington, and Nelson as they rose in dramatic support.

She knew the script. Dear God, it was time. Patrick was beginning his speech.

The churchyard grew quiet. All heads were turned toward the open windows where the magic words like silvered lightning poured forth. All heads but Meredith's—and Benjamin's. She'd lifted her face to his.

His turquoise eyes looked down upon her, bathing her with love . . . with hope, with courage.

"I love you, Treasure," he whispered.

She couldn't speak, but she knew her eyes were telling him of her own love.

*"We must fight! I repeat it, sir, we must fight!"* came the fiery voice from the church. *"An appeal to arms and to the God of Hosts is all that is left us!"*

Oh, and there was also love, she thought, her heart pounding, her gaze locked into Benjamin's.

*"Gentlemen may cry 'peace, peace'—but there is no peace . . ."*

She held her breath. *Here it comes.* She cuddled Philip close, reached behind Benjamin and covered his hand that circled Betsy's leg, and squeezed tight.

A spear of lightning bolted through the sky, but no one moved. The world, for a moment, stood still. Waited.

Patrick's words **rolled like** thunder over her ears. *"Is life so **dear, or peace** so sweet, as to be purchased at the **price** of chains and slavery? Forbid it, Almighty God!"*

The suspended pause. But she heard no silence. *Forbid it, Almighty God!* echoed through her head. Tears blurred her vision, but she wouldn't blink, unwilling to relinquish the sight of Benjamin's beloved eyes even for an instant.

He clutched her tighter. She whimpered softly and instinctively clamped her eyes shut.

*"I know not what course others may take; but as for me, give me liberty or give me death!"*

It was over.

And now, nothing but silence.

And darkness.

But then, pandemonium broke loose around her—cheers, shouts, applause. *"Pah-trick! Pah-trick! Pah-trick!"*

She was jostled—heard familiar voices, a baby's cry.

Dare she breathe? Dare she open her eyes?

"Treasure?"

She smiled. "Where are we, Benjamin?" she asked, her voice trembling. Who cared where they were? They were together—all of them were together.

"Look and see," he said.

She did. She saw him first, smiling radiantly down at her, Betsy's firm little buff-booted legs squirming excitedly about his neck. Philip, still in her arm, was red-faced; squalling at the top of his lungs. Lucy and Sukie both reached out for him—Sukie took him, she believed.

Old Robert, Jack, and Will were dancing an uneven jig behind her. Abraham had run over to another group—was shaking hands and giving pats on backs.

Her head swiveled. The tiny white church was there . . . the churchyard . . . the scattered gravestones.

"We're still here," she gasped in wonder.

"Aye, my love."

Tears of happiness streamed down her cheeks. "We're here! We're here!" she wanted to shout to the heavens, but she could only blubber.

"Why is Merrie crying, Father?" Betsy asked from her sturdy perch.

"Because she loves us," he said, swinging the girl down to her feet.

"We love you too, Merrie," she announced simply. "But 'tis a time for laughter, not tears, I vow." Then, like a sprite, she skipped over toward Abraham without a glance backward.

The church bell began to peal. Tricorn hats sailed through the air. The sky rang with cheers. Meredith's heart rang with joy, and, sobbing like a child, she fell into the warmth of Benjamin's arms.

"We won, we won," she sputtered, hugging him close.

"But the war hasn't even begun, woman," said a stranger walking up beside them.

"Ours is over, sir," Benjamin said with a broad grin, then kissed his wife soundly on the lips.

The man shrugged and left them alone.

Only they'd never be alone again, they knew. For they had each other—and a timeless love to share.

Together.

A chirping sparrow took wing from a nearby oak and joined its mate—they flew toward

Hanover. With faces glowing, Meredith and Benjamin watched the winged pair soar homeward.

"Let's follow them to Fox Haven, Treasure," he breathed against her waiting lips.

Mad Millie's prophesy indeed had come true. Meredith Davis Foxworth had been released at last to be where she truly belonged.

# DANCE of the FLAME

## ELAINE BARBIERI

**Elaine Barbieri's romances are
"powerful...fascinating...storytelling at its best!"
—*Romantic Times***

Exiled to a barren wasteland, Sera will do anything to regain the kingdom that is her birthright. But the hard-eyed warrior she saves from death is the last companion she wants for the long journey to her homeland.

To the world he is known as Death's Shadow—as much a beast of battle as the mighty warhorse he rides. But to the flame-haired healer, his forceful arms offer a warm haven, and he swears his throbbing strength will bring her nothing but pleasure.

Sera and Tolin hold in their hands the fate of two feuding houses with an ancient history of bloodshed and betrayal. But no matter what the age-old prophecy foretells, the sparks between them will not be denied, even if their fiery union consumes them both.

_3793-9                                    $5.99 US/$6.99 CAN

# An Angel's Touch

# Time Heals
## SUSAN COLLIER

Tired of her nagging relatives, Maeve Fredrickson asks for the impossible: to be a thousand miles and a hundred years away from them. Then a heavenly being grants her wish, and she awakes in frontier Montana.

Saved from the wilderness by a handsome widower, Maeve loses her heart to her rescuer—and her temper over the antics of his three less-than-angelic children. As her angel prods her to fight for Seth, Maeve can only pray for the strength to claim a love made in paradise.

__52030-3                                    $4.99 US/$5.99 CAN

# THERE NEVER WAS A TIME
## *GAIL LINK*

**"Gail Link was born to write romance!"
—Jayne Ann Krentz**

Sitting alone in her Vermont farmhouse, Rebecca Gallagher Fraser hears a ghostly voice whisper to her. But not until she stumbles across a distant ancestor's diary do the spirit's words hold any meaning for her.

Drawn by inexplicable forces, Rebecca journeys to the once resplendent Southern plantation where her forebear loved and lost a Union soldier. And there, on a jasmine-scented New Orleans night, she discovers that passion unfulfilled in one lifetime can defy fate and logic and be reborn so much sweeter in another.

_52025-7                                    $4.99 US/$5.99 CAN

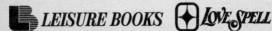
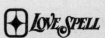

Other *Leisure* and *Love Spell* Books by
Thomasina Ring:
**DREAMCATCHER**
**TIME-SPUN RAPTURE**

## TIME-SPUN TREASURE

Meredith lay limp beneath him, their bodies bonded, moist; their hearts beating a wild cadence, taking far longer than the rest of them to be calmed by the bliss of contented peace.

Wrapped together, neither moved for a long while. Euphoria, like a soothing cloud, enveloped them. His soft breath caressed her ear. Their hearts, at last, slowing—in perfect harmony.

Lifting his head, Benjamin gazed down upon her with a smile of pleasure that matched her own. He patted light kisses on each of her eyes, the tip of her nose, and, with lingering warmth, upon her lips.

"You're a treasure," he said with a sigh.

"You, too," she whispered, aware she'd never been more content. Lord, he was wonderful. Who would have dreamed an eighteenth-century Virginia gentleman would have that kind of skill in the art of lovemaking? No wonder the era was considered Virginia's Golden Age.